H.N. Benson

Awaken the
Demon

Black Rose Writing | Texas

ISBN: 978-1-68433-252-6
PUBLISHED BY BLACK ROSE WRITING
www.blackrosewriting.com

Printed in the United States of America
Suggested Retail Price (SRP) $19.95

Awaken the Demon is printed in Garamond

I want to thank my dearest friend, Tia Cruz, for putting up with all my rambling while I was writing this book and also for her amazing dedication to helping me edit it and her constant support. I would not be able to proudly show this to the world without her.

Awaken the
Demon

Chapter One: Damsel

Laughter fills the room
Excitement, anticipation building,
Justice comes swiftly to those unrelenting,
The weak will never be forgotten
They will be avenged by a dark angel.

She sat on a warped wooden chair, in the corner of a dark tavern. The room was filled with smoke and smelled of drunken men. She watched carefully in the dim light of the candles for the man that was said to roam these parts. It was perfect: a small, rundown town that didn't give a damn if someone went missing, whether it was murder or suicide. She watched as men got drunk and groped the timid girls that were far too young to be there in the first place, many of them were shipped here by their fathers to pay off their debt that they accumulated by too much drinking and gambling, *slavery in payment for stupidity*. It was a cycle that never ended. She shook her head in disgust, just thinking about it made her skin itch.

There was a crash and a muffled scream coming from the room behind the bar, it drew her attention. She looked around the room, but no one so much as blinked at the commotion. She watched the door as a man, half-dressed, staggered out of the dark room. He made his way to the bar.

"Give me another!" he shouted over the noise to the man behind the bar.

He was shortly followed by a young girl in a dress that looked like it had been ripped and sewn back together more than once. She was shaking as she walked past the man and out the front door. She could smell his sweat and breathe on the girl. He had taken her and done what he pleased. The observer stood up, walked towards the bar and sat down on a stool next to him.

"Another drink or another girl?" she asked him, without looking directly at him, as if he was nothing more than trash. He turned his head, not too gracefully, towards her.

"What'd ya say?" he asked, with a hint of annoyance. He was a big man, standing a full head taller than her and almost twice the width. He looked down at her and lost his anger upon seeing a young girl. A smile creeping into his eyes. A shame it was that he thought she was just a petite girl barely in her twenties. He turned fully toward her, a grin placed on his drunken face.

"That girl, just now, how old was she?" She finally looked at him, "Fifteen, fourteen? She looked a little young for you." She didn't back down from him, but she didn't resist him when he ran a filthy hand down her cheek either.

She wanted him to think she was helpless and, even though her words cut him, he didn't pay attention to them; he only saw her small form. "Did you enjoy having your way with someone that was too helpless to stop you?" The look on his drunken face started to shift from happiness to anger, it seems he did hear her words, "Did it make you feel like a man?" He slammed his half-empty mug on the wooden bar and stood up from his stool, sending it falling backward onto the floor.

"You bitch!" he spat. "Ya don't know who you messin' with!" He could barely stand up, he kept leaning towards the bar to keep his balance. She sighed inwardly, this wasn't going to be as much fun as she had hoped. She backed up a step, playing the intimidation card. He took one staggering step towards her and began to fall. He caught himself on a stool and came towards her again. He grabbed her shoulders and yanked her toward him. He was stronger than she had thought. She grinned, *maybe this would be fun*. She collided with his front and lay limp against him, playing the weak damsel in distress.

He laughed in her ear, "Ya thought ya could go against me. None of them bitches could." She felt his huge hands tug on her shirt. That was enough. She had gotten close enough to end his reign of terror. She put her hands around his shoulders in an intimate gesture and pulled his neck towards her lips. She could feel the beating of his heart as she laid her cold lips against his skin

She jumped as if startled when he said, "Have ya warmed up to me?" he paused, and a look of disappointment crossed his drunk face, "I see. That's too bad; I like it when they struggle." She shook inwardly; her anger was building at this fool's disgusting idea of a good time.

She lifted her head to see over his shoulder. The bar crowd had stopped to watch the show. She smiled "You big fool," She whispered in his ear, "You see, I like it when they struggle, too." He tried to lift his head, his anger starting to wane to fear, but she would not allow it. She bared her fangs, and there was a gasp from everyone in the crowd; she used their fearful energy for the finale. She bit down into his hot skin, finding the treasure even a worthless man possessed: Blood. He jolted under the pressure of her teeth as she began to pull the life out of him. The warm, metallic liquid flowed into her like honey. She had craved it, as she always did. He tried to stand up, to pull away from her, but to his surprise, she was much stronger than him. Centuries of life in her vampyre blood will leave many men in awe of her. He pushed down on her shoulders, pulled at her head, but to no avail. He struggled until he became too weak to fight. Then, slowly, he began to slouch, lower and lower until she let him fall from her lips to the floor. He lay motionless, in death, at her feet. She licked her lips and looked around the bar. No one moved; they only stared.

Then, a tiny voice broke the silence, "You're her." It came from the door that led out of the bar. She turned to see the young girl from before. "You're the woman that acts as a vampyre and kills all the evil men. They call you the Rose of Death." The girl wasn't scared, in fact she seemed relieved. She nodded at the girl and left the building.

So, it seems that I'm getting quite a reputation. I should be careful, or I will soon become the hunted, not the hunter.

Chapter Two: Life Before Death

The sun rises in the east
It sets in the west,
So my life starts with the sun
And ends with You.
My Love, you fill my nights with light,
My heart with warmth,
And my Soul with beauty.
I will never be the same when you are gone.

Her life began before the computer, before the television, before the car. It began before modern medicine, during the time when everyone believed what the church said. Go to church on Sundays, go to be baptized, go to be married, and go to repent. When women walked the streets behind their husbands and their children behind them. The children never misbehaved, and the women never spoke of their affairs. Long dresses and petite, useless umbrellas were in fashion, and the streets were full of seemingly happy faces.

She lived with her parents and her twin brother Marcus on their family orchard that was spread out across many acres and sat behind their expansive estate. Their estate sat outside the growing city of Henley. It was near a major river that ran to the ocean and made for a prime location for the exchange of goods from all over the world. The buildings were built with precise measurements, with the finest stone the surrounding land could provide. Her family was well known in this area, and their family name of Talbot was starting to be recognized in other major cities. Though, as quickly as the city was growing, the people there still treated each other as if they lived in a small village. They took care of each other when they could, and everyone knew everyone.

Her father named her Rosina after the rose, he said it has a slight Latin twist to it, even though she had never heard of anyone else with the name Rosina. It came to fit her very well because as she grew her mother taught her how to tend their roses and it became almost an obsession. The roses started in just two flower beds at the back of their home, and she started growing them anywhere there was a spare space of dirt. Their backyard slowly turned into a rose garden with towering bushes of beautiful, full, dark red roses that were larger than even her father's hands. Their color was unique to only their home, the red was so dark that it almost looked black, but when the sun hit them, they glowed a bright red. Her mother crooned over them every time a new one bloomed.

Marcus was a very bright boy, and the townspeople loved him. They were told several times over that she and Marcus were mirror images of each other, which they thought was redundant since they *were* twins. They had the same dark hair, same pale skin, and same emerald green eyes when they were toddlers, however, as they grew they changed, his hair lightened to a brown instead of a dark mocha and his eyes turned hazel, still retaining most of their green, but now with brown and blue infused in them. They were photo negatives of each other by their twelfth birthday. Even so, they still looked alike and the townspeople never let them forget.

The pressure on young women during this era was as high as it was for young men. She was held to the same standards and expected to fulfill her duties to the same degree as Marcus was. He was expected to take over the family estate and business while she was expected to catch the eye of a respectable gentleman. She was as valuable to her family as a good harvest, and she was to catch a fair price for her hand in marriage. What was to be exchanged for her was to be equal to what Marcus was to receive upon gaining head of the family. Their schedule was strict, and nothing but the best tutors would do. They woke with the sun and as soon as their feet hit the floor they were expected to act as the high social standing citizens that they were. Their childhood was short, and there was no time for play, everything they did they were expected to learn something from it or achieve something from it. Even her roses were considered a learning process even though she never saw it that way. She was nearly thirteen when she began having migraines, followed soon by lucid nightmares. Sleep slipped her by while fearing the dreadful dreams would return and the lack of sleep simply led to even worse head pain. Her studies began to falter, and her father would scold her, telling her she was not trying hard enough. She gave her best effort but could no longer focus.

"You need to pay closer attention to what your teacher is saying." Her father said, "I'm not paying her to stand there and have her words fall on deaf ears. You will do better, or you will be punished!"

"But father—" she tried begging him.

"I will have none of your excuses!" he said. "This family has had no shame in all of its generations, and I will not allow a girl to change that! Study harder! Or you will find out what it is like to be a servant!" he bellowed.

She stared at him with tears streaming down her face, she did not want to disappoint him.

"I'm sorry, father," she whispered. "I will try harder."

"Good, that's a good girl," he said. He turned to leave and said over his shoulder, "I will not allow a child of mine to remain in this house if she cannot uphold her station. You will not make me look a fool." He reached for the door when the thud of her fainting body spun him around. Rushing to her, he fell on his knees and cradled her against his chest and felt a hot fever burning through her. He laid his forehead against hers, "I'm sorry my daughter, I have to pressure you. I only want you to have a good home when I can no longer care for you." He had a tear in his eye, he showed this soft side only to her. He lifted her up in his arms and carried her to her room, calling for a doctor.

Her fever finally broke the next day, but she never fully recovered. She was recluse and spoke very little. Her sleeping increased, and she no longer went to her studies. Often sick, her relationship with her family became strained. Her brother Marcus was her only refuge, his love unwavering and strong.

"Rosina," she heard Marcus whisper as he entered her dark room. She pretended to be asleep, facing the wall so he couldn't see her tears. She heard his feet scuff the floor as he walked to her bed and then cool air hit her as he lifted her blanket and climbed into bed with her. He had often shared beds with her when they were little, the felt a connection to each other that they did not with others, as if they were each other's other half. He wrapped his arms around her and pulled her close, he knew she was crying.

"My dear sister, please don't cry, I love you no matter what. You can live in a barn for all it would matter to me. I want to see you smile again and tend your roses. You always had such a look of happiness on your face that reach even your eyes when you would see a new rose bloom, one of your own hybrids especially. You even seemed to like pulling the weeds out of the dirt." He nuzzled her hair. "And if you must cry, do it on my shoulder." He tugged at her arm, trying to coerce her to turn over. She resisted at first. "I know where you are most ticklish, don't make me use the ultimate weapon." She gasped, but remained still. She felt his arm move, and his fingers lightly touched the back of her knee. A small whimper escaped her lips, as she tucked her legs up to her chest.

"Oh, I see, playing hard to tickle?" He reached over again, this time lightly touching the back of her neck. She quickly covered that with her hand. He leaned in close to her and whispered in her ear, "You can't cover this," his breath sent a tingle all the way down her side, and she quickly rolled over, to face him. Her eyes were red and her face wet.

"That's better," he was smiling and pulled her into him, allowing her to cry into him. "I love you Rose, don't ever be afraid to come to me, no matter what, I'm your brother and regardless of what path our lives take, you will always be first in my heart, and I would do anything to comfort you." He stopped talking because he was beginning to tear up himself, was there nothing he could do to ease her suffering? He felt so helpless. She was such a kind soul that she deserved everything this world had to offer, especially happiness. Why, why was she so sad?

"This cannot go on any longer, doctor," he heard their father whisper outside her door. "There must be something you can do for her. Or is sickness not your area of expertise?" he had anger in his voice and frustration.

"There is no need to speak to me so, Mr. Tolbert, I have given her everything I could for the symptoms she is showing. Since the remedies are not working, I can only assume, it is something we have not discovered, or it is something that my "area of expertise" is not needed for, but someone else's is." Another man, the doctor, spoke.

"I apologize," their father replied.

"I understand you are worried, but perhaps someone else, in a different area of work, would be able to help you better. If you'll excuse me." The doctor said goodbye and Marcus could hear him shuffle down the hall and the stairs. His father sighed before he tapped gently on the door and quietly pushed it open. Marcus closed his eyes and pretended to be asleep. His father stopped next to the bed and looked down at them.

"When will you two learn that you are too old to sleep in the same bed." He said, but his voice was soft and a small amount of relief was there for the support she had from her brother, even if he himself failed to give it. He gently moved a piece of hair from her face and rustled Marcus's hair before he whispered, "I love you two more than a man should be allowed. I'm sorry I failed you." A tear was in his voice as his body quickly walked out of the room. Weakness was not an option for him.

"Who's there?" he yelled down the hall to an unheard person. Then, a pause, followed by, I'll be right there." Marcus remained silent and still, trying to hear who would be visiting the manor this late at night.

The room and hall remained silent for a long time before the door swung open and a man dressed in all white, from his fabric cap to his robe and soft shoes. The only color was that of a red shall he had over his shoulders. He wore a long rosary, with marble beads and a cross, around his neck and held a well-used Bible in his hand. He was followed into the room by three other men, which were cover in a brown robe and black rosaries around their necks, their hair cut short and their looks stern. Marcus wrapped his arms tightly around Rosina, who was starting to shake, seeing these strange men come in.

"Shh, I'm here, nothing's going to happen." She gripped him tighter.

"Marcus, come here," his father had followed the men in, he had a look of defeat on his face, Marcus was trying to figure out what was going on. These men were clearly from the church, but what could they possibly want with him?

"If it would be alright with you, I'd like to stay here, with my sister, she isn't well." He said, with as much courtesy as he could, he didn't like to disobey his father.

"That is why we came here," said the man in white, his voice was wise but help a presence of authority that was not to be ignored.

"What do you mean?" Marcus said in defiance of it.

"Your sister is beyond the help of an ordinary man, she needs the help of God to purge the demon that is hiding in her body." He said it sternly, and as he talked, he walked closer to the bed and when he finished he grabbed Marcus by the arm and said, "Now, if you would please vacate this room so we can help your beloved sister." Marcus stared at the man in white. His lack of motion prompted two of the other men to come up to him and replace the man in white and grabbed one arm and one leg and yanked him from the bed, dislodging Rosina from him and she tumbled to the floor. She reached out, grabbing his free arm and crying out.

"Rose!" he called, fighting with the men, trying to get free.

"Marcus! No!" she cried, and the man in white gripped her hand and pulled her back from him, restraining her as he was tossed into the hall with his father and the door was slammed and bolted shut. Marcus was pounding on the door, yelling for them to leave her alone. His father just stood against the wall, not saying anything or doing anything to stop him or to help him. His face was blank as he stood staring off into nothing. Down the hall, he heard his mother crying softly from their room, and his echoing yells, increasing with desperation, filled the entire housed like water in an aquarium.

"Now, young lady, if you don't mind," the man in white said in the room, "we need you to remain calm, what we are going to do is not going to be pleasant or pain free, but I promise you will be free if this illness when we are done." As he spoke, she watched in terror while the men moved furniture against the walls and her bed to the middle of the room. The attached rope to each bedpost and removed her bed covers and pillows, leaving only the mattress and sheet.

"Please return to bed," the white man said. She didn't move, so one of the other men picked her up and placed her on the bed and pushed her shoulders down, so she lay on her back. "Forgive me, my dear," the white man said as the others tied her wrists and ankles to the bed. He reached into his robe and brought out another rosary, this one was silver, and he placed it around her neck. He reached back in and pulled out a silver flask that had a cross embossed on it, holy water. Her brain was so scrambled that she did not realize right away what was going on, but through the fog of her panic, a word seemed to be handed to her: Exorcism. When she saw it, she screamed again and from the hall, she heard Marcus's pounding and yelling for her.

"Help me Marcus!!" she screamed as loud as she could.

"I'm going to ask you to kindly refrain from calling out to him and from any other sounds you are making now, this is a delicate procedure." The man in white was standing over her as he started to pour the water on her face. She squinted against it and tried to turn her head, but one of the other men held her still. The man in white started to speak quickly in Latin, reading from the Bible he had brought. The two men not holding her held their rosaries and repeated what he was saying. She just listened to them, she knew she was not possessed by a demon and that this was not going to hurt her, but she felt like an animal being tied down and not even asked if this was okay. Then, as if her internal thoughts had woken something in her mind she felt a small irritation behind her eyes. She blinked quickly to try to snuff it out, but as he continued to speak the irritation grew to a pain and spread. It felt as if someone was running their nails gently against the inside of her skull. She did not want them to know her pain, so she remained as still as she could and just watched the man in white. Was he cursing her instead of trying to cure her? She tried to look at him closely; she didn't recognize him from church, where had he come from?

He poured more water on her forehead, and this time it burned, and she tried to not struggle away from it, but she knew her skin had turned red and the look on his face was no longer composed. He looked closely at her forehead and saw, not just an irritated round red spot but instead swirls of red that seemed to glow.

"Men, hold her tight." The two free men came around, and one held down her legs, and the other climbed onto her bed and straddled her stomach, holding down her shoulders. She stared at him, and his face was hard. Tenderness had no place for what he was about to do. The man in white spoke even louder and faster and the scratching in her head caused a clawing feeling. She screamed out, the pain was too much.

"Get out of my head!" she yelled before she could stop herself. "Stop!"

"Good!" the man in white said and nodded at the men, they loosened the ties and flipped her over on the bed and retied her. Her hair was pulled up over her head and her neck was exposed. She felt cold water again on her and again it burned.

"Why would you curse me? I'm just a stupid girl!" she shouted at them, and they remained silent, the men holding her down back in place. She felt something cold against the skin of her neck, not a liquid, but something solid. Then, she felt another pain, a quick and intense across her neck, twice, in the shape of a cross and she cried out again. She felt the blood start to run down the side of her neck, and she screamed again as they poured a powder into the fresh wound on her neck. The burning from the water was nothing compared to this new pain. She felt as if her flesh was burning right off her bones, it went straight to her spine and up to her skull and the scratching in her head became ever more intense. She screamed and tried to free herself, by thrashing and kicking her legs, but she couldn't move the heavy men.

The man in white spoke even louder and placed his cold hand on her wound and as if it was possible the burning could increase it did. She screamed until her throat was hoarse and she continued to even without a voice until something came out of her that was not her but something much darker. A howl escaped her lips, and she saw red and then black. She lost consciousness and didn't wake until the next morning.

She felt the warmth of the sun and she lept out of bed to get away from the heat before she realized it was the sun and she was no longer tied, and the four men were gone. She gathered herself but found that she was no longer standing but had already collapsed on the floor. She looked around and saw no one in the room with her. She soon realized that the door was bolted again and she crawled over to it and reached up, unlatching it. She pulled the door open, and her brother slid down from it and onto the floor. When his head hit the floor, he woke to see her looking over him. He quickly sat up and grabbed her, hugging her harder than he had ever, tears were streaming down his face and he kept saying "sorry" over and over again.

She wrapped her weak arms around him and joined him in his sadness. "Exorcism…. What were they thinking?" he mumbled. "Those men will never touch you again," his anger was growing.

She pulled back from him and placed her cool hands on the sides of his hot face and said, "No, let me bear this alone, don't allow them to damage you, as they have me." She leaned her forehead against his as he had done so many times before, "Let me take this one for us both, I'll take the pain and sadness, and you smile and laugh for both of us. You have too, because I don't think I know how to anymore."

"I'll make you smile again, I'll do whatever it takes," he said, with commitment but she could tell he was as lost as she.

"Marcus, please, I beg you to not drag yourself down with this, your love is all I need. Please live as fully as you can. Please," she tried to beg him, not being able to put her feelings into words.

He pulled her close again and just said, "Okay."

Their parents stopped going to Mass on Sundays and instead studied the Bible from the comfort of home. They suffered much on her behalf. The people they once called friends left them, and the townspeople either ignored them or made snide comments behind their back, sometimes not even bothering to try and hide their whispers. As much as her father loved her he rejected her new state, her weakness brought shame to their family, and her mother looked at her with both love and fear in her eyes, she no longer encouraged her to tend her roses, or even leave her room.

She rarely left her room, and she didn't see much of her parents, her food was brought to her by the servant or butler. She spent most of her time looking out the window and watching the leaves blow and wishing she could be out among her roses. Their beauty and silence was always a comfort to her, but she feared leaving her room. She caught the fake smiles everyone gave her. Marcus spent all his free time with her, which as he grew became less and less, but he always made time to come to her, and he often fell asleep in her bed while she sat next to him silently enjoying his calming presence.

Years passed this way, and she was soon sixteen. She had spent her birthday alone except for Marcus sneaking in a slice of cake during all the guests finding their places in the dining hall. She had taken to wearing his old clothes; she didn't need to present herself as a noble since she was no longer seen by anyone. He allowed her to do so because he knew she wanted very little and he could at least do that for her.

On one summer night she, without really deciding to, climbed out her window and down the trellis outside her window. She had been sitting on the cushion in the nook under the window, feeling the warm breeze on her face and she was standing on the ground before she even had the thought that she wanted to be there.

She stood there for a moment, not thinking of going back in but not thinking of leaving either. She stood there for several minutes before her feet just started to carry her across the dew covered grass. The thought of being recognized never crossed her mind as she made her way to town, wandering behind the buildings and through the alleys. She slipped in and out of buildings looking at the many things that were for sale, the elegant cloth that her mother used to sew her dresses and the fine jewelry that glistened in the light of the shops. She had been shopping many times with her mother but had never been able to take in all the beauty of the items that she bought. She was never able to stare in awe at the buildings, the way they were thought out and constructed, they held a beauty all their own. She felt a twinge of what might have been joy rise up in her, and she had to shake herself.

She could smell different foods being prepared and could hear the silver clinking against the china that was brought out for special occasions. She walked by a window that held a group of men raising their champagne glasses in a toast, "Here here!" They all shouted.

"Here's to the woman that was finally able to tie this man down!" a man said and raised his glass to the man at the end of the table who was slowly turning red, while other men threw their arms around him and laughed.

The smells of all the different foods and deserts mingled with the sweet and sour of wines and champagnes, it filled her senses to the point of ecstasy. The laughter of old friends sharing a meal together, filled her with sadness, longing to do so with her family again, and to make friends that did not pity her, but someone that would challenge her and make her laugh as these men were. She wanted to run home and beg for forgiveness, but she knew that even if she did beg, she didn't know how to get better, she was stuck in a dark hole and didn't know how to get out. An intense craving to fill that sadness with something else, a taste of that amazing food, overtook her and before she knew it, she was creeping around the building and trying to sneak into the kitchen. She desired to taste the food that put them into such a good mood, have some flawless creation melt in her mouth and the flavors devour her rather than her it. She thought she could just grab some of that delicious food from the chef who was too busy to notice, when she bumped into something that she never expected.

He stood a good five inches taller than Rosina and was as skinny as a rod, but he was her age, it seemed. He looked down at her with a mischievous smile on his face. His hair was cut different than anyone else's, shorter on one side than the other, the long side reaching his chin in the front and getting shorter as it went back, it was dark, too, almost as dark as hers and he had dark eyes; she was quite sure they were black.

"I wouldn't try that, I've been caught several times already." His voice was deep for someone that looked about sixteen. She looked up at him, questioning him with her eyes. He was well dressed and didn't look like he had been living on the streets.

He laughed, "Before you ask, the answer is yes, I have stuff at home, but it is so much more fun trying to steal it from the cook. For some reason, it tastes…better." He looked up towards the sky, as if thinking, and licked his lips. "Mmmm." She just stared at him, silent.

When he looked back down at her, he wasn't smiling anymore. Instead, he looked worried as he looked at her. "Aren't you the demon child?" he didn't ask with distaste but curiosity.

She backed up preparing to run, a look of terror on her face. She had hidden from the world for so long that she didn't think anyone would recognize her. She had to get away before he raised the alarm. She turned on her heel and ran and ran to get away from him, until she reached the edge of town with the rolling fields before her. She waded into the field until she reached the middle and sat down in the tall grass, hoping he didn't follow her. *What was that? Why did I run? What would he do? Alert people that she was there? And they would simply stone her and return her to her family...* her thoughts made a dark turn and overtook her. She couldn't contain the tears that started to fall from her eyes, she was afraid of being seen, and her imagination started to put horrible images in her mind of how they would look at her and what they would say to her. They would try to purge the demon that was supposed to be hiding in her that she knew didn't exist. *What if they believed me?* Then they would see her as lazy or defective, she couldn't function how she was supposed to... She let out a wail into the darkness only to have it echo back at her. She pulled her knees to her chest and laid her arms and head on them, crying.

"Oi!" She could hear a voice and running steps, then a rustle of cloth and grass. "Umph." The boy from the alley sat down beside her, breathing heavily. She jumped up in surprise and started to run, but he reached up and grabbed her arm, she looked down and saw that it was the boy from the alley, he had followed her. She struggled to get away from him.

"Wait now! I didn't mean to hurt your feelings. I don't believe all the rumors, a bunch of nonsense made up by the church, I imagine." He looked up at her with a smile on his face, "Not to mention, if you really were possessed by a demon I think most of the people in this town would be dead already, not safe as you sneak around in the shadows, cause you know," he motioned to her from head to foot with his free hand, "demon. Ooo." He feigned being scared by raising a hand to the sky as if surrendering, then laughed at the idea. When he recovered from his own laughter he looked at her, and his smile widened; she was captured by it, he had so much confidence and he was the first, except her brother, to treat her as a girl and not a demon.

Once he saw that she was not going to run in panic, he released her and patted on the ground next to him, "come," pat-pat, "sit." She was still leery of him so she sat slowly, sitting in a position that was more of a squat, so she could get up quickly. She faced him, staring at him, saying nothing, just waiting. He reached up a hand and placing a gentle finger under her chin lifting up her face, he kissed her forehead as if she were a lost puppy. She swatted his hand away, *What the hell is going on here? What a strange person*, she caught herself thinking, and it shocked her, *you're not one to judge*. And at that, he laughed at her, "Don't worry, I won't tell anyone as long as you promise me something." He returned to the original subject as if he wasn't just rejected by her.

Immediately she thought of all the things that men wanted from women, and she blushed, "Wha—?"

He laughed at her reaction, "Well now, we just met and you're already putting the moves on me! Haha!" *Somehow he saw right through me!* "You have to be my friend!" His smile faded, and he looked away from her, off into the night, trying to hide his sadness. When he looked back what he said shocked her, "I will protect you, so you don't have to be so strong." There was no laughter in his voice, no smile on his face, just a seriousness that would look much more at place on a man twice his age.

She didn't know what to do, she just stared at him, as if he was made of something other than flesh and bone then it struck her, *this IS strange*, "I don't even know you! Why would you say such a thing?" She was preparing to leave again.

"I can see a person in need in front of me, I will not allow that to go unchecked." His face hadn't changed, he was completely unphased by her, once again, rejecting him. There was something deep inside him, more than was he was willing to show, that caused him to act as such. She did not know what it was, but she felt a twinge of pity and sadness for him. How lonely he must be to befriend the demon child. "I will keep your secret, *and* I will have someone to share my nights with! It's a win-win." He stood up and grabbed her hands, pulling her up with him. She was in such amazement and also a little disturbed, but she had never met someone with so much charisma and fire for life that she just couldn't help her curiosity. She finally nodded to his proposal, and he smiled again. He turned and ran out of the field, practically skipping down the road, leaving her staring after him.

When she regained herself, she yelled after him, "Wait! I don't even know your name!"

He turned to face her but continued to run, backward, "Gabriel, it's Gabriel!" he shouted back at her, and she ran to catch up to him.

That night he showed her how to sneak into shops without getting caught, and they tried on clothes of the rich and fancy and ate delicate treats and laid in beds that were for rent. They spent the night living as they had never done.

"That food was unbelievable!" she exclaimed, forgetting herself, coming out of the back door to the restaurant they had snuck into.

"'Tis just a taste of what you will be experiencing on the Gabriel Tour of our fine city." He said as serious as he could. "Now," he held out a hand, "if you would allow me to guide you to our next stop." She took his hand, without thinking, and he took them to a bench that was positioned alongside the creek just outside of the town.

They sat for a few minutes in quiet, and he tried to break the silence, "Um… so, what kind of books do you like to spend your time reading?" he asked awkwardly, as if he had used up all his charisma.

"Like? Books?" she almost giggled as she said it, "Is that what you're going to ask me, forgive me, but you do not seem the sort for that kind of small talk." She looked at him, "Why not ask me what you really want to?" she leaned into him and squinted her eyes at him to intensify her question. Then she leaned back and said, "Or better yet, allow me to ask *you* something." She didn't wait for him to answer, "Why would you say you'd protect me when you had just met me? How would you even know I needed such a gesture?"

He studied her face for a moment then, "I know not what you mean," he said, playfully trying to hide his smile. As she stared at him quietly, his smile faded, and he looked straight back at her and quickly spoke. "Even now I see your pain and fear. Before you even spoke your eyes burned with need. You fear for your life."

She looked at him questioningly, "I am in no danger," she said.

He elaborated, "As much as you love your family, you want to be away from them because you are so lonely. Being near them reminds you that you can never be loved by them the way you desire. But you also see a monster in yourself, and their disappointment reminds you of that. You fear what you are and what you will become if you stay. However, you cannot leave because that will hurt them even more." He paused for a moment, a look of horror on her face. He gently pushed the hair from her eyes, placed there by the wind. "I also see in you a fire that needs tending. It needs to spread to illuminate all the beauty trapped inside you. You have a passion for life that makes even *me* stumble. You will change this world, Rosina, I am sure of it. And who am I to deny destiny its leader?"

He reached up and wiped a tear from her cheek, a tear she hadn't known she'd shed. After a long moment of locked eyes, she burst out in laughter. She laughed so hard she was bent over, holding her stomach.

"What?" he asked, startled.

After she caught her breath, she wiped her eyes and said, "You are a well-versed poet, my friend, but I believe your humor has gotten the better of your words." She started laughing again. "Destiny's leader," she muttered between breaths.

He stared at her for a minute, baffled and then he too started to laugh, "You're right, you're right!"

"Woo!" she said after they had laughed themselves out, "Thank you for that. I needed a good laugh," she said, with laughter still on her tongue.

"I'm glad I could be of service, milady," he bowed, and they laughed again. "I do mean what I said, though,"

"Yes, I know, but that's a little too scary on point for me, so I'm just going to keep thinking you are a crazy person," she smiled at him.

"Well, I wouldn't need to act as one if someone we both know didn't run around acting as though she were possessed." He gave her a pointed look. She quickly turned away from him as she gasped as if he had slapped her. "I'm sorry!" he said quickly, jumping up to face her, "I didn't mean to hurt you, I was only—"

"PFFT!" she turned back to him, laughing hysterically, "Got ya!" He sank to the ground, looking exhausted. "Oh come now, I hadn't thrust a sword into thy valiant knight's heart, have I?" she said with a giggle.

It was he who looked taken aback this time and he quickly jumped to his feet and put his hands on his hips and pretended to draw a sword, "I am the most valiant of knights, and I would not be wounded by so simple a weapon as a twig," he said looking up his imaginary sword. "My dear lady, do not be so confident in your skills to upset this dragon for honor!" he said without cracking a smile. She was all but rolling off the bench with laughter.

"My noble knight, will thou saveth thee from the beasts of the deep?" she said placing the back of her hand on her forehead, feigning weakness. "Will thou rescue thee from thine tower yonder, beyond the seas of lava?" She sat up straight and said, with a glint of mischief, "Or does thou shake in thine metal boots? Does this twig scareth you?" she reached down and picked up a small stick laying on the ground and held it up as if challenging him.

"Me-lady, I guarantee that small *thing*," he said with mock disgust, "does not even place a shadow of fear in my brave heart," he bent down and also picked up a stick, "On guard!" he said, and she swung her "sword" at him, and he blocked with his. The "fought" all around the bench and up and down the creek until they were exhausted and laughing.

"The sun's about to come up." he said after they had caught their breath, "Allow me to walk you home." He didn't ask her, he told her.

"You have some nerve," pretending to be angry, "I've only just met you, and you want to take me home?" she laughed.

"I recall you were the one already having dirty thoughts about me," he winked at her as her face turned red. "I just want to make sure you get home safely." *He looks innocent enough, but he has a grin creeping up on his face...*

She stared at him for a moment, but then nodded, "It's this way," she pointed towards her home. "You know a good bit about me, but I know very little about you, can you tell me why you are out here and not at home?" she asked, genuinely wanting to know what demons he was hiding.

A dark look came over his face, all traces of his beautiful smile was gone.

"Ah!" She wanted to take it back. "You don't have to answer if you don't want to." They walked in silence for a few minutes.

His rich voice was what broke that silence, "I hate my father."

"Huh?" She was surprised that he spoke and so bluntly.

"I'm the third son, and he expects me to surpass my older brothers, even though his expectations for them are already so high. I can't make any mistakes, or he makes me repeat the task ten times, so I will never forget how to do it properly. It can be as simple as closing the door without making a sound." He paused and looked up to the sky, "I wish I was already able to support myself and I could give him a nice slamming door on my way out forever." She reached out and touched his arm before he realized it. He jumped a little, not expecting it, and she quickly withdrew.

"I'm sorry, that must be horrible," she said, trying to stifle her anger, *how could one be so cruel to their own child?* Even after seeing how her parents acted, she was still shocked, and that shock surprised her.

He turned and stopped, facing her, "Could I ask for a favor?" She nodded. "When we are able, will you run away with me?"

She thought he was joking but then she could see in his eyes that he was serious, "I—" she was going to reject him and tell him he was crazy but the more she thought about it, the more she wanted to go away with him, not today but someday, when the time was right. "Yes." She nodded fervently. "It's a little crazy to think about, but I have always wanted to travel the world, be free of the shackles of a normal life and learn everything about the world. I want to see the temples in China and feel the Nile on my feet." She was growing giddy with excitement, "But! Right now I will just say this: I will go when the time is right, and it no longer sounds foolish to us."

He smiled and pulled her into him, his warmth and scent surrounded her, his excitement and relief obvious. She could feel her heart start to beat faster and her face grow hotter. He pulled away and grinned.

"Why's your face so red?" he said after he looked down at her.

"It's not!" she turned her head away, covering her face with her hands. He laughed a gentle laugh and put his hand in her hair and around the back of her head pulling her to him. The touch shocked her into dropping her hands. He bent down and kissed her. He was so gentle, and he held her loosely so she could pull away. When she didn't, he held her tighter and kissed her deeper until she started to tremble. He pulled away and looked away from her.

"I'm sorry, I've wanted to do that all night." She couldn't say anything, she was still in shock, but she could see that he was blushing. That fact gave her a little confidence and she reached out and grabbed the front of his shirt getting his attention.

He looked down at her. "I'm supposed to be the one blushing." She said in a small voice and he laughed.

"You're right, but am I not allowed to as well? That was, after all, my first kiss." She looked up in surprise, "What's with that look?"

"Nothing," she looked away from him, "we should get going."

"Not until you tell me what you are thinking."
She didn't answer, and when she started walking again and he remained where he was, she gave in, "Fine! You seem like the kind of guy that would have kissed many girls." She looked down and blushed even more.

"I'll take that as a compliment." He reached out, grabbing her hand and started walking. He walked her to the gates of her family's orchard. "I'll leave you here for tonight. Shall we go out again tomorrow? I will meet you here." He didn't even pause between sentences, whether it was excitement or nerves she couldn't tell.

"Yes," she said at a loss for more words. She turned to sneak in the gate when he grabbed her hand and pulled her back to him, kissing her once more.

"I'm sorry, I just am not quite ready to let you go. I'm not a creep, so please don't think that way. There's just something about you…" He covered his mouth as if to stop himself. He let her go and jogged off down the road. She stood there, breathless for a moment. She couldn't believe how good it felt to have someone near her, to touch her to want to look at her. The sun snuck up over the horizon, and she rushed into the house trying to not make any noise.

Many weeks passed this way. Each night they had a different adventure and each night, they came to know a little bit more about each other.

•　　•　　•　　•　　•

He met her at her gate, and they head into town. He took her small hand in his and brought it to his lips, she shuddered at his touch, trying to pull away but he wouldn't let her. "You are afraid of me?" he said over her hand.

She shook her head, and her long hair to swung over her shoulder, coming down and settling on his arm, now very close to her as she was trying to pull hers back. It's silky texture sliding over his skin and sending a shiver up his arm. "If you do not fear me then what is it?"

"I have not been close to anyone in many years. And, seeing the town as we have, I have only observed when people get close to a woman that is not usually a good thing. Men… never allow the woman to say 'no' they just take what they want." She spoke softly, and her voice was shaking.

He brought her hand up to his chest and its warmth spread through her hand. He released her, "I will never do anything to you that you do not wish me to," he smiled down at her, "my heart is in your hands, if you see fit, you may rip it out of my chest." She pulled her hand away quickly and held it to herself.

"I do not wish to harm you, I just know that I must be careful," she said. Then, she reached her trembling hand out and touched his cheek just lightly, barely feeling it beneath her cold fingers. He closed his eyes, and a sigh escaped his lips. He stepped closer to her and gently ran his fingers across her cheek as she had him and then he ran them through her long hair, it cascaded from his fingers like water.

He then brought his arms up and wrapped her in them, holding her tightly, "Didn't I say I would protect you?" he asked with his face in her hair, muffling his voice.

She was silent for a moment then said, "Yes, you did," she pushed him away with her hands on his chest, "but having just met you, I was not sure if you were being earnest or just trying to get close to me to ridicule me."

He looked shocked, "What have they done to you that you automatically distrust everyone you meet?" She turned away, sadness on her face. "I'm sorry." He tried to take back his question seeing the pain on her face, "Forget I asked." He turned her head back to him, she was staring him in the eye, her emerald jewel eyes almost glowing, "I will show you that not everyone in this world is evil." He wiped a tear from her eye as it escaped.

Slowly as the days passed, she started to see a different side of people that she thought didn't exist. He built her up with compliments by telling her things like: she was brilliant and beautiful. He showed her kindness when others shunned her, he smiled at her stories and tried to make her laugh. He helped her when she was sad, he dried her tears, and he lifted her when she fell. He talked to her as if she was any other person, someone that deserved his attention. His eyes lit up when he got excited, and he shared all his loves with her, he loved chocolate, he loved to read: poetry was his muse, he painted, even though he was terrible, he still showed her and when she took in all the magnificent colors and smiled she could feel his relief and happiness. He asked her what she enjoyed what she wanted to do when she was older, what her favorite season, color, food, and books were. He didn't force himself to be with her, she saw genuine joy in his walk and smile when she was with him, and he never missed a chance to sneak out with her, he was at her gate every night.

"Thank you," she whispered at his back, one night he had skipped ahead in his excitement.

He stopped and looked over his shoulder, "For what?"

She smiled because he truly was oblivious to things around him and his honesty was refreshing, "For spending your time with someone like me."

"Someone like you?" he asked confused.

"Someone..." she looked away from him as he turned to face her, "someone so broken."

"You're broken?!" he grabbed her shoulders and looked her up and down, turned her and checked her back, leaned over to check her legs and feet and lifted her hands up to examine. "Where?! We have to fix you," he turned around and kneeled down as if waiting for her to climb on, "Quick, get on, we must find a repairman, who fixes lovely young girls." She laughed at his feigning panic. When she did he stood up and put his finger under her chin, bringing her face up towards his, "We are all broken, some a little, some a lot, but it is what we do with our pain that makes us great or leaves us in the damaged pile." He was so serious, "You are an amazing woman, you are brilliant. You have so much love in you that you are afraid to be hurt by everyone else because no one can compare to you. We all look dim standing next to you. If your love were food, no one would ever go hungry." She felt tears start to fill her eyes, but he wouldn't let her wipe them away, "Let them fall, let them wash away all your pain and fear. Allow them to open your heart to this beautiful world, open it to me, I will always protect it." He bent down and gently kissed her lips as her tears soaked her skin and she quivered with her pain. "Let it out, my beautiful rose, those tears can be your thorns." She felt a wash of sadness over her, and the pain in her stomach rose up to her heart and then to her head where she felt it fall with her tears. She bent her head back and closed her eyes to the blanket of stars and let out a wail into the darkness, she shuddered with its release and with its departure she felt something warm take its place. She brought her head back down, looked at him. Her tear stained face decorated with a smile that he had never before seen. A true smile. He smiled back and pulled her in tight to his body and fell in love with her. Her beauty was shining through, and he was unable to shield himself from it because he did not want to.

•   •   •   •   •

"Come with me." He said to her many weeks later, he had seen a new side of her once she let her walls fall and he couldn't get enough. She was like a tempting candy, you know you should stop eating but you just can't. Now he wanted to show her what she had done for him.

"Where are we going?" she asked.

"It's a secret." He grinned

"You aren't going to do anything weird, are you?"

"Perhaps." He smiled and put her hand in his and walked away from town. They walked until they were well out of town and starting to head up to the cliffs that loomed over the sea.

"You're not going to push me over the cliff are you?" she said only a little fearful.

He laughed, "If I wanted to kill you why would I set up this?" he pointed at the ground where there were a blanket and a basket full of food.

"You don't want me to suspect?" she asked with sarcasm in her voice, but she couldn't help but smile and squeeze his hand tighter.

They sat and ate the sandwiches and drank the fresh fruit juice he had packed, enjoying the beautiful view, the stars reflected off the water and rolling green hills behind them. She closed her eyes and laid down enjoying the peace of the night: the sound of the waves crashing into the stones below and the cool night air surrounded them.

"We should live in the country when we leave this place." she said, loving the calm. They talked every night of all the places they wanted to go see when they finally left home.

"Mmm." He agreed. "With a little cottage and a dog or two. Nothing but us and the sky and grass. We'll live off the land, grow our own vegetables and fruits." When he looked over at her, she was looking at him with a smile on her face. "This is the first time we talked about settling down. I like it much more than anything we have talked about before. He had kindness in his eyes, and a joy that she had never seen, "For once I feel like I belong, you make my world seem like it's not spinning out of control. I can't wait for our life to begin."

"It is only natural that we talk about it, at least once, we can't travel forever, you know." She joked.

"Thank you, you truly make me happy, I think I'm getting the better end of our deal. You are still strong for me, even though I'm supposed to be your protector." He sounded ashamed.

"You fool, I protect you when you are weak, and you protect me when I'm weak. That is how it's supposed to work." She said, with the thoughts of how he had been helping her this whole time even without him trying making her speak.

"But why? I have never had anyone care about me hurting, why do you?" he asked, truly confused.

"Because I love you." Her confidence flew out of her as she realized what she said and she turned away from him, quickly hiding her face. She felt him lay beside her and wrap his arms around her, nuzzling his face in her hair. She could feel his smile and happiness rolling off him; it caused her embarrassment to be replaced with her own happiness.

"I love you, too," he said into her hair. He rolled her over and kissed her, deep and hungry. He found her lips soft, and he pushed them apart with his tongue. She gasped at the invasion, and he pulled away, looking down at her. "I'm sorry, I got ahead of myself."

She shook her head and put her hand on the back of his neck, caressing his skin and pulling him back down to her and reciprocated his moves. She reached up and tugged at his shirt. He pulled up and looked at her in surprise, what he saw was a look of need and love. "I don't know if I can contain myself if you keep looking like this and you keep tugging," he looked down at her hand still grasping his shirt.

"Then don't." She tugged hard on his shirt, pulling it up and exposing his skin to the cold air and her warm hand. This time he gasped. He bent down and kissed her neck, he could feel her warmth. He traced her neck down to her collarbone and slowly undid her shirt, revealing her pale skin. He made a hot trail of kisses down her shoulder then backtracked and went down her body, following his hand as it moved lower, unbuttoning her shirt. He kissed her skin down her chest, between her breast and down her stomach. He gently caressed every inch of her skin as she laid before him, clinging to him, afraid to move. He reached out a hand and laid it on top of one of her trembling hands and moved it up his stomach and to his chest, stopping briefly over his heart. It was pounding so hard she felt it would come right out of his chest. She slowly started to move her hands on her own, around to his back and pulled his shirt up over his head, allowing her full access to all the muscles that she didn't know he had. She ran her hands over his back and his shoulders, exploring these new muscles.

He moved down and slowly slid her pants off, kissing her hips, her thighs and her calves as she moaned at his touch. He smiled as he reached up and pulled down her underwear too, leaving her completely exposed, and he ate her up with his eyes. She was embarrassed, so she decided to even the playing field. She sat up and pushed him down and pulled off his pants. She straddled his hips, teasing him by being so close to him but just out of reach. He grumbled and reached up, putting his hands in her hair and pulling her down to him. He kissed her so fiercely that she was left gasping for breath, his hands still in her hair as he tugged a little on it and she let a moan escape. The sound drove him over the edge, and he sat up so quickly that she wrapped her legs around him and was now sitting in his lap. He kissed her hard and touched her in places she's never been touched with a gentle hunger she feared she would forever crave. He moved her so she could feel how much he wanted her and he reached between her legs to find that she wanted him just as badly. He laid her back down on the blanket and nestled himself in her warm thighs. He was so close to her that she could feel his heat touching hers. He waited to see her reaction.

"We shouldn't be doing this," she gasped, out of breath, but with no desire to stop.

"I know," he whispered in her ear, "but I want you to know how much I love you and how much I need you."

She let out a noise of pleasure, and he could not contain himself. He gently thrust himself into her, shaking with restraint but she was not so patient. She put her hands in the back side of his hips and yanked. He was fully in with one swift thrust, and she rose her hips to meet his. She let out a sigh and a small scream: a mix of pain and pleasure and she whispered to him, "I love you, Gabriel." He made love to her as she gripped onto him with her hands and wrapped her legs around his back. They exhausted themselves and laid in the throes of passion as the night sky moved over them.

• • • • •

They thought their dream would never end and they would be together until they grew old, but deep down they knew that wasn't how life worked, they knew best that fact. The day they had dreaded finally came when Gabriel asked Rosina to meet him in the alley where they had first met. He was in a panic…

"Truth be told the first time I met you I could feel my heart beating faster and I had a burning desire to protect you, I don't know why I had never even spoken to you before. All I knew about you was what other people said. I didn't believe them, and a part of me wanted to find out the truth for myself, I was curious, but when I did meet you all my expectations were blown away. You were more beautiful, more kind, more gentle, and much more heavenly than anything

I had ever had the pleasure of seeing or feeling and I knew in that moment I wanted to stay by your side."

"What are you talking about?" She laughed it off but, when he grabbed her shoulders, she started to feel a fear that was hidden in their denial start to peek out.

"He's sending me to military school."

Chapter Three: The Final Fantasy

With each passing moment my days grew warmer,
The sun burned brighter.
With each passing moment my heart died,
My hands grew cold.
With each passing moment my blood ran faster,
My breathing came quicker.
With each passing moment I lost control,
My skin quivered with excitement.
With each passing moment I fell for you
I fell for you and your evil mind.

"Rose," his smile was gone, and a frown had taken its place. "Something has happened. My family has found out about my 'misbehaving,'" he said with and is planning on 'fixing' me. They are sending me away to the naval academy in preparation for me joining the navy. 'I'll straighten the demons right out of you.'" He mocked his father with a tone of disgust.

She could not find words to speak, but a whimper-like sound slipped from her mouth. He stepped toward her and she backed away. She couldn't believe it, her sun was going to go down and never come back up. The pain she felt was so strong it felt as if it ripped her apart. It was like nothing she'd ever felt before and didn't care to ever feel again. He saw her discomfort and opened up his arms to pull her into an embrace to calm her, but she stepped back away from him. She hadn't meant to, it was automatic: *put a wall up when you lose and you won't get hurt.* She saw the look of abandonment on his face at her rejection and stepped back into his arms. He held her tight and warm against the rush of cold she suddenly felt. She allowed tears to fall into his shirt. He kissed the top of her head, "Shh, it will be alright. I have an idea. I don't plan to go to that school and leave you here."

She looked up at him. He looked so different than the man she had come to love. He now looked serious and firm in his standing. He looked amazing. "What's your plan?" she asked.

"We will run away together."

"You're kidding? Right now?" she saw in his face that this was no joke. "We have no means to run away, we have no money, no place to go and our parents, especially yours, will come after us."

"That will be no problem." he said with confidence. "I will be able to acquire the funds to sustain us until we find a permanent means of income. The term doesn't start for several weeks we have plenty of time to prepare. The plan will be simple: I will pack as if I were leaving for that school and you will wait for me at the old miner's tavern. When I pass by in the carriage, I will simply slip out while it is moving and none would be the wiser. At least until it is discovered that I am not in the carriage several hours later and by then we will be long gone."

"This will never work. What about my family? If I disappear, they will search for me until they find me. They will be tied in knots until I come home, remember they believe I am broken in my head." She put her forefinger on her temple, making her point. "My mother will be mortified if I disappear." *Or relieved,* she did not say out loud. She tried to convince herself and him, even though her heart kept telling her that they could do this. They did not need all of the plush of their current lifestyle. However much she tried to listen to her heart, her intellect was telling her that it would be impossible. And without them being in unison, she felt helpless. Helpless for him and helpless for herself.

He put a finger under her chin and lifted her face so she could look at him. "I will take care of that, somehow, I will ease your heart and your family will be fine, I will make sure of that." He kissed her forehead and whispered, "Believe in us." That was all it took. It was like someone had placed a lantern in the dark and she was no longer afraid.

"Tell me what I need to do."

•　　•　　•　　•　　•

Gabriel's life became much more restricted, and he was able to leave his house less and less often as time grew closer to his departure. "Meet me here, like we always have. Wait for half an hour past ten, and if I don't show, go home, where you are safe." He told her the night their plans started to take root. After that, she did not see much of him, and when she did, only for a few minutes, but most of the time is was a simple note slid under a wooden crate telling her what was happening in his house and more ideas to add to their "Great Escape" as he now called it.

He made an unexpected stop at her house one afternoon, wanting to speak to her parents. She sat in the hallway listening. "I know you don't know me personally, but I know you do business with my father, Mr. Charles Henwood?"

"Oh yes, He is quite the charming man," she heard her mother's voice, and imagined the face he would have made if he were alone with her.

"Yes. He's a force to be reckoned with when it comes to business, if I recall," her father said.

"Yes," Gabriel laughed, "That he is, some say that he loves his business more than his own wife." They all shared a laugh, Gabriel was convincing, but she could tell his was fake. "But that aside, I am sure you have heard that I am leaving for the naval academy in the north shortly."

"Oh yes, of course, congratulations, that is a most prestigious school. Only the best of the best are accepted," her father said.

"Thank you very much, sir, I'm looking forward to achieving my higher goals, but that is not why I came today. I have heard rumors about your daughter and happened to also hear some things about a school in the north, near where I will be going that has a special section specific to cases such as yours."

"Young man, I would watch where your words are leading. Rumors are not the truth." Her father's voice rang out in the silence.

"I understand that, sir," he said, trying to save the quickly sinking ship of a conversation, "however, I have not seen her in town or at church and as her peer I worry about her. I know I have spent very little time—"

She heard a chair scrap as her father stood up, "I will have none of this talk in my home, she is perfect the way she is," she felt a tear well up in her eye, "And we will not stand for a brat such as you to dirty her name!"

"Sir, I did not mean to offend. Please, hear me out, I too care about her, I remember her sitting in church, she was an angel even then, and I only want to help," Gabriel said. "Pl\ease hear me out. This place has many of the finest doctors, and it promises to give the freedom the child needs as well as helping out the parents. They do not mean to keep her, just look after her for a short time, to give you a break, as well as assess her needs and abilities. They do this and then return her to you with all you need to take care of her and even offer a trained assistant, if you would like."

"We will not send away our daughter just because she is different!" her father was angry.

"I do not mean to be rude, however, perhaps you keeping her here is stunting her or there is something that they can do to bring her back up to her old speed?"

"How dare—!"

"Dear, perhaps we should listen to him," she heard her mother's soft voice and imagined her placing a delicate hand on his forearm, "we are tired and if this could help her, what do we have to lose?" Rosina could feel the relief flooding off her mother, and the stress that made her voice tense was gone. She held her breath so she could weather the pain she was feeling.

He finally sat back down and they talked for nearly half an hour more before Gabriel excused himself saying, "I'll send over the paperwork that needs to be filled out and inform you of the date of our departure as soon as we are able."

"Thank you, son." Her father said and they walked him out the door, he glanced down at her and winked, she just stared at him.

She didn't see him at all after that, the days turned into a week, and she started to grow lonely and restless in his absence. She knew that he had not abandoned her, but she couldn't convince her heart, that felt like it had been betrayed and left alone just the same. She began wandering around at night after the time she was supposed to wait for him. She had grown to know the streets well and could hide and disappear at any time she needed to.

She knew she should not be out alone, but she hated being cooped up in her house just waiting for Gabriel. She should be patient, but sitting made her more anxious, and walking helped relieve some of her stress, the stars reminded her of him of how they laid in the grass and just looked up at them and talked all night. She felt a tear well up but kept it from falling. She was lost in her thoughts and didn't notice that she was walking down one of the darker roads that Gabriel had warned her against. She turned around to retrace her steps back to the main road, but someone standing at the mouth of the street. She did not recognize the man, but he was much bigger than she and she immediately began to panic. He laughed a rough laugh, and she could smell alcohol coming from him even though he was almost ten feet from her.

She turned around again to find she was blocked in by another man just as big as the first. She tried to run between him and the wall, but he grabbed her around the throat and slammed her against the wall. A gasp of breath escaped her as her head knocked against the wall and she could feel her consciousness fading. Her head bobbed down against his arm, but the other man lifted it up roughly by grabbing her cheeks with one hand.

"Oh no, sweetheart, you don't get out of it that easily." She opened her eyes and tried to focus on him, but her vision was blurry.

"Please," she whispered.

"What's that?" the man got close to her face.

"Please, let me go."

"I can't hear you." He mocked her and got even closer until he was talking in her ear, "Nothing you say will help you now." Panic shot through her body making her skin tingle. She was frozen, her mind blank, but when he moved back and slid his hand under her tunic, her hands moved on their own. She formed fists and threw them at him as hard as she could, in his face and chest and neck. She tried to dig her fingers into his eyes and push away his face.

"You bitch!" he yelled, and the other man grabbed her hands and held them above her.

"NO!" she screamed as loud as she could as her captor's hand clapped over her mouth. She tried to bite him, but he did not budge, he was a like steel rod. The other man pulled down her pants and underwear, exposing her. She felt her fear climbing to an unbearable height, she couldn't even cry, and her mouth went dry. She struggled against him, crossing her legs and turning from side to side to get away from the second man, but he was too strong, and he just laughed at her as the first man pulled her knees apart and settled himself between her thighs. She screamed behind the man's hand, but even she could barely hear it. She brought one of her knees up and tried to hit the man in front of her, but he grabbed it.

"Thank you, dear." He laughed, and she felt him against her, during her struggle he had loosened his own pants and was ready to take anything she had, whether she wanted to give it or not. She stopped moving, fear blinding her. "Lose your fight already? That's a shame," he laughed as he lifted up her other leg and tucked it around the other side of his waist, he held them there with one hand and yanked up her shirt with the other, tearing it. She started to struggle again and then she felt a cold metal blade on her throat, "Move again and I'll make you bleed." She stopped and stared at him. "That's more like it." He grunted and pushed his way into her. She felt as if he was a searing blade, the pain burned her all the way up her chest, and her tears finally came. She closed her eyes, wishing it was over. He buried himself over and over until he was panting and she was limp. He let her go and she slid to the ground, blood on her thighs and tears streaming down her face, but she made no noise, didn't attempt to move, just sat on the cold ground, empty.

She felt a strong grip on her shoulders pulling her up, "My turn," the other man said, she couldn't even lift her head to look at him, and she felt the cold wall behind her, and his heat grew near. She allowed herself to think of anything but what was happening, trying to escape it when she heard a thud and the grip was gone. She slid to the ground again. She heard a few more thuds and raised her head to see Gabriel was standing over her, shielding her as the two men came at him. He raised his fists and hit them, catching them in the face and belly. It did not knock them down, but it drove the breath out of them and he used that moment to swing out a foot and kick the first man in the head, knocking him to the ground. The other started for him, but thought better of it when he saw Gabriel pull out a short sword. He pulled up the other man and ran away from them. He stay there for a moment, breathing heavy before turning around, dropping the sword and kneeling down in front of her. He took off his coat and wrapped it around her.

"Rosina," he said in barely a whisper, "I'm so sorry." She looked at him, her jewels were now a dull, gray. He pulled her in and held her, and tried to keep his tears from falling, "I'm so sorry." She laid limp in his arms as he rocked her back and forth, the shock still keeping her from believing it was not a horrible nightmare. He whispered to her, "I failed you, I failed…"

"No," her voice was hoarse, "Not your fault."

"Yes," he pulled her face to his, "yes it was, it was my fault for not being here for not protecting you, for letting you get hurt, for—"

"Please," she looked at him, her eyes dead, "just…" a tear fell from her eye, "hold me." Her shock had slightly subsided, and she looked at him for answers, for an explanation to what had happened and why…why her, "why…?"

"Oh Rose," he hugged her as tight as he could and felt her shake, heard her crying, the pain was almost unbearable for him, "I'm so sorry." Her trembling shook his soul, and he kissed her head over and over, not knowing what to do to help her.

"Why? Why? Why me???" he heard her scream into his chest, "Why?"

"Rose…" he grew angry at his helplessness and said, "I'll kill them. I'll kill anyone who hurts you, I'll kill anyone that even thinks about you the way you don't want them to." His anger made him tremble, and when she looked up at him, she saw darkness in his face.

"Gabriel?" He looked down at her, resolve written in his eyes.

"I'll kill them. You'll never have to worry again, you'll never have to be afraid. I'll never leave you alone again." He stood and pulled her up with him. He picked her up in his arms and held her close. "Let's go somewhere else." She nodded

He walked out of the alley and out of town. He carried her to the field where he had first made the promise to protect her, then through it and to the spring hidden by the trees on the other side. He sat her down on a rock just at the edge of the water and took off his shirt, soaking it in the water. He wiped her legs from toes to her hips, cleaning off the dirt and blood. He removed his coat and the remains of her tunic and cleaned her. "I'll remove any trace of him from you, he won't even be in your nightmares." She watched him fall deeper and deeper into despair with her.

"You can't kill them," she whispered. He looked up when she spoke.

"What?" He continued to wash her, "Of course I can, and I will."

She grabbed his hand, stopping his scrubbing, "Please," she looked him in the eyes, his fire was going out, "don't. You will be worse than them, don't sink, please. Keep your fire, please. For me? I need you to relight mine." She started to cry again, "Please."

He dropped his shirt and grabbed her, holding her tight, then he put his hands on either side of her face, and lifted her lips to his and he kissed her hard. He put all his passion in it, his desire to help, her to protect her, to be with her. He felt a shaky hand rest itself on his shoulder and it slowly stopped shaking. He looked at her and saw a new kindness in her eyes.

"I love you so much, Gabriel. I would be gone without you, but you share my pain, and that makes it bearable. Thank you." She leaned into him again and kissed him with as much emotion as he had kissed her. "Never leave me," she said as she pulled him to her, covering her naked body with his and allowed his warmth to spread over her. He lifted her up and carried her away from the river, grabbing his coat as he passed it.

He sat her down in the field and put the coat around her shoulders, but she wouldn't let go of his neck, she kept pulling him down, kissing him.

"Rosina, we need to get you home, you'll get sick." He tugged her arms off him and pulled the coat closed.

"Gabriel," she whispered as she looked at him, "removed that man from my body."

"What?" He knew what she wanted but thought he was wrong.

She opened the coat again and laid down in the grass, her skin was covered with goosebumps from the water and the cold. "Remove him from me," she grabbed his belt and pulled him towards her, "remove all of him." He fell on top of her, and she wrapped her arms around his back.

He pushed himself up off her, "Rose, no." he shook his head, "that will make it worse."

"Please, Gabriel, I can still feel him." He shook his head again, but he was weakening. When he didn't move she pushed him away and sat up, staring at him.

"I'm sorry, Rose, I don't want you to hate me." He was lost, he didn't want to do it, but he didn't want to ignore her pleas. "I can't hurt you."

She turned from him, pulling his coat over her, "yeah."

"Rose," he reached to touch her, and she flinched from him, he stared at her back in shock.

"I'm sorry," she turned back around quickly, "I didn't mean it,"

"No, no, its fine," he smiled at her, trying to reassure her, "I know you are scared and you know I would do anything for you—"

"Let me do it." she said, and he looked at her, confused. "Lay down, let me take back the control." He still wasn't sure what she meant so he laid down in the grass. She stood over him and put her foot on his chest, "I'm taking back what they took from me." She put her toes under the top of his trousers. She leaned down and unbuttoned them and pulled them down just a little then slid her foot down over him. She could feel it pulsing under her touch; she smiled and looked down at his face. He was a little afraid but allowed her to proceed. She ran her foot up his stomach and then his chest, stopping on his shoulder and looked down at him, a strange look in her eyes, one he feared. She then kneeled down, putting her knees on either side of his abdomen, she was straddling his stomach and kissed his neck and chest and slid down to his stomach and hips. She took him in her mouth, and she heard him sigh in pleasure, she licked him starting at the tip, slowly swirling her tongue then moving down until he was completely in her mouth. He grabbed her hair, and she pulled up, licking her lips as she looked at him.

"Do you want to do this?" he asked, through pants.

"Yes." She moved up until she was over him and she slid him inside her. He moaned with her as she took back what was forcibly taken from her. She moved her hips until he grabbed her thighs, leaving bruises, and she knew he was close, and she moved faster until he thrust his hips up and she felt the ecstasy she always found with him, but it was so much more because she took it when she wanted it.

She laid down on him, and their heavy breathing slowed. "Thank you." He wrapped his arms around her, and she heard a whimper leave his lips. She tried to lift up to look at him, but he wouldn't let her.

"Gabriel—"

"Please don't. Let's just stay this way, I don't ever want you to look at me with sadness or fear again." She pushed against him, and he released her.

She sat over him, staring deeply at him a smile playing on her lips. "I will never look at you like that again. I love you, and I know this was hard on you too, I saw that lost look on your face." She looked away, "You should be mad at me, I just used you like a tool."

"No, I am yours to use as you please and if that helps, then use me as much as possible, but don't use me as a tool of your own pain." She just stared at him then, as if someone had lit a candle, realization crept into her face.

"Oh," she felt a pain in her chest and tears started to fall from her eyes, he sat up and pulled her to him and held her as she cried.

"Let it out, it will heal, and I will help it." She cried for nearly an hour before her tears dried up and she fell asleep in his arms, exhausted. He carried her home and woke her just so she could climb in her window.

"Will you be alright for the night?" He asked as she started up the trellis.

"Yes," she said, but he heard a little doubt in her voice.

"If anything happens send someone for me and I will come right over, no matter what. Or, I know how much your brother cares for you, talk to him."

"I will." She said, knowing that she couldn't, she had no one but her brother. She took care of herself, her former servants no longer ventured to her room with food or to help her bath and cloth herself. As much as she loved Marcus, she knew she wouldn't be able to tell him what happened. He held her hand as long as he could then let go and watched her climb into her window. He walked home a new weight heavy on him.

She sat against the wall next to her window, sore, exhausted, and lost. She was thankful for having Gabriel, he eased her mind from the terrible night, and he was the reason she would be able to sleep. She just hoped that she hadn't hurt him in the process.

$$\bullet \qquad \bullet \qquad \bullet \qquad \bullet \qquad \bullet$$

She stayed in more than she went out. She wrote letters to Gabriel when she was feeling the horrible thoughts start to overwhelm her, but never sent them, just piled them under her mattress. After two weeks of not leaving her room, she felt that the time to face her fears had come. She looked at the sky through her open window. She had been watching it all day, the dark clouds were rolling in; a thunderstorm was approaching. This night held more for her than she could imagine. This night she would be ensnared in a web that she would never be able to unweave.

She sat under an awning outside a closed shop and watched the evening thunderstorm. It was unbelievably beautiful with its electrical dances and howling whispers. The rain came down heavy and brought with it a smell of cleanliness that always came with the summer showers. She walked out to the park after it had stopped raining, to feel the wet grass beneath her feet. It was surrounded by trees with only for gaps on each of its long sides to allow for the paths to enter from the streets. She entered on the south side and walked into the dark park, her shoes scraping lightly on the stone path, until she came upon a bench under a fading lamp. She stood just outside of its light and slid off her shoes. She held her face up to the sky and closed her eyes, allowing the smell of rain to fill her and the cool wetness of the grass to tingle on her bare feet.

She felt, amongst the calming aftermath of the rain, a disturbing feeling. A dark feeling, almost as if evil really did exist and it had taken physical form. She stopped and opened her eyes to look around. She did not see anyone at first, then a glint of light reflected on someone's eye caught her attention. She looked over across the park to see a man sitting on a bench several yards from where she stood. She felt a panic shoot through her, but he didn't move. In fact, he seemed to barely even notice her.

He was a tall man, but not skinny; he was built, but not muscular. He was a sleek man wearing a black tuxedo and a top hat. His bow was red and stood out against his white shirt and black jacket. He saw her looking at him and stood up. He had a cane dangling off his left elbow, as he laid his left hand across his belly and slipped two fingers into his jacket between the buttons. He bowed to her as she just stared at him, his motion was not what she had expected. She quickly turned to face him and gave a quick, not-so-lady-like bow herself, but never took her eyes off of him. He did not take a step toward her or make another motion, but she was frightened of him. She turned slowly, so not to allow him to see her fear and started walking away from him. Then, she ran, ran as fast as she could, slinking in and out of the trees scattered throughout the park. She could see the street less than a yard in front of her. But, he was in front of her; he was blocking the exit out of the park. She stopped quickly, almost running into him. His appearance went against all she knew. She didn't hear him running after her and *how did he get in front of me?* She turned quickly to the left and kept running, but he was there. She stopped again and turned fully around and began to run again finally sneaking through the trees. Her cold bare feet slapped onto the stone road, and he was there.

He started to chuckle, low and quietly, as if it wasn't meant to be heard. He looked down at her and grinned. It was evil, but it entranced her against her will. He stood perfectly straight and said to her, "There is nowhere to run, my dear."

"What do you want of me?" she asked, her panic almost choking her.

"Only a little fun," he said.

She started to back away from him, taking small steps, hoping he wouldn't notice. She had fallen into this man's trap as she had several weeks ago with the other men.

"That won't work, I can see your movements with my eyes closed." He said, calmly. "I have played this game many times with men that have a much higher skill level than you." Her curiosity, as well as her fear, caused her to stop moving immediately.

"Are you a soldier?" she asked, before being able to stop herself bend she kicked herself mentally.

"Interesting," he said, taking another look at her, this time he took his time taking in every inch of her. She was starting to itch from discomfort under his stare. "I am no warrior, at least not in your definition of one," was all he said.

There was silence between them in which she thought of trying to leave again. She decided to speak again, her curiosity once again getting the final say. "What is that meant to mean?" she asked.

"That is of no matter," he said, "Right now I wish to speak about you."

"Me?" she asked, surprised. "I am nothing of intrigue." She tried to get him to lose interest. "I am not but a young lady out for an evening walk. I am like all the other young ladies."

"Is that so?" he asked, "I do not believe that." He took a step towards her and leaned down so he was whispering in her ear. "You hide something within you that I can see when others cannot." His breath tickled her as her brothers did, but his was not welcome, so she stepped back again out of his reach.

"I can promise you, sir, that I do not," she said, trying to keep herself calm.

He reached out his hand as he, again, took a step towards her. He laid his hand on her head, sliding it down along her hair until he cupped the back of her head. She tried to pull away, but he held her. With his other hand, he placed two fingers under her chin and gently but strongly lifted her head to look her in the eye. He held her chin with his fingers and thumb as he slid his other hand down further, along her neck and down her back. He then moved it up and over her shoulder and rested it over her heart. She was shaking with fear.

"I can feel it in you," he said, but she thought he meant her fear. "It's heat, just under the surface, screaming to be let out. It claws at you from the inside." He closed his eyes, focusing on her through feeling. He took in a deep breath as if smelling her. "Demon," his whispered.

"What?" she asked, "Are you mad? I am clearly not a demon." She struggled against him but to no avail. "Please release me," she demanded, and to her surprise he did. She stepped back. "Do you wish to make a fool of me, sir?" She dusted herself off trying to get off his touch. "I will humor you no longer. Have a good evening." She turned, even though she feared to show her back to him, and started walking away from him.

"Rosina," his voice rang out in the silence, "You know I do not lie, you have felt it." She continued walking, trying to ignore him. He began laughing, "you cannot hide from me."

She turned back around and snapped at him, "I hide nothing –" but he was not there. A hold hand gripped her shoulder and she leapt away from it reaching down and grabbing a rock off the road and throwing it at its owner.

He allowed it to strike him in the chest. He raised his eyes at her and smiled. She was scared into silence when she looked at him. His eyes were not that of a man but were blackened and his teeth were not strait as hers were, his top canines were elongated and sharpened to a point. "My dear, sticks and stones may break *your* bones, but they will never harm me." He said as he laughed at her fear.

She was choking on it, her fear. She didn't know what to do her mind had shut off and her body refused to move, "Vampyre," was all she was able to whisper.

"Clever girl," he said, pleased, "I am surprised you even know the legends."

He's going to kill me, she thought as she could feel the power coming from him.

"Oh, do not fear me, child," he said as if he could read her mind.

"You will not kill me?" she asked, her voice trembling.

"Not yet, that would disrupt my plans." He gave her a one sided grin that showed his pleasure. "No, I'm going to dig around in your mind first."

Her fear was climbing, "you intend to leave me drooling on the street?" she asked, quietly, she really didn't want to know the answer."

"Oh no," he walked around her, not touching her but taking her in with hungry eyes, "I'm going to break you then I'm going to drain every ounce of blood from your body while its," he paused and took in a deep breath as if his words were causing physical pleasure, "boiling in fear," he laughed and walked away from her.

She stood shaking in the middle of the wet street. She should have run as fast as she could as far away from him as she could but her hatred for him grew as her fear paralyzed her. "You heartless bastard! Were you not also once human? How could you mess with an empty girl? Haven't I suffered enough?" her tears betrayed her as they fell down past her clenched fists. Are you some sort of pervert that has a taste for the young? You… you pedophile!" she knew she was reaching with her name calling and angry rant, but she was so afraid that she couldn't think straight.

He stopped and she heard an angry growl come from him. She only heard one foot take a step before she was slammed to the ground. Her breath was knocked out of her as his cane came across her throat and pinned down. He was atop her straddling her chest his knees holding down her arms. His eyes were angry and his hat laid a yard from them. "Is your mind already destroyed? I can take away that pain now if you wish," his voice was deep she could see a vein pulsing in his temple, his anger barely in check. "I do not waste my time on anyone that has anything less than a brilliant mind. Tell me, girl," he spat the world, "how would a child have the capacity to fear as much as a well-learned mind?" he asked but didn't give her time to answer, "I speak the truth but you spit lies, I no longer believe you are worth my time." He yanked one of her hands out from under his knees and slammed it against his chest. "Feel my heartbeat as I drain your life!" He leaned down near her neck. She could feel her own heart pounding in her ears but her hand felt a different beat, one much slower and off beat from her own.

"Heart... beat," she whispered in amazement, "I was wrong," he stopped and she could feel his teeth sitting on her skin.

"You are a fool," he said against her skin. "How do you think the blood I consume is distributed throughout my body?" He sat up, expecting to see her face stained with tears but she was looking him right in the eyes, her fear had evaporated. He looked down at her for a moment then said, "Are you not afraid to die?"

"If you've watched me as you say then you know there are far worse things than dying. Kill me if you will but don't play with me. I'm not a toy. If its fun you seek you will be disappointed because I'm already broken." She said, and he could see her calm resolve.

"Perhaps you are right." he said and stood and retrieved his hat, holding it in hand with the cane. "What is coming is far worse than anything you have ever even dreamed of," he said facing away from her.

She was still on the road, sitting, not ready to stand. At his words, she looked up and said, "What—" but he was gone. She stood quickly and looked all around her, but there was no sign of him or of him having ever been there. She wanted to find him to ask him what he meant, even though she knew it was a blessing he was gone. *Haven't you gotten yourself hurt enough by wandering around like an airheaded idiot??* She stood in the middle of the road conflicted when she saw a strip of light coming over one of the outer buildings. She ran home as quickly as her feet could move. She had never been out this late, she made sure she was home before the sun started to rise, how could her timing be so far off?

She made her feet move faster. Around the corner, through the square, where people were already getting themselves out of bed and opening up their windows.

Now, up the steady hill toward her family's estate; around the back, through the two pieces of rotting wood in the fence, through the rose garden; up to her window and into her room.

She laid down and covered herself with the soft down comforter and tried to catch her breath before anyone heard her. As she laid under the covers, as the sun hit her window, she tried to wrap her mind around what had happened during the night, but to no avail, her mind was blank, nothing she could think of could explain who or what that man was and all she could do was stare at her wall.

She heard a tapping at her door, and jumped at the sudden break in silence. Her mother came in and saw her looking dumbfounded. Of all the days for her mother to check on her, *why today?* She asked herself. After all, her mother specifically chose to avoid her unless it was impossible or obvious. She saw the sweat on Rosina's face and quickly walked over to place a hand on her face. *Oh no...*

'She's sick, oh no, my darling, you're sick." Her mother had mistaken her heated body as being ravaged with the flu. She called for the nurse to get her some medicine and a cold wash rag for her forehead; she sat uncomfortably by her bed for the rest of the morning, until she fell asleep from the medicine.

While she slept, she had dreams of the vampyre. She dreamt that he held all that she desired and dangled it in front of her. She begged him to give to her what she so desperately wanted, and he did but in the most twisted way he could. He killed everybody in the city. "You wanted me to free you from all your bonds and responsibilities." He cackled, "This is the dream of a child, is this not what you wanted?" his laughter made her ears bleed. "Come with me, and we can rule this world." Before she woke, she saw him kill Gabriel and made her his slave.

She woke in a cold sweat and saw Marcus standing over her with a tray of soup and crackers. There was a glass of water and a glass of orange juice already on her bedside table. She sat up as slowly as she could, to give the illusion that she was weak, and in actuality, it was mostly true. She was young and healthy, but running that far without being properly prepared, leaves one a little sore. When he saw her stir, Marcus laid the tray on the chair that their mother had been sitting in.

"Easy, now," he said putting his arm around her; helping her sit up. "You don't feel hot anymore, you must have had a one-day flue." She felt a little guilty allowing him to be deceived. She felt her face get a little warm, "or maybe you haven't gotten over it yet, your cheeks are still red."

"No, no, I'm fine," she reassured him.

"That's good," he said as he sat the tray on her lap, "cause today is a beautiful day, and it would be a shame for you to miss it." She looked out the window to see the sun high in the sky and the wind gently pushing on the leaves in the trees, the fragrance of her roses was strong, and she breathed in the smell.

"It would be a good day for a walk." She agreed.

"I'm already finished with my studies for the day so as soon as you eat and get dressed, we can go if you are sure you are feeling up to it."

"I'm definitely up for it, I could use some brother-sister time." He smiled at her and turned to leave. *Some time with Marcus should help realign my thinking and help bring me back to reality. I have to put all that vampyre nonsense behind me; it was just a bad dream.*

She wanted to put it all behind her but couldn't help but dwell on it. It was burned into her mind and before she could think she opened her mouth and asked, "Is there really a god, Marcus?" He stopped at the door, and she stared at his back. Without a word, he turned and walked back across the room and slapped her across the face.

"A dream should not be enough to cause your faith to waver," he said. "Mother and Father should be enough to prove that He is watching over you." He turned and left before she could assess what had happened. When she realized that what she said must have sounded like blasphemy. It was too late to tell him that she had seen something that would shake anyone's faith. She saw in him the same pain that ravished her. She knew his temper was quick, and his stress was high. If she didn't help him, he was going to snap as she had. *Not my precious Marcus.*

She sat on the edge of her bed and look out the window into the afternoon sun. The wind shifted the treetops and the clouds slid across the sky in wisps. She let her head hang down and closed her eyes, listening to the birds sing and the running river along the edge of their estate. She prayed, asking for forgiveness, begging for guidance, *"Rosina,"* reaching for a candle to lighten the darkness growing in her soul.

"Please give me strength for him, please don't let him fall as I have," she asked in a whisper.

"I know you can hear me, Rosina"

"God, please help my weary mind to understand the purpose of all this, especially that monster. How could you make a creature like that and expect us to follow the words you set before us?"

"Rosina..."

"I am at your feet, on my knees, begging for your hand to lift me up; allow the knowledge to seep into me and raise me up to the next level of insight, I am ready. Father answer me!!"

"Rosina!!"

She jumped up, listening.

"Come to me Rosina." She ran to the window, his voice was coming from outside.

"That is impossible with the sun still out." She looked down the outside of the house to see no one standing below her window.

"Rosina, my sweet crumpet." She looked up, scanning the landscape around the house, only attendants were to be seen. *"Rose, darling, come to me."*

"No!!! I do not obey you, Vampyre!" she yelled out her window. Some of the servants looked in her direction, and she quickly turned away from the open window.

"You do not? I think you will find that you will, in time." She felt the urge to jump out her window to follow his voice. She turned back to the window, and there was a feeling of a gentle hand on her shoulder, pushing lightly. She resisted the nudge, and the feeling of an arm around her waist appeared and pulled her forward. She put her hands on the window frame and pushed against the feeling that was almost overwhelming. Another push from him and she was going to be climbing the lattice outside her window.

"You can't resist me." She could feel his laughter in her heart and knew he was right. *"I don't want to force you to do anything that you don't want to, but your curiosity is only beat by mine. I want to know you."*

"Why? I am a mere human, of no more importance to you than cattle. I'm only good for a meal!"

"Silly girl" laughter, *"humans are only fun to eat when they play back. And you seem to be a fun toy."*

"I am not your toy!" she screamed again.

"Indeed? Show me then. Show me that you are different than all the rest and don't deserve to be a meal to a higher species." She could feel him laughing at her. He was challenging

her. Somehow he knew just what buttons to push, and the next thing she knew she was halfway down the lattice, still in her nightgown, with her brother, who had reentered her room to apologize, screaming at her to get back inside. She jumped the rest of the way down the lattice and hit the ground running in the direction parallel with the river. She could feel the rush of the water over the rocks hitting in time with her heartbeat, furious and fevered. He was still laughing.

"Foolish girl, you are doing exactly what he wants you to do," she said out loud to herself, trying to snap herself out of this new nightmare she found herself in, but she couldn't resist. He had been right.

She ran with the river, out of the estate and into the forest. She dodged between trees and jumped over fallen branches. Sweat dripped into her eyes. Her breath was coming fast and harsh. She was overexerting herself after her lack of recovery from her morning run, but she didn't want to slow down, not now.

His challenge was not going to be left unanswered.

"What no more smart remarks?" she said aloud, knowing he would hear her. He already got what he wanted. "You grow suddenly quiet. Do I surprise you? Did you not think I would come?" *Why did I come?* "Or did you think I would come and fall right into your trap? Am I not what you thought and you plan to just eat me?" *What am I trying to prove?* She could hear him chuckle, so close it was as if he was holding her to his chest and laughing. His laugh lit a fire in her that threatened to scorch her. He made her angrier than anyone ever had. She was going to shame him for mocking her, vampyre or not, he would wish that he had let her be the day he had lured her to him. He felt her anger and his laughter grew louder.

She could hear pursuers behind her, at least five men, one being her brother, the others were servants or men that worked for her father.

My dear, you are going to blow your cover, if you are not careful. His laughter rang in her ears.

"This is your doing. You called me during the day, instead of waiting for the cover of night. Now I will make you pay for your transgressions." She paused at the words she used, "What has gotten into me?"

"Rosina!" She stopped dead. *Gabriel? How?* She turned around looking for him among the trees. She turned in a circle several times, but couldn't find him.

"I must be hearing things, or this damn vampyre is messing with me." She started running again when she heard footsteps. She turned around so quickly that she almost fell. She was face to chest with Gabriel when she caught herself.

"Ga…briel," she stumbled to say. "What are you doing here?" She wanted to reach out and hug him, but she could see on his face that he was angry.

"Rosina, you need to go home. Your brother took great risk asking me to help get you back home, and I will not see either of us get into trouble because you want to take a run in the middle of the day and scare the life out of everyone." She had forgotten that she told her brother about Gabriel, even if it was only a little, he was a smart boy, and he had figured out that he held a special place in her heart and if anyone could get through to her it was him.

"Gabriel... I'm sorry, but you don't understand!"

"I will hear none of it! You forget how delicate our situation is if you keep acting up you will not be allowed to leave for you 'school' and our plan will fall apart." She saw now that he was not angry, but frightened.

"You are right, of course." She wanted to cry. His words made her realize that she had been a fool and had almost exchanged their dream for a nightmare. *That damn vampyre! I risked myself, my brother and Gabriel to play his ridiculous game.* She started walking past Gabriel towards. As she passed, he put his arm up across the front of her shoulders. She looked up at him to see tears in his eyes as he looked at her. She stopped and grabbed him, wrapping her arms around him and burying her face in his chest. He wrapped his arms around her, and she finally cried.

"Shh, my love, only a little while longer, you only have to suffer a little while longer, and I will take you away with me, and it will be just the two of us." She could hear the sadness in his voice as he spoke, trying to make her feel better. His arms were tight around her as if he was struggling to hold on to something that he knew he was going to lose no matter how tightly he held.

"I love you, Gabriel, and I will take you away." she said, misunderstanding his tight hold on her, repeating his words to let him know that she wanted to save him as much as she wanted to be saved and that she was going to protect him from everything. "We will travel across the sea and forge ourselves a new home in the forest, without all the politics and straight-backs. We will live and love to the fullest, and then we will travel to the next world together and fill it with our joy." She could feel the tension start to leave his body when he pulled her away from him just far enough to bend down and kiss her. His hunger came through his desire, and his need for her, her love and her loyalty. She pushed back her own hunger for him, letting him know she was never going to leave him.

"You better go," he said as he pulled away from her, "before your brother or servants come upon us like this." She nodded, but gripped his shirt in her hands, not wanted to let go. "Rose," he bent down and kissed her again, "you have to go. I will see you soon, when we won't have to part. Never again will I be separated from you, that's a promise."

"Okay, I'll go, but you have to do something for me." she said, reluctantly pulling away.

"What?" he asked.

"You have to bend down in front of your bed every night and pray to God and thank him every day for giving me to you." she said with a laugh.

He laughed a little, then became serious, "I already do," He kissed her hand as her face flushed and pushed her in the direction of her house. She turned to say goodbye but he was already gone.

She looked up through the trees to see the sun peeking through and thought, *I will never again play your games, vampyre, I'm done with you.* He didn't respond to her, though she knew he was there. She didn't wait for it just walked towards her house. She made a promise to herself and to Gabriel that she would not ruin their plans and she would do anything to keep that promise.

She only walked a short way when she met up with her brother. His face was full of an anger that she had not seen on him but was a perfect replica of their father's. She did a double take just to make sure that it was Marcus and not her father.

She said, "Wow, father has trained you well, you even look like he does when he is mad." She kept walking past him to keep him from reacting in a sour way. She heard his laugh coming from behind her.

"Yes, my dear sister but you will give me a heart attack long before him," he said as he caught up with her. She laughed and linked her arm in his, and they walked.

After a moment of silent walking, she said, "You knew about Gabriel."

"Yes," he answered. "I have followed you before. I heard you sneaking a few times. When I saw who you were with I did some research." She looked horrified. "I honestly couldn't find much but did see that father does business with his family and father is a good judge of character, so I will trust him." He paused, "For now," he added. She just stared at him. "Also," he spoke again, "I see how you look with him, he makes you smile like you used to. The only thing I regret is that I could not do that for you." There was a sadness in his voice.

"Oh brother!" she squeezed his arm tighter, "I try not to burden you with my… problem," she used the word as if she didn't know what to call it.

"You will never be a burden to me," he looked at her, "you and I will always be two sides of the same coin, we cannot be happy unless we are both happy."

"You are so right!" she said, "I will lean on you more if you do that same to me," he tried to protest, but she laughed and said, "You walked right into that."

The rest of the way to the house was in silence, he having forgiven her quickly at seeing her still safe. And, although he wanted to, he never asked why she had fled out her window.

•   •   •   •   •   •

As the sun began to set, she grew antsier. Each passing minute drew closer to when the vampyre would wake and stalk her dreams. His whisper still sending chills through her as she lay awake in her bed. She knew that this morning's events would only intrigue the monster more and he would not leave her alone until either he killed her or she killed him. She had declared herself done with his games but knew it would not end there. She was just a toy to him, to entertain him until he grew tired of her and then he would just use her to fill his belly. She tossed and turned trying to find a comfortable position to get some sleep before the nightmares were sure to come, but she could not sleep. She was too full of adrenaline to sleep, almost excited to hear his voice in her ear, one final adventure before she left this place. The thought scared her. *I shouldn't be excited to be swept away by a vampyre that was sure to put me in my grave.* She felt like she had lived her life waiting for this, all that she had done came down to this. *Which is absolutely ridiculous,* she thought, *I want to travel the world with Gabriel, not become some monster's pet.* But still, the lure of him was undeniable and impossible to resist. She grew irritated with trying to sleep and got up to sit on the windowsill, watching the sunset.

That's when his laugh filled her head. *"Were you waiting for me?"* the laughter carried through to his voice.

She snorted out-loud knowing he would get the emotion of it, even if he couldn't hear it. "I simply could not sleep, nothing more."

"I can tell you do not speak the truth. I can feel your anticipation for my call." He said.

"Don't flatter yourself." She said but was surprised at how easily he could see through her. She knew little about vampyres so never knew what powers they possessed. "It is about time for my nightly walk that is all. I am always well awake at this time."

"You do not go for a walk until long after your house is sleeping, down to the very lowest servant. Don't lie to yourself or to me, I know you wait for me. So, come. Come to me and let us have some fun."

"I will not go anywhere with you." She felt his pull, her anticipation growing with each word he spoke.

"No?" he was laughing again. *"Then why does it feel like you are all but jumping out your window?"* he asked. *"Get your boots on and come run with me. I will show you the city as you have never seen it. Unless,"* he paused, *"don't tell me you are afraid. Do you think I will drink your blood on our first date? Don't be silly, I have some manners."* He was laughing again, this time laughing at her fear as if she were a child afraid her mother would take away her favorite toy. She felt stupid; he made her feel that way. Being afraid of a vampyre is normal but he made her feel as though her fears were unfounded.

"You may not tonight, but maybe tomorrow and if not then, then the next night. Why should I come with you if you only wish to toy with me and then throw me out with the trash?" she asked, trying to resist his pull.

"Good question. I may indeed eat you if you are no longer interesting. However, if you keep me interested and excited, then I may just keep you around. It is in your hands, not mine." Laughter.

"Ha! Is that what you tell everyone you eat?" She made sure he felt her doubt.

"No." His answer was simple, and in that answer all her doubts vanished, the truth of it coming through so clear that it felt as if she had never trusted anything in her life. There was no laughter, no fear being pressed through, just a true honest answer. His power amazed her, he could alleviate her fear with just one word; he was truly a beast of the evilest kind.

She hesitated for only a second before she was stripping off her nightgown and throwing on a pair of old trousers and a tunic. Her boots slipped on with ease, she tied them tight, making sure they were ready for a long night of use. She climbed down the trellis and ran towards the river, as she had done earlier. She ran for a short while before slowing to a brisk walk, not wanting him to think she was too excited to get to him. She could feel her heart racing and her blood pounding through her body in anticipation. She walked through the forest by the river and reached the other side where fields spread out across the land. The wheat glowed in the setting sun, making it look like what she would imagine heaven would look like. It made waves as the sea in the wind and rustled gently against each other. She walked through the field towards the west, as if she was walking into the sun, its warmth feeding her excitement even as it faded into a chill. It left her cold and hot all at once.

The wind lifted her hair off her neck, brushing it forward into her face. A soft hand slide across the back of her shoulder, from left to right, caressing her chilled skin through the fabric of her tunic.

"You keep fascinating me, child." She jumped as his breath wisped against her ear. She turned and found herself face to face with the vampyre. His laughter grew louder at her jump. She stepped away from him and gave him her best scowl. He stopped laughing, but his smile remained.

"I am not here to play your games." She said, determined.

"Oh? Then tell me why you are here?" he asked as if he were listening to a child retelling a story that never really happened but he believed it fully.

"I-" but he knew she couldn't answer. She didn't know why she was here, curiosity? *I like playing with fire?* She didn't say.

"You are playing a game of your own that is why," he said, filling in the blanks she didn't even know were there. "You want to see what will happen if you play with the other monsters," he said with a confidence that astounded her, and she realized that he was right.

What does that make me?

"That is not true!" she said, trying to convince herself, but even as she said it she knew she was lying and he did too. But, she was not going to allow him to see it on her face; she looked him in the eye and held her ground. His smile turned into a laugh. "Do I amuse you?" she snapped, he sparked her anger. "Your laughter is making my skin itch!"

"Yes, very much," he said; his smile wider than ever. He took another lap around and stopped behind her with his hand on his chin as if thinking. "Yet, you make me sad: all that brilliance and beauty going to waste, ignored as disturbed, possessed, and aging without being noticed by anyone, that is, except by me."

"There is someone that notices!" Gabriel's face appeared in her mind, and she could feel her anger surfacing. "He sees and -"

"He is taking advantage of it," he interrupted her, "knowing that you can use your talents to get him away from a little hard work."

"No," she disagreed.

"He wants a life of freedom and fun, but doesn't want the responsibility. He's a rich boy, and he doesn't want to have to work for himself, he wants to use his parent's money and live his life on the high." He responded, calmly.

"No!" she said, slowly getting angrier.

"Oh yes, my dear," he said.

"Don't call me that! I am not your pet, and I am not your 'dear!'" she said, clenching her fists. "You don't know what we have, we have love, and that is something lost on a beast like you. You are nothing but a manipulative, murdering, monster!"

"Ooo fiery." he giggled a little, "Amazing." Before she knew what she was doing, her anger took over. She pulled her fist back and swung as hard as she could, aiming for his nose. He was too fast, grabbing her wrist and pulled it to his lips and kissing her folded fingers.

"Gah!" she yelled and ripped her hand out of his grasp. She knew he let her as she could feel his strength. She wiped the spot where he kissed her roughly on her trousers. She held her arms stiffly at her sides turning away from him and started walking back towards her house. Every time she was around him, it only took a few words and his stupid laugh to spark her anger. She was not used to being out of control of her emotions; he had to be using some sort of trick to get a rise out of her.

"I am NOT playing your games!" she yelled over her shoulder, she could still hear his laughter. Again he was too fast; he was in front of her before she knew he had even moved. His hands were on her shoulders and his face was mere inches from hers. His eyes were wild, full of a new hunger, and she could see his fangs that he was no longer trying to hide behind his lips.

He leaned in closer so he could speak into her ear, as if he didn't want her to miss what he had to say. "Do you really believe you have a choice? You *are* my pet now. You do not pull the strings in this puppet show. *I* am the puppet master, and you will do as I say." With each word she could feel her fear grow and for the first time in her life, she thought she was going to lose control of herself completely. She thought she *was* going to die when he was finished playing with her. Maybe she would wish for that. She did not know what he had planned for her when death would sound so sweet. She felt herself begin to shake, not physically but in her soul. Her brain felt like it had been battered around in her skull.

He leaned back and put his hands on either side of her face and lifted it up, examining the fear and resignation on it. "There now, that's more like it. My dear, obedience is the key to happiness, but don't lose that fiery spirit. I do get bored quickly." He grasped her chin roughly with one hand and lifted her face further and kissed her cheek, marking her as his. She didn't say anything, didn't move just stood shaking in her skin. He let go of her and started walking opposite the way she had, leaving her standing in his shadow. "Come, my darling, we have much to do tonight."

The night came and went in such a manner. He guided them around town and filled her with the history of the buildings and bridges. She stood in silence, not understanding why he would do something so trivial. He was more of a tour guide than a monster of the night. She couldn't say anything because she feared another outburst from her guide. She found something to be truly afraid of, something that was more cunning and dangerous than her mind could handle. She didn't know when he would strike or what he would do. He was unpredictable. She quaked in his presence, but her heart leapt at the sight of him. The adrenaline was almost paralyzing, so much so that she wished someone would recognize her, but no one did. She suspected he had something to do with it; they passed within inches of many people she knew from church who acted as if she was not there.

As the night progressed, the streets became more deserted, and candles were blown out as the town slowly went to sleep. He started to enjoy himself, getting even more, drunk on her fear. *No, it's as if I'm not here, his love for these old buildings is causing it. Is this what he was like before he was changed?*

"Have you... ever done this before?" she whispered, half hoping he wouldn't hear her.

He stopped mid-step and turned to look at her, as if trying to read what she meant in her face. She trembled, thinking she had misstepped and that he was going to punish her. For a moment he just stood there looking at her, in silence. Then, he looked away, slowing caressing each building with his eyes.

He let out a sigh before he finally answered her, "The history of this town is lost to its people, going unknown to the children and elder all the same. It was built with the sweat and passion of men, yet it is allowed to rot as the new century and its new inventions come." She was taken aback at his answer, she expected a sarcastic remark and got the opposite. "The hard work of men is now the writing of documents and newspapers, not the building of a fence or the shepherding of cattle across the land to feed a man's family. Now all a man has to do is be quick at tongue and slow to sign his name and exchange money with another rich paper pusher." He stopped, still not looking at her. She could feel sadness and anger for a world now lost coming from him. He turned around to keep walking and then stopped again, looking over his shoulder at her he said, in barely a whisper, "Someone should know." Then he started walking again, leaving her in wonder of the thing she saw in front of her. She was no longer fully sure he was all monster, a glimmer of human had shown through when he was talking, not cocky or manipulative, just pure human emotion: pure…sadness.

She followed him, but this time it wasn't out of fear but out of curiosity. She wanted to learn what he knew and a small part of her wanted to help him. She no longer saw a monster, but a man lost in time, desperately clinging to a world that was already gone. She followed him until the sun began to rise over the hills, shining light on the old buildings, casting a rainbow on the streets. Squinting, she could almost see them as they were when they were first constructed. She stood in awe as she imagined them, sturdy and whole. She could hear the sound of the hammers and the scrape of the metal trowels. The laughter, of the men after a hard day's work, ringing out as they walked to the pub.

"Don't think about it too much," he whispered gently into her ear, and she jumped slightly. "I would hate to see you shed even a single tear when I have already shed too many." She looked up at him and found that she *was* close to crying.

She stepped away from him and turned to face him, "Don't you worry, now, I don't plan on shedding any of my tears for you."

He broke into a laugh that was more genuine than anything she had heard from him. "That's my sweet." He said, then leaned close to her and whispered, "Don't let anything in, be strong and unmovable. That's why I like you so much. You are me."

"I am nothing like you." And just like that the moment passed and they were back at each other's throats'.

He winked at her and said, "If you say it enough, you might just believe it. But I do think it is time for you to head to bed." He leaned down and kissed the top of her head before she could move and then he was gone, leaving her standing alone in the street, angry at his desire to ruffle her feathers.

The time for Gabriel's departure drew closer, and she became more anxious. But as she grew anxious for their plan to finally be put into motion, she became more excited to see the vampyre, who was showing her a different side of the city that she never knew was there. He took her to the tops of buildings and showed her the lights and how the city breathed. He carried her from roof top to roof top using his quick reflexes and supernatural speed and strength. She felt like she was flying, something that she never thought she would experience. But even with as much magic he showed her, he never missed a chance to fire her up. He was no human, and she could not allow herself to forget that. But amongst the arrogance and laughter, she saw a man that/who strangely reminded her of her father, teaching her and guiding her towards knowledge and soon she came to think of his human side as an older brother. He let her in very little, hiding his past and his true emotions. She knew very little about him.

One evening he offered her something that shook her where she stood. "Do you want to live forever?" he asked.

"What, you mean be like you, a blood sucking, life draining monster?" she said without even pausing to think about it, "I think I'll pass."

"I can give you the means to finally control your future, not to have to play these games anymore. You can be strong, vibrant, whole." he said with a hint of desperation in his voice.

"You think I need your 'gift' to be strong, vibrant, and whole? I do not, I only need to be patient." She said.

"Patient for what? For that *boy*," he spat the word.

"Yes, I will be patient for that 'boy.' He is all I need." She said, quietly. She could hear his irritation.

"He will use you only to cast you aside when he has no more use for you. Is that what you want?" he did not like her rejection. He wanted to keep her to himself, and now that she was within his grasp he was not going to let go.

"He will not—"

"I can give that to you," he cut her off. "to such a degree you will wish you had not wanted it in the first place." He grew angrier with each word; his voice grew darker with each breath. "I will show you what I can give you, I can give you what you so long for!"

She moved away from him, "Why are you so angry?" she tried to keep from trembling.

"You wish to be human?" he asked as if in disbelief, "I offer you a wonderful gift. I offer you strength and eternal life, and you reject it?!"

"I don't want to be like you." She said softly, "You are in pain constantly, and you feed off humans to live? Tell me what kind of life is that??" She knew her fear was at its highest and out of stupidity she said, "You are a monster!"

He thrust out his hand and grasped her neck, choking her. She gasped for breath and clawed at his unrelenting grip. She had been wrong: her fear rose and became unbearable.

"Please…" she gasped.

"Please what?" his eyes glowed with hunger she had never seen. They were pure black with a need that she couldn't even conceive. She was staring into the eyes of the devil himself.

"Please…" she tried, but couldn't breathe. She was fighting to stay awake as the dark hands of unconsciousness tried to pull her under, whispering sweet promises to her. "… release me…" He let go of her throat only to wrap his hand around the back of her neck. Held her tight to him in an embrace of death as he sank his fang into her neck and pulled the life out of her. She wanted to scream, to cry, to whimper, to do anything. All she could do was stare at nothing with her mouth gaping in disbelief. *He's going to kill me, drain my blood to satisfy his undying hunger, I'm going to be just a meal, food for him. I am nothing more than cattle to him.* She felt like a mouse that was captured by a cat and played with until she was exhausted and then finally was killed. She could feel the warmth of oblivion at her back and the darkness once again grasping at her. She wanted to give in, the temptation almost unbearable, but she fought. She weakly pushed against his chest as he held her in his iron grip. She pushed as hard as she could, and finally a sigh escaped her mouth which gave way to her shouting at the top of her lung the simple word: no. *No, I don't want to die yet, I'm not finished here.*

Her heart slowly quieted in her chest, she couldn't hear it or feel it; she lost the strength to struggle but not the will to fight. She thought that she had lost when she felt him lift his head, felt the pulling stop. She glimpsed his face, his lips red from her blood and his cheeks pink while his eyes glowed with new vigor. She looked at him with hooded eyes. His smile was gone as she finally faded into unconsciousness. With just enough energy to wonder why he had not killed her, she heard him whisper, "I will release you from this life."

She faded in and out for a long time after that. He continued to feed from her, she could not discern how many times or for how long she was with him. The last thing she remembered was him feeding from her only to force her to drink from him in return. She didn't want to, but she couldn't tell her body not to. She had lost all control of herself. His blood burned her body as it filled her, her blood vessels surged with each drop. She could feel it from her mouth to her heart and all the way to her feet. Her skin burned so badly that she yelled out, begging him to stop, but he was not there. She could not feel or see him through the haze he left her in. She reached around finding a stool and pulling herself up to her weak feet. She used the wall to find her way to the door of the room she was in. She pushed on the door and as it gave way she stumbled out onto the street. It was raining, but even the cold water could not cool her searing skin. She could feel the darkness gripping her once again. She tried to run away from it, but her mind was sluggish and she could not move her feet. It consumed her, and she fell into the darkness.

A consuming hunger woke her. She ached all over, sore and insatiably hungry. She opened her eyes expecting to see the sun and her room with her brother waiting to mock her for being out in the rain and getting sick again. Or to smell a bowl of hot soup and hear her mother quietly crying from worry. That is not what she found. She found darkness and the dank smell of rot. She lifted her hands to find what was covering her in darkness, but instead of a soft blanket, she felt something hard and wooden. She felt around above her and beside her, all wood. She was laying in something rectangular. She thought maybe she was in something that the doctor had concocted. When she yelled out the sound did not leave the box, as if someone had covered it with a very thick blanket. She pushed on the top of the box hoping to lift up the lid, but it was heavy, too heavy to just push open. She started to panic. She screamed and yelled and began hitting the inside of the box until she could feel her hands bleed. She stopped and started to cry. *Why is no one helping me; why did they put me in the box and why aren't they letting me out?* She laid there for a long time trying to figure out what had happened and lead to her being put in a box? What did that vampyre do to her and where did he go when he was done? Did he believe she was dead? That seems unlikely since he could feel her heartbeat, but why would he leave her if she was still alive?

Maybe he was trying to get to her again, trying to break her, like a wild mustang.

She decided it was his doing and tried again to open the box again. He was not going to get amusement on her behalf any longer. She could not open the lid with her hands so she to kick the box as hard as she could repeatedly until she heard the wood crack. She pushed up on the weakened wood to create a whole big enough for her to climb out. What she found was not some sort of weight or a blanket, but dirt, dirt that began filling the wooden box quickly. She didn't think, just pushed her way out of the hole as the dirt fell in and dug her way up, or what she hoped was up, not allowing her panic to stop her. Finally she dug to a level where the soil was not so heavily packed and punched her way through to find air instead of dirt. She could feel the wind in her hand and used that as a goal. She pulled the rest of her body out of the dirt. She laid on top of the dirt for a long while just feeling the grass under her face and the wind blowing fresh air into her lungs. Then the thought hit her like a huge stone: *grass? Dirt? Wooden box?* She looked around and saw to her horror that she had just dragged herself out of the ground. All around her were smooth stones and wooden crosses that bore names of people she didn't know. Her panic grew when she realized she was in a graveyard, the church rising in front of her like a horrible omen, she had been buried. But why? She was not dead, so why would they bury her? She looked around again, trying to find the marker for the grave she had been in. If this was some twisted joke by the vampyre she was going to kill him, even if it really killed her. What she found was a temporary wooden marker that bore her name. She just stared at it in shock. *I'm not dead…*

She slowly lifted herself to her feet, feeling unbelievably weak, and wandered through the grave markers. She saw the light from the sun start to rise over the horizon and heard blowing of horns and horses scuffing their feet on the ground. The sounds caused a single thought to shoot through her, through the horrible thoughts of killing someone and being buried alive… *Gabriel.* What day was it, had he already gone? Would he even want to see her now, now that she was… dead? *No, I am not dead, I couldn't possibly feel alive and be…dead.* She stumbled towards the sound of the horses. She needed to find a road so she could figure out where she was, which graveyard was she buried in, the shock had still not fully set in. *It's just a terrible dream…* She reached the road and realized she was in the graveyard that was only a short distance from Gabriel's house. She stayed on the road only long enough to reach the fields that stretched for miles directly opposite the front of his estate. She veered off into the tall grass so she could see the gates to his house. As she stood there, horses and a carriage came out. She saw his family crest on the side of the carriage laden with luggage.

His father was holding his mother, she was gently wiping tears from her eyes. "I just can't believe that he turned out this way." she heard her say. It did not occur to her that she was half a mile away and that she could hear and see them clearly.

"I know, dear, but this school will straighten him up, and he will be ready to take over the family business when he returns. He will learn what responsibility is and that there is no time for the weak. That girl started her path to the grave the day she was possessed. He should be grateful that we kept him in or he would be buried right next to her." His father spoke of him and her as if they were a disease. She felt as if a hot dagger had been plunged into her heart and the pain spread. It was more intense than the burning of her own death.

I am too late. She stood staring at the scene in front of her, not believing she had lost so much time. *That fucking vampyre!* The carriage passed by her and she saw him. Gabriel was looking out into the field, staring at nothing and then he saw her. And he jumped as if he had just seen a ghost. She raised her hand to wave at him. He just remained still, staring, like he didn't believe she was really there. She saw tears in his eyes; he was crying. Why was he crying? And then he was gone, the carriage took him away; away from her. Her life shattered as his carriage became smaller and smaller and the grave loomed in her mind.

She stumbled through the grass to the road and ran after him. She ran faster than she should have been able to with bleeding feet. She could barely breathe, and when she did, it felt like she was inhaling shards of glass. She kept running until a shadow caught her eye. She looked to her side, but it seemed to be stuck in the side of her eye. She turned, and it stayed in the corner of her eye. She shook her head ignoring it. *I have to catch up, he's not going to stop if I can't catch him he'll really be gone.* She realized then that they had been children. In all their planning he never told her where his school was or even in what area it was located. She did not know what stops he planned to make on his way there. She kept moving, she could see the dust from the carriage, still ignoring the shadow that was becoming larger. She stumbled, her legs were tired. She fell to the ground, scraping her hands and knees. The shadow was engulfing her now as she crawled. She slowly sank to the ground, and the shadow completely consumed her vision.

"Get up you fool! You can't pass out on the road!" a voice screamed at her from somewhere, she could not see anything, so she trusted it. She had fallen forward, so she reached her hands out as far as she could to her right, the side nearest the field. She could not find the edge of the road, but was too far away. She slid on her belly until she felt the dusty road turn to grass. She grasped it in her sore hands and pulled, but grass gave way before she moved, so she dug her hands into the soft soil and pulled herself off the road and lost consciousness.

She jolted awake to see the sun going down. Before she could think about how she had lost all opportunities to follow Gabriel a smell caught her attention. A sweet metallic sent was in the air, carried to her by the wind. She got up and slowly followed that sent, retracing her steps back through to the graveyard. She glanced back just long enough to see her name carved into a temporary headstone. She wanted to stand and stare at the wood until it made sense, but the smell was pulling at her. She had forgotten about it, but now it was growing so intense that she couldn't ignore it anymore. She took off in the direction of the smell as fast as she could.

As the smell grew stronger, she began to hear a beating. It was weak at first then became stronger as the scent grew stronger. She finally came to the edge of the forest and saw a campfire, but that is not what she was longing for. It was what was lying beside it that she wanted. She saw a man a barely breathing man, in a sleeping roll his left side was wet with blood. She walked into the campsite and kneeled down beside the man. She wanted to ask if he was okay, but instead grabbed his shoulders and drew him to her sucking blood from his neck so hard the skin stretched thin up to her teeth and mouth. The blood filling her mouth tasted so sweet and fresh that she could not stop drawing it in down her throat, satiating the hunger. Between gulps and slurps, she heard the man's heart beating inside of his chest. Shocked and gasping she withdrew and backed away.

He whimpered when she stopped, but not in pain. "Please…please help me… the pain," he said and touched his side, "Please just kill me."

She could see the fear on his face, almost smell it. She was repulsed by what she was doing, but her hunger for his blood and now his fear overrode her thoughts. She was drinking again all the while his heart was weakening. She felt her skin start to burn and laughter echoed in her mind. She thought it was her going insane. She loved the taste of the man's blood; it was sweeter than any cake, saltier than any sauce, more nourishing than any meat, and more satisfying than any exotic delicacy. She couldn't believe that she enjoyed it, but the repulsion was overcome by instinct. Then, his heart stopped. She stopped drinking, the blood was going sour, it was tainted with the man's death.

She laid him down and wanted to run when she heard another muffled moan. She looked across the fire to see another sleeping roll, this one much smaller. She watched it twitch, and a small head poked out from the end. It was covered in thick red hair, and its eyes were half opened. A child crawled out from the comfort of the roll and stared at her. His eyes then roamed over the campsite and found the man. Shock and sadness filled the child's face. He ran over to the man and started screaming: "Pappa!" over and over, pushing on the man's shoulder, causing him to move slightly back and forth. His screaming filled her ears, piercing through her. She had caused this pain. *The man had a child, and he still wished for death?* She watched the child, now covered in tears and blood from his father's wound, and realized her hunger had not diminished. She shook her head, taking steps back. She wanted to get away from the child before she was overcome again and… *"Eat him…"*

The taste of blood filled her mouth. This was much sweeter, innocent blood held a different flavor. The meal didn't last as long, but it quenched her thirst. She stood over the lifeless body of the child; his fear still burning her skin. She was screaming and tears flooding her face. *What have I done?!* She turned and ran away from him as fast as she could. She was clear of the forest in a second and was standing in the middle of a field before she even decided where she wanted to go. She stopped running, the speed sending shocks through her, She didn't want to have any new strengths or cravings. She tried to ignore it and soon she was overwhelmed with emotions: sadness, despair, fear… all of it mingled, and her mind became muddled.

She clumsily made her way across the rain flooded field towards a familiar place. She did know where her mud-soaked feet were taking her, now that blood stained her lips. She was horrified at how much she had enjoyed its taste and even more the feeling of killing. She tried to push the child's freckled face out of her mind, She was overwhelmingly thankful she had not been completely lucid when she took his life. With each step the mixture of the child's fear and her sick satisfaction began to fade; as it did the hunger began to grow again. It pushed out the disgust she felt towards herself.

In the silence, the voice she didn't realize she was listening too had also gone quiet. What was that voice? Was it her? Was it some sort of survival instinct that had formed a presence of its own? Had it grown stronger because she had already died? Or was it something completely different? Perhaps it was the vampyre illness. Was a vampyre not someone who suffered a disease but possession? Had the vampyre forced another creature into her body? She looked down at herself and saw she was shaking. She wanted to wash herself not to remove the blood but the feeling of violation. Possession was the only thing that made sense. It spoke and had a personality separate from her own will. It knew that she needed to consume blood even before she could fully process what had happened to her.

The hunger yanked her out of her panicked thoughts as it reached an almost unbearable peak as she finally found her destination. She stopped walking without thinking and looked up from her feet. She stood at the edge of the road across from the welcoming gates of her family's estate. It was painfully obvious that she could no longer call it home.

She heard whimpering coming from inside the house, and without thought rushed across the road through the gates. She had to help whoever was in pain…she came to the closed front door and stopped. A dark chuckle escaped her as she thought *I'll be no use. I'm no use to anyone, just a burden that is nothing but pain.*

An even darker voice splintered its way into her thoughts, "*You'll just end up eating them…*" the voice was back. A tear leaked down her cheek, then another… "*That's right, cry for the life that is now lost to you. But, isn't that what you always wanted?*"

'Not this way…" she whispered.

While she was fighting within herself, she did not notice that the whimpering had stopped, replaced with footsteps. The sound of the door lock scraping back brought her attention back. She quickly jumped for a hiding place behind the close-by bushes but wasn't quick enough. Someone's warm hand gently clasped over her wrist, and a soggy muffled voice said, "Rose?"

She felt a fear rise up in her that even overcame her fear she held for the vampyre. Fear of what they would think of what she had become, the word she couldn't even mutter in her thoughts. But she feared, even more, to break his heart again by crushing the relief she felt flooding from him.

"No, she is gone, you saw her buried." She said knowing it to be the truth.

"Do not lie to me. I knew it was all just a bad dream. I must get Mother and Father, they'll be so relieved." He released her and turned in a rush to re-enter the house, but it was her turn to grab him. She wrapped her arms around his chest, putting her face against his back.

"No," she whispered, "it is best if they think me dead, for I truly am. Your sister died, and you buried her," she spoke without thinking but knew she was right. "I am nothing more than a dark shadow of her." She had started to cry again. He loosened her grasp and turned gently around and embraced her, she never lifted her head.

"My dear sister, no matter what shape you take," he said, his voice gentle, "I shall always recognize you and love you. You belong here, in our home, as you always have, with us, your family, who love you."

"No." She could feel her frustration growing. He was so kind, she should have stayed away, ran the other direction, he did not deserve this pain, she had already done enough. He didn't understand what she had become.

"D*emon*," the voice whispered.

"Rose, you are trembling, what happened?" his concern evident, "You must be freezing, you are covered in water."

"*He's mistaken,*" the voice laughed, "*He thinks the child's blood is water!*"

"Come inside by the fire and –"

"No!" She could take his kindness no longer. *I don't deserve it!* The child's face flashed before her eyes, slowly turning into her loving brother's, his smile gone, turned to horror. A silent scream lingering on his dead lips. Blood covering the tear in his throat… She pushed away from him; he stumbled back a few paces as her hunger pulsed through her. She could hear his heart beating, or maybe that was the pounding in her ears from her bloodlust. "No! Don't you see what I have become?!" she screamed, desperately trying to reach him.

"Rose…" he looked startled as he caught his balance finally looking at her. Her eyes were black but putting off a red glow. Her mouth was still covered in blood; her tears were staining her muddy cheeks. Her teeth pointed and ready to draw his blood. Her skin was pale, but blushing from the excitement of the past kill and the promise of a new one. He took another step back, "Rose?" She could see fear starting to darken his eyes, but what he did next surprised her so much that her hunger lessened. He stopped himself from backing up any further and swallowed his fear. He looked straight at her and said, "I do not fear you, whatever form you take, whatever you do or have done in this darkened state: I will never fear you, and I will always love you."

"I cannot stay here any longer." She whispered, she could tell her was forcing herself. The love they once shared, shattered before her eyes.

"Okay," he said, again surprising her, "but when you are ready to allow me to help you, I'll be here, waiting." She just stared at him. "Whatever this is," he motioned with his hand, encompassing her new features, "you have to handle it on your own, like you do everything else. If I were to help you, what good would that do? You wouldn't learn anything if I gave you the answer." He ended with a smile, which shocked her even more than anything he had done up to that point. He came close to her and placed his hands on her shoulders and kissed her forehead. He leaned next to her ear and whispered, "Just promise me one thing: you will come back to me when you do." He turned quickly away from her and returned to the house, closing the door behind him. As he did, she could hear his heavy breathing and smell the salt from his tears.

She turned away from the house and the city that bore her and left it behind. She couldn't bring herself to look back, she knew she was truly exiled. She left, tears burning her throat and the hunger consuming her.

She felt that new presence within her, it was a dark presence that pushed to feed. It whispered evil things to her, giving her the plots of her worst nightmares that were the reality that she now lived. She tried to ignore it, but when she did, its dark demon fingers crept in, and she lost control. She had to get away, far, far away, where she could never hurt anyone.

CHAPTER FOUR: THE HOLY LIGHT IS SO BRIGHT

The darkness creeps in, fills the empty spaces
Trembling, quivering, pounding,
Sadness overwhelming.
A bright light shows the way,
Consuming the darkness that is within
A hand on the shoulder, guiding, forgiving,
Beauty Blinding!

The pounding increased; the burning radiated through her skin, as she walked towards nothing in a state of bare consciousness. She knew what she wanted and what her body craved; she knew they didn't coincide except for the part where death was involved. She wanted to die, to kill what she now called 'demon,' but the demon wanted to be the killer, to feed on others. She did not know how to do the first, but she did know that if the demon did not feed it would die. The question was: how long she could fight the demon for control before it took over and did what it wanted. She knew if she tried starving it, it would take control of her. She stumbled around and wished she could blame it on the dark, but she could see better at night than she could during the day. She assumed the great night vision was because she would burn to death in the sun if she was not running for a hiding place when it rose. She wandered for an indeterminable amount of time. She could have been stumbling around for weeks or years, she couldn't tell through the haze. She only clearly remembered when she felt the hunger gnawing at her.

She could hear heartbeats in the distance and turned away. She tried to avoid them but she couldn't fight the growing excitement in her arteries. The anticipation of fresh food was almost unbearable. She could already taste the sweet metal on her tongue and the warmth filling her from the inside, not like the burning she was feeling now. The demon surfaced and all her senses began to tingle. She knew the blackout would soon be upon her and she would wake somewhere she had no recollection of. It had been happening over and over since she left her village. She refused to drain any more people after the child with the fiery hair but the demon refused to starve and would take over. She would lose days, waking up covered in blood in a place far from where she was. She knew what had happened because the demon thought she needed to see what it had done. In her nightmares she saw their faces, men, women, children, young, old, innocent, evil; none escaped the demon's fangs. She could feel its dark burning fingers grasping at her. She didn't want it, but she had no choice.

She longingly looked out at the forest on the horizon. She wished to escape into it. Then, she looked to the village just south of it, laying before the trees. She could smell the fires warming the homes and stew a mother was making for her family. The soft humming of a man working on a wooden toy for his unborn son or daughter made her heartache. She would visit there tonight, even if she didn't want to, the demon always won in the end. She closed her eyes and started walking towards the village. As the distance became shorter, she expecting the demon to take control. This time it didn't consume her. She remained in control but was directed, by the hunger, towards the heartbeats of the villagers. Perhaps if she fed then the demon would stay at bay or perhaps the hunger was the demon, she could not distinguish between the two. She crept across a field full of wheat hiding in the shadow of the trees and mountain. She entered on the western side of the town as the sun was still setting, its rays haloed her and set her skin on fire, the wind blew on her gently, but it didn't extinguish the heat. She made her way around the village looking for an easy meal, trying not to awaken the village to the monster she was, trying to give them some peace. If only she could control her hunger and the demon and take one life instead of as many as she could feed on. She knew the demon feed every human in its vicinity; she always woke with a saturated body and not have to feed for several days.

She hurried around the corner of a building and leaned against the cold stone. She closed her eyes for a moment, enjoying the heat leave her body. She let out a sigh of relief. She listened every day sounds the few dozen villagers. The farms were small, and the buildings neglected. This village was dying. She could see it everywhere, thanks to the man who sired her vampyre. She knew the signs, the sagging roofs, the creaking doors, cracked and patched stone walls. She opened her eyes and looked out past the building to see an old man trying to repair his wagon. The wood was so rotten, however, that pieces just kept flaking off. The man did not give up, though. Watching him made her long for a will that strong.

"Will he fight for his life or will he beg for death?" The demon always looked at each person as a meal and tried to decide which would be a good kill or which would be of no excitement.

"I'm not going to kill *him*." She whispered to it, "he has a family, he is their caregiver."

"They all have a family; many of them are the caregiver. But they all die eventually, whether by your hands or time's." She shook her head trying to get the voice out of her head, but it cackled at her attempt. *"You have to kill someone that is the way of nature. You need to feed just as they do, that is just how it is."*

"They don't kill other people; they kill and eat animals," she protested.

"They are animals! Just as you are an animal. They all are, no matter what they eat they are animals." She tried to ignore it, but she knew she could not deny that she needed to feed. Hunger was clawing inside her, and the demon waited impatiently to take over. She could already feel its darkness creeping in. She turned from the man and walked further into the village. She crept from one building to another, keeping out of sight as she had done as a human. This she was good at, but killing and feeding without getting caught was something she was having trouble with.

"Have confidence in your power, and you will not fail." Her demon would say, but she faltered most times and ran away before she even reached her target, panic choking her.

She made it to the center of the village where several men finishing up their days business or making their way to the local pub, which doubled as a general store. She watched them disperse and go their separate ways. A young man walking alone caught her eye. He could not have been more than seventeen, and he looked sickly. His skin was pale, and his arms were thin from lack of use.

"Good eye." She followed him until he walked behind a building and she decided that now was the best time to strike. She approached him slowly, trying to keep him from hearing her, but he turned around as she scuffed her boot on the ground. He looked surprised to see her then his eyes widened and fear covered his features; she knew her eyes must be black with the hunger, but she had hoped that they were not noticeable in the growing dark.

She walked closer to him trying to keep him from yelling out, but she was too slow, and he sounded an alarm, "Help! Monster!"

"Fool you have super speed and you WALKED to him??" the demon screamed at her.

He turned to run away, but she panicked and grabbed the back of his cloak. She pulled him to her, wrapping her hand around his mouth but in her fear she pulled too hard. She could feel the bones in his neck crack, and he went limp, the sound of it vibrating through her body and she dropped him quickly as if he was on fire. She stared at him lying on the ground, disbelief filling her as she stood frozen there beside him.

"What a waste. Well, I'm sure he wouldn't have tasted very good anyway——" She turned around at the sound of footsteps, many footsteps. They were coming from all directions, she turned again to see several men stepping out from behind one of the buildings carrying some sort of weapon: pitchforks, torches, shovels. *"That's cliché."* the demon said in disgust.

"What do I do?" she asked desperately as her voice tremble and her legs grew heavy.

"Well, unless you want to massacre this whole village, I suggest you run for it," it said as if talking to a child.

"But they are everywhere," she said.

"You are a vampyre!" it said, pointing what she, for a second, had forgotten, *" Pull yourself together and use the strengths you have to get yourself out of here. Or I will be forced to do so and your pathetic conscience will not like how I do it."*

Its words knocked her legs loose, and she looked around, trying to find an escape route. The men were closing in on her, and they grew angrier when they saw the body of the young man lying on the ground.

"You'll pay for that, you bitch!" one said and charged at her. She didn't think just reacted. She jumped, meaning to just get out of his way, but she jumped much higher than she had thought she could. She was eye level with the roof of a building before she fell back to the ground. She landed hard on her feet and fell down on her backside and scratching her palms as she tried to catch herself. The men stopped for a moment, all rethinking their resolve when another charged at her. She could smell the alcohol on him and knew he was looking for a fight and she just happened to be an available target. She rolled backward over her shoulders and landed on her feet just in time to see his axe come swinging down and crash into the ground. He yanked it up and tried to swing at her again. She jumped back again and slammed into one of the other men. She tried to pull away from him, but something was stopping her. She looked down to see three dirty pieces of metal protruding from her abdomen, they made a parallel line to the ground on her left side, beneath her ribs. As soon as she saw them a red hot pain shot through her. She stumbled forward as the man released the handle of his pitchfork. They all gasped as she fell to her knees, bleeding. They started cheering when they thought she was going to die. Only she didn't, she just remained there, on her knees, with the fork sticking out of her back. The pain had started to subside, and she felt the urge to yank it out of her body. She reached behind her and grasped the splintering handle. She pulled as hard as she could, sending pieces of wood into her palm as the wood cracked under her strength, and slowly the metal came free of her body. She dropped the tool as soon as she was free of it and bent over as the pain dissipated. She looked down to see that the wounds were healing, leaving only holes in her tunic and blood soaking her. She couldn't believe it almost as much as they couldn't. She heard them all take a few steps back and whisper "monster."

She looked up from the ground and felt a smile curl up on her face. She enjoyed their fear and was not quite sure why until she heard her demon's laughter. It loved it, and her smile grew as its joy joined hers. She tilted her head down again, hiding her face from the men. "Oh, I see." She said as her skin began to tingle. "This is what an animal feels like before the hunt?" She could barely contain her excitement.

"Where did your spines go?! Get her!" she heard one of the men say and then some murmuring followed by the scraping of shoes of the ground. They were coming closer with more caution. She looked again to see them holding up their 'weapons.'

"Use that energy. Feel the excitement flowing through your body and use it!" widening her smile she flashed her fangs. She could smell sweetness coming, and it grew as they stared at her. She did not move allowing it to flow over her. Then, when the anticipation was too much, she stood, slowly. She looked around her, taking in each and every one of their faces. One was foolish enough to step forward.

"Demon, you should leave this place!" he said, his fear apparent. He didn't want to fight her, he knew he would lose, but he had to defend his home, for honor.

"Demon?" she said, "That does seem to suit me." She tilted her head thinking about it, and she could hear her demon laughing.

"He would be tasty."

She nodded and took a step towards him, he twitched but didn't move. She took another step and another until she was close enough to reach out and grab his dirty tunic. She grabbed it gently, "You would be tasty," she echoed her demons words which scared her, but her high overtook it. He flinched, and that made her grab the cloth tighter and pull him to her. He stumbled not expecting her to be able to pull him almost clear off his feet. He slammed into her, but she didn't budge, and he slid down to his knees.

She leaned over him and whispered to him, "Defend your home, animal, defend it against the demon that is hailing fire down on you." She bent down to his neck and sunk her teeth into his skin. She did not drink right away, but instead let blood run down his shoulder and chest, allowing the men to witness her imbibing. Her glowing red pupils stared at them and they gasped and backstepped in unison and were ready to run. There anger stopped them however and they started to stomp toward her and their fallen comrade. She had not anticipated them to come at her again. She had hoped they would run in fear, but she forgot how stupid humans could be; they would willingly die for a cause that didn't mean anything. Killing in the name of a god that abandoned them long ago was something they volunteered for. Before she was able to pull away from the man and protect herself, she felt several metal objects slice through her body. The man's body fell to the ground, not dead but soon to be. She fell down beside it, bleeding out of several places on her body. The warm blood that she had just swallowed flowed out of her, staining her skin and clothes and pooling on the ground around her. She felt weak, her vision going dark. She fought it, pushing it back. She put her hands on the warm ground and pushed herself up as they continued to stab and beat her. Her instinct to survive flared along with her anger at being beat by these weak beings, *I am the hunter here!* She struggled to her feet, leaning over her stomach as more wounds were inflicted on her as quickly as the old ones healed.

"I've had enough!" She felt power flow into her from the demon, she assumed, and the sweet smell returned and the attacking stopped. Her skin was on fire, but she ignored it; every time the demon interfered she felt as if she was going to burst into flames. She turned around looking at them and then she ran as fast as her feet could carry her in her weakened state. She heard them coming after her. She looked up the road to the horizon and with it a field of corn. *If I can make it there…* she could feel her strength leaving her and the blackness pushing in. *No… Not yet, I'm not ready…* she begged the demon.

"You will kill us!" it shouted in her head.

No, I'm almost there

"You will never make it! Let me in!" A surge of power overcame her but it wasn't helping her, it was overtaking her. She knew she had lost, but she tried to fight it and with each step she became weaker until she was crawling, leaving a trail of blood behind her. The men drew near, and she finally gave in, collapsing on the ground and allowing the blackness take over. The last thing she heard was the cackling laughter of her demon coming from her own lips and then nothing.

•　　　•　　　•　　　•

She woke in the middle of the field that she had been running towards when she lost consciousness. She dreaded what she would find and when she opened her eyes she saw her worse nightmare come alive, again. She lay in the middle of the trampled wheat, there were bodies everywhere around her, she recognized some of them from the night before but there were many she did not recognize. When she tried to look away she saw women and children among them. She stood on shaky legs, her body drenched in blood as well as mud and wheat from beneath her feet. She couldn't move, she was frozen, amazed at what she had done; if only she was not so weak.

"Say something!" she screamed to the demon that always was quiet after a night of killing. "Tell me why you do this! Why did you need to kill all of them?! You killed everyone in the village!" She was shaking, anger building up in her along with her fear. She was afraid of what resided inside her, and she did not know how to control it. "Will it always be like this?" she whispered to herself. She turned away from her massacre and walked towards the woods. She would rest there for days, knowing the demon would be silent, its evil belly saturated with the blood of all the villagers. Deserving or not, they were dead, and their blood was in her or on her.

As she sat covered in blood, her despair made her delusional mind wandered back to the one thing it could latch onto. His face was distance; she could barely picture it. What would he do in this moment? Would he draw her near and gently wash the blood from her, comfort her? Would he smile at her like he used to? OR would he look at her with false love on his face but fear in his eyes as her mother had? Would he not worry for her feelings and allow his to fear paint his face white and terror cause him to flee?

"You fool," his voice laughed in her ear. "I could never fear you." She could almost feel his warm hands on her face, wiping away her hot tears. He laid a gentle kiss on her forehead. "I love you, remember? Your form will never change that." He echoed her brother's words.

She was calming when she realized he was an illusion. She had abandoned him when he needed her and did not deserve to think he would care for her if he knew she was not dead.

"I can't come back to you, my love," her voice shook as she spoke to the stars. "You deserve a better form of me."

"Soon," she heard his voice again, and she laid her head on a tree and allowed its smooth sound to wash over her and she was soon sleeping in its warmth.

She took advantage of the demon's absence and walked for days, pushing the limits of her abilities. She walked in the sun until the burning was unbearable; she did not have the will to allow it to consume her. She tried to jump from high places and heard her bones crack. She lay where she landed for hours in pain until she healed. She tried to drown herself in the river, but found she didn't need to breathe. She tried over and over to kill herself, but she was either too weak to allow it or her body healed too quickly. So, she sat on the forest floor, in the cold, until the hunger stirred again. She slowly walked towards the closest village; she could hear their hearts and knew one would stop beating tonight.

She made it to the village and told herself that this time would be different: this time she would be in control; she would kill only the one she wanted and none others. She could hear her demon laugh.

"You're finally back?" it didn't answer, but she felt its presence. "Tsh." She pushed it aside.

She hid outside the town pub waiting impatiently for someone to exit. She was about to enter and lure someone outside when the door swung open, and a man was tossed out onto the street.

"And don't you come back until you can pay for you mead!" the man who did the tossing said, then muttered, as he turned to return to the pub, "you filthy rat." *Perfect*, she thought and caught herself grinning and shook her head. *No, this is just so the demon doesn't get out.*

She watched the man try and fail to pick himself up several times before she emerged from behind the building and walked towards him, her pace brisk but quiet. She was standing next to him before he or she realized it. She bent down and reached for him. He swung his arm up, trying to hit her; "I said I'll pay when the crops come in!" He kept swinging at her until she grabbed his wrists and pinned him down. She saw his fear when she realized she was holding him so tight his hands were losing blood circulation and were turning white.

She released him and said, "I'm not here to collect your debt, I was simply trying to help you up."

"Oh…" the look of dumb returned to his drunken face. Clearly he had drank far too much, and would owe the barkeep much money when the "crops came in." He nodded at her and allowed her to put an arm around him and lift him up to his feet. His warmth soaked into her and she could feel his heartbeat; her mouth started to water. "Thank you, miss," He mumbled in her ear, sending waves of hunger down her whole body. Stifling a shiver, she amazed and pleased that could that this drunken rat smelled so good? She shook her head to clear it, the edge of her vision beginning to darken. She slowly walked him to the side of the building and leaned him against the wall. "Thank you," he muttered again.

"Don't thank me." She said as she took in his whole appearance, he didn't appeal to her human ideas of attractiveness, but her demon was leaping with excitement.

"No one stops to help a drunk man lying in the street. That is unless they want something, and there is only one thing I can offer you." She almost felt pity for the man, he was just a fool that didn't know when to stop, not a person that she would deem worthy of death, but then again none of the men or women, or children the demon had taken deserved their untimely demise, why should this be any different? *I have a conscience,* she thought to herself.

"*Unlikely*" the demon interjected, "*but go ahead and hide behind that if it makes you feel better.*" She shook her head again to try to shake out the voice, but this time it did not work, and it let out an evil cackle. She was ripped from her thoughts when the man lounged for her and she quickly learned what he had to offer. In her moment of shock that he could even stand on his own, let alone try to tackle her, he spun them around and had her pinned against the wall. He was attempting to rip open her coat to access what was underneath, but by then she had recovered and grabbed his wrists and spun him back around and slammed him against the wall, cracking the stones all within a fraction of a second. He opened his mouth, but was unable to speak as she stopped him by lunging for his throat and plunging her fangs into his sweating flesh and drawing forth what she and the demon craved most: the sweet nectar flooding through his veins. She heard him gasp and try to rip his wrists from her grasp, but her hands were made of steel, and he was shackled in a prison of her making, and the only way out was his death.

She pulled his blood from him in large swallows feeling her skin burning and ignoring it. She indulged in his sweetness until she could feel his life fading and she pulled away and looked into his dimming eyes as they looked at her full of a terror that he would never understand. "I've only one thing to offer you as well, rat..." She leaned into him and whispered, "death." And she began to laugh a deep-throated laugh. She released him and let him fall to the ground like the trash he was. *It seems I was wrong, he does deserve to die*, she thought and she and her demon laughed in unison.

•   •   •   •   •

She had new drive and ambition after that kill. It was her first kill where she did not succumb to her demon resident. She now knew if she fed when she needed she would remain in control.

"It's time I embrace this curse and learn a bit about what's going on here." She pepped herself up, even if she was trying to convince herself she was stuck like this; it was either choose what she ate or live a life of darkness and blood. "I'm taking control now, demon," she said to it. She pushed her limits, this time not trying to kill herself and learned about her strengths: physical strength, speed, and the ability to lure her victims to her using the release of pheromones; her weaknesses: sunlight, eating from the innocent children left her weak. She thought she must have some sort of affinity for the evil or maybe that was the only time both she and her demon enjoyed the kill and were completely in unison. Evil, deserving kills left her in control and not taken over by the demon. She avoided blackouts and lost memories by feeding on the evil. She made it her ambition to find a man or woman worthy of death before she became too hungry. If she did that, the demon would not take over do what it needed to keep them alive. Even with all her exploration of her new powers she often forgot she had them and neglected to use them. She was scolded often for it by the demon. She noticed subtle changes in her personality; she became more confident with each kill. She used what men liked and lured them without using any special ability. She enjoyed the kill as much as her demon, she even craved the chase, the fear, and the eventual death of her victims. She also found out that vampyres, no matter how much she believes it, may not be damned purely based on their being a vampyre. She still had her conscience, which she took to mean she still had her soul. She could also be on holy land. That she found out by accident while running from the sun; she entered the first building she could find open to her. She didn't realize it was a place of worship until she turned around, leaned against the heavy oak doors of a church, and looked up at a crucifix nailed behind the altar. She panicked but after several moments of not "bursting into flames," she realized that she was safe. That didn't stop her from running from it as fast as possible as soon as the sun had set that night.

Her travels led her to a village that was packed full of thieves, murders, rapists, and abusers. The place was called Wolford. People fled there under the pretense of trying to find God again and repent for their actions. The clergy allowed this because it was home to one of the most ancient cathedrals in Europe. She had learned of it while she still attended church with her family. She, well, she and her demon, would be very happy there. But she had to figure out what she was going to do if she stayed there long term; someone was bound to see her and start to question her reason for being there. This place was like prison, if she did not have a group to protect her or display her dominance she would surely have to flee, even she couldn't kill everyone. *That would defeat the purpose.* These men who were trying to fake finding God tend to get jumpy when someone new shows up. So, as soon as she arrived, she headed straight for the cathedral. She wanted to remain hidden not stand out, *what better place than the cover of God?*

She had been wandering for so long that, besides luring her prey, she had forgotten how to speak to a human. Her encounter with the men of the church frightened her. She stopped before reaching the massive building that now seemed much larger. She fought with herself, *I cannot do this, a man of God is going to know immediately what I am.* The faces of the bishop and his priests holding her down, pouring holy water over her and down her throat, caused her to freeze, stop breathing, and then she felt her heart stop. Her panic rising and she started to sweat.

"*These men cannot hurt you,*" her demon spoke up. "*They are nothing, but blood filled sacks of flesh. If your deceit does not work, you can kill them. I thirst to taste a holy man!"* It cackled.

"I have already decided to not kill any more innocent people. As tempting as it may be, these holy men will remain unharmed." She replied as if saying it out loud made her resolve stronger, even though her fear was steadily getting the better of her and she thought of the boy she killed in her panic.

"If you so desire to snake your way into these men's hearts and have them trust you," it paused as if what it was going to say next hurt it, *"I will guide you."* She felt a warmth spread through her, and it calmed her. She both welcomed it and hated it. She felt dirty taking its help, knowing she needed it. And she felt her legs loosen and she looked down at them, as if they had betrayed her.

She lifted her hand to her face and wiped off the sweat and took a deep breath, letting it out saying, "Let's get this over with." She walked around the side of the building and entered using the side door to avoid creating a commotion. The huge building was dark but for a few candles lit at the altar. No people were praying, which she expected, but there were also no priests or deacons or anyone else scurrying around, reading, praying, or copying manuscripts, as she *did* expect. She stopped to listen: only one heartbeat was near her. She still had trouble though narrowing down the scope of her senses, so she mostly shut them almost completely off. She made her way through the pews towards the lit candles, not making a noise. She went past the altar when she saw no one there, and down a narrow hallway to the right of the altar towards the back of the building. She was halfway there when she heard a man muttering. She stopped and listened to determine where it was coming from. A light appeared in the end room. She was going to continue to the door then thought better of it. She cleared her throat and called out, not wanting to startle him, "Hello? Is there anyone there?" She heard a tumble of what she recognized as books falling off a desk or table before the light got brighter as the door opened the full way. A young man emerged wearing a dark robe and a surprised look on his face.

"Can I help you?" He tentatively asked, the candlelight playing on his soft skin. His dark brown eyes that were in laughing contrast to his light brown hair.

"I'm sorry, I did not mean to startle you, but there was no one in the main part of the building," she said looking up at him, since she was only as tall as his shoulders.

"Believe me, my child, that is not the reason I am startled." His voice lost the surprise and cascaded over her, it was much deeper than she had expected coming from a man that she realized could not be much older than her, he looked barely twenty years old.

"Oh?" she asked, not allowing her confidence to falter so quickly. She knew the demon lent her its strength but that did not stop her from fearing for his safety, she was afraid that at any moment it would jump on him.

"Yes, no one comes in here, I haven't seen another soul come to pray or ask for guidance since I arrived two years ago," he said with a sadness playing in his eyes.

"Really? No one in two years?" She feigned surprised. "I thought this was the holy city, a place to come to be forgiven for all your sins and be allowed into heaven?"

He let slip a chuckle before catching himself, "Of course it is," he said cheerfully that was only half faked. "Now, tell me what I can help you with."

"Well, I would like to find God again. I have been traveling for many years and would like to return to my home without the weight of my sins to bear. I wish not to shame my family; they expect me to marry a charming man and take my place as mother of his children." She said as smoothly as she could, she had practiced it over and over again on her way here, but she could still hear her voice shake and she cursed herself, even with the demon she may yet end up making a mess. If she were human, she could have said that piece and even added some dainty body language, her hips straight, her legs together, hands clasped together before her, her head down slightly and a pout on her face. As she was now she came off scared and desperate and even a little angry, the former was good, but the latter gave her away.

"Do not take me the wrong way, my lady, but I do not believe you," he said, clearly having seen a liar before.

She hid the fear that tried to creep up on her face and said, "I'm sorry?" she asked, actually shocked.

"What does a young girl, of what maybe 17, have to ask forgiveness for?" he said, raising his eyebrows, and she feared him more than her own demon; her heart could not bear to be rejected, its fragile pieces barely holding together again.

Once again she had to hide her fear, but inside her demon was cackling, "*We could just kill him.*"

"And if you are as young as I see you for, you have not traveled long, if at all.

A young woman's father would never allow her to travel alone, especially one that is to be wed to an upstanding gentleman. He would do quite the opposite; he would shelter her and keep her pure and innocent." He said, his knowledge of the world was showing, and she cursed herself for not thinking of a secondary plan to lean on.

This time she could not hide her fear, but instead of a shaking breath, a small laugh escaped her lips, and before she knew it, she said, "You are quite smart for a deacon of such a young age, you are how old? Nineteen? Twenty? I promise you I have done plenty to not be allowed past the gates of heaven and gaze upon the heavenly father's face. And I may look young, but I am much older than you for I have had hardships that no one should endure." She almost gasped but stopped herself, she knew this was the work of a demon but she agreed with every word and now that it was out she could not take it back, so she had to allow it to happen. (go with the flow?)

He was not fazed by this, "I too have been through much, but I still am in God's graces. There is no reason you cannot find your path back to Him, if that is what you truly wish, I will be your guiding hand. However, I would be remiss if I did not say that I can almost taste you anger. You came here for some reason, though I do not know what. I ask again, what can I help you with?"

She was grinning at him, she had found a true person in this deacon, or priest she noticed by his offended look when she had said such, someone she could not hide from. It scared her and exhilarated her all at once; she could feel the demons excitement while her fear grew. Its confidence leaked into her even more and she grew brave, "Fine, priest. I have a proposition for you," she swung her long dark hair away from her face, revealing her smile. She was careful to hide her fangs, and also her earnestness, "I will clean up this town for you and the rest of your brotherhood in exchange for one thing," she paused waiting for his response, which he gave by merely folding his arms in front of himself and raised his eyebrows once again, "you act as if I am here on behalf of the Vatican." *He is never going to buy that! I look like a child!*

"Forgive me this time for not understanding, you'll do what? And why? And a girl of your age with no training cannot 'clean this town,' as you say, with her bare hands," he looked her up and down taking in her dirty boots, torn coat, oversized trousers and the lack of a bag. "I must admit you are a skilled liar, but you don't back up your lies with any truths," he was shaking his head.

"Good priest, I assure you that my hands are all I need," she said, thinking, *I knew it*, her was panic growing.

"*Calm yourself*" she was scolded.

"But, I understand your skepticism. Allow me to stay here under the pretense of working for the church for a short time, and if things do not improve, I will leave,"

"*Or I'll just kill you,*" her demon added.

No, he is a man of God, innocent, she thought.

"*A man that will reject you and cast you out as soon as he learns what you are, and he WILL find out. Can you handle that? I doubt it, you will go mad, and I will finish him for you, to relieve the pain…*" She blinked, surprised by what the demon said. Even as she knew it to be true, she still didn't want it to happen. She used that fear to build up a wall and strengthen herself.

He looked at her for a long moment, then nodded, "Fine," he paused and looked around the large, empty building, "but there is only me. The men of this village allow me to live if I send letters to the Vatican telling them things are improving, and they are on the path to righteousness."

"Does that mean I put you in danger by being here?" her concern getting the better of her and her wall started to chip already.

"*Foolish girl!*" she was scolded again, "*What is the point of my helping you if you go soft?!*"

"Perhaps, but you should worry about yourself before you worry about me," he said, but he was grateful for her concern.

"My dear priest, I assure you that *I* have nothing to worry about." Her confidence shifting from feigned to real, if she was sure about anything it was that she had no trouble killing, that made her frown, wearing on her soul, but her demon smiled inwardly, "*That's right, we are good at killing.*"

He gave her a sideways glance, almost as if he was trying to see into her mind and find out what she was hiding. She stared straight back at him, allowing him to see exactly what she wanted: nothing. "I will prepare you a room. I assume that you will want to stay here?" At her nod, he turned away and entered a room closer to the front of the church. She sighed when he was out of sight and smiled a little to herself having accomplished what she wanted without having to harm the priest.

She heard rustling around and the soft sound of a bed being made and curtains being opened. She waited for a few minutes until he returned holding a folded piece of cloth, the same color as his robe. "You are mad if you think I am going to wear a robe, father," she said.

"If you want them to believe you work with me, you must dress the part," he said as she gave him a defiant look, after a brief standoff between them, she finally took the robe.

"I will wear this if you will allow me to alter it as I see fit." She couldn't afford to have a long piece of cloth tripping her as she chased down her victims. *"You learn quickly,"* her demon laughed.

"If you mean by shortening it and remaining in those awful trousers and boots then I say, 'no.'"

How did he know? She chuckled, hiding her surprise. "I will replace the trousers and wash the boots if that will please you." Again he thought about it for a moment and then finally nodded.

"I will prepare some supper, you must be famished." He looked at her again, "It does not look as if you eat at all." She smiled at the irony but he mistook it for one of gratitude. "Do not worry you will be working for your meal." Her smile only widened.

•　　•　　•　　•　　•

She found that she could consume small amounts of food without her body violently removing it. But, she was able to talk her way out of dinner with the young priest by saying she wanted to get to work as quickly as possible. That had gotten her another sideways glance and a grunt of, "to thyn own self be true." which made her smile. She had taken the robe and shortened it, washed her boots and was out searching for new trousers.

She spent most of the next few nights getting to know the town and its residents; most of them were men that liked to enter the pub at close to dusk and not leave til several hours later. A fight broking out ended the night every night. The barkeep would not allow the fight to remain inside his establishment. He kicked them all out and slammed the door after the last man tripped out into the street swinging at the guy that had stumbled out before him. There were a few stragglers who had not exited the pub with the rest but before that. They preferred the shadows as she did, looking for a victim as she watched them as her own victim. They were the pickpockets that preyed on the drunks fools fighting each other or the men looking for the-not-already-occupied prostitute or woman that was stupid enough to walk the streets alone. Those doing everything but watching their purses were all a potential victim.

She memorized the streets and the buildings, making a mental map of the different areas. Each section had its own style of 'governing.' Some sects would merely kill someone for stealing, if he got caught, others would torture that person for days or weeks then kill them. Some would take their freedom and force them to be a slave. She watched the daily lives of the people. She learned of their reason for being there; the place was overrun with thieves, but that number was equal to murders. Many of the men that were condemned here forced their family, if they had one, to come to this place with them. Their families lived in fear and were treated as slaves to do the work and be the man's entertainment by way of being a beating bag when he felt like it. They lived like kings in their own homes. There were also women sentenced to live here. They were scarcely seen unless they were as ruthless as the men, carrying and using weapons as they pleased. There were, to her surprise, shops and restaurants in the village, ran by men that had truly come here to reform or members of some sort of gang that ran the business for darker reason. On the surface they looked like a typical business, but in the back women and children were forced to work. This was to get back the debt owed to them by their father, whom they had already killed. She chose to avoid the darker sects of the village, she feared what she saw would cause her to lose the little control she had. Those areas would ignite her temper, and she knew she would gladly allow the demon to take over.

She entered the front of the cathedral after a night of observation, closing the large oak door as quietly as she could because it was very early in the morning, the sun wasn't even coloring the sky yet. She realized that she didn't need to when she looked up the aisles of pews to see the priest kneeling in front of the altar. There was a lit candle on the floor in front of him, his hands pressed together in front of his face that was bent down, his lips moving so slightly that she was not sure they were actually moving. She stood watching him for a moment fighting the urge to make a comment about his misplaced faith, but she thought it better to not bite the hand that feeds. She remained silent taking him in, something about him made her just want to watch him, to not look away, he gave off a calming feeling that was impeding on her new life of chaos, and she was not sure she liked it. She stopped staring at the peaceful creature and walked silently down the far aisle towards the hallway that led to their rooms. She tried not to disturb him, but she didn't make it to the first row of pews before he spoke.

"Would you come pray with me?" she stifled a sigh and stopped but made no move towards him. "You've been here for days, and I have not seen you pray once." He said without lifting his head.

"I do not pray, priest," she said with a snap. She quickly cleared her throat, trying to cover her anger and started again, "What I mean to say is that I have not prayed since I was young and do not wish to begin again."

"Why?" he asked, again without looking at her.

"I'm sorry?" she asked. Those were the only words she could speak politely.

"Why did you stop praying?" he asked again.

"Tsh." She started walking towards the hall again. She really wanted to avoid this conversation.

"Please tell me," he said.

When she looked at him, he was looking at her with curiosity in his eyes, instead of judgment. "I want to know." His voice was gentle as if he was talking to a small child.

Images of the failed exorcisms came to the front of her mind. She saw the priests and bishop standing over her, cursing her, condemning her, shunning her, cutting her. She felt a tear rise up in her eye but quickly wiped it away. "Why do you want to know? Do you want to try to fix me? That's been done, priest, to no end."

"I do not wish to do anything, I simply want to know a little more about you. You take comfort in my church and I know nothing about you, especially where you stand in your faith." He watched her shift from foot to foot, uncomfortable. She didn't really want to talk to him about anything meaningful, just what was necessary to stay there until it was time to move on.

"Please, Rosina, I do not want to pry; I just want to know you a little more." He crossed himself and stood up, carrying the candle to the shelf with the other candles. Then he walked to her and extended his arm, "Would you like some tea?" She looked at him, trying to figure out his plan, but wrapped her hand around his bicep anyway and he led her to the kitchen. He boiled water and collected two mugs as she sat stiffly in the hard wooden chairs at the table, watching and studying him. It was obvious that he was trying to comfort her. *He sees right through me.* She didn't let any emotion show on her face, just remained a stoic stone.

"Would it be better if I shared a little about myself first?" He asked over the sound of clinking.

She thought for a few seconds then said, "Sure. Let's try that."

"Okay." He paused for a moment, thinking. "Before I came here, to this village, I was lost, not just from God but in life. I did not know where I was going to end up, I thought I was going to end up dead in some ditch somewhere, and no one would even know who I was or bother to bury me. I decided, then, that I would not make my life about me; I was going to fill my life with the lives of others. I was going to help them because I was never helped. So, I walked into the church and never looked back. And, to be honest, when they looked for members to come to this village, I was afraid. I was going to look for any reason to not go, but then I realized I acting cowardly, just like those that refused to help me for some ridiculous reason or another. So, I volunteered. I came here to guide these lost souls back to God." He turned around and placed the teapot down on the table in front of her.

"That's a lovely story, and I commend you for being a man of worth, but that has nothing to do with God and my faith." She said, amazed at him, how he pulled himself out of the mud but she still didn't want to show him her scars.

"Actually, it had everything to do with Him. He was my guide and allowed me to do what I needed." He sat down and added some honey to his tea. "I want to know what drove you from God. Not because I want to preach to you or try to 'fix you' but because I want to know what kind of person I allowed to stay here; should I trust my judgment or should I be afraid that you'll kill me in my sleep if the urge overcomes you?" He paused, and without changing his tone, he said, "I know I'm tempting prey, being a meek, weak priest, but I *will* put up a fight."

She stopped her hand, with her cup to her lips, and looked at him over her cup, not sure if he was joking or if he was serious. But, she saw a smile playing on his lips, and she let out a laugh that she didn't know she still had, which she quickly covered with a drink.

"Oh, you do laugh? So nice to know." He chuckled and took a sip of his tea, "Oo, that's a bit hot." He blew on it before trying again.

There was only the sound of their mugs chinking on the table and their sipping for a long moment then, "I didn't know I could still laugh." She said it in a whisper, but he still heard.

"Everyone can laugh if they have the right person to give them something to laugh at," he said.

"I haven't had anyone in my life for too long." She said, the sadness creeping in.

"I would offer you a promise of friendship, but that would be empty. I don't know where your path is going to take you or what your past is, but I can promise this: As long as you are here, I will be your companion." He took a sip of his tea, "But I must warn you, I am pretty stubborn."

"I can see that," she said with a small laugh in her voice.

"You have not seen anything yet." He smiled at her.

She quickly dampened the mood. "I stopped because I took a dark path." She said quietly, hoping he wouldn't hear her but he looked up from his tea and watched her face. She saw him look up and quickly turned away.

When she didn't say anything more, he said, "You don't have to talk about it, I want you to, but if it is too much you don't have to." He reached across the table and put his hand on hers, "Letting it out might help you heal, even if it is a little." She quickly pulled her hand away from him. *I will not get close to another person.* She saw defeat on his face as he refilled his mug.

She watched him, he seemed so sure of himself, so flawless, so pure. *"Until you get your hands around his throat."* Her demon said.

She placed her mug back on the table and got up. She walked out of the kitchen and out the side door that led to the courtyard. The sun was now starting to creep up over the hills, but she was still in shadow behind the buildings surround the courtyard. She stood in the cool air, swimming in emotion that he seemed to be good at stirring up. She let out a sigh, echoing the one she heard him give as she left the room. She wanted to tell him why she didn't pray, she wanted to tell him everything, to let the gates open and all her fears and pain spill forth unto him and have him really help her. She knew that that was not possible, though. She knew that if she told him her truths that he would kill her on the spot. She was too far from his grasp and she needed to keep it that way, she needed to get herself under control. She could never trust anyone the way she has Gabriel, never again. She had to handle this burden alone, but she had to give him something. She had to satisfy his curiosity so that he would quit digging, looking for answers. He was a man on knowledge, and she knew that he would not quit until then. She physically shook herself, trying to relieve herself of her emotions and decided on what she was going to tell him. *Only enough to sate his curiosity*, she reminded herself.

She returned to the kitchen and sat back down at the table where the priest was still sitting. He sat up, surprised at her return, but also trying and failing to hide a smile growing on his mouth.

"Sorry," she said, not looking at him directly but into her cup of tea.

"Oh, no, don't be," he said, generously, "it was not right for me to push. I am glad you are back though."

"I went down a dark path, one so dark that I couldn't see anything but myself." She said without preamble, "I thought I was helping those around me, but I was really hurting them. Though, I tried to make amends it was too late. Then, I dragged in the one I loved the most and drove him down. I was raped mentally and physically and left to die. I did things that I cannot take back, and God has let me go down this path by myself. He has not stopped me, saved me, or removed me. I'm living proof that God does not care about us." She stood up and left the room as fast as an upset human would have. She didn't want to see how he would react or hear any words of encouragement. She ran to her room and slammed the door. She paced the worn stone floor. Her tears started to fall for the first time in many months.

"Stupid priest!" She had finally built high enough wall to keep her emotions separate from herself, to allow her to live with what she was and what she's done, but in just one sitting with him he tore them down.

"He will hurt you as all those others have, he will abandon you, like trash!" the demon-fueled her fears.

"I know!" She yelled at it just as a light tap came from the door.

"What?!" she yelled at the door and viciously wiped away her tears.

He slowly opened the door a little and she heard his voice come through the crack, "Can I come in?" She stared at the door, she half expected him to just come in. "I didn't mean to cause you pain. I just wanted to talk to you. We pass each other in the hall everyday, but we do not speak. To be honest, it has been lonely here since the others left and you seem very interesting." She could almost hear him mentally kick himself.

"What I meant was, you are interesting and I would like to get to know you and not be so lonely, if that leads you back to God then my work would be done but if it doesn't I'm not going to hold you to it.," he paused, "That's not right either," he said quietly to himself. "I just want to get to know you. I don't want to preach to you, just be a friendly face to you." She waited to see if he was done amending himself before walking to the door. She opened it the rest of the way a smile on her face and tears in her eyes.

For the first time he saw her vulnerable, and he had to really look at her. She was no longer just an interesting subject he would help, but she was an actual woman, a very dangerous and hurt woman. He had catch himself as he was staring at her in a way he shouldn't.

"I didn't run away because of you." Her smile faded. "I ran away because I'm afraid of my past. I'm afraid that if I light the candle in the dark all the nightmares will haunt me and I'll never be able to get away."

He cautiously wiped a tear from her cheek, "I know you don't know me, but you can trust me. I will not allow those demons to harm you. It is my job to help, not to harm."

His soft voice was soothing to her ears, and he drown out her real demon, *"You can't trust him!"* it wailed.

"Ok, priest, I will tread these waters, but I do not take kindly to being betrayed." She smiled again, "And I have to quit this thing you call laughing."

He chuckled at her and said, "Shall we finish our tea?" She nodded and followed him to the kitchen.

"Priest, what *is* your name?" she asked.

He just laughed and said, "Father."

•　　　•　　　•　　　•　　　•

She came out of her room the night after they had talked. She and the priest stayed up talking about shallow things, such as the town, the history of the cathedral, his work. They parted as the night wore down and the sun was beginning to light up the dark sky. She slept well, even though she didn't dream, she felt as if she was more rested than she had been since she left home. She stood in her doorway, not sure where she should go or what she should do. She heard a shifting of paper and decided to see if the priest needed any help. She walked towards the end of the hall wear she saw a candlelight illuminating a room whose door was open. She walked in and was taken aback at what she saw. Shelves lined all four walls from the floor to the ceiling and each one covered in books. Old books, new books, large books, and small books, each well used.

"Wow." She said, taking in all the books, reading over the titles and noticing that there were old bibles but also Greek mythology books, Asian texts, and European novels. The range of literature in the room astounded her.

There was a thump of a book hitting the ground as the priest jumped and spun around from the wall, dropping his book. He made a surprised noise. "Rosina! When did you get here?"

"Just now," she said without looking at him. "This is amazing. I didn't know you had such a wide taste in…" She opened her arms and motioned to the entire room, "for lack of a better description, knowledge."

"I am a man of the cloth, it is in our nature to learn as much as we can about the good and evil of the world." He said, almost brushing her off.

She ran her fingers across some of the old tomes and pulled one out after reading its title. "I don't think this has anything to do with that." She held up the book. The title was almost completely worn off. *Mythology of the Ancient World.* She put it back and pulled out another one and read its title saying, *Languages of the Far East.* "What does this have to do with good and evil?"

"I learn about the old religions in order to learn about the human behavior and reactions to things unknown and undefinable." He came over and took the book she had replaced and opened it to reveal several pieces of parchment tucked into its pages, she looked at them and saw written notes.

She leaned in to read them. Most of the pages were in a language she did not know, but amongst the original language was scribbled in English highlighting a certain point or translating a word for his reference. He had studied every word, every sentence, and paragraph in that book and had taken notes on all of it. She looked at him, seeing him in a new light.

"I had nothing when I was younger, so I fill myself with knowledge of everything to fill up the emptiness of my past and to help me understand why people do what they do when they do it to others. I want to know why people choose to rape rather than woo or steal rather than work for their food as everyone else does. Why do they believe that they are better or don't have to do things the way everyone else does." She could see the fire in his eyes grow, and she felt her heart sink as he described her. She took what she needed from people that were unable to defend themselves, and she stole and killed for her own gain.

She fought with herself every day for it, but she had not discovered any other way to sustain herself. *What makes my life more important than theirs?*

"Is something wrong?" he asked as he saw her eyes unfocused and her shoulders tense.

"Huh?" she corrected her stance quickly, "No, nothing. I'm just amazed at you."

"There is nothing to be amazed about." He closed the book and gently set it back on the shelf. "I simply fill myself with something that I love." He took the other book from her and placed it back on the shelf as well. He turned to pick up the book he had dropped but kept watching her as she stood there, grasping her left arm with her right hand. "What is bothering you?" He asked her again. She shifted again and looked at him.

"Nothing, really. I was just thinking." She said, clearly lying, but she was not giving him any more.

He stared at her for a moment then shook his head, "What did you need?"

"Hm?" She was distracted again.

"When you came in here, what did you need?" He asked again.

"Oh!" She said, seeming to snap back to reality, "I heard you moving stuff around, and I was coming to see if you needed any help."

He looked at her but didn't answer, waiting to see how long she would stand there, oblivious to him. "If you want to help me, you can pull all the books about the Romans out and place them over there," he pointed to a corner that already had several books sitting on the floor. "I have accumulated so many books that I need to organize them, so I know where to look when I want to read something particular."

"Okay," she nodded and walked to the wall next to the door and started at the bottom. They worked in silence for over an hour before she stumbled upon a book about Asian forms of war. "AH!" she exclaimed.

He spun around and rushed over to her as if to aid her. "Are you hurt?"

"Huh? Oh, no," she said, staring down at the book.

He paused, just staring at her, a slight annoyance creeping into his posture. "What is wrong then?" He didn't realize she was consumed in the book, or rather what about the book had consumed her.

"This book, could I borrow it?" she asked as sincere as she had ever been. *This could help me control myself, the Asians have been practicing control for centuries.*

He just stared at her.

She finally tore her eyes off the book and looked at him, he could see the excitement in her eyes.

"I will allow it, but can it wait until after we are done with the work?" He turned around to hide the smile on his face.

"Okay!" she placed the book back on the shelf and got back to work, all but dancing with excitement. The worked for the rest of the evening, the tension in the room all dissipated as her mood improved with each book she touched. He tried to hide his happiness at finding a kindred spirit, but there was still much about her that he didn't know and he was already gathering information on her behavior in a small leather-bound book hidden in his room. He hoped he was wrong about her, but the more time he spent with her, the more he feared that she was not all she appeared. (tia's note about it being too early to have him suspect she's not human)

She was there several weeks before she decided it was time for a real hunt. She followed one of the men looking for an after-drink-roll-in-the-hay, walking loud by enough to subtley attract his attention. She learned that the best way to catch prey was to allow it to come to you, allow it to get close, allow it to think it has the upper hand then strike, taking it by surprise. She watched him glance at her several time over his shoulder before he turned off down an alley. She kept walking straight, knowing he would reappear shortly. She did not walk more than a few yards before she heard him behind her. She pretended to panic, looking over her shoulder several times as she increased her pace. She heard him start to run to catch up to her and she also started a slow run allowing him to think she was running from him but also allowing him to catch up to her.

She smelled him before he touched her, grabbing her around the neck and pulling her to him. She screamed, and he covered her mouth. She bit him lightly, and he let go, cursing at her. She screamed again, and he stupidly put his hand back over her mouth. He dragged her into another dark alley and slammed her face-first into the stone wall of a building. She kicked back at him, and he jumped back, regrouped and came back with more force. Pressing his body against hers and reaching around her, trying to remove her robe. She felt her body start to heat up, the pounding of her hunger growing stronger and the demon at the edge of her consciousness. She couldn't contain her excitement and let out a loud laugh that caught him off guard.

He turned her around so she was facing him, "What is so funny, bitch?!" At that she laughed even louder, with her hunger her strength and desire to kill grew, flooding her with power that was much stronger than adrenaline and she was drunk on it.

He slapped her to get her to stop, and she looked at him with her glowing black eyes and said, "I have only one answer to offer you." Before he could pull away from her and run, she grasped his shoulders and slammed him down against the ground and quickly straddled over his middle. She felt his heat and excitement falter; she bent over him and sunk her teeth into his neck and allowed his nectar to flow into her waiting mouth. She devoured him slowly since it had been so long and he had been eager to get started; she wanted him to suffer while she enjoyed him slowly and gently where he would have done it roughly, in a hurry. She stopped short of his death and looked down at him as he struggled to hold onto his pitiful life. She whispered into his ear, "I laugh because a rat like you can never have a girl like me." Her demon howled in laughter, it enjoyed when she let her vampyre nature out. She took what was left of him, draining him until his death filled her with an ecstasy that she had never experienced. It was so intense that it took her breath away and the demon was satisfied and silent. The men here are truly evil, and their death would satisfy her and her demon to their delight and not only would it satisfy her hunger but also her own dark desires.

•   •   •   •   •

She returned to the cathedral shortly before the sun rose. She was so distracted, holding on to the feeling the death of the rapist had given her, that she was startled when the priest started talking to her.

"I want to ask you what you have been doing, seeing as you are quite literally glowing," he looked her up and down, "but I am afraid of what you might say. Especially since I scared you when you are usually the one that is always sneaking up on me. You actually jumped," he looked at her sideways, "I really do not want to know."

"I'm just doing my job." She answered with a grin. "If you do not mind I'm going to rest for a while, my job is quite exhausting." She went to her room and closed the door laying down on her cot. She was going to allow the endorphins to swim around her body as long as she could. The warmth that usually flew from her far too quickly, lingered and she could feel it in her skin. When she looked down at it, she was startled to see that it was, in fact, glowing. She could see a slight red color coming from her arms and hands. At first, she just stared at it, almost hoping it would disappear if she stared long enough, then when it didn't she jumped up and ran to the basin and poured some water on her arms and started scrubbing, trying to get the tingling to stop, to wash off the glow.

When that did not work, she opened her window, allowing the cool night air to flow in before it slowly slid closed again, trying to cool herself. She stripped off her robe and trousers leaving her standing in the cool air in just her undergarments. When she still felt like the heat had been turned up, she ripped off what was left of her clothes and throwing them violently into the corner. The wet clothes knocked stuff off the table as they hit it and slid off the other end, sending the lamp crashing to the floor, shattering the glass and soaking the floor in oil. The warmth that she had been enjoying now drove her to fear, and her skin started to burn hotter as her fear grew. She flipped the desk stool over and ripped off one of the legs and propped open the window. She poured the remaining water over her head soaking her hair and making it cling to her naked back. The chill air was blowing in the window, but the heavy drapes were blocking most of the window and hindering the wind. In her panic she tore them clear off the wall, bringing down the metal rod that held them down with a crash. Then at last, the wind was blasting into the room and over her wet, naked flesh. She lifted her head towards the ceiling and closed her eyes, focusing on the cold of the air, willing it to cool her skin. She stood there for what seemed like hours, but the heat only dimmed. Brisk footsteps filled the hallway, and the priest came rushing in her room. She slowly turned, forgetting that she had shed her clothes, watching as he looked over the now trashed room before his eyes finally settle on her and she saw him blush and avert his eyes. When he found her torn robe on the floor, he handed her the bed sheet. This time she blushed as she quickly covered herself.

They stood in the cold room, as the silence filled the air. Finally, the priest cleared his throat and when she looked at him, he asked, "What happened to you?"

She tilted her head and thought it strange he asked about her not his room in his church in his town. She could see in his face that he knew she was warring with her emotions and was able to read her so clearly. The heat in her skin that had finally settled into an annoying simmer roared back to life, he made her feel even more naked, could see straight through her as if he could read her thoughts and that vulnerability caused her temper to flare.

"What business is it of yours, priest, what happened to me? You, who cannot even tell me your name, are concerned about me?" Her anger causing her words to run away, she felt possessed by the same power that fueled the hunt, and she said things that were harmful and made no sense. "Are you asking because you fear my emotions will run away and those felons," she pointed to the village beyond the front doors of the cathedral, "will find out I am not sent from God and will come after you?"

She lowered her voice and started stalking towards him, a grin on her lips, almost a smile, almost showing her fangs, her demon behind that dark turmoil that was raging within her. "You know, I can take care of them for you. All of them. In one night." Her enjoyment of the idea was clear and with every word she spoke she took a step closer until she was within inches of him.

He could feel her heat and smell the blood on her breath, though he did not know that is what he smelled. He stood his ground, as she did this and then, when she had finished, she merely looked him in the eyes, remaining silent and he didn't even twitch. Now shaking with rage, her skin burned all the more and the once sweet blood that filler her now curdled within her.

"Do I not scare you, priest?!" she had an angry smile on her face, "I scare many, but not you?" She said directly at him, trying to get him to show some fear. "Do you not wonder how I do it? How could one so 'young' and 'untrained' and lost clean up this God-forsaken town? And do not jest yourself, priest, He has forsaken it." At this, she saw a slight twitch in his hand, and a fire start in his eyes. She chuckled outside as her demon wailed inside. "*So quickly you learn, how to hunt, how to kill and how to hurt those that would hurt you.*"

"I've heard rumor of people like you," he finally spoke, his voice quiet and tense, "Godless hunters of your fellow man: bounty hunters that kill for profit but hide behind justice and God." His statement took her off guard, he thought she was a bounty hunter? *If it were that simple.* "I will not allow you to defile this sacred place. I have seen the true justice, the justice of God. He wishes not that his children be extinguished but that all his children be forgiven and saved from —"

She let out a loud, "Ha!" which stopped him. "He wishes all his children be saved?! What about me? I carry a demon that he has yet to save me from. What say you now, priest? Am I not one of His children? Or am I forsaken? Your faith is misplaced; not everyone can be saved, and it is just to remove them for the sake of His children that can be." She turned from him and walked back to the window as if talking to God rather than the priest, "I hope that when the day comes when I become a threat to His sheep that the farmer will shoot me as he does the coyote." She whispered to the night, "I hope that the bullet is not far off, for at least then there will be some peace." She lowered the sheet to drape behind her. She held it in her hands but let it sag to the floor; she was trying to put out the fire raging in her soul and on her skin.

This is not what I want. I never wanted to hurt this man who was so kind to me. Why do you make me do this, demon?

"I do not do this, you do this. Your anger has led you down this road; I am merely enjoying the show." It cackled at her growing guilt.

The priest was looking away, holding his tongue. He was seeking for the truth amongst all her words, looking for something, the skeleton she was, without all the fluff and hard shell. What was she really trying to tell him? He knew she did not truly possess a demon, but perhaps some tragedy or another even that causes her pain and keeps her from being more than an angry, violent woman.

She felt him look at her, could feel his eyes on her and then she heard him gasp. She spun around to see what was wrong only to find him staring, in awe, at her. She immediately moved her hand clasping the sheet to her chest to cover herself when he walked over and stopped her, saying, "No, don't cover it. It is beautiful." She was confused and just continued to stare at him as his cold hand moved to her wrist and lowered it, lowering the sheet as he did. He stared at her until she felt uncomfortable physically and emotionally. The change of atmosphere, from fear and anger to guilt to some semblance of calm, in the room was like riding in a cart that had misshapen wheels. She moved again to cover herself. He stopped her again this time taking the sheet from her completely, pulling it up to her chest and covered her front, leaving her back exposed. She grasped it quickly, grateful for the overage.

He turned her back towards the dirty mirror that was forgotten in the corner and said, "Beautiful. I did not know you had these." He stopped staring her and asked, "Is this the demon that you carry?" She was even more confused now than she had been and seeing this he pointed at the mirror. She looked over her shoulder at herself reflected in the dust, and it was she who gasped this time. Reflected in the mirror was her prtially naked back; red glowing markings covered her skin. He was right, they were beautiful as they swirled and intermingled forming one large design that covered her entire body from the base of head down to each toe and finger. The intricate patterns were nothing like she had ever seen and as beautiful as they were, they scared her. In all the tales about vampyres, she had never heard one about them having any sort of markings. Unless they received some sort of marking, like a tattoo or scar before being changed they had no outwards markings. They healed far too quickly leaving their skin unblemished. She saw that these markings were not put on her from the outside but were coming from within.

When she didn't answer him, instead kept staring, he put his hand on her shoulder and turned her to face him. The look on his face was soft, not full of pity or sadness, but of comfort, "You didn't know." He wasn't asking her, but telling her that he knew just by looking at her. She looked at him, as if seeing him for the first time. He truly was an angel sent to help those in need, maybe he was right when he said he wanted all of Gods children saved, but it was him not Him, that was driving him, his pure soul and kind heart. She looked at him in a new way as if she could actually see a halo over his head.

He saw her expression change from confusion to one of understanding, and if he was honest, it scared him a little, but he was never going to tell her that. "Rose?" he urged her.

"No, I didn't. I've never allowed my emotions to get this much out of control," *because the demon takes over*, she didn't say. "Maybe that is why my skin burns when I get excited. I have always been unusually good at deceiving and, well, let's call it hunting." He gave her a sideways glance. "maybe this is my punishment."

"Or reward." He said.

She laughed a sarcastic laugh, "Reward for doing what?"

"God's work."

"Augh. You are *stuck* on that." She said with a snap. "Like I said earlier, He has left me behind, I'm merely floating through till my hunter comes along."

"You are doing His work. And do not give up so easily, you have so much life left, so much to live for." He said.

"I'm doing my work, it makes me happy, and I do not get paid for it. I never said that I wasn't going to make that bastard of a hunter work hard for my heart." She said with a little bit of a laugh. "But you, Angel, keep trying to convince yourself that I am righteous and am sent from God when I am very much not."

"Angel?" he asked, the corners of his mouth twitching, trying not to smile.

"Yeah, you know, like one of those guys up in heaven with God. You have the halo and everything." He looked at her with his head cocked to the side, trying to understand what she meant, she laughed at his look. "Don't think too hard, you'll hurt your pretty little head. You aren't the only one that can see into someone's heart. I can see your beautiful heart, she pointed at his chest, "and glowing halo." She made a ring with her two thumbs and fingers and held them over her head as if putting on a crown. He still looked at her without saying anything. She smiled at him, "you came in here, and instead of asking what happened to the room or why I was going crazy, you asked about me. Seeing right through to the root of the problem, me, you knew something was wrong with me. Even after I badmouthed your precious Father, you still showed concern for me. I could be confusing it for trying to put me on the right path, but I'll take it as concern from one human to another, because no one," *except Gabriel,* "has ever looked at me like that. And no one has tried to help me with no benefit to themselves." *Except Gabriel.* The last bit was out of her mouth before she could stop it, and he grabbed onto it.

"And that is the first time you have been *completely* open with me." He moved to sit on the bed, it squeaked as he sat down on the old mattress. "I do like that smile on your face, it is more beautiful than all those tattoos. If that isn't worth living for, then I don't know what is."

"I'm sorry?" she asked. "I don't live for my own smile, that doesn't make sense."

"No, think deeper." he said. "Happiness makes you smile and that is worth living for."

She could not believe what she was hearing, he wanted her to be happy? "You are saying I should try to be happy?"

"Yes, isn't that a worthy goal? That is something that not only He would want but what I would want."

"What?" She was sure she had heard him wrong, he wanted to help her be happy? There was a moment of silence between them, and for the first time it wasn't an awkward silence. She spoke first, because she couldn't contain herself, she was on some sort of high that had nothing to do with the blood, but all to do with the angel priest, "Are you saying that you can help me be happy? And if so, why? How would you benefit?"

"Is it so hard to believe that someone would want to help you without any gain to them?" He asked as if it was nonsense to expect anything in return for his help.

"Oh right, it's His will." She said sarcastically.

"No! It is mine!" He shut his mouth quickly as if he was trying to stop himself from admitting that he *was* doing something for himself and not for God.

"Oh." She said, giving him a little of his dignity and not drilling him about it. She didn't want to delve deeper into the emotions of a priest, she would only get hurt, she knew he would not allow himself anything that God had not bestowed upon him and he would in turn hand out whatever it was to the people around him, keeping none for himself. She covered herself better with the sheet, using it as if it was a toga, and sat down beside him. Her leg bumping him unintentionally, but instead of jumping back from her, as she expected, he let it rest against his, so she left it, it was comforting, his warmth different from the burning she felt in her skin every day, it was calming not razor sharp and painful. "You really are an angel," she whispered, "but not because God sent you here."

"Thank you," he whispered back, not asking what she meant, feeling a different warmth than she was growing in his heart. Then, there was more silence. They sat on the bed, and she watched as her tattoos dim to nothing as the heat of her anger faded. He clasped his hands together, trying not to fidget, getting agitated that he couldn't keep himself calm, he was at a loss as to what was happening. He stood suddenly, "I think I'm going to go… pray and then go back to bed." He hurried to the door and removed himself from her presence before she could even look up at him.

He leaned against the other side of the closed door, breathing heavily as if he had just been running, praying was exactly what he needed, he was going to seek guidance from someone that had more strength than he. His heart was pounding as he lifted himself from the door. Before he walked away he heard a muffled, "Good night, Angel," coming from the other side of the door and he could hear her real emotions coming through, her gratitude that was rooted much deeper than he knew. He was no angel, for he coveted something that was forbidden. He had no idea what was happening. He had always had control over his emotion and was never once tempted by a woman, but when the most damaged one fell upon him, he was tempted beyond belief, as if the devil himself had stopped by to pay him a visit.

He hurried away from her door and to the altar to pray. He lit as many candles as he could find and kneeled down before the crucifix and prayed for guidance to be led from temptation and from the woman that was pulling at his heart without knowing.

Chapter Five: Temptation is Such a Fleeting Desire

The wind howls over the mountain
The rain falls heavy on the ground
The deep burning grew brighter
The darkness surrounds and suffocates
The end is nigh
Death is here
No escape for the needing soul
There is no savior for you.

The weeks passed in the church much more comfortably. Instead of avoiding the priest, whose name she still did not know, she would seek him out. She enjoyed his company, she felt as if she was more her old self around him. He also loosened up and was gaining the courage to go out more and talk to the people: spread his words to the people he was supposed to be helping. They had heard rumors of a dark angel of death that was killing people that acted out of line and assumed it was something the church was behind. None of them chose to openly be rude to the priest. However, if anyone tried to make an attempt to silence him, she was there to silence *them*. She had to stop several times to make sure that she wasn't dreaming; how was it possible that she had found a place she belonged and felt at home? She had caught herself actually pinching herself several times. When she yelped, thinking she was alone, the priest poked his head around the corner and asked what she was doing. She lied every time, saying she stubbed her toe, which, of course, he did not believe, and he would remove his shaking head without asking any more questions.

She still hunted at night, especially when people seemed like they were staying in line with the priest. She had taken to wandering the streets and actually taking in the town as it was. Seeing all the crafts and foods that were made and how the people interacted with each other. She learned that some of the people who moved here had actually done it to make their lives better not only for themselves but their family. They had done something that society couldn't forgive but their family could. To stay together and not be tormented constantly, they moved with them. That is true love, something she had almost forgotten.

She had been invited in many times by these kind families as she had been walking the streets alone. She gracefully declined, but couldn't help her smile. There were people out there, other than the priest, that had pure kindness in their hearts. She could not believe that she had found it here, of all places. When she finally moved on, this village would forever leave a mark on her heart.

"So, Angel, where are we going to today?" She entered the kitchen where the priest was brewing tea.

"Would you stop calling me that?" She had taken to calling him that since she thought it was softer than calling him *priest*, which was so unfamiliar, and she didn't know his actual name. He said this very statement every time she did; but she could tell by the smile in his eyes that he didn't mind; in fact, he actually liked it. "And I thought we could go out in the daylight, we might get more people to come listen when the sun is out, warming up the air."

She paused her movement to dry the teacups, not knowing what to say. She could not go out into the sun, she would burn, but if she told him she would be uncovered and probably burned anyways. She cleared her throat, "Okay, if you want."

"Good, we'll head out at eight tomorrow morning?" That could work; the sun won't be high in the sky, which means there would be plenty of shadows.

"Fine, but I'll warn you now; I am not a morning person." she said, trying to make a joke.

"I would be more surprised if you were." He chuckled as he sipped his tea. "You better stay in tonight, get some sleep, I know your tempter, and I would hate for one of our students to go missing because he looked at you wrong while you were sleep deprived." He looked up from his book at her.

"*Our* students? Ha! You can have them; I'm just here to keep the order." She made a fist and punched her other palm so punctuate her statement, Angel laughed at that. "And I'll slap someone silly if that someone 'looks at me wrong' regardless of my mood."

"They are your students indirectly, you were the one who convinced me to go out and speak to the people again. I am beginning to think you really *are* sent from God, in the form of a Sister teacher."

She spun around almost dropping the cup in her hand, "Are you saying I'm a nun?!" He looked up at her over his steaming tea, her reaction surprising him, "because I think that I have proven over and over that I am not a person sent from God. I kill people, you know?" *Keep it together,* she gave herself a pep talk, *you keep reacting like this and he's going to know your secret!* "I mean, figuratively, I kill their bad spirit." She covered up her slip quickly.

"Ha ha! He will discover your secret soon enough, you just can't help yourself. You will slip and he will die!" she ignored her demon's harsh words.

"You're right, just the reaction to the robe was enough to prove that, because you know those nuns just *love* their robes." sarcasm was dripping from his words. She turned around to hide her smile, but she knew that he could tell when she was smiling, even if he couldn't see it. The thought of her beautiful smile made him smile, but he wasn't quick enough to hide his when she spun around with a wild remark about to drop from her lips, but his smile stopped her.

"What are you smiling about?" She got a surprised look on her face, "Don't tell me you are trying to picture me in a nun's robe?" she gasped, as if finally understanding something, "If you are picturing me as some sort of naughty nun or something you are going to end up on the floor with a sore head." She was shaking a dripping plate at him.

He kept smiling at her, "I promise you that I am not; I am a man of God, and I do not desire to 'imagine' such things, but I do believe that if you keep dripping water on the floor of God, I'll make you scrub the whole cathedral."

"Psh," she made a noise of disbelief, "every man is a man of God and every man desires—"

"This is a house of God, remember." He tried to interrupt

"Sex." she finished anyways. He gasped and gave her *a watch-what-you-say* look. "Admit it, there was at least one point that you craved a woman's touch, her soft hands on your cheek or chest, or perhaps her warm lips on yours, trailing down your neck," she leaned over the table, looking him straight in the eye, but his eye traveled briefly down her long, creamy neck to the low line of her robe before catching himself dend looking back up to her face. "I thought so," she stood up straight with a smirk on her face. She returned to drying the dishes.

It took him only a moment to recover, "I most certainly have never coveted…" he cleared his throat, "sex." he finished quietly.

"Uh huh," she said as she winked at him over her shoulder, her hair swaying across her back as she turned her head back to the bowl of soapy water. He watched her wash the remaining dishes, her hips swaying as her hands moved back and forth in the water, a slight hum escaping her soft lips, like the nightingale's soothing song. "You never answered me, where do you want to go in the morning?"

Her question imposed on his focus, "Huh?" he tried to recover, "I mean, I was thinking the town square, plenty of room for people to gather. Now, if you'll excuse me, I'm going to go prepare." He stood up, nearly knocking over his chair, and left the kitchen.

"Well, that was strange."

"And don't forget what I said about tonight." He yelled back. "I see the clouds coming in, there is going to be a thunderstorm tonight."

"I'd never miss a chance to experience a thunderstorm; it is one of the more enticing things that God has created." She yelled back at him, and she received a grunt of disproval that made her laugh.

•　　•　　•　　•　　•

Down the hall from the kitchen, on his way to the chapel, the priest was in disbelief of his behavior and even more of the thoughts he was having. It would seem that the girl was right, every man was weak to temptation, but what she was wrong about was that all of them acted on it. If he didn't get himself together, though, he would soon no longer be allowed to wear the cloth of a priest. He knelt in front of the altar and prayed, asking for the strength to defeat the temptation that the devil had laid before him. He asked for a reason for such a temptation. Was God trying to show him what the men in the town went through? Was it to allow him to see what they see, feel what they felt, and be able to teach them to allow God to guide them back onto the path of righteousness?

"Thank you, Father." He got up, lit a candle and head back down the hall to the library, excited to get started. He nearly ran into Rosina on her way out of the kitchen.

"Woah, watch it!" she joked with him.

"I am sorry, but please excuse me, I have work to do." He said, serious, without looking at her.

"Hey! What is going on with you? You've been acting weird the last few days. If my addressing you as Angel is really bothering you that much, I'll stop," she put her hand over her heart, showing her sincerity.

"Huh?" he looked up at her, "Oh, no, that's not it. I've been inspired. I know now that God has been tempting me for one reason."

"Tempting you? How?" she asked, confused, "You've barely left this building other than to preach, and I've been with you the whole time you are doing so." She was clearly missing something.

"That is of no matter, all that is important is that I know how to help them now. I know how it feels to be tempted and how to overcome it!" He hurried on past her. She could feel the air shift in his absence because he left so fast.

"Well, okay then," she shook her head and proceeded on down the hall. On her way by her room, she reached in and grabbed her cloak. She was going to need as much strength and focus tomorrow if she was going to go out in the daylight, she needed to feed, and she was not joking about missing the thunderstorm; it was her favorite natural occurrence, and for some reason, it calmed her.

"You love the chaos."

•   •   •   •   •

She dined on a barmaid that lured men to their death with her ample bosom. The maid would allow them to do their business and then kill them, rob them, and dump them. She was allowed to come to the town to increase the 'diversity' of the place. The thinking was that with a few less respectful women amongst the men, they would have other things to do than beating, stealing from, or killing each other. Rosina believed that the women may actually be making it worse, since they liked the naughty ones and because of this, the men tried harder to impress them.

After she finished dinner, she wandered down to the field on the east end of town, close to the river. She sat down on the top of the hill and enjoyed the warm evening air. She could feel the electricity of the coming storm and her anticipation grew. The clouds rolled in, making the black sky dark blue, she could trace the outlines of them with her eyes, the electricity flowing through them bringing them to life. The bolts of lightning were jumping from cloud to cloud, as if they too were growing excited to leap from the heavens but it wasn't yet time. She laid back on the soft grass and watched as the build up to the storm progressed.

As she lay there, she thought of all the summers that she and her brother had run home in the rain, the lightning at their backs and how their mother would scold them for making a mess of the foyer and how they could have caught a cold from getting soaked. That did not stop them from doing it again and again any chance they got. She was lost in her memories when the soft sound of grass being pressed flat drew her attention. She looked up from where she laid to see the priest standing next to her, looking down at her in wonder.

"I thought I said that you should stay in tonight." He said.

She sat up and asked, "Are you here to collect me, then?"

He sat down beside her, "No, I thought I would come out here and be closer to God."

"By sitting in the rain?" she had disbelief written all over her face.

"Who was it that created the rain? And the thunder? And—"

"Okay, okay, I grasp your point." He settled himself with a smug look on his face. "Are you sure that you are a man of God? You seem to enjoy proving me wrong." She had a little pout in her voice.

"I am quite certain. But what harm is it to have a little fun now and again?" he asked with a chuckle.

"You're allowed to have fun?" she looked at him in feigned shock, "I did not know that." He gave her a sideways look. She put her hands up as if surrendering, "My apologies, priest. I will never again make the mistake of assuming you aren't fun." She snickered at the look on his face.

"Can we please just enjoy the night without talking? Silence is a beautiful thing, you should give it a try sometime." She just looked at him in disbelief. A loud clap of thunder pulled her attention back to the sky, the rain followed as they watched large drops fall from the sky. She allowed herself to be consumed by the storm and a smile encompassed her entire face. There is only one thing that she would miss when she died and it was not the sun but the thunder. She stood up and walked down the hill to where it was level and closed her eyes allowing the water to fall on her and soak her, she could feel it down to her bones.

The priest remained where he was and watched her, wondering what she was doing. She was just standing in the rain at first, but then she actually started dancing in it, she was relishing it. For some reason, she was at peace in the storm, in the midst of all the chaos and turmoil she was at peace. *I really will never understand this woman,* he thought, then stood up when the rain began to thin and walked towards her. He touched her shoulder, and she turned to face him, a smile on her face.

"You truly are a mystery to me." He said.

"I thought you could read me like an open book, Angel."

"I can read most people, but you are more like a stone wall rather than a book; I can detect subtle things from you, but the real story lies hidden."

"My story is the same as any other, there is sadness, happiness, anger, and then death which brings peace." She replied.

"You are kind of morbid at times." He said with worry.

"Not morbid, just honest," she replied. "I am saying what others will not, death happens to us all, eventually."

He nodded, "But most people focus on the living part of life, not the death part."

"In case you haven't noticed, death is my particular specialty." She said, looking sideways at him, mentally kicking herself.

"What did I tell you?" Her demon cackled loudly in her ear.

He nodded again, "Unfortunately, I have," he didn't even flinch, "but that's what I'm here for, to show you the good things about living."

She scoffed at that. "You can try, Father. But, whether you believe it or not, I get quite a bit of enjoyment out of 'living.'" Her stubbornness was more than what it seemed, she was not allowing him to help her, *who could possibly hate God so much that they would avoid His guidance,* he thought.

"I can see your wheels turning, Angel, you need to just enjoy what we are given, as you would say. Take in this beauty." She raised her arms and motioned to everything above her, around her and beneath her.

"I only have one question." He said, demanding her to look his way.

"No," she said firmly. "No more questions, no more prodding, just enjoy." When he opened his mouth to protest she put a finger over it, quieting him. She stepped closer to him, stopping any further protest on his part and whispered in his ear, "Just enjoy what God has given you and me," her warm breath on his neck was enough to silence him. All he could do was nod in agreement, but he was enjoying something that she wasn't, and he was going to keep it that way. She felt his hesitation and backed up. "Is there something wrong?"

He shook his head, "No, nothing." He turned away from her, about to walk away, but she put a hand on his shoulder and turned him back towards her.

"Tell me, Angel, what is bothering you?" she insisted.

"Nothing. Nothing that God will not be able to help me." He avoided her eyes, looking everywhere but into her face. She saw this and gently touched his hand on his cheek guiding his sight to hers.

"Dear Angel, you do not need to suffer alone; I am here, if for nothing else but a listening ear," she leaned his head to hers, placing his forehead against hers and closed her eyes. "I can help ease your pain, you have helped so many others, it is time someone helped you."

"God helps me," he whispered, but he too closed his eyes and soaked in her warmth and kindness.

"He has made it so that everyone can help each other when He is too far away to help Himself." She said.

"He is never too far away." He disagreed gently.

"Then why do you struggle now? My sweet, kind Angel, why does he allow you to do this alone? Or perhaps He *has* sent me, for you, not for them," she meant the villages, but he knew that.

His heart was beginning to beat faster, he had never felt a temptation so strong. It was wrapped up in such beauty and sweetness, he almost didn't recognize it. Would he be strong enough to overcome it? He sent up a silent prayer asking for strength. "There are so many temptations in this world and I have been unaffected by them all, until now, until you. I don't know if I have the strength to resist it." He put his hands on her hips, before she could say anything. He didn't pull her in or push her away. He just held her where she was, also holding himself still. "The demon inside you is no match for my demon it would appear," he tried to make a joke, but it was strained as if he really was fighting off a demon.

"I would debate that with you, but you are struggling with it much more than I." He could feel the muscles in her face move, and he knew she was smiling.

He lifted his head so he could see it, and it light up his heart, she was truly an angel in dark clothes and he could resist her no more. His grip on her waist tightened, and he pulled her towards him until her body was against his and his breath came in quick, heavy draws.

She looked into his eyes and could see his torment; his hot breath on her face was causing her skin to tingle, and she realized what he was fighting: his temptation was *literally* her. He craved her but was not allowed to have her. *What kind of God would wish his sons to go without love? To give up the most basic needs of life, companionship and touch, the warmth of another?* She was filled with a desire to show him what he was living without and that it was not a sin to crave another human. She put a hand on the back of his neck and another on his back pulling him even closer to her. She leaned in and kissed his cheek, allowing him to reject her if he desired; she didn't want to be the cause of his hatred towards what was meant to be enjoyed. She heard a quiet moan leave his mouth from deep within and she could feel he was barely holding himself in check, tightening the chains on his desire. She wanted to break those chains for him, to be his guide. She leaned in again and trailed a path of soft kisses from his ear to the corner of his mouth and finally taking possession of his lips with hers. She gently pushed into him with her lips, not wanting to scare him. At first, he simply allowed her presence there, but then he pushed back with his own lips. There was a hunger so fierce in his kiss that her breath was taken away and a moan escaped her. At that, he pushed more furiously into her, and she pushed back, running her hand along his neck and into his short brown hair. She could feel her skin start to burn, but she welcomed it, for she knew her hunger was not for his blood.

He pulled away, his lips swollen, and looked at her, the red glow from her markings illuminating his face, "I… I… I can't…"

She put her lips over his again, to quiet him and whispered against him, "Yes, you can. God made us to bond with each other, to not be alone, to not hunger for love." He nodded, allowing her to guide him, rejecting all that he had learned. She pushed herself into him, sucking up his intoxicating scent. Her skin felt like it had erupted fire, and she kissed him more viciously, giving in to her own need as he ran his hands up and down her back and over her hip, feeling ever curve within his reach. She was caught up in the heat and placed the hand from his neck under the top seam of his robe, feeling his hard body. This took her a little by surprise; he didn't seem the one to worry about body figure. Her cold hands on his skin snapped him back to reality, and he pulled away from her as if she had slapped him.

"God does not want this! He put me here to help others; not to be tempted by pleasures of the flesh! It is forbidden, my mind should not be clouded with this filth!" he said in a panic.

"Filth?!" she felt his words hit her like a wall. "I may not be a perfect little angel, but I am far from filth!" And this time she did slap him. The smack reverberated across the field, and he stumbled back a few steps holding his left cheek. "God doesn't care if you choose to love or not, that is why it is a choice! He does not demand that you remain alone. That is why he made us such social creatures (in pairs, a man and a woman, or man and man if you so desire), or do you CHOOSE to forget that?!" She ran away from him towards the town, the opposite end from the cathedral. She felt her hunger for his body turn to hunger for his blood, if she stayed near him tonight she just might kill him.

•   •   •   •   •

He watched her run from him, he could see her tears, but whether they were from anger or sadness, he did not know. All he knew is that he should have restrained himself and not drew her into his weakness. He should have just left her alone or handled her better; she was a delicate flower, and he just smashed her. He could feel himself falling, falling hard into the pits of his own mind and the sadness was overwhelming. He couldn't even bring himself to call after her, to stop her and explain to her that he didn't mean what he said; he did not mean to hurt her, to push her away. He needed to tell her that he was attracted to her, and feared that he may be falling for her quirky habits and overconfident personality, but God forbids it.

He stayed in the field for several minutes, even though they seemed to drag on for hours in the cold rain and harsh wind. He just stood, not thinking, not moving until he felt the rain stop and it drew him back out. He slowly made his way back to the cathedral and stripped off his wet clothes and threw them, to be forgotten, on the floor. He then kneeled before his personal alter in a room across from his, locking the door behind him, so no one could defile it.

"Forgive me, Father," he began to pray, "for I have sinned. I have gone against your ways and sought solace with another and for that I know I must be punished." He opened the drawer below the altar and withdrew a slender wooden handle that had several pieces of leather attached to one end. He bowed over his knees and, holding the wooden handle, whipped his back over and over. He did not cry, he did not gasp in pain. He remained silent and continued to abuse himself until he had lost so much blood that he could no longer keep conscious and fell the rest of the way to the floor, lying in his own blood.

•   •   •   •   •

Rosina returned to the cathedral just before dawn, hoping she could avoid the priest but he was waiting for her. He was sitting in the front pew, his posture tense. But it wasn't his posture that she first noticed, as soon as she entered the cavernous worshiping area she was completely overcome by the smell of blood, his blood, a lot of it. She cursed and turned to leave, "Wait." He barely spoke, and a normal person may not have even heard him. The plea in his voice caused her steps to falter, and she stopped at the door. She didn't want to be in the room with him, when he smelled so… tasty. She had to get away from him before she gave in to her need to feed on the oh-so-available blood that he was offering her without knowing. She covered her nose, hoping it would stifle the smell, but it only did a little and she held her breath to extinguish her burning desire. She didn't say anything just waited. When she had grown impatient and was unsuccessful at ignoring her thirst, she put her hand on the door and opened it a small amount when he finally spoke. "I'm sorry."

The fresh air from the crack in the door was helping tremendously, and she was able to turn around to look at him; he was facing away from her still, "Sorry? You're sorry? That is all that you have to say to me? Sorry?" She demanded, angrier than she had any right to be.

"Yes," he said softly, "that is all I can offer you."

"Is that right? Why is that, priest? Are your thoughts all jumbled? Has God not told you what to say? Or are you not man enough to admit that you *are* just that, a man, a human man? A human that has needs. God is lying to you if He is telling you that it is a sin to love, all human emotion and motivation towards one another is based on love. Love is the reason He is so desperately trying to save us!" She turned to leave again.

"Perhaps you are right, but love is not meant for everyone." He answered her many questions with a vague response. "I chose not to be loved, to not covet the simple pleasures. That was my own decision. I did it so that I could help others out of my love for Him."

"Do you really think that is enough?" she asked, her anger growing. "I may not have as much wisdom as you, but even I know everyone needs someone."

"I have God," he turned around at looked her straight in the eyes and said, "That IS enough." There was a long moment of silence while she stood at the door thinking about what he said, her hunger just below the surface and despite her better judgment, she walked up to the pew where he sat, now facing the altar. She sat down next to him and faced the altar without saying anything. She put her hand on his leg and looked at him, trying to curb her hunger even though she could now feel his warmth and pulse in his leg. She promptly removed her hand and placed it along with her other hand between her thighs to keep herself in check. She could feel her skin start to warm, her markings making a soft appearance, and her mouth water, she had to do something to get her mind off of it. Clearly, he could not tell she could smell his blood. He was acting so casual. What he had done he did not want her to know about. He had cleaned up, so she wasn't about to give up the fact that she could, indeed, smell it because that may give away that *she* was *not* human.

"If you are truly fulfilled then I am sorry. I am sorry I put you in a position that you did not want to be in. I'm sorry I forced you to feel the way that you did, to feel cornered and to push you over the edge all at the same time." He didn't say anything to her, just sat and absorbed. She could feel her heart sinking and was surprised that it was. *Why does this priest affect me so?* She thought.

Her demon chimed in, "*it's because he is covered in blood!*" She shook her head, knowing that it was wrong.

He sighed and looked over at her. "No, my child… I mean, no, it was not you, it was me. I made a promise, and I broke it. I not only betrayed God, I shamed myself and I hurt you." She could only stare at him. "I allowed my emotions to overtake me and that allowed the devil in." She made a noise of disbelief, but he put his hand up to quiet her. "I am no better than those men out there," again he put his hand up before she could speak, "as easily swayed by my needs and desires as they are. How is it that I think I can help them, when I am no different?" She didn't know what to do. She knew he was hurting, but she was never good at comforting anyone, especially a man of God, the same as the ones that had shunned her and proclaimed her possessed and evil. It was even worse because she was trying to get away from him. Fidgeting because all she wanted to do was sink her fangs into his calling flesh, taking him in a very different way than she had planned for last night. She turned away from him while he continued to belittle himself and mumble on about how awful he was.

Then a thought struck her, and she slid off the pew and knelt before the alter speaking loudly, "Oh Holy Father on high, please hear my words and head my pleas." She heard the silence in the room as he stopped talking. "Forgive me, Father, for I have committed the gravest of acts against you and your children. I am one who murders, steals, and manipulates your most innocent and sickly. I walk the path of darkness and enjoy the many steps I have taken thus far. I do not regret what I have done save one act that has led another down my dark path. One who is devoted to you, Lord, in every way, has been led astray by myself. I ask, Father, that you forgive me for leading him such, I did not wish to stain his brightly shining light or make crooked his halo and break his wings, for Father, he truly is an angel sent from you to guide the tainted and dirty back to your holy embrace."

She could feel his eyes on her, in shock of her prayer. He knelt down beside her, crossing himself and whispering "In the name of the Father, the Son, and the Holy Spirit, Amen." Then he sighed as if a weight had been lifted from him and he turned and hugged her so swiftly that she was knocked over and he landed on her. She stifled a laugh as they plummeted to the floor and a cloud of dust erupted from under them. She wrapped her arms around him, embracing him and feeling relieved that she was able to undo one wrong that she had done, one on a list of many. He was whispering "thank you's" in her ear, and she could almost swear that he was crying. She could still smell his blood, but the scent was overcome by the smell of his happiness, at least that's what she thought that smell was, and his salty tears. He lifted himself from her and helped her to a sitting position; she could see the light returning to his eyes.

"I know that it was my fault. You did not vow yourself to God, but you went to our Father and asked for forgiveness for me. No one has ever done anything like this for me. I have always had God, but no one else." She gave him a puzzled look. "I was mostly grown when I made my way to the church. My parents abandoned me on the street. I never knew my brothers and sisters, if I had any, and I do not know who my parents or grandparents or cousins or uncles are. All I have ever had is God."

Noting his awkwardness with people: "That explains a lot," she mumbled behind her hand, pretending to cough.

"What?" he asked.

"Nothing," she answered, hiding a smile this time.

"Okay." He looked confused but continued, "I never had anyone show such kindness to me as you have. I do believe that may be why I fell into the devil's trap," she looked at him aghast, but he ignored it, "You are so... hmm... What's the word I am looking for?"

"Devilish?" She said with a wink, which got her a look of exasperation from the good father. She gave him a grin in return.

"Different." he finished his thought, "You are so different than anyone I have ever met."

"More than you know, priest," her devil piped up.

"Different how?" she asked, curious.

"Well, everyone I've interacted with has either been a man of the cloth or a criminal, so I guess maybe you are just normal compared to all that." He seemed at a loss, as if he didn't want to belittle her, but at the same time, it was the truth.

"Thank you, I guess?"

"I don't mean it in a bad way; it is very much welcome and refreshing. It's a change, and I like it. To a point, but as you saw, that led me to commit a crime against God."

"I see. If you are done...um... what's the word? Demeaning? Yes, demeaning me, I'm going to head to bed." She put her hands on the floor to push herself to a standing position when he grasped her wrist, gently, stopping her and making her turn to look at him, concerned.

"I am not demeaning you, I am praising you. There is so much to you; you are kind, gentle, and seek to help other even though you have no obligation to. I just don't understand it."

"You haven't traveled much, have you? For a man of God, you do not know much about his children. My mother was as kind as she was beautiful. She helped anyone that needed and she stood up for those less fortunate, even then she had to stand against the church to do so." He could see the sadness in her eyes.

He looked at her, and she could tell that he was reading her like he always did. Before he could ask her about it, she continued, "And my father and brother were almost as saintly, they went out of their way to be kind to others and gave away the food from our fields that we didn't need to feed ourselves, there was always surplus and always mouths to feed. And Gabriel," she paused before continuing as if lost in the thought of him, "He helped me the most in my time of need. Without even knowing me, he took my hand and lifted me up and gave me back my desire to live and sparked my drive for being happy. He made me see the world in different colors." She paused again, looking past him. Her eyes alight with a passion that she had failed to leave behind when she left her life behind.

"You loved him, didn't you?" When she just stared at him, he said, "Gabriel? You loved him?"

"Yes," she whispered, dropping her head down so she was looking at the floor, "I loved him, and still do," She looked up after a short pause, "but that's not the point," she said, her voice normal again, "the point is that I am nothing compared to them, I do what I do for myself."

"Even including what you did for me just now?" he asked, doubtful.

"It was nothing; I just hate to see people saddened by something that shouldn't sadden them." He could tell there was more to it than that and gave her a look that said, 'come on, out with it.' She put on a stubborn face, lips tightly sealed, but after a moment of his boring stare, she caved in and said, "Fine! That *is* true, however, there is something about you, Angel, that has gotten to me and I want to do anything that I can to make you happy." She stopped talking at the look of pure happiness on his face. *That is slightly unnerving,* she thought. She didn't have the chance to say so because he was once again upon her, once again catching her off guard and knocking her to the ground. This time, however, he wasn't hugging her, he was kissing her. She was shocked at first, *isn't this what we just repented for?* But she couldn't bring herself to push him away; instead, she wrapped her arms around him and immersed herself in him, the warmth changing from hunger to comfort and a little lingering love for Gabriel leaking out from her heart and mixing with her confused feelings for him.

She had never been this close to a human that was bleeding and not have to fight every second to keep from draining him. He sat up with her in his arms and kept her close to him. The embrace was different than before, This time she dreaded it ending, dreaded that he would take the heat with him and she would remain, cold, colder than ever before. She could feel tears start to well up in her eyes and pulled away before they could fall and quickly blinked them away. She knew she had to distance herself from him, or she would destroy everything he had worked for and leave him broken and alone.

"Well, if that's that, then we should get ready for your little meeting with your 'holy congregation.'" She said, and he snorted at her expression but nodded. She got up and turned away from him, glad to be out of his embrace and miserable to not be in it at the same time. She started making her way down the hall leaving him behind emotionally and physically.

"Wait," his voice stopped her.

"What?" she asked without turning around.

"What exactly happened between us last night? You were talking of love and how we should not live without it, but you have left behind someone that you love dearly." She felt as if he had just nailed down her coffin, the pain was fresh in her mind; she had foolishly torn down the wall between her past and present.

She turned around and beamed a huge smile at him. She laughed at him, allowing a little of her demon to show, hiding her pain. "My dear priest, what happened was not love, no, it was lust. The reason so many people get into trouble, as you can see," she waved her hand between them, so he knew what she was talking about, "is what happened to us."

"Oh," she could hear the hurt in his voice, and it broke her heart. She had not been lying, but she also felt for him, not as she felt for Gabriel. She knew no one would ever make her feel like that, but she still felt some sort of longing for the priest. Maybe she was lying to herself as much as she was to the priest.

"I'm sorry, love is a dream long lost for me, as it is for you. I thought you would understand. I did not mean to hurt you. I just wanted to show you that it was alright to seek comfort in another. I have since been shown that that was not the right thing to do. And, unfortunately, it is not the worst thing I have done."

He looked away from her, his eyes dead, a new pain growing in him, or perhaps an old one, abandon. He didn't love her and knew she didn't love him, but she was so cold about how she said it. She felt a knife go into her heart at seeing him. She wanted to go to him and comfort him, but she was afraid that she might end up mending the hurt, a pain she needed to encourage for his own good, by saying something that she did not mean just to stop his pain. Her frustration was making her angry. That she cared so much for this man and couldn't help herself coupled with the thought of Gabriel and how she was betraying him drove her mad. She could barely contain herself, but her hunger was back and burning her from both the inside and out. The smell of his blood doubled, and she knew if she did not leave, she would kill him and there was no coming back from that. She could deal with him hating her but not with her guilt over his death.

He stood up, but kept looking at the floor, "No, it makes sense. You don't have to defend yourself. It isn't that I have fallen in love, I just needed to understand. This is uncharted territory for me, so it is a little confusing," he let out a little chuckle that she knew was fake. He walked past her to the hall and to a room that she had never seen him enter before. There was shuffling and the sound of cloth on the floor and then the smell of fresh blood drifted towards her. She stomped her foot on the ground, adding another crack to the already crumbling floor. She closed her eyes both is shame and hunger; how she wished it was dark and she could drown her pain and his in the sweet nector of someone else's life.

•　　•　　•　　•　　•

Several hours after the awkward exit of the priest, he reappeared looking his normal self, quiet and confident. She sat at the table only half reading one of the many books that were around the building, trying to ignore him but couldn't help but wonder what had happened that he was fine now. She looked up over the top of the tattered book and watched him move around the kitchen getting something for breakfast.

"Do you still wish to accompany me?" He said not turning around and startled her.

"I'm sorry?" she asked stupidly and kicked herself inwardly.

"To the gathering this morning," he reminded her.

"I was not sure you still planned on going out since you had injured yourself." She couldn't stop herself from saying it, and it was out before she could even try. He whirled around and faced her with a look of shock on his face. Before he could recover, she added, "I meant since it was so late I thought you may have gone back to bed or decided not to go."

He straightened his face and turned back around to what she thought was bread and butter, "I promised them I would be there and I cannot let them down." She snickered, once again unable to stop her stupid self. "I will take that as a 'no'."

"I will come with you priest. Don't think I will go back on my word, either. Do not insult me, I may be a woman but I have honor."

"Then you will cease your laughter. You may not believe in them, but I do, and I will do anything I can to help them." It was she who looked up in shock. He had used her very words against her. She got angry and hurt. She stood up from the table so quickly that her chair flew across the room and she was on him, turning him around and slamming him against the counter before he could even take a breath. She lifted him by his shoulders and stared at him, she could feel her skin burning, and her demon was wailing in delight, *"kill him, fill yourself with this holy man!"* He was so shocked by her movement that he couldn't speak; he could barely breathe, but he was staring straight into her eyes, and in the reflection of her in his eyes, she could see why. Her eyes had turned black and glowing red because of her anger and hunger that had been gnawing at her since she returned to the cathedral. For a split moment, she didn't care. She was about to show him just how dangerous she was and that she could snap him like a twig if he ever tried to purposely hurt her again.

"Don't you try to turn my words against me," she growled at him, her anger barely contained, "You are no man of God if you try to hurt someone because you were scorned. I do not love you, and you will have to live with that, but try to hurt me again like you just did and you will not live to regret it." She dropped him without warning and walked away from him. He fell to the ground rubbing his shoulders. "To think I found a friend in you. What was my stupid mind doing thinking something like that? I'll be outside waiting for you to get your holier-than-thou ass together." She stomped away and grabbed her cloak. He remained on the floor and watched her leave and heard her slam the door. He was still in shock of what had just happened. How was she able to lift him with such ease and why did her eyes change color and did he see fang in her mouth? Was she truly possessed by a demon and he had been mistaken? Was it was his job to save her?

They walked toward the town center in silence, she against the walls, equally glad for the distance as much as she was for the shade. But even as she walked, hood up, avoiding him, she could feel his eyes on her every few minutes. It was as if he was waiting for her to burst into flame and if she let her irritation get to her, he just might get to see just that.

They remained silent for several minutes until she finally said, "If you have something to say, out with it, or else quit staring at me or you're going to lose that smug face of yours." He didn't say anything but he did stop staring at her.

They finally reached the town square and there were actually people gathering, more than she had thought would come. She leaned against the furthest building and allowed him to trek to the temporary podium. He began his speech and the people started gathering closer to him to be able to hear him. As time went by more and more people came, including an individual that did not at all seem interested in the priest but was instead staring intently at her. He also had his hood up, but she could tell that he was a tall, well-built man with rough skin, he looked like he was made for running *"or perhaps chasing."* He piqued her interest, and she immediately put him in the enemy category, her foul mood getting the better of her.

Her demon whispered to her, *"We can grab him and take him down the alley and no one would notice, he doesn't belong here anyway."* She nodded inwardly, but decided that she would just watch him for a while and if he made a move then she would make hers. She didn't want to risk exposing herself just because a pervert had locked on to her. She would take care of him later. She looked away from him and back to the priest, ignoring his intent gaze. After another hour of preaching the priest said a prayer, and he joined the crowd, talking to them and answering questions. She was in amazement that this little plan of theirs had worked. She was shaking her head at them when she realized that the man in the hood had moved and was now walking right towards her. She lifted herself from the wall and faced him, trying to look nonchalant. He was walking fast, but instead of stopping in front of her, he grabbed her arm with more strength that she had ever encountered in a human, which made her smile, and kept walking, dragging her along.

"If you want to talk all you had to do was ask." She said snidely.

At her remark, he shoved her into the wall, pressing his hand against her shoulder and in a deep voice said, "Don't play your games with me, I know what you are and what you do." She was truly surprised by the quick hard movement but also with what he said.

"What are you talking about? You must have me confused with someone else, there are plenty of women in this town that can take care of your needs." At that, he pushed her harder into the wall, clearly not pleased.

"Don't play with me, vampyre!" At that, all of her playfulness failed, and she immediately went into attack mode, but refrained from acting on it.

"You clearly have had too much to drink, Mr. ?" she paused to allow him to tell her his name, but when he did not fill in the blank she continued, "There are no such things as vampyres. They are just myths." She made a noise that showed she believed he was crazy, "You need to go talk to the good priest over there, I hear he can help the lost lambs."

He made a growling noise that almost put her growl to shame and shoved his face into hers. The movement caused his hood to drop and reveal his long dirty blond hair that he had tied back at the base of his neck with a piece of leather, and a face that has not been shaved in several days. His eyes were a dead gray, even in the heat of the moment they had no fire, perhaps verbal battle is not what he sought. With his nose pressed against hers, through clenched teeth he snarled, "You know very well I speak the truth, vampyre, and I've come to kill you for your crimes and the murders of dozens of innocent people." His hot breath was caressing her face and neck, and she smiled at him showing her fangs, *this will be fun. Finally, an opponent that can keep up and knows what is coming for him!* She and her demon agreed, not for the first time today and it was starting to scare her, but first things first. She started to laugh hysterically at him, and punched him square in the chest causing him to let her go and grasp his middle gasping for breath.

"You think these people are innocent?!" She spat at him, "they are far from it, so far that God himself has abandoned them! And if you think you can kill me, you are welcome to try, but know this, I will take great pleasure in stopping you and…", she ran a finger up the side of his prickly, unshaven neck, stopping under his chin to pull his face towards hers, as she leaned down to put herself within inches of it, "tasting your delicious, angry blood." He growled again and made a grab at her, but she jumped back, against the wall and laughed.

"You are a fool," he said to her. "There is nowhere for you to run and you wouldn't dare reveal yourself in front of all the people, especially the priest that you seem to have some strange attraction to and who loves you." A look of shock passed over her, but she quickly hid it under a fake smile. "The sun will burn you if you run and he will banish you if you kill me in broad daylight." He chuckled as he watched her smile fall from her face replaced by a small amount of fear. She thought of the priest and how she had already disappointed him and she got angry that this man was trying to use him against her. The familiar burning started on her skin and she could see his surprise when her red markings appeared along with her glowing eyes.

"No one will ever harm that man or use him to harm me!" She leaned over again and grabbed him by his neck and held him there, unable to breathe.

"*Kill him! Kill him!!*" Her demon screamed.

She shook her head and whispered, "I cannot kill this man, he is innocent, and Angel will see…" He took advantage of her distraction and kneed her in the stomach making her double over more from surprise than pain. He pulled out a silver dagger and plunged it into her, missing his mark because she saw it coming and moved. Not fast enough, though, to get completely out of the way, the silver blade plunged into her left shoulder. She yelled out in anger and grabbed him again, swinging him around and slamming him against the wall, knocking his head into the stones and then throwing him out into the street. She sent his dagger after him, missing his head by inches, causing it to clatter on the ground, next to him as he lay unconscious on the ground. She hurried back to the cathedral before he could come after her, or any of the townspeople came to investigate the noise. Though she had a feeling he already knew where she was staying, she hoped that he would not come after her, she would not bring further harm to the priest. She stood in shock, replaying what had happened in her head and came to the only conclusion that made sense, *if there are vampyres then there have to be vampyre hunters…*

She could hear the priest's footsteps and hurried to her room to clean herself up. She removed her clothes and washed her wound, it hadn't healed as fast as she expected but it was still healing at a rapid rate, silver must cause a reaction that slows healing, she made a mental note to avoid one of those silver daggers to the heart. She heard him calling from the front door and quickly put on new clothes and dried her hands. She opened her door and headed back down the hall.

"Rosina?"

"Here!" she said as she emerged from the hall.

"What happened, one minute you were there and then you were gone, and you're wearing different clothes?" he was probing for answers that she didn't want to give, she had no way of explaining a stab wound.

"Would you believe I tripped and fell in horse manure?" she lied. "I can be so absent-minded sometimes."

"I've never seen that," he replied, "but I won't call you a liar, especially after what happened this morning."

She had completely forgotten about having threatened him this morning, "Oh. About that," she said in a small voice, "I'm sorry, I have a hard time controlling my temper. Are you alright?" she asked truly concerned. "I didn't hurt you too bad, did I?" She moved closer to him grabbing his robe, trying to pull it away from his shoulder to see if he had a bruise, but he pulled out of her grasp and turned his back away from her.

"I'm fine," he said, but she didn't believe him and made another grab at him, this time succeeding in lifting his entire robe up and over his back revealing the fresh wounds from his self-whipping. She quickly dropped his robe, and it fell back over his skin. Her hands were over her open mouth as she stepped back from him.

"Did you do this yourself? When? And Why? Was it because of me?" she frantically spouted out questions. She knew he had been bleeding the night before but never expected this. He put his hands on her shoulders and shook his head.

"No, it is because of me. Giving in to the pleasures of the flesh is forbidden, so I needed punishment." He said it so calmly that, even though it was not her nature, she wanted to get hysterical because he wasn't even affected by the act of self-mutilation.

"It was because of me, I pushed myself on you." She moved to lift his robe again, but he grabbed her hand and stopped her.

"No, it wasn't. I should have said no, but I didn't. Its fine, it's over now, and everything is as it should be." He said as if that was the end of the conversation.

She looked at him in disbelief, almost angry that she had caused this. She was also a little surprised that his blood no longer seemed to affect her, perhaps the rush she had gotten from the hunter had masked it, or she just wanted his blood much more than Angel's. "Since I am the one that started all this, allow me to at least make sure it is cleaned properly." He stubbornly remained still and looked at her, but she could tell he was in pain from the wounds on his back, and he finally gave in and agreed to her cleaning them.

He sat down on the floor of the altar, and she boiled some water and got a few clean rags and gauze to wrap his back with. She removed his robe and his chest was different than she had expected, there were small scars here and there all over his smooth skin, but he was in good shape: she could draw the outline of his muscles with her fingers, but she did not want to start what they had just got out of. As she stared at his chest, he started to get antsy. He worried that he might be adding to the wounds. Under her intense gaze, he was starting to feel the heat in his blood that was the same as the night before and he didn't want to fall back into the trap. He turned and laid down on his chest, forcing her gaze to his back. He heard an audible gasp when she saw the full extent of the wounds, but she didn't say anything just dipped the rag into the water.

"This is going to hurt, but please bear with me." He smiled when he heard her say 'with me,' having her there meant more to him that he thought it would. She gently put the rag on his back, and he didn't even flinch. She slowly cleaned his back from top to bottom, rinsing the rag over and over. He could hear her humming and almost fell asleep under her gentle touch and soft music. When she was finally done washing him, she bent over and kissed his shoulder. She purposefully missed where he had whipped himself, but her kiss burned the most out of all the wounds. He pulled in a breath and caught her scent. It was a smell that he couldn't place, it was sweet and strong and somehow stubborn just like her.

She sat back up and reached for the bowl of bloody water, when he grabbed her outstretched arm and sat up facing her. His chest glistening with the runoff water from his back, his face shadowed. "I'm sorry, I didn't want to hurt you, but I wanted you to feel the pain I felt. I felt abandoned when you said you didn't love me, even though I couldn't do anything even if you did. It stabbed my heart like a knife. I hate being here alone, I love God and love doing His work, but it is lonely, very lonely and when you came out of nowhere and requested to stay here, I thought God had finally sent someone to me, someone I could keep, even if it is just another kind soul on the same path I am. I never expected to feel this way. I was so solid before you, so set in my ways and consumed with my need to help others. You came with your beautiful long black hair, mysterious eyes, swaying steps, and stubborn attitude. It was as if I never had any center because I just collapsed at your feet and begged for your attention like a kitten begging its mother for milk." She let go of the bowl and grabbed his hand that was over hers and held it as he spoke, blushing a little as he praised her. But she felt as he felt and knew the pain of loneliness. Now she understood why she had grabbed onto him so hard and why she felt she needed to make him happy; in some indirect way making him happy would also make her happy.

"You are so amazing," she said when he had finished, "I am so glad I met you. I had thought God had abandoned all men, I thought all that is good was dead," a tear had welled up in his eye and fell over on his cheek. His world was crumbling in front of her eyes. Before she thought about it, she reached up with her hand and wiped it off with her thumb, placing her hand on his cheek. She caught herself and pulled it away, but he grabbed it and put it back.

"You are so comfortable and warm, don't leave or I will be cold again." She was surprised at his words, it was as if he had read her mind.

She leaned her head so her forehead was against his and closed her eyes, "I'm not going anywhere, you can count on that," he let out a sigh, and his shoulders lost their tension.

"*Liar.*"

He leaned into her and wrapped his arms around her and let her in completely and finally, let down his defenses. She could feel his aura and his goodness, and his holy light shone brighter than ever. His head was on her shoulder and lifting her head to the sky she let the light bathe over her, and tears of joy ran down her cheek, and she wrapped her arms around him.

Chapter Six: Desire Leads Thy Only to Temptation

The trap is set
The beast approaches, unknowingly,
Creeping, stalking, hunting.
Its jaws open revealing long, sharp fangs,
Claws extended, grasping for its prey.
The trap collapses under its weight,
Splintering, shattering, crumbling, failing.
But the prey does not give up,
Raising against the beast it strikes it down with one swift swipe.
Down it falls, crashing to the ground,
All around shaking, defeated,
By the small, forgotten flower.

After helping the priest get himself back together as much as she could, she returned to her room and finished putting herself back together. By now the wound had closed, but there was still a flaming red line where it had been. Still in shock, she covered it quickly and laid down in her bed to try and get some sleep. It, however, eluded her. All she could do was picture the blond man and how he had almost killed her. And what she was going to do about it. She had made a decision when she came to this town that she would no longer kill innocent people. She would feed on the evil and keep herself, her demon, and her conscience happy. No matter how much the hunter pushed her buttons, she couldn't kill him outright, because he was not evil, in fact she was the evil one that he was trying to remove from the world. She laughed at herself, she WAS looking forward to the day when someone killed her, begged for it, she just didn't think it would be this soon, and quite frankly she wasn't ready for it. But if she had to choose, she would allow him to kill her before she killed him. Just the thought of it made her demon whale and try to fight against her so she decided she would have to try to reason with him. She had to laugh again because he didn't seem the man who wanted to talk, just kill, she could see the spark in his eye when he stabbed her. She shivered in excitement but also in fear, he had come too close today.

"No matter what happens, I have to keep him away from Angel. He doesn't need to be brought into any more of my problems." She said to herself, and that seemed to settle her, and she was finally able to drift off into sleep, being out in the sun and not feeding finally took its toll on her. She was glad that she had yet to dream as a vampyre, because she was not haunted by the faces of those she had killed and those that will try to kill her in the future.

When she woke, the sun was still in the sky, she had never had this happen, she always slept when the sun ruled the sky, but the thought of a faster, wiser predator hunting her, gave her no rest. She rolled over to try to go back to sleep, but it evaded her, so she got out of bed and ventured out into the kitchen, only to find it empty and cold. She looked around, but couldn't see or hear the priest anywhere in the cathedral. She was just beginning to worry, and it was *strange* when she heard the heavy wooden doors open and shut and then heard a whistled catchy tune. It drew her to the front of the cathedral where she saw Angel coming in with an armful of old books and a jostle in his step. She stopped with her hands on her hips and waited for him to notice her.

"Oh, hello!" even his voice was a little higher pitched than usual.

She stifled a smile and asked, "What's got you so happy?"

"I just got my hands on some old tomes! And I am over the edge excited to read them and share with the town." She shook her head. "Just because you do not enjoy the written word does not mean everyone else does," he said with a joking attitude.

"It's not that I do not enjoy them, it's just that I have too much adventure in my life to add to it with fictional stories," she replied.

"These are not fictional." He said, stubbornly.

"Fine then, with other people's ... adventures." She tilted her head and raised an eyebrow as if asking 'better?' He simply nodded and started whistling again, walking past her to the back rooms of the cathedral where the library was filled with the rest of his collection of books. She shook her head and made her way to the door, she was almost there when she heard him call at her from down the hall. It was muffled, from him being several rooms away, so she acted like she didn't hear him. She wanted to get out of the building to clear her head and prepare for her meeting with the hunter. But just as her hand found the cold metal of the door handle, she heard him again, this time louder because he had come back out of his library, still with his nose in a book. She stopped but didn't turn around, she had an itch in the back of mind, making her eye twitch.

"You really should read some of these stories. And before you reject the idea, just take a listen for a moment. 'The giant fell with a great thud, and all the towns were saved,'" he began reading a passage out of the book he held. "'and though the young man was small and sickly, he found the strength, through God, to fight his demons and rise above them to help those with more need.'" He stopped and looked up at her, she could feel that itch again, along with his eyes on her back. He didn't say anything else, just waited… and waited… *and* waited until she could not stand his patience and assistance and she let out a very audible sigh, and slouching, turned around with a snap showing her irritation. When she turned around she did not see a smug look, or even a smile showing and he knew he got to her; what she found on his face was seriousness and concern without a hint of playfulness. She immediately stood up straight, the itch becoming almost too much to bear, she raised her twitching hand to try to scratch it, but could not reach it.

Frustrated, she growled at him, "What does this have to do with me or anything else?" Her irritation growing from her lack of rest and so much time in the sun. Every second with the priest seemed to rub her as if she had no skin, it was painful, and it left her feeling exposed.

He stared at her for a moment, still serious, still silent.

"What?!" she said angrily.

He didn't flinch, but calmly answered, "It means everything." She waited for him to elaborate, but when he didn't, she turn around again to leave. "There is something wrong," he said, hitting her already raw nerve.

She stopped and turned around again, "What?" she questioned.

"You know I'm right, you haven't been the same since this morning. Tell me."

"You must have me confused with one of your fictional characters." She snapped.

"You know I don't. I can get you to talk, that's the truth, don't make me pull out the glory of God to get you to speak, and trust me, He has better things to do." He said, half joking.

"Like helping you to get your head on straight." She said with agitation and got a glare for her remark.

"Tell me, Rosina. I know there is something troubling you." He said, the concern in his voice almost making the twitch unbearable.

The use of her name threw her off, but she had vowed to keep the priest out of this mess. "It is nothing, just a man I've been trying to confront is proving elusive. It is… frustrating." He gave her a look of disbelief, but didn't push. He planned to follow her instead. Since she likes to be a closed and sealed book, he had a feeling he was not going to get any real information from her also tightly sealed lips.

    •   •   •   •   •

The sun was still spilling over the horizon hitting her skin like liquid heat. Its light filled the street she stood on as it fought to stay above the hills and reached its last tendrils of fire up into the blood red sky. The burning in her flesh became worse, adding to her already irritated skin. She knew, without looking, that her markings had returned sometime during her attempt to escape the priest's insistent questioning. *He had given up rather quickly,* she thought, going against everything she knew about him; which, given the time to actually think about it, wasn't very much. This thought made her feel sad, which she didn't understand. She shouldn't feel sad for not answering his queries. The more she thought, the less she understood about her emotions toward him and the situation as a whole. Maybe her time here was over and she needed to move on. She paused at the thought and found that she agreed with it and for the first time in weeks her demon howled in anguish almost splitting her already pained head in half.

"You leave and we starve! You lack the ability to feed as needed!!" It screeched. She fell to her knees and clasped her head, holding back tears and a scream clawing its way up her throat. The pain seemed to remain forever, but when it finally subsided, she raised her aching head only to see that the sun was still making its slow descent into the horizon. She braced herself on the wall and pulled herself up only to find that she was so week she could barely stand. Her head was spinning and her skin was raw from the still glowing marks on her skin. She hung her head, if she didn't feed soon she would lose control to the demon.

"Yes, yes," it hissed, *"Let me show you how it's to be done, the true way of our kind!"*

She fiercely shook her head, *NO! You would destroy this whole village*, she thought. The demon's laughter brought to mind an evil witch rubbing her hands together and 'he-he-he'ing at the success of her evil plan coming to fruition.

"I won't allow it!" she yelled out loud as if that would make it truer. All it did was get her a look from a nearby shopkeep. To which she responded with a comment that earned her both a scowl and a look of fright from him as he scuttled back into his store and slammed the door. She growled at him, but remained against the wall, feeling like she needed to catch her breath, even though she knew she really did not need to breathe at all. She leaned her head on her chest, weak.

She felt as if she was about to lose consciousness, the black was creeping into her vision, when she heard a door creak.Lifting her head he saw a young couple stumble out of the back of a run-down tavern. Their cheeks were flush, hair tousled, and they smelled of sweat and excitement. They giggled as they stumbled down the steps and fell down onto the stones of the street. He was the first to get to his feet, he reached out his hand to her and lifted her up, *"what a gentlemen,"* the demon interjected. She rose from the ground and right into his arms. They embraced and kissed each other with such passion it left even Rosina breathless. When their lips parted she smiled at him, her eyes lit up with love for him, and when he smiled back and whispered something to her they got even brighter. They held hands as they turned her way and started walking towards the street she was on.

The girl felt Rosina watching them and looked up, letting out a gasp as she saw Rosina's glowing skin. She stopped and moved closer to the boy, wrapping her arms around his. Rosina felt a sadness, she thought had buried away, rise in her with such an unforgiving ferocity that she fell back to the ground. Being near the priest and his steady light had torn down all her barriers and given her time and safety to allow the past back in. How she missed Gabriel, his soft, warm touch on her frightened skin. How he gently kissed her and wiped away all her tears. Tears such as the ones that burned her cheeks now. Then the sadness turned to anger. She was angry that it was all torn away from her and how she was being punished for her vampyre father. How dare they flaunt their love in front of her? How are they allowed to have each other when she had her love ripped away and was left to have this miserable hell of an existence?! Her anger lit another fire in her, and her eyes turned black with it, glowing darker with her hate. Her demon howl with laughter, it knew what was going to happen, it loved it and Rosina allowed herself to enjoy it, too. She did not allow her conscience to speak. She was on her feet and walking towards them before she realized she had the strength to even stand.

She imagined how sweet it would be to drain the girl, full of fear while the boy beat helplessly on Rosina, trying to save her as his anger built and hope faded. Then she would drain him, savoring their warm, sweet nectar, filling her heart and fueling her rage and her own hopelessness. She would leave them dead, together, like the infamous Romeo and Juliet. Her demon laughed and cheered in its evil voice.

She was almost to them. The girl's fear was so strong she could almost see it, but she could *smell* it and it smelled so good.

"Devour them!" the demon screeched, *"Devour their foolish love!"*

The boy pushed the girl behind him, guarding her from Rosina. She could not help but laugh at his futile attempt. She was less than five feet from them when a voice rang through all her hateful thoughts. She stopped to listen, thinking she actually didn't hear it, but then it as there again. His smooth, silky voice, calming her, stopping her. She turned around and whispered, "Gabriel?" but it wasn't Gabriel that stood there in front of the now overbearing oak doors of the cathedral. No, it was another angel that stopped her.

"No, dear, its Samuel," she was in awe at finally hearing his real name, but not surprised. His name fit him better than anyone else's ever had. "But, I'll gladly step in for him until you find him again." She could feel her anger melt away, and her eyes turned back to their bright green, but they filled with tears because she knew she could never be with him again, not like this. Samuel motioned for the young couple to leave, telling them they shouldn't be drinking so much at such a young age. Rosina knelt down on the ground allowing her tears to fall unchecked from her eyes, until she could no longer contain her anguish and she wept uncontrollably, wailing into the setting sun. The sky was blood red, like the pain burning her heart, burning it right out of her chest. She clenched at it and doubled over allowing her tears to soak the ground in front of her. Her emotions took over, and there was nothing but blinding pain. Pain that was stronger than anything she ever felt, including her descent into hell when she became the devil and lost her family. Samuel knelt beside her, putting his arm around her, pulling her towards him and holding her as she cried for several minutes until her tears dried and she was left shaking in his arms. She was starting to mumbling, "Why did this happen to me, why-why-why…?" He held her as tight as he could, hoping to stop her trembling and allow her to think a bit clearer. He would find what the true root of her pain was. If it was Gabriel's absence, then why did he leave her and how did she end up here, alone in the middle of a villain infested hell?

Her trembling slowed and resembled the chills one gets when thinking of or witnessing a repulsion. And then she stopped mumbling and lunged, pushing her hands against him, wriggling away from him and staring up at him with her black eyes. Her movement had been so fast that he almost lost his balance. He was not able to actually see her move. He just saw her new position right in front of him, while it had left him barely upright. Her hands shot out and grabbing his shoulders, and he was under her on his back on the cobblestone street. She was only inches away from his face, with hunger in her eyes that he almost missed in their deep darkness. Shock briefly showed on her face before she yanked herself away from him and ran at inhuman speed away from him down the alley and out of sight. He lay stunned on the ground for several minutes trying to figure out what had just happened and how she had gone from a weeping mess to a monster with incredible strength and speed that he had never seen in her.

"Is this how she is 'taking care of the bad guys?' What is she hiding from me? And even more, why can't she trust me enough to tell me?" He spoke aloud, trying to put the pieces together, but what he did not speak was that he felt. His rejection had only helped the rift grow in her heart. He feared that if he did not help her fix the fire in her soul, her anger and hate would turn her heart to ice. She would be lost to him, and any happiness that he hoped for her would never be found. He stood up, dusted himself off, and made his way back to the cathedral and to his old dusty tomes hoping for some answers.

•　　•　　•　　•　　•

She put a small amount of distance between her and the cathedral and stopped behind the nearest building that she could hide behind. Her eyesight was almost gone and sweat was covered her burning skin. She collapsed on the ground, having used up all the energy she had to get away from the priest before her hunger took over and she drained him. She was mortified that it did not matter who the person was or what he meant to her. When the hunger took over all he looked like was a meal, a piece of meat filled with delicious blood. Her mouth started to water, and she wiped it violently, angry at her body's reaction. She was fighting the darkness, knowing that, if she didn't feed her demon, it would take over and she would not like the results she would find when she woke. The darkness was creeping further and further into her vision, but she couldn't stand, couldn't walk, or run, to a food source. Her only hope was that by chance somebody would come strolling down the street. The demon had its eyes set on one particular person, and if she did not satisfy it, the priest would pay the price. That is something she could never forgive herself for, and she fought harder against the darkness.

Gasping for breath with sweat dripping off her face, she heard what she thought was her saving grace. She turned her head just enough to see a pair of scuffed leather shoes and prepared for the kill. A deep laugh caused her to pause. The next thing she knew a rough hand was jerking her head up by her hair, to look into a pair of dead gray eyes, shadowed by dirty blond hair and her subconscious said what she had not the energy to: *Shit.*

She tried to suppress the shiver that was rising. It was not only from the hunger she was fighting, but also from the fear of him finding her in this state and knowing he could easily overpower her. She would lose unless she let loose the demon. *More innocent blood on my hands…*

"Well, look what we have here: The monster. The demon of legend, crouching in a dirty ally barely able to remain conscious. And was that a shiver I felt? You're not afraid of a human, a weak, slow human, are you?" He laughed again and pulled her face up until she felt as if her neck was going to snap. She stopped a grunt of pain that was trying to escape. *I will not allow him to see my pain, it is a weakness.* She could feel the demon agreeing, almost as if it had nodded its invisible head. *I need blood, I'm not strong enough to take down a normal human let alone a man that has been trained to kill my kind at our full strength.*

He laughed again at her, "Does that hurt, little girl?" his last words striking her with more force than she expected and her anger started to grow again. She knew she shouldn't allow it, knowing that it would only help to allow the demon: it fed on her anger.

"You stubborn fool! Let me out, or we will both DIE!" it howled at her. She knew it was right, but she would rather die than take another innocent life. If it was her

time she was willing to go, but she would be damned if she was going to let him know how easy it would be! Her anger was growing, anger at his remark and anger at being at his whims. She was angry at not being unable to move away from his dirty, blood-stained hands, vampyre blood, but blood none the less, the blood of her kin. She was surprised at how much it hurt to have that thought in her head. She had not met any other vampyre other than her sire and he was not a good example of something that she would long to be near or miss if it was gone. But, she knew that there had to be others out there, others with a different perspective on life and a different heart. Maybe one that could save her from all her pain and anger. The thought gave her a little energy, and she pulled away from his grasp, not as hard as she had wanted to, but at least he was no longer touching her.

The demon was pressing on her, so close she could feel it as if it was pushing on her skin from the inside, trying to get out. It being barely held under wraps but for her fragile will to keep it in. She knew it would only be moments after it was out that the hunter would be dead, her vision was completely black but for a tiny spot of light that was more like a pinhole in a canopy. She growled at her weakness, but even that was so quiet she doubted he heard it.

He knelt down in front of her, grasping her chin and forcing her face towards his. "My dear monster, I do believe today is your lucky day. I am supposed to kill those that walk the earth when they aught not to, but I must confess, I do so love the hunt. Putting you out of your misery might be the humane thing to do, but seeing as you are not human, I'm not going to. You see, I can't kill something that doesn't run away, or what kind of hunter would that make me? I am driven by the chase, the fight and the final defeat of my enemy much like you do when you drain a human." He said comparing them in a twisted way. "The only difference is that you hunt those that cannot possibly fight back, I fight and defeat things that I shouldn't be able to defeat and that is a great sense of pride for me." He laughed with self-consumption and arrogance, knowing that she could not do a damn thing about his mockery. He knew she was weak and he was allowing her to live and fight him at her full strength. He was mocking her by saying that even then she could not win. He was tormenting her: she was going to die, not today but soon.

She grunted in response to his speech. Then finally found her voice, "Nice speech," she whispered in his face, "do you give it to every vampyre you kill? Does it make you feel better about the life you chose, about the lives you have taken," he was about to protest, but she kept speaking, "Yes, lives. I may not be human, but I am living, I am here, I exist, and that is what living is, not a heartbeat, not behavior or emotion, but existence. I still have my soul, and I still walk on this ground." She moved her eyes to look past his arm and down toward the stones that make the street. "I live not for myself, but for those I care about and I do not kill for a living as you do. I don't hunt down those that you deem evil or not of this world for sport, but for survival. I have to hunt and kill to live, I kill as little as possible and if I could feed without killing I would, but humans slaughter thousands of animals to feed yourselves and do not blink. I know they are not the same as humans, and I would trade a human life for that of a sow, but I cannot. I feel their soul crying everytime I kill." She stopped and took a deep breath. "I have been this way for only a short while, and already I know what I do is wrong and evil. I know, because I am taking from this world, I will be dragged straight to hell for all I am." She paused, "What about you?" she asked but didn't give him time to answer. "I *will* meet you there, I know this," she whispered. She took a heavy breath allowing her words to sink in and could see in his eyes that she had struck a nerve. She thought she saw a tiny light flicker there, but it went out before she could be sure. "Do not be so quick to pass judgment on me when you live a life that is just as tainted." She gave her last bit of energy with those words and slumped in his grip which was gone as soon as he noticed that she had given up, given in to the idea of it being her time to go. She fell to the ground and scraped her chin when she landed, but she didn't have the energy to regain even a sitting position. She heard him stand up quickly and start to pace near her as if fighting the urge to kill her.

"No, you don't get out of this so easily. You're not allowed to give up!" he shouted and was angry that she had given in, but not for a reason she thought he would have been angry. He wanted her to fight to live, he had seen in her something that he had never seen. She teetered on not believing in God, but what the priest saw in her was starting to show. He couldn't kill her because she was not evil; she was pure, innocent, even with all the death she had brought. She was trying to make it better to cleanse herself, to help people she didn't even know and only feed on those that God would deem evil and would forgive her for killing.

He let out a sound of anger, yelling at the new night. "You are not allowed to do this, demon! You have killed so many innocent, you have no soul, you enjoy the kill and the blood!"

"We do enjoy the blood", her demon agreed.

"You are empty." He started out angry but now sounded like he was trying to convince himself, "You go against everything that I have ever seen or learned, this cannot be. I cannot kill you." He turned to face her, crumpled on the ground, helpless, so small, so young. "How dare you!" he spat softly at her then turned and walked away.

•   •   •   •   •

Samuel was sitting at his desk, behind a pile of dusty books that was higher than him, reading and searching for anything that could help him figure out what was wrong with Rosina. She seemed human enough. One with many problems and a painful past, add that to her young age, her solidarity and distance from home, and mysterious markings that seemed to appear whenever she was very emotional. When she ate, she really didn't; her food was moved around, but the same amount remained on her plate when she was finished. She slept all day and went out at night, which he thought was only a small quirk but now reconsidered, especially if she was traveling alone and kept the very same schedule: night was a dangerous place for a young woman. He went through books with the information he had gathered, separating out things that she couldn't be: werewolf: she didn't eat enough to sustain the metabolism the change required; ghost: she was solid enough; banshee: well obviously, and the list goes on. After what felt like hours he was left with two possibilities: Demon and Vampyre. Both seemed unlikely because she was held up in a cathedral. Not all the stories were true, however, demons could be very powerful and, as the bible tells it, they were born of an angel who fell to earth. They may be able to enter a church. God had hoped that the fallen angels and his followers would return to his side so he may have allowed them to enter to be closer to Him. Vampyres are said to be soulless and cannot enter holy ground, but the information on them ranged from one end of the spectrum to the other. Most of it was based on hysterical stories from witnesses to the supernatural. Very few of the stories, if any, could be trusted.

He stood from his desk rushed to the front of the church, barely keeping himself from stumbling over the pile of books on the floor and out its heavy doors in hopes he could find Rosina. A terrified anything was dangerous, but a frightened demon or vampyre means a demon or vampyre that is angry and very powerful. When he emerged from the cathedral he paused and listened for any sound of her, wishing her to not have gone far in her current state. He caught the sound of a voice coming from a nearby alley and went in that direction. He reached the building beside the alley. When he looked around the corner, he saw a large hooded man walking briskly in the other direction. He was about to shout out to him when he looked down and saw a mound of clothes laying on the ground. At first, he thought it might just be discarded clothes or a blanket until it groaned. He rushed over, recognizing the sound of her voice. The other man walked away, ignored, while he rolled her over to reveal a scraped face that was covered in sweat. She opened her eyes just a sliver and all he saw was the glowing black he saw earlier. He wanted to shy away, but he remembered that when he needed her, she didn't hesitate. He bent down and gently lifted her up off the ground. She groaned something unrecognizable and when he started to walk towards the cathedral, intending to lay her in bed and do whatever it took to make her well. What he thought was her fighting off a darker power was perhaps closer to reality than he realized.

"No, stop," she begged, "hungry."

He looked down at her, her eyes closed again, "I will cook you something when we get back to the cathedral and you are laying comfortably." He said forgetting she wasn't human. He did not retract it because he wanted to help her and that was his way of saying so.

"No," she said a little louder. Her fear was building, but she could do nothing but try to plea with him. She knew he was stubborn. If she could convey how much danger he was in, and that she could not live with his death on her hands, he might leave her laying in the gutter where she belonged. "No food," she hesitated, she did not want to reveal what she was. He was a man of God, and she didn't want to taint him with her dark passenger. "Hunger." She tried to stress the word, but he didn't leave. She tried to move, but she was at his mercy. "No!" she stressed as much as she could in her whisper of a voice, "blood," she finally conceded. She could live with him rejecting her, again, and sending her from this place, as long as he was still alive. If there was anyone that deserved to live it was him, above anyone else.

"I see." He said, cool, calculating. She was surprised when he didn't put her back down and walk away. Instead, he changed his direction towards a part of town she didn't visit much. A dark place she was saving for a very dark time. There were so many evil people lurking the shadows, she couldn't possibly get in, kill just one person, and get out without being seen by anyone. No matter how quiet or quick she was. He wandered further and further into the heart of the dark corner, walking with confidence he shouldn't have had. He finally stopped at a building with all the shuttered closed and not a sliver of light sneaking out of any cracks, doors or windows. He put her down against the door and whispered, "Trust me." He tapped on the door and quickly retreated around the corner. *If this doesn't send me to hell…* he thought. She could smell his fear that had started to build as he made it to the door. What was waiting for her behind the door, what had he condemned her to? She heard heavy footsteps approached the door and it creaked as it was opened and she fell backward into the dark room.

"Well, well, well, what do we have here?" a large man with a large belly, who smelled of alcohol and body odor, looked down at her, a rotten tooth smile on his face. He bent down and roughly picked her up, throwing her over his shoulder like a sack of potatoes and slammed the door shut behind him. Even with her vampyre vision she couldn't see much, she blamed that on the lack of light and her foggy vision. "We have a new one!" he yelled, and she already wanted to kill him after only spending a very few moments with him. He slammed her down on what she could only guess was a cot. A cot that was made of wood and covered with more wood and a very thin piece of cotton. She wanted to kick the bastard in the nuts who had thrown her on the cot like piece of Samsonite luggage. She was trying to figure out how she was going to do that, when she heard several more men coming downstairs that were located somewhere to her right.

"Oh she's cute *and* young," the first man said, "That'll be good for business. The clients," he said the last word with a little laugh in his voice, "do enjoy them young and 'unable to resist' if you know what I mean." He let out a laugh as if it was the world's greatest joke.

"Yeah, we know what you mean, you moron," said a third man. "Just shut up and get her clothes off." Panic rose up in her lightning fast, her weakness leaving her more vulnerable than she had ever been. She could hear more men moving both upstairs and down and thought she heard women upstairs, crying, begging to be released. She tried to listen closely to the feminine voices coming from rooms upstairs. She heard several women weeping, begging, desperate to get out of this dark, dirty place; some wailed for freedom, while others pleaded for death.

She could feel her skin burning, and amongst the women, she could hear tiny voices. She closed her eyes, blocking out her own horror to hear these voices clearer.

"Mommy…" a just audible voice rang in her ears, a tiny heart skipped beats, and tiny lungs filled and emptied rapidly and the smell of a tiny bowel releasing in fear. Her eyes snapped open in anger, children? Here, in this place? She finally realized this was a house of sex. A brothel perhaps, in any other city. But here it was not something the victims agreed to, they did not get paid, they were slaves. They were brought here to be used and degraded and neglected. If mothers could not keep their children safe, they were stolen away to be abused for the pleasure of demented men.

"Even I would not allow this, they are more demon than I. They must pay…" the demon whispered disgust heavy in its voice.

She nodded her head and said quietly, "You will die here tonight." The men stopped and laughed.

"Are you threatening us?" asked the third man.

"Take it how you will, but know that it is true." They laughed again and continued towards her. "Whenever you are ready." She was talking to her demon this time, "kill them all."

"Huh? What was that you brat?!" one of the men said and raised his hand to strike her.

She closed her eyes and allowed the darkness to take over; she heard it howl with excitement and a laugh of evil pleasure escaped her lips. It didn't belong to her, but she wholeheartedly enjoyed it. Before she lost consciousness her sight cleared and tainted red, her weakness was completely gone. She leaped up faster than she had ever done and was on the closest man, ripping his throat out; blood sprayed all over the floor, walls and her and she was laughing as she did so. She lapped up the blood from his gushing throat and ran her hands up and down her own skin, smearing the hot blood all over herself. Then everything went dark, and she was no longer aware of what was going on around her.

Chapter Seven: Temptation Leads Only To Pain

She wept for the lost
The ones left behind
Those who will be forgotten.
Those she will pass by and never notice
Those she will never meet
And more for those she has already met.

She stumbled out of the house into the street, glowing so bright she lit up the walls of the buildings around her. She was smiling a wicked smile and she was covered from head to toe in blood. She looked up to the sky and let out an evil cackle that the priest had never heard come from her before. That bothered him less than the blood and the look of pure joy on her face. He remained hidden around the corner he had fled behind. He prayed he was right about what she was and that he wasn't sending her to her death. He heard the screams of both the men and women inside, but did not care to look. From the sounds, he deduced that she had regained her strength and massacred all the people in sight; there was no better word for the violence he heard going on inside. When the door opened, he found assumption correct as she walked out into the moonlight. If not for all the blood she would have looked almost god-like with the moon bouncing off her dark silky hair and her markings flaming on her wet skin; a smile on her face that showed, for the first time, a truly happy smile, one that went to her eyes, still glowing, and even radiated down her whole body. Even her posture seemed joyous.

She stood there for a long while, enjoying the night and savoring the residual fresh blood flavor on her lips and tongue. The joy in her eyes was suddenly replaced with a deep gray dullness and the color in her tattoos faded to nothing, and she fell asleep standing, before crumpling to the ground. He lept out from his hiding spot and ran to her before he could even think of what he was doing. He knelt down beside her to make sure she was alright and noticed she was sleeping peacefully, even though she had just fallen straight from a standing position to the stone ground like a dead weight. He made sure that she had no broken bones or injury that he would make worse by moving her before he picked her up, holding her in his arms like she was a sleeping princess.

He took her to the river, laid her in the grass and removed her blood soaked clothes and threw them away from them into the woods near the edge of the field. He lifted her again and slowly put her into the water and washed her as well as he could, scrubbing with his hands to get the blood off her skin and out of her hair. He removed his robe and wrapped her in it and carried her back to the cathedral. He laid her in her bed, leaving her in his robe, thinking disrobing her twice in one night was pushing the inappropriate line just a little. He covered her in the heavy blanket he dug out of his wardrobe. She was still sleeping when he closed the door and went to pray for her and his soul.

• • • • •

She awoke under a heap of blankets, so warm and cozy that she forgot for a moment the nightmare of the night before. She laid there wishing that she could remain like this forever in the cocoon of warmth, shielded from the world. She thought of this and then wondered why it was so terrible that she wanted to hide? Then the illusion shattered and all the horrible images flooded her mind reminding her of the carnage she created last night starting with her trying to feed on Angel and ending with the bloodbath she was sure she left behind when she allowed her demon out because she was too weak to control it. She was so mortified by her actions that she pulled the blankets over her head like it would actually hide her shame and erase all the evil. When the blanket settled on her she got a face full of air, the scent of it settled on her. It smelled of old wood and cold stones and the priest, Samuel. She threw off the blanket as if it had burned her and lept off the bed to see that she was in her room at the cathedral. How had she gotten back here? After last night there was no possible way that he would have brought her back here she should be laying on the cold, hard street, covered in the blood of her demon's victims. It was more than she deserved, but he had taken her in again even after seeing her dark side, a side she knew would be her undoing.

She tried opening the door as quietly as she could, but it still creaked. She hesitated, and when she did not hear footsteps, she proceeded to open the door far enough for her to slip out. She stopped when she was fully out in the hall and listened for the priest. Any noise she could hear was coming from the far back of the cathedral, so she made her way to the closest exit which was in the kitchen. She was planning on sneaking out and getting as far away as fast as she could. She made it to the kitchen and had her hand on the door when a hand reached out and touched her shoulder. She grabbed it and whipped its owner around in front of her, slamming him into the door and pressing her arm into his neck. She was so close to him that his breath warmed her face and she could see in his eyes her own face, red with anger and eyes darker than the blackest pit. She withdrew from him, his own chocolate eyes showing a variety of emotions. They looked confused, as if he was not sure if he should be afraid, angry, or sad.

She took several steps back, because she knew *she* was afraid. She walked harshly into the table making it slide and several dishes to fall off it, clattering on the floor in the silence that seemed to be suffocating her. The hot tea in the now-broken mug filled the cracks in the floor making its way to her bare feet, burning them when it was finally successful. She could feel her skin blistering but was frozen in place. The feelings she felt while hiding in the bed were like a walk through paradise compared to the emotions clawing their way around inside her chest now. She could hardly breathe and brought her hand to her chest and grasped the fabric covering it, gasping. She was so overcome she couldn't even form a thought, just stood there grasping; gasping, and slowly dying.

He just remained against the door, not even bothering to straighten himself. Still missing his robe, he felt a little exposed, but he refused to allow her to see. He wasn't sure why he had saved her; looking at her now, he thought that he may have made a mistake. She could lose control at any moment and devour him. At the same time, he pitied her; she was clearly trying very hard to contain whatever was running rampant in her body. And the way she looked right now, he didn't see a demon or a vampyre or any other monster for that matter, just a very scared girl that was so lost she had no way of finding her way back, maybe even with his help. She watched him watch her but remained unmoving, as if she was frozen by something stronger than her. He pushed himself off the door slowly, but that movement seemed to break her free, and she tried to jump back. She slammed into the table again, and she looked down behind her to see what she hit, like she had forgotten that she just hit it not moments ago. The look that overcame her was that of shock, like someone had shot her in the heart. She released the fabric of his robe, that she just noticed she was wearing, and quick as lightening yanked the bottom of it up and over her head and threw it to the floor leaving herself only covered in her glowing marks. He now thought of them not as a gift from God but from the devil, yet he still thought them the most beautiful thing he had ever seen.

She jumped over the table to get away from the robe. He had complete control over her, and he didn't even know it. He was everywhere, his warmth on her skin, his smell in her nose, his beautiful words in her head. She grabbed her temples, digging her nails into her skin and making her bleed. "GET OUT!" She yelled as loud as she could, "You don't belong here! This is mine!" He moved from across the room, an emotion finally on his face, one of fear. She moved further away from him, "Get away!" She backed up until she had her back against the cold wall, it sent chills up her naked skin. He finally made his way to her, having no where to go with the wall at her back. He reached out for her, but she swatted him away with great strength. But he didn't stop, no matter how many times she swatted his hands away, he kept trying until finally he got angry at her stubbornness.

"FINE! If you wish to fight this alone, then do so somewhere else! I have already allowed you to taint this magnificent house of God far too much and I will no longer stand for your childish behavior!" She looked him in the face, shock in her eyes; the Angel of this hell had never raised his voice before. "You told me once that you were older than me because you had endured many more hardships than me. But all I have yet to see is a scared girl running away from something that she, if she were a woman as she claims to be, would face down with her feet planted firmly on the ground and her hands on her hips, welcoming any trial." He turned to leave the kitchen but stopped to look back at her, "You are a fool and a child, you are no woman, and you no longer deserve my pity."

She stood silent as she watched him walk away from her. She felt as if her heart was being ripped out, the further he walked from her the more it hurt. She finally gave in and ran after him, colliding with his back and wrapping her arms around him, her face between his shoulders. "I'm sorry." She whispered and felt tears start to wet his shirt. Then she quickly withdrew, remembering how his back was wounded and how much it must still hurt. "I'm sorry, your back —"

"No, it doesn't hurt." And she collapsed back into him.

"Angel." She whispered, and he couldn't help but smile.

After she had cried herself out, he retrieved his robe and gave it back to her. She put it on, glad for the cover, and he made her a cup of tea as she cleaned up the broken dishes. She gasped as she cut her finger on one of the sharp edges. He grabbed a towel to wipe it off but by the time he got back to her she had it in her mouth and was licking off the dark blood.

"Don't do that," he scowled at her, but when she pulled it out of her mouth and held it up, he could see that there was no cut. Either he had seen wrong and she didn't cut herself, or it had somehow healed already. He looked up at her temples to see only dried blood where she had dug her nails into her flesh, but no actual cuts. He looked at her quizzically and when she realized what he was looking at she quickly went back to cleaning.

"Oh no, you are not going to run away from my questions."

"I don't know what you are talking about." She tried to joke but the laughter that was once in her voice was gone.

"I know that you do." He gently placed his hands on hers, stopping her from moving. "I also know that you are scared, but I want you to know that no matter what you say, I will not reject you."

She just kept looking down at her and his hands until he squeezed hers, a small but reassuring gesture. "I don't know what happened. One day I was a normal, rebellious girl the next I awoke in a dark place that I soon found out to be my own grave. I dug myself out and ever since I've been taking each day as it comes, just trying to make it through the long hours of night without allowing the darkness within," she grasped the tunic just over her heart, "to take over."

She stopped, and he knew she wasn't going to say anything more unless she wanted to, and that would take time and patience. So, he bent over and kissed her head and whispered into her dark hair, "Thank you,"instead and helped her finish cleaning up the mess in silence, content silence.

•　•　•　•　•

She moved through the next few days much like she had before, but it was different in many ways. Firstly, she was very conscious of how much the priest was watching her, dissecting her every move and word. Secondly, she was a little foggy at times, and she floated through rather than lived through the days. Thirdly, there was the absence of the hunter. She didn't remember much, but she didn't believe that she had really made that much of an impact on him that he would leave town.

She wasn't left wondering for long when she and the priest were "working off their sins" by cleaning the stained glass windows, the pews, the altar, the candelabras, and so much more. A pounding came from the front door that caused the whole building to shake. They looked at each other, and the sound came again. Samuel put down his rag and walked to the door going on about how they had finally done it, people were starting to come to the cathedral to pray…

He opened one heavy door and was shoved violently to the floor, hitting is head on the stone and knocking him unconsious. Rosina gasped and ran to his aid only to be met by a man larger than any she had ever seen. He stood even taller than Samuel, but was three times as musclular, his hair was white with age, long like the hunter and tied back but for a few pieces that had fell from their restraint. He had several scars on his old, bearded face, but the one on his neck drew her attention. It was a large red area, looking like someone had taken a knife and cut out a huge chunk of his neck as if trying to rid his flesh of something. His eyes were lit with a fire so fierce as he looked at her that she was almost knocked over with just his glare. He wore a long leather coat that hid many weapons, from the cross around his neck to several silver knives, also with a cross embedded in them. He had a large, two-handed axe on his back and several guns, ranging from several small pistols to a large shotgun, also resting on his gigantic back. She was struck with an image of honor and duty.

A smile decorated his scarred face, but even with it the hatred coming from him was so pungent that it made her cough. His voice was deep with time, and she assumed maybe cigar smoke, "Found you." Was all the warming she had before he had lept the space between them, several feet, and landed heavily ontop of her, choking her with his enormous, calloused hands.

"Hunter" was all she could gasp out. He laughed at her and squeezed tighter. Her vision started getting darker, not from lack of breath but lack of blood to her brain and her demon spoke up, *"Let me have him, let me out!"*

No, this one is mine! She thought back, ready for battle.

"You seem like an honorable man," she said close to his face in a fake innocent voice, batting her eyes, "You'd never hurt a lady," she said ironically, because he was, in fact, hurting her.

He paused for only a brief second before responding, "You are no lady, demon!" *If you only knew,* she thought.

She brought a hand up to his wrists, grasping his left one with just one hand.

It barely wrapped halfway around, but she pressed her fingers down around it anyway. She looked him straight in the eye and stopped gasping for air, holding her breath and allowing her anger to heat her up. Her eyes were going black, the red glow lighting his face. She twitched her hand and broke his wrist with barely any effort. She wasn't sure she could do it, not having ever broken anything intentionally, that includes the boy's neck from the long-ago village. Her anger almost subsided as she tried to hide a smile of success. He withdrew quickly, taking many steps back. She got up and dusted herself off.

"Now, shall we try this again?" She asked, not expecting an answer.

"Yes, I think so." He said quickly drawing his shotgun, aiming and shooting in one quick movement, but she was quicker. She sidestepped the bullet and ran to him, throwing a right hook and connecting with his jaw, hearing an audible crack. His gun clattered to the ground, forgotten. She ran full force at him tackling him into the street, her anger making the motion much more violent than she had intended but she enjoyed it all the more because of it. She jumped up quickly, grabbed him by the hair and threw him back into the cathedral, slamming the door, all in one motion. The old hunter was dazed but back on his feet quickly and she was back on him before he could react. She had her fingers dug into his shoulders, her legs wrapped around his waist and her fangs were less than an inch from the flesh of his neck, but he had gotten his uninjured arm up between her chest and his and was blocking her from biting him by pushing against her shoulders and collar bones. She roared as she squeezed her legs, causing him to grunt and fall to one knee. But he was still holding up his muscular arm, keeping her from her treasure. She brought her hands up and boxed his ears causing him to finally weaken his resistance. He also used the opportunity to fall forward and cause her to lose her balance. She had to release her legs to catch herself. As she twisted to put her hand on the floor to catch herself, he caught her around the stomach with his injured arm, grunting with the pain. He hauled her back up putting a blade deep into the front of her shoulder as he swung his free arm around in front of her. She let out her breath, not expecting him to move so fast, but he just yanked the blade out and stabbed her again, this time in her chest, a little lower than the first puncture. She was taken by surprise when he yanked it out, again, and readjusting himself, tried to reach lower. He swung his arm again but she caught it this time. She dug her nails deep into his forearm, causing the wound to bleed immediately. He hit her in the back of the head with what she found out to be his own rock-hard head. She was dazed for only a moment but released him during that brief second. He also released her and she jumped away from him and turned to face him. He was panting, but didn't show any signs of the head hit having hurt him. He drew another gun from inside his jacket and took aim. She ducked several shots by rolling to the left, leaving her now facing the door and his back to it. He stopped to load his gun, which even she thought was painful to watch because of his broken wrist, but she wasted no time attacking him again. This time she grabbed one of the heavy candelabras and swung it full force at him knocking the gun away, and he landed on his back on the floor. She hoisted him up to his feet. She continued to try to strike him. Even in his state, he was still almost able to keep up with her, *Another worthy opponent, hahaha!* She hit him a few times in noncrucial areas before she backed up away from him because he had backed into the wall.

She dropped the candelabra with a loud clatter and grabbed him by the throat, thrusting him up the wall as far as her shorter stature would let her. She looked up into his face, full of hate. "Oops," she giggled, "I should have told you: not too long ago I gorged myself on so much blood that, quite frankly, I'm surprised I'm not sweating red. I'm feeling very, very good and very angry that this is the second hunter that has come after me in as many weeks. On top of that, you endangered the life of someone I hold dear." Her anger dripped from her voice.

"But! I can I say this:" she continued, "it is great to not have to hide what I am. I can finally let the beast out!" While she had been talking he had pulled out a knife and decided just then to ram into her side, reaching between her ribs and into her heart. Her battle anger shattered. The pain was unbearable. She released him and doubled over, blood flowing from the wound along with it her energy. "Oh god," she whispered, as she watched it.

He brought his hand to his jaw and shoved it back into place, he grunted with the movement. Clearly it was painfull for him, his skin was already starting to bruise. "That's ironic," he said, a little labored. She scrambled to get to her feet, falling back down and opting to crawl backward towards the altar. He was walking heavily towards her, his broken wrist held against his stomach. She was losing so much blood and the demon was scratching to be let out, what was left of her anger drained as she feared she was going to have another bloodbath on her hands. She refused to allow it. She used a pew to lift herself up off the floor, blood soaking her left side. *"Let me out! You will kill us!"*

He was upon her in no time with his axe in his uninjured hand, poised to kill. He held it steady but not as confident as he would have been with both hands. He intended to cut her head off and when she realized that she was terrified. For first part of this battle, she wasn't truly angry, not really the way she knew her anger to be, she was just having fun, freeing her beast without fear. But now she was afraid and, with her fear and anger growing, her markings appeared on her skin, lighting up the cathedral and giving her a little strength. The markings also caused him to stop and stare at her.

"What are you?" he asked. "They sent me here to kill a vampyre. Yet here you stand in front of me a vampyre but not. Is this what caused Johnathan to stumble?" He paused for a moment, thinking. Then continued, "It matters not, you are evil, and I am here to kill you." His shock was short-lived, and he was back on his path to death. He swung the axe down on her, and she was just barely able to bend back, causing him to miss. The blade slammed into a pew beside her, and she stumbled to the floor, growing weaker by the second. *Why am I not healing??* She continued to slide herself away from him with her hands, reaching the alter as he yanked the axe out of the pew. He raised it for a second strike when another deep voice resonated through the room, stopping him, a look of irritation on his face. He lowered his axe and turned around with a huff.

"Stop!" the other man said, again.

What now? She thought.

"You cannot hurt her!" The hunter leaned on his axe, moving just enough for Rosina to see that the original hunter had returned and was now…*saving* her? That didn't make sense.

"Pray tell me why should I not kill this evil creature, Johnathan, traitor?" hunter number two said, spitting the last two words as if they were poison on his tongue.

"She was made out of evil, but is not evil. She is different than any vampyre I have ever encountered. She struggles every day, trying to make a different path for herself, one of good. Just take a look at where you found her, in a house of God with a man of God." He pointed at the unconscious Samuel that was still sprawled out on the floor.

"Evil is evil, boy" the older hunter spat at him.

Johnathan moved around the outside of the pews and came around to stand beside Rosina, who twitched with mistrust. He put a hand on her shoulder trying to reassure her and to tell her to trust him. She didn't move because she lacked the strength but gave him a look of discontent. "If you will not listen to me, old man, then you will have to kill me as well!" He raised his free hand and shot at him, hitting him in the shoulder and knocking him to one knee. She could smell blood starting to seep out of him. While he was bent over, Johnathan lifted Rosina and put her on a pew in the first aisle. He knelt down in front of her so he was eye level with her.

"You must feed or you will die. I cannot defeat this man, he is very strong and very stubborn, he will still try to kill you even if he, himself, were dead." She just stared at him, the man that, not a week before, had been hell-bent on killing her himself was trying to help her. "I know you don't believe me, and you don't trust me, but you will have to take a leap of faith here as I am." She continued to stare at him. He clicked his tongue as if out of ideas, then he surprised her when he turned his neck towards her and pulled his collar down, baring his skin and pulsing artery to her. Her mouth started to water, and her hunger became overpowering. "Just please do me the favor I did you and not kill me." She heard him say as she grasped his shoulder and pushed his head even further to the side. She then leaned into his neck, smelling his warm flesh: salt and iron, so delicious. She sank her fangs into him as gently as she could. At first, he gasped then he let out a sigh of relief. She pulled blood from him and could feel it start to warm her from the inside. Her wound closed up, and part of her strength returned. She felt him grab her knee and squeeze; she stopped feeding but left her lips on his neck. She gently placed her tongue over the bite and licked it, trying to stop his bleeding. She had never had to keep her meal alive so she wasn't sure what she was doing but thought it might help. She heard him sigh again, so she lifted away completely and saw that the bite was already healing.

He twisted around and sat down, his back against the hardwood of the pew, looking exhausted. For some reason she felt bad at what she had just done, leaving him weak and vulnerable. She shook her head slightly, trying to remove the feeling, but she couldn't. He had trusted her not to kill him and in return she gained the power she needed to defeated the old hunter. The thought of him sacrificing himself, both in body and mind taking a leap of faith on her, believing that she is different, something new, angered her. She was angry at the world for teaching him all the wrong things about judging someone based on a category she fell into and him for his stupidity. She let out a growl that would do a wolf proud and lept across the room into the old hunter, who was slowly getting to his feet, knocking him down. He used her momentum to continue the motion into a roll, so he ended on top of her, his hand holding a blade to her throat.

"You're quick, old man, but no longer quick enough." She already had the blade out of his hand and thrown across the floor, landing under a pew out of sight. A look crossed over his face so quickly that she thought she was seeing things. It wasn't fear, but it did seem like his ego had just taken a blow. She was faster, much faster than he was now and he knew that only meant one thing: his death.

He recovered quickly and drew another blade, he saw her smile over the polished blade and then it, too, was scraping across the floor. He watched it crash into the wall, and when he turned back toward her, he was met by a palm being shoved into his chin, thrusting his whole head back and further damaging his already cracked jaw. He quickly grasped his jaw and backed away from her. She was laughing now. She got up slowly and walked over to him. Looking down at him with her devil eyes as he knelt down, trying to collect himself. She spoke to him, "You are a fool," but he didn't get to find out why because he swung his foot around trying to catch her ankle but she saw it and jumped. She didn't notice, however, that he had followed through with his other leg and did catch her, knocking her down. He had hoped that would give him enough time to at least get to his feet and prepare for the next attack, but all he managed to do was turn over onto his belly. In one fluid motion she pushed herself off the floor and landed on the old hunter, grabbing a handful of his long salt and pepper hair, yanking his head up. She leaned up so he could see her, her eyes glowing with hatred. He took notice of her markings, actually studying them, the intricate red swirls and lines that flowed along her body. He couldn't help but think them beautiful, think her beautiful, with her fair skin and long dark hair. But with a strenght that he knew didn't come from being a vampyre. He pictured her in simple clothes with her green eyes and the wind blowing her hair, she looked nothing like a demon, instead, he imagined her as an angel. That image was shattered when she showed her sharp fangs and spoke with a dark voice.

"I'm going to end this now," as she spoke, she leaned closer, smelling him, caressing his neck with her free hand, and he felt himself giving into the warmth of death. He always knew there would be someone that could beat him, but he never thought it would be such a fledgling, perhaps that is what gave her such a bright light rather than a darkness. She had not been poisoned by the older monsters, maybe Johnathan was right and that is why he was defeated. Her pure desire was to change the way she was to live, break away from the beaten path.

She wanted so much to rip open his flesh and taste his wise, old, honorable blood, but she couldn't. As much as she hated him, he was not evil and therefore wouldn't kill him. She leaned back and pulled his head back more and then smacked it off the stone ground, knocking him unconscious.

She stood up and searched him for any more hidden weapons. She came up with four more hidden knives, two pistols, a small throwing axe and several globe-like glass containers; some with clear liquid, which she assumed were filled with holy water, she laughed a little to herself, and some containing a black power. She turned one over, watching the powder move and looked closely at it, confused. She stood there staring at it when she was startled by Johnathan walking up behind her. She reacted by punching him in the chest so hard he doubled over, a hand clutching his chest and gasping a little. Then she perked up, as if remembering something and punched him again, this time in the arm.

"Okay, I understand the first time was for startling you, but what was the second one for?" he asked.

"For trusting me! You are a bigger fool than he!" She pointed at the old hunter on the floor. Which drew her attention back to the glass bottle in her hand, "And what is this?" she held it up so he could see it as he rubbed his sore arm.

"Sorry?" was his response to her accusation. And answering her question, he said, "It's supposed to be some kind of explosive. Something new the old bastard was working on. The normal bow and sword weren't good enough for him," She turned and looked at him thinking he was crazier than she thought and God help her kind if he ever succeeded in creating a large explosive. "And you are entirely too easy to spook for having supernatural senses." He earned himself a punch in the other arm for that but continued, "However did you managed to stay alive this long?"

He took a step back when she turned again to him, but she had a thoughtful look on her face, "Mostly luck." She answered as she gently set the explosive bottle down. Her demeanor was completely different than it was when she was fighting, she was almost childlike. She made her way quickly over to Samuel who was still laying on the floor. She knelt down beside him and lifted his head gently off the floor, checking for blood. When she did so, she realised she was doing a very human, very unnecessary action; she could tell by scent alone that his blood was not among the scents in the room. She gently put her arms under him and lifted him completely off the floor and carried him to his room, laying him down on his cot. She grabbed a discarded bag on his floor and brought it up to the kitchen where she grabbed some rope. She returned to where the old hunter was laying, still unconscious and tied up his hands and feet. She started gathering up his weapons, including the ones that had went astray and placed them in the bag.

"No matter how many times I have seen the strength of your kind, I am still amazed. You are so small, yet you easily lifted a man at least fifty pounds heavier than you." Johnathan remarked, staring at her.

Without missing a beat, she replied, "Thank you for the compliment but I have to make an observation of my own and as much as I would hate to hurt your manliness," she stumbled a little over the word, but went with it, "but you aren't as …" She paused, thinking, "Grrrr," she motioned with her hands, making them into claws up by her head, showing her teeth in a growl and making her look like an angry cat. Her gesture had him hiding a smile, "as I thought, especially after all that big talk."

"As I recall I had you cornered, not once, but twice. I could have killed you, but didn't. She stopped her motion to collect the weapons and looked at him, her anger beginning to rise. She realized that it wasn't the comment about her being weak, she already knew that, but he was disrespecting her, something she never knew herself to get too overly irritated about. He stopped chuckling at her when he saw her looking at him, her eyes, that had returned to their normal green, were darkening. She dropped the bag, it landed with a thump of metal on stone and she took a quick step in his direciton. She clamped to his shoulders with her hands before he could blink. She leaned into him, baring her fangs. She could smell his fear growing, but it was soured with something else, a scent she did not recognize, but based on his lack of defense, she assumed it was guilt. She leaned into his neck, but instead of biting him, she gently kissed his warm skin, when she did she felt him jump just a little. She pulled back from him, her anger completely gone and she smiled.

"Now we're even," and she returned to packing the bag.

He stood in shock for a moment then joined her in her quest to gather all the weapons. When they finished, she went to the door and whistled out it. A young boy came running. She handed him some coins and told him to find the dirtiest, most arrogant travel coach owner, she wouldn't object to a farmer with a wagon full of manuer and bring him to her. The boy ran off, and she went to the kitchen to gather a bucket of water and a rag. While she waited, she scrubbed the blood off the floor and the pews. He grabbed a rag and joined her. She thought it was weird how he had made himself right at home and voluntarily helped her and was friendly with her, a vampyre. She decided his goofy behavior must be from the lack of blood. Otherwise, he would have never been a hunter, not with that high level of comfort around a vampyre that he was supposed to hunt and kill.

When he spoke again, she was surprised at how serious he was, perhaps he recovered much faster than she expected. "Why didn't you kill him?" he had a solemn look on his face, somewhere between confusion, sadness, and anger. "I've never seen a vampyre spare a human's life, especially that of a hunter's."

She stopped scrubbing and answered him with a snide remark, "Perhaps there is more you do not know than you think." But she knew the truth, he probably knew more about her own kind that she did.

"That's not it," he ignored the shallowness of her answer, "Vampyres, most of them, consider themselves warriors and to provide death is the most honorable thing to do when an enemy is defeated. Especially after a battle between two closely matched opponents. It is much sweeter, spicier, and fulfilling. It is very hard to resist, and most do not try."

She watched him as he replaced some of the sconces and the candles knocked ascue during the fight. "It is clear that you have done your fair share of studying." He let out a soft chuckle as if to say 'You have no idea.' "Well, lucky for you both, I'm 'no lady.'" She quoted the old hunter. "I can't kill him just like I would never have or will kill you. You are innocent."

He knocked over a candle he just set straight and said, "Excuse me, what?" He stared at her in shock, "Innocent?"

She had gone back to cleaning but his reaction stopped her and had her looking at him, "Yes, innocent. Does this confuse you? Should I elaborate?"

"That would be most helpful," he said.

"She tilted her head to the side, thinking, confused at what he was confused about, but after a moment she straightened and continued, "You do not rape, you do not steal, you do not torture, I could go on, but in essence you are not evil, you do not deserve to be fed to my demon."

"My lady, I fear you are mistaken." He replied, "I have stolen, killed and tortured."

"For survival, not for pleasure. You kill what needs killed, to protect those you care about. You steal to live. I doubt you are paid sufficient amounts, considering your line of work," she looked at the bulge in his coat that hid his pistol, "and I'm sure you didn't enjoy the torturing of my kin to find the whereabouts of an innocent child being held captive or something along those lines?" a smile played on her lips, "Because in that case, I will have to change my mind and kill you after all, which I will not lie, I would enjoy," a smile broke over her face, showing her teeth and her fangs.

"No, no, I didn't enjoy it, it more painful for me than for those of your," he paused, "kin." He hid a smile, but it faded to nothing quickly.

"I was merely having a laugh, I have no intention to kill the man that just saved myself and another innocent," she looked back the hallway towards the priest's room, misreading his change in mood.

At first he didn't respond, then, "No, of course not."

She heard the lie in his answer and walked to where he was standing, staring at the candles. "You have something you would like to share?"

He jumped a little and continued to fix the candles, even going beyond by wiping the dust off and relighting them. She stared at him, a look of displeasure on her face. Finally, he spoke, "It's just that I still can't believe this is happening. I know you are young, in life and in this new world you find yourself in, but the young ones are the ones that fall into the darkness and end up more than animals than masquerading humans."

She could see the pain in his eyes and hear the sadness in his voice. "No matter what you see in front of you here, or how you perceive me, don't let it fool you. I do enjoy the hunt and the kill. The blood is like nothing I have ever experienced. I believe it is the closest I will ever get to be in heaven and it comes with a hefty price. It would be all too easy to give into my demon, but I have been doing that for far too long already and, even though it is said a vampyre does not have soul, I feel that it would be much worse if I didn't watch myself, I would completely lose myself and go on a rampage and kill everyone I come into contact with…" *"Sounds delightful!"* she tried to not agree, but sometimes, when she was in a mood, she felt the urge to do exactly that and she knew that would drive her completely mad.

"I wish all of your kind would stop for just a second and see the world the way you do. If they only saw that it is their nature to kill but they don't have too, I wouldn't be here, I would be home with…" He trailed off and for the first time she saw him truly raw. Before she had a chance to ask, he put his hand over his mouth as if trying to stop himself, but she could see the tears in his eyes. He reached up and grasped a necklace that she hadn't noticed he was wearing. It was tarnished and dented, barely still in one piece, but still, it was the one thing that was holding him together. She wasn't sure what to do, she was never good at comforting people.

She stood there awkwardly for a moment, then she put a hand on his shoulder and squeezed. "Who was she?" she said as gently as she could. At first he didn't answer, then it was as if a floodgate had opened and all his emotion came flooding forward. She had never been hit with such strong scents and feelings; she couldn't filter them, and it almost knocked her down, the weight of them was so much.

"I was young when I first saw her. She was standing in the middle of the street, her head tilted back, so her face was towards the heavens. She had her eyes closed as if taking in everything just by feeling and hearing it. The sun was setting behind her, and she seemed to glow in its rays; it was only dimmed by her radiant smile. She turned to me and opened her eyes, but she was already smiling at me as if she knew I was there. 'I can feel a thunderstorm coming. It will be beautiful with such a warm day proceeding it.' All I could do was stare. She grabbed my hand and started running towards the hill under the great oak tree that stood right outside our village. She didn't ask me with words but with her touch, I knew she wanted me to watch it with her. We stayed all evening, she did most of the talking because I was too shy to speak. But as the night rolled on and the clouds descended on us, I became more comfortable with her and found that I had fallen in love with her in that short time. I didn't even know her name.

"Ah! Did you see that?" Her voice was like that of an angel's. She jumped up and looked up at the clouds as the lightning started dancing across the sky, tickling the clouds and causing them to moan with delight. He stood up beside her and watched the most amazing display of beauty he had ever seen. His eyes never left her face. He watched as happiness seemed to light her up straight from her very soul. She was so beautiful, and she only became more so when the rain started to fall, and she reached out her arms to catch as many raindrops as she could. Her dress and long golden blond hair were drenched; her gray eyes closed and her rosy lips turned up in a smile that seemed brighter than even the lightning. She turned around in a circle and ended

up facing him, somehow he thought she did that on purpose. Her eyes wide open, even gray as they were they were more like diamonds than stone and differed greatly from the clouds above her.

"You are supposed to be watching the lightning, why are you looking at me?" A smile grew on his face, reaching his eyes as he reached up and touched her cheek. She didn't flinch at his touch but melted into it. He leaned in and kissed her soft red lips. He thought she would pull away and run from him, but she reached up with her hand and ran it through his rain-soaked hair; he felt his heart jump. When he pulled away, she asked again, "Why are you looking at me?"

Without even thinking he said, "Because I love you."

Her face flushed but she smiled again and said, "I love you." From that day they spent as much time together as they could. And they grew closer. They married, a simple, but beautiful ceremony, with only family. They built a home together on the edge of their village and before they could settle they discovered their family would be expanding. The baby came, a girl, and she grew, and they loved her more than they thought they ever could, and they loved each other more and more as their daughter grew. Everything was perfect, and he was more happy than he ever thought he could be until a man came to town and changed everything. This stranger also thought that his wife was a beauty and set out to make her his. She rejected him, but he couldn't accept it so he took her life. He stole her light and made her a monster...

"She was such a strong, kind, and gentle woman that I thought if anyone could handle the change, she could. Hell, I thought she would try to avoid killing to feed altogether; the thought of killing even a small animal, even one that needed killing, mortified her, killing a human would destroy her. But as it was, I was dead wrong. It seems the gentle, kind ones are the ones that cannot handle the evil that comes with the hunger of being a vampyre. We tried to work through it, I had faith in her, she was still my beloved.

"I woke one night to screaming. I quickly ran outside to see our village in chaos. People were running past my front door yelling about a demon an I should get my daughter and run as fast as I could. I couldn't believe the sight, but I ran inside to wake my wife and daughter. When I opened the door to my daughter's room I was met by a most terrifying sight. My wife, in her white nightgown, held our sleeping daughter, but she was covered in blood, her mouth dripped it and her front was no longer white but dark red with the blood. It was from her many victims, I did not care to guess how many. Her eyes were looking down watching our daughter sleep, a wicked grin on her face that just wasn't her's. She heard me come in but didn't look up, didn't move at all. For a moment it was silent, until I moved towards her a fear in me like I have never felt until that day nor any day since. She started speaking. Her voice was soft, as it had always been, reassuring and kind, 'Join me, my love. This life is exhilarating, I've never felt this alive. We can be together forever and we never have to watch our daughter grow old and die. John,' she whispered as she brought our daughter up to her chest, holding her close, I thought that this was just a lapse and she would recover, but I saw her fangs and they were moving steadily towards my precious angel's neck…

He rushed to her, 'NOOO!' His greatest fears about to be made real. She shoved him back through the door, splintering the wood and wounding him. He sat up just in time to see her sink her teeth into the innocent flesh of his daughter. She drained her as he begged from his position on the floor, barely able to move, 'You can't, she will forever be a child, you cannot condemn her to that hell. Please, I beg you!' but she didn't head him please. She drained her daughter and tried to get her to take her blood to replace that which she had taken. But she had done it wrong, she had taken too much and her precious child was dead at the hands of her once loving mother. She died without ever waking, without ever making a sound or a cry.

When she realized what she had done, she lost her mind and destroyed everything in the room and then she came at him. She grasped him around the throat, 'This is your fault!' she hissed. And knelt to bite him too but he had grabbed a dagger kept under the table just in case this had ever happened. He had hoped he was wrong for thinking he would ever need it, he could live with her being angry at him, but this…

He sat in the pool of blood soaking into the floor, unable to move, barely able to breathe. She was gone, they were both gone…

He left his house and set it alight, leaving everything that he had ever known or loved and went to find the people that killed these demons. He knew they were there, in the shadows. He wandered for years, slumping at one pub then another until he stumbled into Rome and a man cornered him, questioning him about his wife and child and his destroyed village. When he spouted about vampyres, instead of thinking him a drunkard fool, he took him to God's Order of the Hunt

She was overcome by sadness. Before she realized it, she was hugging him and repeatedly saying 'sorry.'

He gently pushed her away, and she was grateful, she hadn't noticed that the small meal of his blood had already started to wear off and she was craving more of his blood. "I know, but there was nothing anyone could have done, not even me…" He trailed off again, and they just sat in silence for a while until she heard him pray, praying for his wife's soul and his. And then he begged for Rosina's to be saved from the darkness that had overtaken her. She was so taken aback by his request that she actually gasped out loud. He ignored it, "Amen. I—" There was a small tap at the door, she didn't move, not hearing it because she was so enamored by the hunter. He looked defeated, "Are you going to answer the door?"

"Oh! I didn't notice..." she quickly went to open the door, it was the boy from earlier, a smile on his face from ear to ear. She could smell why, the scent of feces was wafting into the cathedral. She looked out the door and saw what it was. The boy had found a farmer that was heading out of town with a less-than-clean cart, she couldn't help but grin.

"Thanks!" She went to reach for a small token of thanks in the form of coin.

"No! Thanks, but that was fun." He was grinning as he hopped away.

She turned to the farmer, "Thanks, I'll collect the 'goods.'" She went to the old hunter laying on the floor and his bag of weapons, she reached for him when Johnathan spoke up.

"You had better let me if you don't want the whole town to know about you."

"Ah, that's probably a good idea. Thanks." He lifted up the hunter, and she collected his bag. He unceremonially dropped him into the dirty wagon. She paid the farmer and walked back to the hunter, he had begun to stir.

"I'll give you your weapons back to take with you only if you remember that I spared your life. And, since you seem to be a man of honor, you now owe me a life debt. You can no longer hunt me. If you do, remember this: you will not leave in one piece next time, because I *will* be stronger and I *will* happen to lose my conscience that day." She tossed the leather bag with his guns and knives at him, hitting him hard in the face. He grunted, but didn't say anything. She nodded at the farmer without looking away from the hunter.

He grumbled at the dirty wagon, and she leaned in close to his ear; he flinched, and she enjoyed that fear, "I could just kill you right now if you'd like," She made sure her breath reached his neck and she could see goosebumps growing where it touched him.

"Why didn't you just kill me anyway, why play games with me?" he was defiant right up to the end, she actually respected him for that.

"Because I can't," He looked at her, waiting for more, but she didn't provide it just turned and walked back into the cathedral.

When she closed the door and turned back towards the inside of the massive building, she noticed that Johnathan was standing in the middle of the room. "Well, now that my mess has been taken care of, I best be on my way," his composure was completely back in place as if he hadn't just share the rawest thing with her, the same thing that had caused him so much pain. When he reached the door, he bent and picked up his own bag that she hadn't noticed he had dropped. He turned to leave but paused and turned back around.

"Does your friend," he motioned with his chin towards the hallway that led to their rooms, "know about you?"

She was only slightly surprised at his question, she had been waiting on his inquiries about Samuel since the very beginning of their relationship. "He suspects something about me, whether he knows the truth I do not know."

"After all he's done for you, including putting up with your sour attitude," he could read the surprise on her face, and he smiled, *she really was a baby. I've never followed and observed a vampyre so easily,* he thought, "Don't you think he deserves that much?"

"I think its better, for him and me, if he doesn't know. Either he will preach me to death, or I'll kill him first." She meant it as a joke, but it came out wringing of the truth.

He gave her a "really?" look, "You wouldn't kill him, you love him." A look of shock covered her face again, but he kept going, "on some level he means more to you than Gabriel," again the surprise was apparent, but it was quickly replaced with anger.

"No one means more to me than Gabriel! He saved me from my life of loneliness. He loved me when no one else should or would! He took me away from everything!"

"He gave you an escape, allowed you to run away! He didn't help you! He didn't love you!!"

"And Angel doesn't either! The only person he loves is God!" There was silence for a moment. "Why are we fighting over this? The other day you wanted me dead now you're concerned about who I love or who loves me? That doesn't make sense. What are you up to?"

"I'm just concerned." He said nonchalantly.

"Don't you try to pull the wool over my eyes!"

"Okay, Okay," he put his hand up in defeat. "We've been watching this town, with all its filth. It is a perfect place for a vampyre." He shrugged his shoulder and looked at her as if to say, 'and we were right.' "He could feed and 'change' people to his heart's content and form a colony of his own, and no one would notice. This vampyre would have to be a cast out, making him weak and vulnerable to rage. We feared that when the other men of the cloth left, that a vampyre had indeed sunk its nasty claws into this place. But we watched, for a long time, this young priest tries to do good, try to help these people that don't deserve it. Then you came along and he accepted you into his," he looked around the cathedral, "home, no questions asked," he stopped, at the look on her face, one of disbelief, again, "Okay, maybe a few questions, but you get my meaning. And he has done nothing but help you, and yes, love you. Though he denies it because he took an oath to God and he intends to keep it. He may love you, but he loves God more." She thought about that for a moment and it made her feel a little better, a little less like a fool for having allowed him so deep under her skin, at least he was feeling the same itch. He pulled her out of her thoughts, "And he deserves to know." She didn't know how long he had been talking, but she nodded.

"Uh-huh," she muttered.

"Okay, then I'll be leaving," he said.

"Be safe, If you ever need anything, I owe you my life, so find me," she offered.

"Well, you are turning my life upside down with so much new knowledge about your kind. And I just didn't want the priest to wake up to a dead monster, pardon me. That might cause a small amount of turmoil." He was brushing off her gratitude.

"While it is true the good priest would have woken to a dead vampyre, if there was anything left, if not for your timely entrance, but I give you my word. If you ever need anything, you can seek me out, and I will help you. But! I will not be degraded to the level of carrying heavy objects for you when you are old and odorous," she had been joking in that last part, but she could feel the air shift, ever since he revealed himself to her, he was different, even when he tried to pass off a joke, it was missing any amusement.

"I think we are even, I had something that needed protected and you did it." When she looked confused, he continued, "Hope, faith, etcetera, it may have been a long time coming, but it's here now and I never want to let it go." He said seriously then, "I promise you my life is entirely too exciting for me to grow old, I'll die long before I'm odorous." He forced a chuckle, that was superficial. She forced a smile, "But since this hope comes with you turning my whole world upside down, I'll remember your offer when I need it, thank you." He bowed his head to her, showing her respect and gratitude, something that he must have picked up in his travels east, she quickly returned the gesture and he turned to go.

Samuel stood in the shadow of the hallway, leaning against the wall, listening to Rosina and the strange man bicker and then talk fondly about him. He couldn't believe what he was hearing, but it was because everything that was said by this stranger was true. He did love her but he loved her the way he would a lost kitten and he had suspected she wasn't what she seemed but deep in his heart he still stubbornly hoped he was wrong. A vamypre? The truth heard out loud flipped a switch in him, this seemed more real than seeing her covered in blood and glowing, and yet he still wanted to jump out and save her when he argued with her and comfort her when he upset her, but something held him against the wall, as much made of stone as the wall itself. He was mortified and relieved all at once and overcome with a fear born from the realization that he had befriended and trusted a creature God had cast out and didn't even notice and fear that she was capable of so much destruction. He didn't fear her abilities, he had no doubt that she would not harm him, but that she keeps it deep within her under tight wrap, allowing her anger and sadness to build up. He feared those restraints would snap and he would lose her to a power-drunken rage.

The sound of the door closing and her happy sigh brought him out of his thoughts; he scurried down the hall back to his room, tripping several times because his legs didn't seem to be in agreement with his fleeing. They may be right, but he didn't want to chance her anger. He had to shake himself mentally, to be afraid of her was ridiculous. He had not seen what had happened just moments before with the old stranger, but he still needed to pray. He did not know how to proceed, and he knew God would not allow him to stray down the wrong path.

Johnathan pushed the door closed behind him, and she leaned against it. She let out a sigh whether of relief of his absence or happiness that someone knew her secret; she didn't ponder. She could have asked him all the questions that were swimming around her head, but she decided that she didn't really want to know about the behavior of her kin. She was her own kind of vampyre and she liked writing her own rule book. The thought make her smile, but it quickly faded when she thought of the angel that had offered her salvation. How could she explain to him what she was? Would he too try to kill her? Cast her out? Leave her alone, again? Or would he accept her or try to save her? She shook her head and decided that she would just take whatever he had to give her, even if that meant her death, its the least she could do, and the thought of dying at his hands didn't scare her, it was almost as if a wash of peace came over her. Then Gabriel's face crept into her mind and she felt the tears start to well up in her eyes.

She shook her head violently and marched to the kitchen. She thought she heard a door close and could smell Samuel's recent presence, but she quickly put that out of her mind as she went in search of a manuscript in his massive library. After several minutes and doubt that she would find it, she finally found what she was looking for. She let out an "ah ha!" of triumph. The thought popped into her head, *Why would Samuel have such a book?* Then *OOH, now his toned muscles make sense.*

She quickly vacated the building to the courtyard beside it. It was a perfect place for her to blow off some steam, at her *full* potential. She could feel her demon's smile burning inside her soul. She sat cross-legged on the cool grass and opened the text across her lap. Dust drifted out of it as she leafed through the pages, taking it all in. She held in her lap a complete manual to an ancient art form of fighting. It was written by an Englishman visiting China and was allowed to stay at a monastery and study there under the condition he not take profit in what he learned. The book contained everything from novice to expert form, stance, movement, combat, defense, and even weapons use. She turned to page one and gently sat the book on the grass, meditating for a short while to prepare herself. Then, she started with the basic form, positioning her feet under her shoulders, knees slightly bent, arms up and rigid, elbows bent, fists held loosely closed, one up near her head the other lower, in a defensive position. The first form took her across the grass and back covering basic punch and block combinations.

She was out there for hours, mastering every detail of the stances and motions down to her very muscles, which should be tense and which should be relaxed. She eventually commandeered several bags of grain and tied them up on a dead tree at the corner of the yard, making it look like a scarecrow. She practiced hitting, slow at first allowing her body to memorize the movements. Then, she quickened her pace, hitting the bags with as much force and speed as she dared. She kept quickening her pace, *faster, faster,* she thought, *harder,* until she was hitting it so fast and hard her knuckles and feet were bloody, not having time to heal before she struck again. She enjoyed the pain, it helped to drain away her fear and anger and the aches in her heart. She hit the fake man the more she thought, thought about her family, brother, her vampyre sire, Gabriel, Angel, Johnathan… her pain, loneliness, anger, sadness… The more her emotions rocked through her body the harder she hit until she was yelling with every hit, tears falling down her face unchecked. The thought of her being exiled by the priest made her fears bubble over, and her instincts turned it to anger; her adrenaline coursed through her body, her flesh turned red and her eyes black. She hit the now bare wood with all her strength, punching clear through the wood sending splinters in every direction. The hit left the ground looking as if instead of hale falling from the sky, wood did. She remained still with her arm in the wood, blood flowing from all the wooden slivers projecting out of her flesh. She slowly removed her arm from the tree and stared at it. Her body was already starting to heal, the wood would soon be part of her arm, and she did nothing to stop it, just watched. Until she heard a door slam and a man's voice, that she recognized as an angel's, yelling at her. She turned to see him running towards her, but couldn't hear what he was saying over the sound of her heart pounding in her ears. He was upon her quickly, asking her something and pointing to her arm. He quit trying t talk when it was clear that she couldn't hear him, so he just reached down and yanked out a piece of the wood, the pain was minimal, but it still got her attention. He kept pulling out the wood splinters until her blood loss caused her to collapse to the ground, landing on her knees. Her anger was almost gone, ebbing into the tears now flowing like rain from her eyes. She could hear him again, "are you insane??!!" she thought he was saying.

She let her head fall down onto her chest, and her sweaty hair fell over her face. "Sorry, I'm so sorry…" she kept repeating, *maybe I am insane,* she thought. She was going to give into his warmth and allow him to help her, but then she realized she was just taking the easy way out, *"Coward."* She wasn't sure if that was her or her demon, but it didn't matter, it was the truth. She pushed him away from her, hard enough that it knocked him down on the grass. She stood up, anger in her eyes and yelled a sound of frustration.

"Stop it! I don't need your help, I don't need you to save me. Don't you understand, I'm beyond help! I'm a fucking vampyre for god's sake! I don't want this, I don't need this, I don't need you!" she regretted the words as soon as they fell from her stupid mouth. She was so mortified that she just stared at him, her eyes black, waiting for his response. But what she got wasn't what she had expected in any scenario of this situation.

"I know what you are," he said. She had wondered if he suspected, "And I've been praying," she knew, "I was hoping to have more time to think on this and approach it gently, delicately—"

"There is no delicate or gentle way to approach this!"

"Please!" he raised his voice for the second time against her, and she saw real fear in his eyes. She quickly closed her mouth with an audible sound. "I need to get this out." *before my fear stops me*, he didn't say. He took a deep breath, "I want…" he closed his eyes and let out his breath, "need you to bite me." He opened his eyes to see her reaction. She had a look of half puzzlement and half amusement on her face.

She stifled a snicker, "I'm sorry, pardon me, I think I heard wrong?"

"Bite me, make me like you. Make me a vampyre. Make me immortal so I can spend eternity spreading God's word, starting with these lost, violent souls that live in my town. I do not want to walk amongst them as weak as I am. If my words do not reach them with kindness, then the wrath of God will!" He was getting excited at the thought. She could almost see his eye already glowing, *gold,* she thought, *how fitting.*

She put her hands on his shoulders to calm him, she could feel him shaking, a heat rising from him. He jumped a little when she touched him.

"Angel," she whispered and pulled him to her, embracing him. "I cannot." He stiffened and pushed her away.

"Why?! You do not wish me to have your power, your strength? You wish to keep it all to yourself, don't you? I should have known! A demon like you could never help the good! All you want is to kill! You're a murderer just like them!"

At that moment she wished all that were true, so she wouldn't feel the pain shooting through her soul. She could give him what he wanted without thinking of the consequences. She wiped a tear from her eye, pretending she had an itch. "Do you feel better?" she cocked her head, and gave him a snide look. "You listen to me now. I will never place this curse on you." She motioned with her hands from her head to her feet. "I will never allow a soul so pure as yours to be soiled by this darkness, this madness. Do you not see what it will do to you, what the mere thought of it has done to you? You will be swallowed by its hunger, its desire." She pictured Johnathan's wife, causing her to want him to see the truth even more. "You will no longer exist, your body will be filled with only anger and sadness. Your happy smile will never again light the room. Your kindness will never warm another heart. Your words will never save another soul for they will be gone, the meaning vanished or tarnished by evil. And, my beautiful angel, your wings will blacken and God will forsake you. You will no longer be his but that of the darkness, the demon within. He sat in the grass, hunched over tears falling him. She sat next to him. "If *your* words cannot reach them, no one's will and the wrath that you speak of will not be that of God's." He remained quiet, still, barely breathing. She didn't know what to do so she just sat next to him, hoping he would understand, almost praying he would forgive her.

He stood up so suddenly that she gasped at his movement; without saying anything, he walked back into the cathedral. *No, not yet,* she thought, *if he ever will. I'll have to be patient.* She became frustrated, she never had to care about hurting anyone's feelings. She growled and walked over to the destroyed wood of her punching dummy and stared at it. She then moved to the tree in the furthest corner to the front of the cathedral. It was old, hundreds of years. It was tall and wide, the branches spreading out from the corner in all directions. She looked up at it and couldn't see the top, just the leaves, bright green, reflecting its life, beautiful and strong; she envied it. It loomed over her, but it also calmed her. She had walked over with the urge to hit something, but now that she was there she felt a different need. She ran quickly to the front of the cathedral and gathered a candle and white cloth and returned to the tree. She tied the white cloth around the old tree and knelt down before it. She lit the candle and cradled it in her hands as she closed her eyes and tilted her head toward the heavens. And she prayed: prayed to a god she barely believed in to help her, help her make him understand, help guide him to the truth, help him see what she was doing was not for herself but for him, for his heart and his soul. *Please, please, help him, help your precious child find his way back to your light. Take his hand and guide him back to himself and to your embrace.* She begged with all her might, and when she was done, she found she was exhausted. She laid down in the grass, looking up at the stars and slowly drifted off in the cool, crisp air of night, dreaming of a vampyre priest. She fell asleep to a nightmare, a monster backed by the name of God, destroying everyone who didn't listen to his words and she shuttered in her sleep as a tear fell from her eye. *I did this,* was her last thought before the darkness took her.

CHAPTER EIGHT: PAIN GIVES SO MUCH PLEASURE

She knew she couldn't have him,
But she just couldn't resist him.
His beautiful voice filled her very soul,
His warmth settled her shaking nerves,
His gentle hands soothed her trembling heart.
He is pure and she wants to dirty him,
Take him and cover him with her sin.
She wants to release the monster,
Allow the demon to take control,
Show him what she really is.
She can't,
It will destroy him,
But she can't resist...

She awoke to the burning of the sun. Her skin was on fire, and she jumped up from the grass and bolted into the coolness of the stone cathedral. She slammed the door behind her, and turned toward her room, moving quickly and she ran right into the priest. She almost knocked them both over, but she was able to keep on her feet, he barely seemed to even notice. She apologized fervently, but her sorry's were met only with a grunt. He straightened his robe and continued walking towards his library. She stared after him, but when he didn't re-emerge, she went to her room and laid down; she heard him leave shortly afterward.

Over a week passed this way. She would ask him something or try to talk to him and would only be met by grunts or nods. He was avoiding her, not physically but mentally he had shut her out; he was a stone wall. She knew he was upset, knew he needed some space and time, but she grew tired of this game. She told herself to be patient but when almost two weeks had passed her temper got the better of her.

She was cleaning in the kitchen, her back to him, as he leaned against the counter drinking and reading. She was trying to have a conversation with him, but his pauses were a little too loud, and his grunts were a little too quiet. She slammed her hands down on the wooden table, it creaked under the pressure. "That is enough!" she heard him gasp, but say nothing. She turned to him and looked at him. Even though he didn't hide that he was avoiding eye contact, he didn't turn away or try to leave.

"I have waited patiently for you to get rid of this childish attitude you've been walking around with but, I'm not putting up with it anymore! You didn't get what you wanted, be an adult and get over it!" He still didn't look at her. She grew angrier and took a step towards him, "Look at me, damn it!" When he still didn't look up, she walked over to him and grabbed him with both hands on either side of his head forcing him to turn his face towards her. He kept his eyes to the left and away.

"Are you really this mad that I didn't turn you into a monster?" she asked, he shrugged his shoulders. That made her even angrier. "Fine! I'll give you what you want," *but don't hate me when its done,* was her only thought before she grabbed his shoulders and forced him down to his knees. He was looking at her now, looking up as she looked down, her eyes black. She could see the fear in his eyes, but she ignored it. She bent down bit him on the warm flesh above his collar bone, she did it gently and held him gently. She felt tears against her lip that had fallen on to his skin and realized that they weren't his, but hers.

She barely sank her teeth into his skin, keeping herself from drawing blood. She barely held onto him, but when he tried to pull away, she wouldn't let him. She feared what he would see, how he would react. He pushed against her with his hands, but she only gripped him tighter until he spoke.

"Please," it was ragged and barely audible, but it shot directly to her heart. She let go of him, and he sank the rest of the way to the floor. She didn't move and didn't look at him, *what have I done?* His breath was shallow and fast, and sweat had started to bead up on his skin. He had been so very wrong…

He slowly reached towards her frozen form, hesitating only for a moment, placing his hand on her thigh, grasping the fabric of her trousers. She jolted when she felt his hand, he felt it even through his body, it reflected his own fear: fear that he was wrong, that she was actually going to do it: take him and change him. He was thrilled at first, but when she clasped onto him and so easily forced him to the ground, he had feared her for the first time. He knew she had felt his panic when she held him so gently, but his fear only subsided when she released him, and he saw his fear and sadness reflected in her eyes.

"Thank you," he said, "I didn't know, I didn't know…" and she moved, but it was more like she finally ran out of strength for she fell to the floor as her legs gave out. Her hands hit the floor with a smack as she tried to brace herself for the fall, her elbows and shoulders buckled when she landed, hard, on the stone floor, tears falling from her face.

"I'm sorry," she whispered, desperate for him to hear her words. She looked him straight in the eye, her eyes now back to their normal green, "I had no other choice. I couldn't get through to you any other way."

"I know, please forgive me," he said, earnestly. "I did not mean to put you in such a terrible position."

"No, it was my own fault. I should not have kept this from you I will get my things and be gone by night." She tried to stand, as she turned away from him, to leave before he could move but then he reached to her again, grasping her wrist and pulling her back towards him. The unexpected change in direction caused her to fall. Again she landed on Samuel, knocking him down to the floor. She braced herself with her hands on either side of him, below his arms, which were thrown out to help catch himself. They were inches from each other. Her on her knees which were between his thighs and he sprawled, legs wide and hands flung back holding him up only a foot from the ground and their noses less than six inches from each other.

"I'm so sorry," she said and started to move off him.

"No." he whispered and sat up fully. "Don't be," he raised his cold hand to her face, cupping it. She was warm with emotion, and he could feel the tears on her skin. He pulled her towards him and whispered gently, "I will protect you, so you don't have to be so strong." He knew it was a lie, but was shocked to find that he actually did want to protect her. He wanted to keep her safe from the men that would hunt her, those that would love her, from herself and himself, from his-greedy-selfish-self. Something changed in her, she became less rigid and she slowly nodded. She closed her eyes tightly as if trying to block out something. What he didn't know was that he echoed Gabriel's words to her on the night he had found her in tears for the first time, the night they met.

He pulled her closer and kissed her, her eyes flew open in shock. It was gentle at first then it became hungry, as if he was claiming his mate, angry that someone had hurt her, even though the someone was him. He was trying to heal her wounds with his kiss. She was stiff and could feel his emotions, every one of them. Then she reached up with her hand and ran it through his short hair and gave in to him. Her mouth was soft and sweet when she finally let him in. She understood what this kiss was and could feel his joy that she trusted him, not knowing it was false trust. He brought his arm down and put it around her back, pulling her against him, embracing her, filling himself with her. He pulled his other hand through her beautiful dark hair, and she let slip a small moan before she could stop herself.

She knew it was wrong, but she couldn't resist. This kiss was one of anger and regret, he was trying to make things go back to the way they were before he knew the truth, but she knew it could never be that way. His warmth was so inviting, so soothing and his hands were so gentle on her, she couldn't help herself but give in. She knew this man and knew he would never hurt her intentionally. She knew he was at a loss for what to do to fix this, so he was turning to the most primal, animal choice: physical comfort, the need to feel another's hands on yourself, craving it in the most basic way. He needed to *feel* that she was still there, that she wasn't leaving and that she wasn't in pain. His need touched hers, his desire stirred up hers. It brought to the front her human monster, something that hadn't shown its head since Gabriel…

Oh, Gabriel! They broke their kiss and she dug both hands under his robe, touched his skin, and guided her hands over his shoulders and neck. When that wasn't enough, she pulled the cloth up over his head, leaving him sitting with just his trousers and the bandages that covered his still-sore back. She started ripping them from the front only pausing when he grunted in pain, but she couldn't get them off fast enough, so she started biting them, and they fell off him in tattered strips. She pushed him so he was laying fully on the cold floor. She straddled him, pulling off her own robe to reveal her sleeveless shirt and her glowing skin. He was once again struck with awe by the beauty of her markings. He couldn't keep himself from reaching up and touching her, her arms, her neck, and he timidly reached for her belly. He lifted up the bottom of her shirt and placed his hand on her burning skin.

"You've seen all of me before. Why so shy?" she asked, grinning.

"That may be true," he said, around a frog in his throat, "but that was in a completely different context." He cleared his throat, "And I've never had such a strong urge to touch you…" She was shocked by his honesty. She leaned down and kissed him, a strong kiss, and she accidentally nicked his lip with her fang, she sat up covering her mouth, saying sorry over and over.

He only grinned, a bubble of blood on his lip. "Don't worry…" She looked at him, *masochist?* She couldn't stop her smile as she bent down and licked the blood from his lip, her eyes turning black with the introduction of it, and her drive doubled, she now understood why vampyres always mixed sex with feeding…

She made a trail of kisses down from his lips to his neck and down his chest and stomach. She loosened his pants, happy at his reaction to her touch. He was working on driving her crazy with his hands, pulling her hair and removing her clothing, kissing each of her fingers. He sat up, and she was sitting facing him in his lap, unable to get to his pants now, she grumbled and he laughed. He kissed her neck and her shoulder, focusing on her collarbone, driving another moan out of her. She ran her fingers up his back and over the muscles on his arms.

"We shouldn't be doing this," she said, out of breath.

"I know…" he said, but there was no regret in his voice

"We can't do this," She said, panting, sweat beading on her skin even though it was so cold that she could see her own breath. He was kissing her hot skin, as he knelt over her.

"I want to show you how much I love you…" His breath was hot on her skin, and she blushed deeper. He drove her crazy, but she loved him and wanted to show him just how much. He loved her when she didn't deserve it, and he protected her from every evil, obvious and hidden.

"I love you, Gabriel," she whispered in his ear, and he let out a soft sound of happiness and invaded her body as she screamed out his name…

She stopped and pushed gently on him, moving him away from her. "You will break your vows to God for something like me? I'm damned, you know that and yet you keep giving in to me." She had sadness in her eyes, and he could feel her withdrawing from him again.

"You are not a thing, you are a woman. A beautiful, strong woman, who has been placed in a bad situation and has come out on top. If there were anyone that I would break my vows for, it would be you." He looked at her pointedly, as if saying, "look at what we are doing." She could hear the genuine honesty in his voice.

"Allow me to be strong for you, Samuel," she whispered, "Since you have been strong for me." She stood up and collected her clothes, not dressing but staring at him. "You are a very handsome man. It takes everything I have to not just ravage you, but you cannot see clearly. You have found what many men fall victim to. I will not allow it!" She turned and, holding her pants up and her shirt to her chest, started to the door, taking one last look and biting her lip. She was obviously very upset with her decision but holding strong to it anyway, she left him sitting half-naked on the cold stone floor.

"What just happened?" he whispered to himself. Then, as if a bell went off, he was struck by a realization: she had just saved him, in more than one way. "Thank you…" he whispered, not thinking she could hear then her voice traveled down the hall.

"Don't thank me, I'm still struggling with this 'not ravaging you' thing." He couldn't help but laugh. He got dressed and made his way to the front of the cathedral. He lit the candles that had gone out and knelt in from of them to pray. She followed him in. She sat in the front pew and just watched him. He felt her staring at him and looked over his shoulder to see that the hunger in her eyes hadn't subsided and she was biting her lower lip again, her legs crossed tightly. He chuckled to himself.

"I can always change my mind if you don't stop laughing at me," she said, her voice tense.

"I'm sorry, my lady, but it is not something I am used to." he responded, still smiling.

"What part of it? You've never made love, so I'm sure all of it is something you're not used to?" she said, pointing out the obvious.

"It is much simpler than that," he replied, his smile faltering. "I'm not used to someone being attracted to me. No one has ever looked at me with that look in their eyes." She blushed.

"Tsh." She turned away from him.

"Could you help me?" he asked.

"Huh?" she stupidly responded, mentally kicking herself.

He turned to face her. "Since I cannot have your strength and scare appeal, can you help me reach those out there that won't be moved by just my words?"

She was shocked by the sudden change of subject, but she recovered quickly.

"I'll help you by protecting you, but I'm not going to threaten anyone. If your words cannot reach them, then they are truly lost and you should just give up on them." She said, trying to be straightforward, but it came out sounding cold.

"I see." He said, discouraged.

She sat up, feeling his change in attitude. "I didn't mean to offend you, that's not what I meant. I just don't want to lie to you. Not anymore," she whispered the last, "I was so afraid of losing you."

He stood up and came to sit beside her, "I appreciate your honesty. I was just hoping for a different answer. I know it is wrong to punish those who turn from God, but I think He will overlook it if I help lead more of his children into his good graces."

"You're thought process is not wrong, but that is not how I imagine that he would want it done. He forgives everyone who asks for it, right? But you are someone that is supposed to lead by example. Don't you think you will lead them to do more wrong if you use me as a weapon; they'll think its ok if you do it."

"You're right." He sat silently for a moment. "What about you?" He asked.

"What about me?" she asked.

"You said earlier that you were damned," he said. "Will you allow me to save you?"

She laughed, "I don't think even you can save me."

He looked distraught, "You just said everyone is forgiven if they simply ask, then why don't you ask?"

"Because even God can't forgive someone who killed innocent children, their mothers, and anyone she could get her hands on because she has a demon that cannot be satisfied. Not to mention, how many more will I kill before someone kills me? I cannot be sustained without killing, the meal wears off almost instantly." She said the latter, disappointed. "So it's either them or me. Even if I choose to die, my demon won't allow it. It takes over, and the damage is much worse because it doesn't have a conscience. Well," she paused and looked at him, but not in the eyes, "I'm sure you saw the results of your little trip to the dark side of this town, the brothel you left me it. The bloodbath that I left behind was done by my demon because I was too weak to say 'no.'" she looked down at her hands that she held tightly in her lap. "It even killed the women and children that were held prisoner there. It didn't matter to the demon, all the demon saw were toys and food."

There was silence between them for a long while. She could tell he was thinking, trying to find a way around her words that were the truth more than anything else was. She thought he had given up and she was about to leave to go for a walk. It was night now, and she needed some fresh air. Even after seeing him so vulnerable and becoming stronger because of that vulnerability, she was still thinking about him sprawled out on the floor begging to taste her, and she was losing her restraint. She shook her head, trying to clear out her fantasies of him. She never thought another man would drive her wild the way Gabriel did. But, this feeling was different than it was before, this was more primal and lacked the love that she shared with Gabriel. Her heart started hurting thinking about it and she got up to make her way to the door.

"I'm heading out for some air." She said.

"Wait, Please let me help you." He begged.

"Did I bump your head on the floor earlier or are you just that stubborn? It can't be done." She said, half joking.

"If you don't want it then it can't. But if you let me help you, we," made a circle between the two of them with his finger, "can."

"Why is this so important to you, priest?" She was starting to lose patience.

"I don't want you to go to hell." He said, very straightforward.

"When I do, I'll make Satan work hard to punish me. He'll have his work cut out." She grinned.

"It's not a joke, Rosina." He said, with a scowl, stopping her laughter.

"Woah, Okay." She put her hands up as if blocking his words, "But can you please just listen to me? If there is a hell, I'm already going there just because of what I am, I cannot live without hurting people. So, please don't waste your energy on me."

"You're being selfish again." He said, and she could have swore she heard a little pout in his voice.

"Huh??" she asked, dumbfounded.

"You won't let me help you. You won't allow God in! It is as if you *want* to be miserable. You want to be punished every day because you did something wrong once. You deserve better than that!" "*He loves God more than me*" echoed in her mind.

"You're a fool, Priest." She said again, but more gentle this time, "I caused my family so much pain, got them excommunicated, lied to them. I ran away from home, betrayed the man I loved, and befriended a monster. I knew what he was and still didn't run away. I was a stupid girl, and I need to pay for what I've done! And that is all before I became this," she motioned to herself, "This beast that kills innocents for fun. This living hell is what I deserve!"

"No! You're an angel that needs to go to heaven." She was shocked at being called an angel. "You need God's grace and his embrace. I'll help you find the path." He said desperately.

"STOP IT! I can't take it anymore! You're a constant reminder that I'm no good! I'm leaving!" She ran to the door and slammed it against the wall when she yanked it open.

That fool! He has no idea! Trying to praise me, make me forget what I really am! Trying to teach me, to get me to find "the path" again. THERE IS NO PATH! No path to the good side in the sun. There is only darkness and evil, and I relish in it! She stomped through the village, not seeing or hearing things past her rage. After all the time they had spent together, he thought he could change her, though she needed guidance, and, even though he may be right, she did not want it. She had found a delicate balance between her and her demon, and he wasn't going to step in and screw it all up again, causing her to fall back into the darkness when it took over her.

"Right now it sounds pretty good, though doesn't it," it piped in amongst her jumbled, angry thoughts. *"I could show you the 'path' that is suited for those like us, the way of the vampyre, the way of a demon."* She stopped dead in the middle of the street, surprised, but not by what the demon had said but that she actually agreed with it. It would be nice to just let loose the demon and show the priest exactly what she was, allow the anger to overcome her and relieve all this built up tension. *It is completely ridiculous that I even care what he thinks. I should have just killed him when I got here, and I wouldn't have had to deal with any of this. All these emotions and having to walk a wire, so I don't upset him.*

She paused. "That's not it," she whispered out loud.

She shook her head violently and furrowed her brows as if trying to grasp the concept. Why had she tried so hard to please him? *No…* She was a vampyre! She didn't need anyone's approval. She had only one person to please, and that was herself, *no…* That was only because she couldn't kill herself to stop from annoying herself, *like I'm doing now…*

She let out a growl of frustration, "That's not it! He was just trying to help me."

"He wants to use you to do his work, like you're a puppet."

"No… That isn't be true… is it?" she was starting to doubt herself.

"Yes, it is." The demon confirmed.

There was a loud crashing that drew her attention to a close by the alley. It was followed by three men coming out of the mouth of it. All three were looking at her with a hunger she understood all too well, though she thirsted for Samuel's touch and Samuel's blood. They thirsted for control and they were going to try to make her the tool to achieve it. A tall, slightly built man with long hair and a dirty cap lead them and the two shorter, scrawnier men following him. One with red hair and one bald, but with a scraggly beard. The two shorter men were slouching, and each had a hand under the front of their coat, holding something; she presumed it was some sort of a weapon, most likely a knife. The leader walked tall and straight towards her, not hiding his intentions. He walked to her and circled her dragging a light hand across her back and up her neck to her cheek as he came back around her front.

He stopped in front of her as the two others stood behind her, snickering, or what passed for snickering, at her. The leader didn't say anything, but put his other hand on her other cheek and forced her to tilt her head towards his face. He bent down to kiss her, and an evil laugh erupted from her. She was emotional, and now she was getting angry that these men were trying to toy with her. They were going to be one of the mistakes she was telling the priest that she couldn't be forgiven for.

Her vision started to get dark around the edges, her eyes going black. He stopped as she pulled out of his grasp and bent her head down. She looked up at him through her lashes. She was smiling at him and her fangs were in full view. *Now we hunt, together!* She thought, and the demon let out a laugh that matched hers.

"Yes, now we hunt together." She repeated out loud. She heard the leader make a noise of confusion before she gave in to the demon. This time instead of her blacking out, her vision cleared and she could feel the familiar burning of her skin start. All of her previous heightened senses and strengths were doubled.

Drunk with power, she threw her head back and laughed. The two short men had backed away from her, but at the leader demanded they attack her. They started towards her and seeing them do this she jumped from her place in the middle of the street to the closest building. The two men that had tried to circle around her, ran into each other at her absence and tumbled to the ground, but the tall one stopped and whirled around to find her once again back on the ground and no more than an inch from his face. Before he tried to back away, she grabbed him by the throat and pulled him to her, kissing him with a furiousness that she never felt before.

When she pulled him from her, she said, "You couldn't have made this easier for me. Almost as if the rabbit lay down in front of the coyote. At least make it a little fun for me. I do so love a challenge." She laughed again and shoved him away. He stumbled backward and fell to the ground. The bald man recovered and once again made an attempt to catch her. She turned to him and grabbed his outstretched arm, twisting it around until it was behind him and she heard it crack as it was dislocated. "Run, little bunny." This time her laugh was almost a screech. She shoved him away as well. As he whimpered from the pain in his shoulder, he ran as fast as he could to get away from her. "I'll give you a head start, 1…2…3…" She started counting and the other two men ran in two different directions. "Now that is more like it."

She ran after the first, the red-headed one, who had gone back down the alley they had come from. If she couldn't see him, she could have followed all the noise he was making, knocking things over trying to get away from her. "Aw, you poor little, blind rat. Lost in the dark are we?" She grabbed his flailing arm and threw him against the wall, hearing his head hit the wall with a loud thump. He started to droop when she caught him and stood him up again. "Oh no, you don't get off that easily." She sank her teeth into his neck with a burning anger. She ripped instead of piercing his neck. Hot blood came bubbling out of his flesh, and she lapped it up, getting it all over the front of herself , staining the priest's precious robe. She didn't finish him, but the wound would, and she didn't want the hunt to be over yet.

She left the alley in pursuit of the bald man. He was going slowly because of his hurt arm, perhaps she had broken it? She grabbed him by the back of the neck and threw him through the window of a close-by house. He plummeted through the window and into the living room of the house. The glass from the window shattered and scattered all over the floor. The man and woman of the house jumped up in surprised. The woman grabbed her small son and pulled him to her as Rosina stepped on the window frame and in through a missing window.

"I'm sorry for the mess," she said, kindly to the couple. "I'll pay you for the window, or actually," she paused and looked down at the bald man, bleeding from the cut he got going through the glass, "*he* will." She picked up the bald man by the shoulders and stood him up. She bit him and drained him almost to death as the family watched in horror. She reached in his coat and pulled out a purse of money; she tossed it to the homeowner as the bald man fell to the floor.

She looked at the little boy, "This is what happens when you don't respect women. Don't you forget it or I'll find you." She winked at him, and turned to leave. She shouted over her shoulder as she stepped back through the window, "Listen to your mother and father, boy!"

She walked back into the street, stripping off the bloody robe, wiping her mouth with it, and discarding it in the dirt, leaving her wearing her sleeveless tunic. "Now for the real fun," she said to herself with a half-smile. She stood in the street for a moment, allowing the wind to bring her the scent of the tall man. It took her a little by surprise when she found that he was standing on the edge of the street, just out of the light. She turned towards him and stood, waiting, but when he didn't emerge she yelled to him, "Come out, come out, where ever you are!"

She heard it before she saw it, a swoosh of something thin and smooth passing quickly through the air. She put her hand up in time to catch the small knife he had thrown. She had just a second to look at it before two more came at her. She jumped towards him, gripped him by the front of his coat, and threw him out into the street. He fell, but rolled over quickly, pulling out a cross and putting it up in front of him, "I've heard of demons like you, vampyre," he spat.

"No, I don't think you have," she said snidely, "I'm one of a kind." She didn't know just how right she was. He started praying in Latin. She walked towards him and stopped a few feet away from where he knelt.

"You know, that's funny. Oh—," she put her hand to her chest as if her heart was in pain, "please stop," she croaked, falling to her knees, "it's so painful." She doubled over on herself. The man stood, still praying, and daring to step closer to her. He stopped quickly when he heard her laughing. She looked up, grabbed his wrist, and stood up so quickly he couldn't follow her. She ripped the cross from his hands and held it in her free hand. "Where do you think I have be living in this rotten town?" She motioned to her robe with the cross, "and I was wearing a priest robe." She gave him a look of pity, as if he was so stupid it actually hurt her. "Do you think I just wore it for a gander? I was LIVING in the cathedral. So trust me when I say, if that place didn't cause me to burst into flames, this pathetic piece of wood isn't going to either." She crushed the cross and let the splinters fall to the ground. She could see the growing fear in his eyes, *"good, let him fear us, as all of them should."*

"You are going to die now, and you will never harm another person. You will appease my burning appetite and fuel my rage!" She sank her teeth into his sweating flesh and pulled his blood from him in large draws. His life faded away and flowed into her, igniting the demon's fire. She could feel it all over her, engulfing her and she reveled in it. She dropped the man and indulged in the beauty the man's death had bestowed on her. Her skin felt like it was on fire and her heart pounded with all the blood she had consumed. She looked down to see the magnificent scrolls all over her body glowing bright, and she smiled and closed her eyes. Her euphoria was short-lived, though, because she heard the familiar beat of the priest's heart. She opened her eyes and was looking straight at him. He was standing several yards away from her. The horror apparent on his face, his mouth open and his eyes wide with fear and something else. Shame, she recognized after a moment, she had never seen it on his beautiful face, she was immediately regretting her actions.

"I told you, Priest. You can't save me! Do you see what I am? You think you can save this?" She motioned to the dead body and her bloodied robe. "Even you can't fix this" Her shouting was starting to cause people to look out their windows, those that weren't already looking. Her high was starting to wear off, and she was starting to feel strange. She thought it was because she had never joined with her demon before, but she was starting to feel week. Her vision was starting to feel hazy, and her legs were trembling, losing strength. She fell to the ground, her limbs going numb. She heard Samuel gasp and start running towards her.

He knelt down by her, "Rosina, what's wrong?"

"I do—don't know," she could barely speak.

"Haha, I never thought you would fall for that, but when I saw how angry you were, I knew you would be easy prey. If there is anything I know about a vampyre it is that when they are angry they don't think before they hunt." She recognized that deep voice.

"You!" Samuel said, "What are you doing here?"

"To kill your little vampyre girlfriend, of course. I have to finish what I started."

"No…" Rosina was gasping for breath.

"What did you do to her?" The old hunter's footsteps stopped close to where she lay on the ground.

"Just a little concoction I've been working on. I put it into the beer of each of the taverns, assuring it would get into your system no matter who you fed from. It won't keep ahold of her for very long, but I only need a moment." He pulled out his pistol and pointed it at her heart.

Samuel threw himself across her, "You'll have to kill me to get to her."

"Tsk tks, priest. I'll give you a chance to change your mind. Move, and I won't kill you, but if you don't then that's fine. My orders were to kill the little bitch no matter what, and if that means casualties outside her, then I have the 'go ahead.' But, to be honest, I don't want to kill a man of God. You *are* still a man of God, right? She didn't corrupt you?" Samuel just glared at him.

"Hmm." Rosina was starting to gain feeling back in her body, she sat up, but she was still weak.

"Ros-"

Seeing that he had wasted his opportunity to kill her while she was paralyzed, the old hunter yelled, "No! You've ruined it priest!" He took aim at Samuel's head, but Rosina pushed him down just in time and took the bullet in her arm. She grunted with pain. "Ah, I see. You are still sluggish, this could still work." He chuckled and took aim at her again. "Before I kill you, I think you should know that you are the reason that Johnathan was removed from the Order. He has no home and no family thanks to you. You played your devilish tricks on him, and he was deemed unfit to be a crusader against evil."

"But they let you stay?!" Samuel yelled out before he could stop himself.

"Yes, because I was betrayed," the hunter answered. "They saw it fit to give me this opportunity to prove that I am not also brainwashed by you."

"Because of me…" she whispered.

"Yes, because of you he has nothing. He wanders around like a bum, drinking and starting fights with anyone that he can. Pathetic." He spat on the ground to express his feelings on the man. Sadness spread through her, and it cleared the rest of the poison out of her body. She lept up from the ground and was on the old hunter before he could even comprehend what was going on. She knocked him down on his back and sat down hard on his chest.

"No, your group, and those like them, are the reason, so close-minded. I'm a vampyre, I *should* be hunted. But, if something good happens to someone and they take a new path to something better then they should not be punished! They should be celebrated!" He tried to push her away but she didn't budge, anger had flared in her and she was not allowing him to walk away from this again. "I thought you had honor. I let you live because I thought you were innocent," she said, a sadness in her voice and a tear in her eye. "But it appears that, not for the first time, I was wrong." She put her hand on either side of his head, "go in peace, 'man of God.'" She said as she twisted his neck and heard it snap. He fell limp. The people around gasped. She looked up at them and they dispersed, afraid of what she would do to them.

She stood up, not facing the priest, ashamed. "I have to save him."

"Yes." He said, as if expecting it. "I'll come with you," he said without thinking.

"No, you have to stay and clean up my mess," she said quietly, guilty, "I cannot."

"Unless you plan to kill all of the men in that Order, you're going to need a trick up your sleeve to win them over and have them come to the conclusion that their punishment was too rash. They must know that you are not a threat and that Johnathan made the right decision in not killing you." He talked as if he had been thinking this over for a long time even though they just got the new. "I think I'm that trick, I am a man of God just the same as them. If they see that you live with me and help with my mission here, they may look fondly upon you."

She wanted to protest. This was happening because she existed, *she* needed to correct what that had caused. However, she really didn't have any idea how she was going to help Johnathan. She could tell that Samuel did, he was a negotiator for God, after all, he convinced men to come back to the church. He may have a better handle on this than she.

"Clearly you've put more thought into this in the last few seconds than I have," she paused, not wanting to willingly drag him into this. But, somehow she had started to care about the hunter. Seeing his love for his wife and child and the pain he had gone through shot straight to her heart. She felt she had to do anything to give him back the family he had now, he needed the Order. "Fine, but you had better keep up. We should leave as soon as possible." He nodded.

CHAPTER NINE: PLEASURE WILL FADE WITH SADNESS

The darkness hides many things
Hope, Love, Happiness.
Many things hide from the darkness,
Smiles, Laughter, Dreams.
The darkness is created by many things,
Hunger, Lust, Desire.
Many Things flourish in the Darkness,
Evil, Hatred, Pain.
How do you illuminate the Darkness?
Can one person light up all the hidden secrets?

They returned to the cathedral and packed for the trip, Samuel did some digging in his many books and found that the Order was based just outside Rome. They discussed what their plan was upon arriving, he suggested that they try to reason with them. She agreed as long as, if they didn't change their mind, she got to kill them.

"I don't like this side of you." He said. After objecting, saying it would defeat the whole purpose of their mission, he finally gave in to her stubbornness.

She just shrugged her shoulders.

They prepared a covered wagon with a horse so they could split shifts driving; she would sleep during the day and him during the night, to make better time. She was restless during the next day, she woke several times and, after what seemed like days, night was finally upon them.

"Are you sure you want to come?" she asked him from the front door. He walked up and face her full on.

"This is not a burden you should carry alone," he said, as if he hadn't witnessed her evil.

"Even after you saw what I did to those men yesterday, you still see me as delicate, like I'm a lost puppy," she replied.

"No, I think of you as damaged," he corrected, and she was taken aback. "You need help keeping it together. Think of me as your twine that will keep all your emotions contained." She glared at him, and he stepped up to her and put his hand behind her head and pulled her into a kiss. When he pulled away, he laughed and walked out the door.

"Stop doing that! You should be repulsed by me!" She yelled out after him. He just laughed. "Gah!!" she closed the door behind her and followed him to the wagon. They made their way out of town, quietly riding into the darkness. "Thank you," she whispered.

"Mhmm."

•   •   •   •   •

The further they journeyed from the little village they had made their home, however temporary, the more darkness the priest saw, not just in the night, but in the people they came in contact with. No one had a generous heart, they all were full of greed and a hunger for more. They would not help even a man of God without a price. He went hungry on those nights, even though he had money to give he was ashamed of these people and pitied them. He did not want to add to their greed or be in their presence while they destroyed themselves. Rosina loved those times as much as he hated them. She was always filled after a visit with one of those people. She came back to the wagon with glowing eyes and blushing skin, filled with fresh, warm blood. He shuddered at the thought. How had he missed this? Had she really been trying that hard to hide her demon self and now she was showing off? Or was he really that dense? She had caught him looking at her several times while she was like this. She smiled but then quickly hid her face from him. He became more curious about her even as he wanted to distance himself from such a creature. Did he really love her that much that he was willing to stay with her, even knowing that she was a killer? No, it was an intellectual love, he had stumbled upon a treasure that no one had ever discovered, and he wanted to be the first to study it. He wrote in his journal during the long periods of time he had alone while she slept, he took in the bright sun while she hid in the shadows.

He hid his notes from her, afraid of what she might do to them. He could picture her yelling at him, 'What right do you have?' and tearing them up. 'I don't want people to know about me…' she would hide her embarrassment behind her anger or she would be eager to share all with him, finally able to, and he didn't really want that either.

They had been traveling over a week without much incident. She was keeping to herself while they were both awake, except the occasional excited outburst: "Did you see that building! What amazing structural design!" "Those flowers are so beautiful, I wish I could see them during the daylight!" It seems there was still many things he had to learn about her. He smiled to himself during these times, and she would chastise him, "What are you laughing at?" he just kept smiling, *I love to see you smile, even if for just a moment. I love to see that you aren't worrying or sad. I wish I could tell you that it is alright to be happy. Let me take care of you.* He mentally shook himself because he knew that would never happen. Even if she would allow it, God was the one that had to take care of her, not him.

They were getting closer to their destination; the open fields and forests were turning into vineyards and the distance between villages became shorter, the buildings growing in number. They were on the outskirts of one of the larger towns when she decided it was time for a more exciting meal than what she had been getting.

"I'm heading into this tavern, are you okay to stay here?" she asked as she hopped down from the wooden seat.

He knew she didn't want him to accompany her, but he said, "I think I'll join you, I could use a hot meal." She stared at him for a moment then nodded once and went inside. He tied up the horses and made his way in behind her. The tavern was full of howling drunk men and promiscuous women with very little clothing on. He felt dirty just stepping into such a place, but he was more concerned about Rosina. He wanted to make sure she didn't do anything that she couldn't take back, something that would hurt her against the Order. Not that he could really stop her if she went into a rage, but he could help prevent someone provoking her.

"Look who stumbled upon our little slice of heaven." He turned to see a tall, red-headed, busty woman looking at him but talking to another, slightly shorter, blonde.

"Oh? Are you lost, priest? Or did you finally realized that we are the true gifts from God?" she asked, smiling sweetly.

He looked at them, nothing but kindness on his face and in his voice, "My dear, you truly are gifts from God, but I am here merely to watch over one of my flock."

"Aw~ are you sure? We can take care of him as well, so you don't have to worry." The redhead said.

"Or is it a her? We can do that too," she roguishly grinned at him.

"That is quite generous of you, but I will have to decline." He smiled back at them, and they finally gave up and walked away, muttering that he wanted his 'flock' member all to himself, "probably his lover…" "Man of God, more like a man of men…"

"I try to be kind and look what it gets me…" he mumbled to himself.

"Samuel!" he heard Rosina's voice over the crowd and slowly made is way over to the furthest corner where she sat at a table just watching the people at the bar. He sat down and was shortly followed by a young girl in an apron. She had her hair up in a bun and was covered with flour and what smelled like boiled potatoes. She placed a plate of steaming pasta and sauce in front of him and a mug of water beside it. He thanked the girl but looked at the food in amazement.

"You said you wanted a hot meal. I ordered you their best pasta," she said to his confusion.

"Oh," he was overcome with happiness for some reason, and he couldn't help but smile.

"Its just food, no need to get all emotional," she said, but grinned back at him.

"It's not that. I came in here afraid of what you had in mind. But, now I see you just sitting here, almost enjoying the atmosphere." He looked at her, a new idea of her creeping into his mind.

"Don't get ahead of yourself. I'm here to eat, too." He stopped mid-bite and stared at her over his pasta. "How do you think I feed? I just barge in and grab someone and drain them right there?" He choked a little on his food in surprise. She wasn't looking at him. "That's not how it works. Don't you know the hunt is the best part?" she turned and look at him this time, a glint in her eye when she winked at him, then she turned back towards the bar. "I have to find the perfect one and then get them to follow me to a secluded place and then –"

"Okay! I don't want to hear the details. But I appreciate you shattering my image of you. She smiled a wide, toothy smile at him but, when she realized that he was really upset, she reached across the table and laid her hand on his. He repressed the urge to pull his hand away.

"I'm sorry, I shouldn't have been so blunt, but I don't want you to have any illusions about what I am. I'm not happy about this behavior, but I have no choice, there is no other way. And I don't want you to have any surprises when we get there, they are going to try to poison you against me."

"I have no illusions about what you are and what you can do. I just don't want to think about it." He paused to look at her, "I appreciate you're honesty, though, even if I did have to wait for it."

She heard the bite in his voice, and it struck her hard. "I'm sorry, but you understand why I did it, right? Would you have ever let me into your cathedral if you had known?" He didn't answer right away. "That's what I thought." She turned away from him again.

He could feel her pain. "You have not given me time to answer." She gave him a glare from the orner of her eye, without turning her head. "I've never been faced with such a situation. I would not have known how to handle it. From all the legends, I would be a fool to just trust a vampyre without a second thought. I got lucky with you, but most of your kind don't act like you. I would have been dead as soon as they stepped through my door. You cannot condemn me for thinking this way."

"Hmmm." Was all she said because she was focused on something else he followed her gaze to a man just entering the tavern.

He slammed the door against the wall on his way in. He was angry, but the smell of blood and death was what drew her attention. His hands were red with it, and he didn't even bother to wipe them off when he sat down at the bar and ordered food as if it was nothing. The barkeep warily watched him but took his order and said nothing. He was hoping this time the other man would have won. He didn't want such an evil man in his tavern, scaring off reputable customers, but he could never make a move to remove him. His family would be out in the street before his corpse was cold.

She watched him, a hunger stirring in her; she felt her demon's attention on him as well, "*He smells tasty. Let's have a bite, shall we?*"

I think we shall, but let's have a little fun first, she thought. She smiled as she stood up and made her way to the bar, leaving the priest behind without a second thought. When she finally made it through all the groping, disgusting men, her anger was high, and her eyes were black. She leaned against the old wooden bar and tried to collect herself. She wasn't allowed to for long when she felt cold liquid hit the back of her head and soak her hair and clothes on its way down. She turned around ready to give some drunk idiot a piece of her mind only to turn to a scene she didn't expect. The drunk man was being held by the throat, his feet barely on the floor, and a knife very close to piercing through this flesh and into his stomach. The man holding that knife was the very man she was hunting. She couldn't help but smile, *"This IS going to be fun."* her demon howled with laughter. Before she could even think about her next move, the situation changed, again.

Samuel had placed himself between the two men. He could see the escalation of the situation and Rosina getting herself into trouble. She had a look of shock on her face as she peered at him under the other man's arm. She could only see the back of his head, but she could hear him trying to talk down the angry man. She had a moment of pause before the bloody-handed man released the drunk man and threw Samuel over the bar. He crashed into the many bottles of liquor, shattering most of them. He didn't reappear for several minutes, but by then Rosina's emotions had gone from concern to rage. She took his place in front of the man. She didn't say anything just removed her cloak and robe, folding it and placed it gently on the bar. Her skin was glowing, and her eyes were black, and she didn't try to hide it.

The man was surprised but recovered quickly, "What are you looking at, little girl?"

She felt her rage flow through her body. She had her head down, and her face covered by her hair, "mine…" she whispered. She didn't know what had come over her, but she felt a different kind of anger in her. *Samuel.*

"What did you say?!" he asked angrily. He leaned down so he was at eye level with her and his nose almost touched hers. "Do you know what I do to little girls that disrespect me?" When she didn't answer, he grew angrier. He grabbed her head with his two dirty hands and made her look at him, undeterred by her black eyes, "I take them to a filthy bed because they are nothing but whores, then I take from them all their innocence. They scream and try to fight back but they can't," he said with a smile. "I take whatever I want from them," she watched his face as he told her. He was worse than she thought. Flashes of her experience as a weak girl flooded her senses; she could even smell the men that had taken from her what was not theirs. This man had the same smell, but it was much stronger. She also notices that his face was getting red not from rage, but arousal. She looked down and saw that he was growing hard at the thought of forcing himself on a helpless girl, "and when they finally give up, when their very soul breaks, I take the only thing they have left. I twist their scrawny necks and leave them, naked, in the streets for everyone to see what garbage they are!" He had excitement in his voice that pushed her over the edge.

She reached down and grabbed him in his instrument of destruction. He had a look of shock on his face, but he smiled, "Do you like that? You are as sick as—"

"Do you feel like a man, a tough guy? Being so strong, overpowering so many people?" As she talked, she tightened her grip, and he became more concerned. She pulled him closer to her with her other hand, pulling him by the back of his head, easily overpowering him. "You're nothing," she whispered in his ear, "Nothing." He was starting to panic.

"How-?"

"You will die tonight, but I'm not going to do it quickly. I'm going to take everything you have, and when your soul breaks, I'll leave you in the street, so everyone will know what garbage you are!" She removed her hand from his lower region and ripped off his pants for the whole tavern to watch. By this point, they had formed a circle around the commotion, careful not to get too close, but close enough to hear what was being said. He brought his fist up to hit her, but she was too quick, and she slammed him against the bar, nearly breaking it in two. "No, not yet, you don't get to die yet." She whispered to him again. She held him there with her hands, and she stepped up on the bar and dragged him up on it and stood over his half-naked body. She ripped off the rest of his clothes and straddled his stomach. She leaned down to his ear, he flinched. "Does this make you excited?" she reached down and grabbed him again, "Tsk, that's too bad, and here I thought you were a real monster," she smiled and showed her fangs, "like me." She released him and bit down into the skin on his chest, just enough to hurt and draw just a small amount of blood. She did this the whole way down his chest and stomach then she bit his arms, taking her time at his wrists and fingers, making sure she gave him the most pain in those evil fingers that had caused so much. It was much harder to keep his blood out of her mouth and it mixed with the blood of the man he had killed, the blood that was still on his skin. Her hunger was growing. *Not yet* she told herself, *he needs to suffer.*

She could hear people murmuring, "Is this some sort of erotic show?"

"How is she overpowering him?"

"He's allowing it."

She had completely blocked out all the other people in the tavern and how they could see her now. She started to have a fear build up in her, she had never put on a show, now they will know what she is and hunt her…

He moved to tried to get her off him, and that brought her back, *I don't care!* She bent down and bit into his, now deflated manhood, he jerked at the sudden pain and his body reacted to it. She bit down as hard as she could, almost biting it off completely. He yelled out in pain. Then the blood began to flow, she licked up some of it but also sealed the wound with her saliva, so he couldn't die, yet. She stood up and kicked him in the head. He put up his arms to block her, but she kicked him hard enough he hit himself and his arms went weak, not broken, but severely bruised.

She looked down and could see the fear in his eyes. She knelt down again to get close to him, "Is this what it felt like for those girls?" She stood up again, and he took advantage of it and swung his legs to the side knocking her off the bar. She landed in front of it, the crowd stepped back quickly. He dismounted the bar and grabbed her hair, forcing her up. She clawed at his hand, but he ignored it. He slammed her against the wall and ripped her shirt, leaving her exposed to everyone in the tavern.

"No, this is," he held her hands above her head with one of his giant hands while the other ventured down to her pants. He fumbled to get his hands in then as she recovered from the pain that shot through her back. She rammed a knee up between his legs, hitting his already injured area. He gasped and loosened his grip just enough for her to slip her hands out from his grasp. She grabbed his shoulders and pulled herself up on top of him, wrapping her legs around his waist. She could feel his warmth, and it only made her sick. She pulled his hair back, yanking his head with it, exposing his neck. She plunged her fangs into his flesh, and his blood came flooding forth. It was hot and thick. She pulled it from him in great gulps.

"We are both monsters," he whispered, as he gasped for breath, but he was no longer fighting against her. His will had been broken. "At least I was taken down by such a beautiful woman… who would have ever thought that would… have… happened…" he started walking towards the back door, carrying her with her, "I'll give you this parting gift, let them think you and I are lovers and they won't hurt you…" She stopped drinking and looked at him, he had a tear in his eye, "We… can't help… what… we are… can we?" He made it out the door and slumped against the wall. He turned his head to give her better access, "Please…" She paused for a moment, rethinking everything that had just happened, but then continued, draining him until he had nothing left to give. She got up and looked down at him. He was slumped against the wall, in a dirty alley, he deserved nothing more, but she felt a twinge in her heart, so she went back inside and grabbed his clothes. Everyone was staring at her, her lips had blood on them, and her skin was red from the fresh meal and the fight.

"Who would have thought that a girl like you would make a lover out of that man…"

"You really are a match for him. Where were you when he was ravaging the village…"

She ignored the people in the tavern as she made her way back out to the alley. She tried to redress him but in the end, only managed to put his pants and shirt halfway on and laid his coat over the rest of him. She looked at him and wondered what he had said to her…they couldn't help what they were. She was a vampyre and killing was infused to her every cell, she couldn't live without it, but he was simply a man who didn't want to control himself

She picked up a bottle and threw it at him, "You bastard! You were just selfish! I can't stop myself, but you could have! Don't compare yourself to me! My hell is worse!" She picked up another bottle and threw it at him again and again and again, tears were falling from her eyes. "I can't stop being this way. You had a choice, and you made the wrong one!"

"Rose?" she heard her brother and Gabriel and Samuel all speaking to her, calling to her, all she had to or will have to abandon someday. She, a monster, doesn't deserve their company, their kindness, their love… "Augh!" she screamed into the night sky, "Why?!" she threw her fist at the wall, hitting it over and over, her hands becoming bloody…

"Rose!" She heard it again.

"Go Away!" She screamed back at it.

"No." She felt arms go around her. He stopped her hands and trying to calm her, but her tears didn't stop, they would never stop. She was turned around and pulled into a warm embrace, she cried into his coat, whaling.

"Let it out. All that pain, let it out." She cried harder, until she couldn't breathe and then she slipped into the darkness of exhaustion.

•   •   •   •

They traveled in silence for several days. Samuel couldn't bring himself to talk to her about what had happened; he didn't have the words to make this better. She had looked in a mirror when she looked at that man, she had seen a monster. She said she knew she was a monster, but she was never faced with the reality of it, never seen what others see. She was going to have to face this alone, as much as he wanted to help her, he couldn't. She was in a dark place, and it showed, she didn't feed, she didn't speak; she didn't even bother to cover herself after having her shirt torn. He had to wash and dress her after the tavern, while she sat with a blank stare on her face. She didn't try to stop him, just allowed him to do so. They were getting close to their destination, and he was hoping she could pull herself together. This was her quest, and she needed to stand up for herself and for Johnathan, if she had any chance of helping him.

"We should be there within two days, have you thought about what you are going to say?" He asked. Silence. "I was thinking you should just be your usual self, your personality should win them over pretty quickly." She mumbled something. "What? I couldn't hear you."

"I'm a vampyre…" she murmured.

"Yes, I know. That's why I think we should focus on who you are and not what you are." He said.

"I kill people," she murmured.

"I know that as well, but only to feed and you choose very carefully who you… eat." He tried to reassure her.

"Vampyre…"

"Not by choice," he was still talking calmly.

"Stop it! I'm a monster! I don't deserve to be defending someone that is fighting the world's evil, which includes me! He would have been better off if he hadn't met me. You'd be better off if you hadn't met me… Gabriel, Marcus, mama, pa…"

"If he hadn't met you, his life would still be that of a narrow path following orders from people who don't have the right to give them because they are closed minded. They never thought that your kind could be gentle and giving and caring. They are the ones that forced your kind to be evil. They had to defend themselves against the words and weapons of man!"

"Forced… right…" she said sarcastically.

He ignored her and kept going, "If Gabriel and Marcus and your family hadn't known you, they wouldn't have known the kindness that rises above all other kindness. You gave your all to protect them and to give back to them all they gave you." He paused to take a breath. She was looking at him in wonder. "If I had never met you, I would never have known love. You fill me with so much of it I feel like I'm going to burst. You fill my home with joy and life. I never thought I would ever see that in that shell again, but you brought it back. You gave me a new flame for life and a vigor I had lost. I was in despair, and you gave me hope." He turned to her and grabbed her, shaking her, "Don't you understand? You are so beautiful, if you weren't here they sun wouldn't be as bright, the flowers not as colorful, and our hearts would be empty!" He pulled her to him and kissed her with such a force it knocked the breath out of her. He pulled away from her, his face flush, "Don't you see what you do to me?" He let her go and turned away from her. She still didn't say anything, and he fell silent.

Day came, and she slept, he ran over in his head what he had said to her and wanted to take it back. He felt like a fool, nothing he said made her feel better, in fact, it probably made her feel worse.

CHAPTER TEN: SADNESS CAN SAVE

Crawling, scratching, biting,
Fear overwhelms and suffocates.
Tears fall like fire from her burning eyes,
Ice forms in her heart,
A wall of stone surrounds her love.
She watches as he walks into the neverending.
She is chained by her fear,
Everything is being consumed and her light is going out.
She screams, but no noise is released,
It wells up inside her and she burns with it.
Nothing will quench its heat.

They reached the outskirts of Rome shortly before sundown the next night. As they approached the old city he was struck by awe, he had heard of its beauty and magnificence, but nothing could compare to the view he now looked upon. The buildings were built with careful calculations, stones used to form the very hills around them. Tall and filled with power centuries old. He looked up at them, their colossal columns made to stand for thousands of years, holding up intricate sculptures that were slowly starting to lose the long battle against the wind but still as beautiful, if not more so, than they were the day they were carved. He made his way up the cobblestone road towards many buildings that lined the outskirts. He found an inn, tall like the other buildings, but it was newer and all white. The building was smaller than the outside led on, but it was well kept. It only had six rooms, but each room had a balcony and large French doors. The beds were immaculate, white fluffy linens with large white pillows. The floor was polished wood, and the high ceilings were painted with golden scrolls and swirls that only made the clean white that much brighter. He put their bags in the room before stabling the horses. When he came back to the wagon, she was awake and staring out into the setting sun. Her face was red and it took him a moment to realize she was burning. He quickly removed his coat and placed it over her.

"What are you doing? You're burning," he said slightly irritated at her recklessness.

"Hm." She made the noise, not caring what the sun did to her.

He shook his head, "We are close, I can try to set up a meeting with them tomorrow, but I'm not certain on where their headquarters are."

"I'll find them." She said jumped out of the wagon. He wanted to go after her, but he didn't want to drive her away. He decided to wait for her, however long it took. *Love, huh?*

She tried to stay in the shadows, avoiding the sunlight. She was about to head into the adjacent building when she heard a familiar voice, "NO! 'm nauh ready 'oo leabe!"

"Sir, you've had enough and are causing a disturbance. The guests have requested you to be removed." There was some rustling and then a slamming door. She crept around the building, staying in the shadows, and saw Johnathan sitting on the ground wiping a bloody nose on his sleeve. Her thought of "That was easy," evaporated as she looked at him. The smell of alcohol hit her, and it was so strong her eyes started to water, she covered her nose with her hand and made her way over to him. As she got closer she saw how bad he looked, his clothes were all torn and dirty, his hair a mess, and it seemed and smelled as if he hadn't bathed in well over a week. She walked deliberately loudly when she approached and when he looked up at the sound of her footsteps, she slapped him. The crack of her hand on his cheek was loud in the silence and he stared at her in shock with his dirty hand on his cheek. His eyes were bloodshot and half closed, he was so drunk he couldn't even look at her properly, she had the urge to slap him again, but held back.

"You rat!" she yelled at him. "You are not allowed to be a drunk idiot. You are not allowed to fall apart!" He just stared at her, eyes half closed, as if she were a dream. She reached down and grabbed the front of his jacket, pulling him up.

"Wha—" escaped his mouth before she shook him, his head bobbing back and forth like a rag doll, her anger was growing and yet a deep pain was nesting into her heart, a sadness that she couldn't handle, this is what her parents must have felt when she "fell ill" or what Gabriel felt when she didn't show up to run away with him… She felt her skin start to tingle, burning with the sun and now her markings.

"Roshe?" He slurred, she released him, and he swayed then fell back to the ground.

"Yes, you fool!" She sighed with irritation and relief. "What the hell are you doing?"

He scoffed at her, "Wha doesh i' loo' 'ike?"

"Wasting my time." She turned, wanting to leave, and walked to the wall and leaned her forehead against the cold stone.

She heard a new set of footsteps and a man's voice. "There you are! You son of a bitch!" he sounded angry, and when she turned around she saw he was talking to Johnathan, he wasn't much better off then he but the new man clearly wasn't drunk. "You aren't getting away this time," He grabbed his shirt front and pulled his fist back to punch him.

"Hey!" Rosina yell at him, he hadn't noticed her, "I'm only going to say this once, leave him be, I'm not in the mood."

He spat in her direction but continued to look at Johnathan, "Oh ho! Having your whores talk for you now?" She could feel a twitch in her eye, and her skin grew hot, she let out a small growl.

"Wouldn't... do... that..." Johnathan stuttered between heavy breaths. "Vampyre," he pointed a slack arm at her.

The other man glanced at her then started to laugh, laughing so hard he let go a Johnathan and grabbed his stomach. She held her temper in as he mocked her. "She?" he looked at her, "Vampyre? Ha!" he walked over to her, standing a head over her, he bent down at the waist so he was at eye level with her. He looked at her, not hiding it as he scanned her from head to foot. With each second her anger grew. He reached his hand out and pat her on the head.

"What are you gonna do? Bite me?" he thought that was terribly funny as he walked away laughing, brushing her off as if she were a dog.

Her temper was getting the better of her, and she decided that he would make a good meal, *soothing to the soul.* "Don't ever," she said through grit teeth, and he stopped walking, "treat me like a dog." He turned with a smirk on his face and a snide remark in his mouth, both fumbled when he saw her black eyes and burning skin.

She looked at him, enjoying his faltering bravado, "Didn't your mother ever teach you how to treat a lady?" she gave him a closed mouth grin. "or that you shouldn't tease the monsters under your bed?" she gave him a full smile that held no joy, showing her long, sharp fangs. He went pale, fear flowing off him in waves and she drank it up. He let out a whimper and turned coat, running full speed away from her. She let out a laugh of excitement and her demon said, *"Let's hunt!"*

She leapt from her position up onto the roof of the closest building, the clay shingles cracking a little at her landing, she had to catch her balance, still not used to the ability to jump so far. After she recovered, she ran along that roof and jumped to the next, chasing after the man. *"This would have been better in the dark."* Her demon said about the slowly setting sun, she nodded in agreement.

"Any more fear, though, and he'd be dead of heart failure before we've had our fun." Her demon howled with laughter. She jumped off the room, landing right behind the man; startled, he stumbled as he stopped and turned to see what was behind him.

"This is my favorite part, right before my prey gives up," she leaned into him and whispered in his ear, "they always fight the most right before death," she heard his hard intake of breath and smiled. He was frozen in fear, and she straightened up and took a step, and he fell, as his feet tripped on nothing. She stood over him, looking down at him. "Who's the dog now?" She laughed as she yanked him up by the front of his shirt. She was about to feed when she heard a scraping noise. She looked behind her to see Johnathan slowly sliding down the wall of a nearby building.

She glared at him, her anger towards him starting to wear on her own patience. "I prefer to dine alone."
"Innocent…" he mumbled.

She paused for a moment, not sure what he was talking about then it slowly crawled into her mind. This man, no matter how irritating, was innocent, he was not the person she should be preying on. She dragged the man over to Johnathan, very irritated and short on patience.

"What do you propose I do?" confusion was written on his face, "He will not forget this! By this time tomorrow, I'll be the most hunted animal in this region. Your vampyre hunting friends will not hesitate to kill me!"

"Suggest." He said, and she waited for him to elaborate, but he just stared at her.

"Suggest? That's all you've got?!" she said shaking the man in her hands, he had passed out with fear, "I'm starting to wonder why I came here."

"Forget." He mumbled, she stared at him, her eyes black.

"Forget? Did all that alcohol ruin your brain?"

"*Let's just kill him and solve the problem.*" She wanted to agree, but she didn't want evil to win again.

She finally gave up on patience and grabbed and shook him again, "Tell me old man!!"

"Suggest…. that… he forgets."

"I could talk him to death, but he's not going to forget it, no matter how sweet I talk to him."

"Bite him."

She just stared at him.

"Bite, don't 'ink. Push wha' you wan'" She was still confused, but *if it doesn't work, I'll just drain him*. She bent and bit the man on the muscle above his collarbone, she tasted the blood that was coming from his wound and had to resist drinking it up. She thought as hard as she could, *forget what happened here*. She felt a surge of warmth leave her and enter the bite she had just made, but nothing else. She released him and looked at his face, trying to see any change that would tell her if it worked. She didn't see anything, and she was about to sink her teeth in again and drain him when he let out a sigh. She looked at his face again, and the look of fear was gone, his eyes had gone hazy and he was relaxed. She let him go, and he slumped over.

She turned back to Johnathan, "What the hell was that?" He just smiled at her, a crooked smile.

"Augh!" she grabbed him and dragged him around the closest corner and poked her head out to watch the man. He stayed slumped for a moment then seemed to wake up. He looked around himself as if not sure where he was and stood up, dusting himself off, still looking around, lost. Then, as if he recognized the area he made an "ah" noise and started walking the other direction.

"That's new," she whispered to herself then saw Johnathan sliding down the wall she had propped him against. She grabbed him and dragged him, stumbling behind her to the closest stream she could find, and she threw him in. He splashed around trying to get his legs under him, when he couldn't, she removed her clothes, down to her cammies and undergarments, and climbed in. She put him upright on a large stone and undressed him, tossing his clothes on the shore next to hers. He shivered in the cold water and slumped over onto her shoulder. She shoved him back in place and splashed more water on him. He was slow to rouse from his drunken stupor, and she was getting impatient. She pulled her hand back and swung, meaning to slap him again but this time he reached up and stopped her, grabbing her wrist.

"Could you please stop that?"

"Tsh." She pulled her hand from his grasp, "It's good to see you back to your old self." She stepped out of the water and started redressing.

"Why did you pull me back? I've got no need to be conscious of this world, can't you just let me be happy in my own?" He leaned his head on his hand.

"No," she turned to look at him, "You said yourself that I had a conscience, so when I found out that you had been forcibly removed from your precious Order I couldn't just sit by and wait for you to wither away." She finished dressing. "If you had a desire to die," she stepped back into the water and grabbed the front of his shirt, "I haven't fed on an innocent for quite a while, and I'd be lying if I said I didn't crave the sweetness of that pureblood." She leaned closer to him and he just turned his head, giving her better access. She pushed him into the water, "You're pathetic! You don't deserve for me to kill you, I don't waste my time on rats!" She got out of the water again and walked towards town.

She heard splashing behind her, then the sound of sliding cloth and, "Wait!" She didn't stop, but she slowed her pace, and she could hear him running to catch up with her. When she glanced behind her, she saw him running in just his pants and his shoes and coat in his arms.

"What do you want?" she asked, but she could tell her irritation was muffled by relief.

"Why did you come here?" he asked.

She stopped and faced him. "Because you were dishonored because of me and that doesn't sit well with me."

"What did you have planned?" he said, covering up his surprise, "Were you just going to march in the front doors of the Order's stronghold? You'll be killed before you even reach the gate. It's not worth it!"

"It's not *worth* it?!" she said, gritting her teeth, "You're life is not worth it?" she demanded.

"My life?" he said, as if he didn't understand.

"Yes! We both know that without that drive towards something you will succumb to insanity. I already see it and in such a short time in such a short time."

She motioned to his current state by waving a hand up and down at him. "As much as I don't like you killing my kin, I can't live with you giving up. I know you I don't know them and I don't owe them anything, and from what I have heard they aren't a good group anyways." She took a deep breath, her skin was starting to burn again, she couldn't give in to her frustration, or she would lose him.

"My life is not worth yours." He said quietly.

"What are —"

"My life will soon be over, I'm already in my thirties, which in my line of work is old, I don't have much time left, but you, you have eternity. Don't throw that away for someone like me."

"Someone like you?" she gave a sarcastic laugh. "Who exactly do you think you are? Are you so low that you don't think you are worth saving? Or is it that you want to meet your wife?" He stared at her, a look of shock on his face. She softened her gaze and her tone, "I know you miss her, and if you want I will send you to her."

She waited for his answer, when he remained silent she said, "Please don't make me do that. I know it's what you want, but please don't ask me to kill someone I care about, I may never recover, and then you will have to look down from heaven and watch the demon destroy everything." She said with honesty and fear in her voice.

After another long moment he said, "I do miss her, so much, every night, when I lay alone, I think of her, I can still smell her and feel her warmth. Even with the horrible memory of her killing our daughter, I cannot stop loving her, longing for her." He paused again, clearing his throat, pushing down his sorrow, "but I can't leave this place this way, knowing that we were wrong…"

"You couldn't have saved her." She whispered.

"I know!" He stopped, "but I didn't even try, I can't allow another man to lose his wife to the monster." She nodded as he composed himself, "What can I do?" he asked, she smiled.

"Glad you're back." She explained how they planned to talk to the council.

"That priest knows how to do his research," he commented.

She told him that they had no intension to cause a fight. They just wanted to show that he hadn't been wrong in sparing her. "If they didn't believe you then we'll just have to show them."

He had a glint in his eye when she was done, "That might work," he said, and she smiled.

"Would you be willing to tell us where the headquarters are and any information that would help us convince them and," she looked him in the eye, excitement on her face, "you know, to stay alive?"

He hesitated but then said, "I will share what I deem necessary for your quest, but you must swear that you will not share this information with anyone."

This time she hesitated, he glared at her, "Fine, I cannot foresee a reason to share this information, and it is likely they will change everything after I've been there anyways." She turned and started walking back towards the inn that Samuel reserved and was waiting, patiently. She was grateful that the sun had finally gone down and she didn't have to skulk around corners and in the shadows but it also hid her emotions from Johnathan, fear that he was lost to her and relief that he wasn't, he didn't need to know, he didn't need to worry about another woman, especially another woman that was a vampire. They arrive at the inn and made their way up to the room, she could smell tea coming from under the door and knew he was in there. She knocked once before opening the door to find the priest sitting at the table on the balcony. He stood when he heard her come in then stopped when he saw the strange man with her, the man who he had seen her talking to, the one who had confirmed his fears about the woman who brought the sun back to his sky.

She saw the fear in his eyes, but it passed as he pushed it down and came to greet them, he extended a hand to the new man, "I'm Samuel, a priest—"

"I do not mean to be rude, father, but I know who you are." He spoke in soft tones, "it is a pleasure to finally meet you." He reached out his hand and placed it in Samuel's, shaking it with a strong movement, "Ah, sorry, I'm no used to niceties, I'm used to be attacked as soon as I enter a room."

"No, it is quite alright. I'm rather pleased to meet you as well, forgive me, but I overheard the two of you talking before you left our church. I usually do no hide but, as you can imagine, I had just gotten some disturbing news." He glanced at Rosina, she turned her head away from him, in shame.

"Ah, so that's how you found out, I am truly sorry for that, but I see that you two have worked out your differences?" Neither answered and he tisked at them, "Once again, I'm sorry.

"No matter, we are not here for that, we are here for you." Samuel recovered quickly, back to his normal, calm self.

"I'm sorry for that as well." Johnathan said, shame hovering over him.

"I believe it was inevitable, you would have eventually run into Rosina and had all this happen, I'm just glad that I'm still around that I can help." He said, a light in his eyes.

"You get too excited helping people, Priest." her demon chimed in.

"Thank you, father." Samuel nodded and then went to his bags to pull out the books he brought, laying out maps of the city and what he believed was the headquarters of the Order.

"Shall we?" Rosina spoke for the first time.

"Do you mind if I used a towel while my clothes dry?" She had forgotten that he was standing practically naked and quickly moved to the closet and pulled out a towel. She turned as he disrobed again and wrapped the towel around his waist, settling at the table with Samuel after hanging his ragged clothes on the balcony railing.

"You really know a lot don't you?" Johnathan asked Samuel.

"I have many books." He said, a little too excited.

"And by many he means a vast library that takes up a better part of the back half of the cathedral." Rosina chimed in. Johnathan gave Samuel a *'really?'* look, and he nodded.

"This building here," Johnathan pointed to a building on the city map, "is the front of our headquarters, it doesn't look like much, but we like it that way, keeps from drawing attention. The actually building leads underground to here," he drew a line with his finger to a building much further into the city, Samuel followed with an ink line, circling both buildings. "It's easy to get into the first building but to get to the secret passages you need to know the riddles and have the keys, which you get from the riddles. I'll walk you through them." He went into great detail about several of the traps that they had to pass and what the answers to the riddles were. Samuel took notes as fast as Johnathan talked, Rosina faded in and out, she was thinking further ahead. She had thought about it many times over, infiltrating the Order and killing everyone there, protecting her and her kind, but she had to retrain herself from that if she wanted to help Johnathan.

"Once you get to the main building you'll have to get around the guards, I assume that you do not intend to kill them," he glanced at Rosina she replied with a fang-filled grin.

"No, we do not want to kill them," Samuel broke in, also looking at Rosina.

"Ok, this is where you will need a silver tongue. I do not know what will happen, but I do know this, they will try to kill you, Rosina, you must not retaliate, allow them to take you to the council."

"I doubt they will allow me to live long enough to see the council." She said, confident.

"I know they won't, which is why the father will have to go without you." He said looking down at the map again and avoiding her gaze.

"What?! I'm not sending him alone into the secret den place of killers!" She came to him from her position against the wall and was within inches of him, "are you insane?!"

"Rose." Samuel tried to get her attention.

"They will kill him just because he consorts with me, a vampyre!"

"Rosina!" she looked up to see Samuel, still seated and calm. "They will not kill a man of God for that reason only, they will have to investigate me to be sure that I have not been put under some sort of spell." She started to protest, but he cut her off, "If they kill me then you can smash in their window and kill them all, you have my permission." She stared at him, he laughed at the look of surprise on her face.

"Well, when you put it that way…" she said, a hint of worry in her voice, "but you have to promise to try your best to not be killed, I can't drink that much blood."

"You did pretty good at the brothel." Johnathan spoke up.

Both Samuel and Rosina looked at him in surprise. "Just how long have you been watching us?" Rosina spoke first, and this time Samuel looked at her in surprise.

"Us?" he asked.

"Oh, you heard that I was a vampyre from him but you missed the part where he said they had been watching you?" She had a laugh in her voice.

"Me? Why me?" he asked genuinely surprised.

"Something about your town being a cesspool of temptation for a rogue vampire. I'll tell you all about it when you get back from your suicide mission." She made light of it so he wouldn't worry. Johnathan's words ran through her mind, and Samuel's death haunted her.

There was silence in the room, the calm before the storm. Samuel broke it, "I guess I should probably get rest if I'm to break into the infamous vampyre hunters' headquarters." He gathered the papers and started tucked them neatly into a bag.

"Before that," Johnathan said causing Samuel to stop cleaning up, "we need to talk about the council." Samuel quickly got his notes back out. "There is a Master, he leads the council, he is old and wise, he is the one that you need to win over, but also he has two seconds in command. One is young but wise beyond his years. He will listen and make an informed decision, and the other was once a hunter but was injured, so he took a place in the council. He harbors a deep resentment for the bloodsuckers." Rosina grumbled. "Sorry, habit." He shrugged his shoulders, "there are four more members, but they are merely placeholders. You need to convince the Master and the seconds, everyone else will follow their decision."

"If two of them are willing to listen, then I will direct my words to them, and hopefully they will be easy to win over," Samuel said.

"Just use your words cautiously. Even if they are open to listening to you, that doesn't mean they are open to changing the ways of the Order. They are, after all *the* vampyre hunters."

"Yes, yes. I'll watch my words." There was silence again only broken by Samuel, "thank you for breaking your oath and helping us."

"Don't thank me. It may not work, and you are doing it for me so it's the least I can do." Johnathan said, appreciation in his voice, "I'll let you rest now."

"I'm going out," Rosina said without preamble.

"I'll go with you," Johnathan said. She looked at him with irritation, "I know, you prefer to feed alone, but I'm a night person, perks of my former job. I will leave you alone."

"You think I'm going to let you go to another tavern and drink yourself into a stupor?"

"Don't worry, I'm just going to enjoy some night air," he redressed himself and made for the door.

"I'm not going to take care of you." She said after him, she closed the door quietly after him.

"I know."

She fed quickly, she didn't want to be out long, but she was dwelling on the priest too much, and she needed to take her mind off it. He was risking everything for a man he had just met all because he was kind. She knew she had to leave him after this, she wouldn't allow him to come to any more harm because of her or anyone else.

She made her way back to the room, it was dark, and Johnathan had not returned yet, if he ever planned to. She stood over the bed where Samuel laid, he was breathing lightly. *Peaceful,* she thought. She placed a gentle hand on his cheek and ran it down over his jaw, *so peaceful.* She knelt down and sat against the wall closest to him and allowed all her worries to surface, she could hide from them in the dark. *He could die and for what? He is doing me a favor, but why? He owes me nothing. And if he does die what then? How could I possibly live knowing I had sent him to his death? And the massacre that will ensue after, my demon will take over and kill them all, all those innocents and what's to stop it at that.* She knew he demon was strong, but how strong, would it ever be satisfied, would it stop or would someone have to stop it and would there be anyone left that could do that?

She closed her eyes and let the fear take over until tears started to run from her eyes, her skin was burning when a cool hand touched her cheek. Her eyes snapped open, and she looked up to see Samuel kneeling before her, a smile on his face.

"Still green." She had no idea what he was talking about, "your eyes, they are still green even though your skin is alight. It's so beautiful." He ran his hand up her arm, the coolness causing her to shiver.

"I'm sorry," she whispered as he leaned his head down, laying his forehead against hers. "I can't ask you to do this."

"You didn't ask." He said, and she scoffed at his words, "I'm glad to do it, this is what I was born for." He felt her warm skin and knew she was worried, "Do not be afraid, my beautiful, black rose, I'll come back to you for your scent will always call to me."

She closed her eyes and drank in his aura, "You are always comforting me, saving me, why are you so strong, even tonight? Can I not care for you just once?"

He laughed, "I do not profess to be strong, but will you come lay with me? I need your warmth to help me sleep, and so I know what I'll be missing if I fail."

"Don't talk like that." Her voice quivered.

"Will you come lay with me?" He stood and extended his hand to her, she took it, and he led her to the bed. He laid down, and she hesitated, afraid that she would never be near him again. He reached up and grabbed both her hands and pulled her into the bed, into him. He held her in his arms and pulled the covers over them both. She just laid there until she couldn't hold back anymore and she wrapped her arms around him and held him as tightly as she dared, her face buried into his chest. He ran his hand through her hair, taking in every part of her that he could, filling his senses. He buried his face in her long, soft hair, nestled in it. He breathed her in, she really did smell of roses. Roses and vanilla beans. He felt tears coming to his eyes and tried to stifle them, but she smelled the salt in them and lifted her head.

She lifted her face and kissed away the tears that were coming from his gentle brown eyes that seemed to have lost their light, "No," she whispered, "that light cannot go out, you can't do this, you must stay with me." At her words, his tears flowed more freely, "Please stay with me, forever." She bent her head back down and rested it on the warm flesh of his neck. She kissed his skin. He put his hand under her chin and lifted up her face to his and gently kissed her.

"I will always be here." And he kissed her again and held her. She couldn't stop her tears now, and hers mingled with his, as they slid down her cheek and he held her close and kissed her deeper until he couldn't breathe and parted from her. He looked at her, her skin lit his face, and he smiled, "So beautiful." And he kissed her again, on her lips then on her nose and her cheeks, her forehead and her chin.

"I want to eat you," he whispered in her ear and then he kissed down her neck and she gasped in surprise. She didn't make a smart remark about how she should be cooked first or that he should be ashamed because he was a man of God, she just grabbed on to the muscles in his back and held on.

He took her in, her taste and her sounds, her breathing quickened and her scent changing with her emotion. He kissed every inch of skin that he could reach, her neck, her shoulders, her collarbones. He bit what she would allow, especially her neck, until she pushed away and without saying anything asked him if that is what he wanted. When he nodded, she pushed him into the soft bed and slowly removed his shirt. She kissed all his hard muscles in his shoulders and arms and made her way down his chest and his stomach. She stopped at the top of his trousers and worked her way back up to his neck where she nibbled, playing with him, but not breaking through to the blood.

"It's okay, go ahead." She stopped and looked up at him in shock. He nodded, "I want to know what it feels like." She waited for a moment, just staring at him, waiting for him to come to his senses but when he didn't, she knelt back down and bit him on the muscle of his chest. He took a quick intake of breath but when he let it out it wasn't that of pain but pleasure. She licked the little bit of blood that surfaced from the bite. She lifted his arm to her mouth and kissed the tender area of his wrist, she looked at him to see his eyes closed and him biting his lip and a smile played on his face. She bit gently into his soft flesh and pulled some blood from him, just enough to stir her hunger and cause him to moan, deep in his throat. She smiled as she sealed the wound with her tongue. She straddled him, sitting gently on his hips, bending down to kiss his neck, giving him a moment to change his mind before she sank her fangs into his neck, wishing him pleasure instead of pain. She pulled his blood from him and he bucked against her, his pleasure was reaching its limit and she lifted up from him, licking the wound, sealing it like the others. She looked at him, sweat gleamed on his skin and his eyes were half closed as he looked at her. She smiled down at him.

"I never knew," he whispered, "it was that good." She laughed as she watched him, "come here." He reached up and pulled her back down to him and kissed her, a new hunger in his kiss than before and it took her breath away.

"I could say the same." She breathed, "This is the most fun I've had without having sex."

"Let's not stop there." He sat up and pulled her in close, "will you make a man out of me?"

"I cannot, I don't hold that authority, but I can drive you crazy while trying." She reached between them and under his trousers and found him. He was warm and pulsing, "I want to eat you," she echoed his words in his ears, and she pushed him back onto the bed and pulled him out. She placed her lips on him, teasing him, then she ran the tip of her tongue on him causing him to say her name, a plea in it she had never thought she would hear.

She smiled and took him in her mouth, playing with him with her tongue until he grabbed a handful of hair and pulled her up, "You're going to ruin me." She bit down on the tip of him, and he yanked her up again, this time he pulled her fully up to him and kissed her. He yanked her pants off and put his hands on her hips and pulled her up to meet him. She took all of him in one swift thrust, and she called out. He ripped her shirt off to completely expose her as she sat atop him. She moved with him, her hips moving up and down, back and forth in rhythm with his. He sat up and ran his hands up and down her body as she moaned with pleasure. He pushed himself up into her as far and hard as he could until that wasn't enough and he pushed her down into the bed and moved fiercely as she called his name, scratching him as she clung to him: pushing him to the limit. He bit her right above her collarbone, hard enough to draw blood. He stopped as he realized what he had done.

"I'm sorry, I didn't —"

"Lick it." She said, barely able to contain her passion. He bent down and slowly licked the blood coming from his bite, and she bucked under him, moaning. "I can't take it!" He joined her in motion, and when she called out one last time, he joined her in oblivion.

They lay panting on the bed, sweaty and exhausted. "I'm sorry," she whispered.

He turned on his side and leaned up on his elbow, "Why?"

"I corrupted you. Not only did I ask you to go on a dangerous quest that could kill you but I finally led you to temptation."

"Stop." He said firmly, kissing her, and she did, "Don't you ruin this." He pulled her into him and held her, she resisted at first but then she gave into sleep as he drifted off she felt his breath, soothing, slowing as he finally found rest.

Chapter Eleven: Beware the Demon

The beauty of the moon is dimmed only by your eyes.
The red dancing on your skin,
The heat from your desire.
Your anger will ignite them all,
Be careful they are your only way out.
They will push you to the edge,
They will force you to choose,
They will drive you mad.
But don't turn from them,
They will save you from death and
She will save you from them.

The sun rose, filling the room with white light. Rosina awoke to the warm scent of Samuel. She rolled over to find that she was alone in the bed. She lept up and looked around the room, listening for any sound of him, but there was nothing, only silence, then a creek.

"Samuel?" she opened the door to find a man but not the man she was hoping for.

"You sure have quite a way of greeting your guests." Johnathan motion to her naked body. She quickly retreated back to the bed and grabbed a sheet to cover herself.

"What are you doing here? And where is he?" she demanded.

"I'm here to look after you, to make sure you don't do anything stupid. And he…" he paused to look at the rumpled bed, "already left," he tore his eyes off the sheets. "I just came back from taking him to the entrance to the headquarters. If he's as smart as he looks, he should be past the first riddle by now."

"He left?" she stumbled around putting on her clothes, "without saying goodbye."

"By the looks of it, he did say goodbye." He looked at the bed again, "That's one of the best ways to say goodbye." He smirked.

"If you don't wipe that off your face," she pointed to his smile, "I'll do it for you." She felt her skin start to tingle with irritation. "How could you let him leave without even waking me?"

"He met me out front. I assumed he had woken you, but I am seeing now that it probably was a good idea that he didn't. I'm going to guess that you were going to follow him?" She stopped trying to find her other shoe and looked at him. "You're a little more predictable than you think. It's actually kind of painful just how much you are." She threw her already-found shoe at him, but he dodged it.

"Show me where you took him." She had seen the map, but she was too consumed with worry that she neglected to study it well enough to know where the entrance was.

"No." he said, sternly.

She shoved him against a wall, nearly breaking a hole clear through it. "You will show me where you took him or I will end your miserable life."

"That wouldn't make any sense," he said between pained grunts. "You cannot interfere or he will be killed and then they will hunt you *and* me. Remind me again why you came here, if you just want us to die."

She knew he was right, but she didn't want to allow Samuel to go alone. She didn't want to leave it up to fate, she wanted to load the dice. "You have to trust him. You have to believe he will be alright or you are just insulting him." He said, and she nodded and released him, turning away.

"Can't I care for him? Can't I just watch over him?" she mumbled to herself.

She heard him sigh. "I will take you there, but I will not allow you to go in after him. If he is not in contact with us within two days, we go in and get him." She turned to him a look of horror on her face, "They will not kill a human without reason. They will fully investigate him and have a trial if they find him suspicious. That gives us at least a week, but we have to give him time to convince them. I gave him all the tools, he just needs to use them properly." She was silent for a long moment then nodded. She put her shoes on and grabbed her coat, making her way to the door.

She covered herself from the sun, but she could still feel its heat through her coat so she stuck as close to the buildings as she could without drawing attention.

"We can perch up there," Johnathan pointed to the bell tower of an abandoned church. "It will hide you from the sun, and we have a good viewpoint of the entrance." She nodded, she was feeling weak from the sun. They entered the church with a loud creaking objection from the doors. The place was covered in dust from lack of use and looked like there had been some sort of fight before the doors were closed for good, but even it was covered with a layer of dust. The broken pews scattered, leaving the stone floor open and accessible, as if someone had cleared it purposefully. Right in the center was a circle that held melted candles and letters she recognized as latin. There were bloody lines on the floor, some intentional and some smears that looked like a drag marks.

"They say that the crusaders exercised a demon in here." He caught her looking around and answered her unasked question. "The truth was that there was an especially powerful vampyre shacked up here and it took almost the whole Order to trap him and bury him underground. He killed most of them before the end."

"Who was he?" she asked.

"They call him The Dracula."

She looked at him as if he was jesting, but he was looking around the building as if he could see the battle playing out.

"No one knows his real name, but he was the most powerful vampyre that anyone has ever fought so, they gave him the name of the legendary first vampyre. Whether that was him or not, I do not know. But, I doubt that Dracula would have allowed himself to be captured so easily." He continued walking.

"Easily?" she said, taking another look at the room.

He turned to look at her, "Once this is over you should see if that priest of yours has a book on Dracula and his reign of terror." He opened the rotting door to the tower and started climbing the spiral stairs.

"Perhaps. It wouldn't hurt to know a little about the beginnings of my kind." *But I'll have to find another way to learn it.*

The stairwell was almost completely dark, she welcomed the cool air and stones. She took off her coat and leaned against the wall, all but rolled herself over the stones, cooling her burning skin, "ahhhhh."

He stopped when he reached the top and had to force the door open with his shoulder. Light filtered the first few steps and she had to put her coat back on to enter the room where the bell used to be housed. She quickly took shelter in the shade against the wall under one of the large opening facing the entrance to the headquarters. They waited, through the day and into the night. She was getting restless and paced impatiently back and forth in front of the missing bell.

Night came without a single clue that the priest had made it into the headquarters or that he hadn't. She couldn't take the waiting anymore and rushed down the stairs to the door, planning on marching into the headquarters to find out what had happened. Johnathan grabbed her arm before she could reach the door and nodded towards the street. She looked down from the tower to see a man walking towards the church. She rushed down to the main floor, reaching it just in time for the man to open the door. She met him as he looked up to see who was there.

She grabbed him by the front of his shirt, noticing that he was wearing similar clothes that both the old hunter and Johnathan wore, she saw the knives and guns under his coat. She slammed him against the door, "Where is he?" she demanded.

He didn't move only said, "I would watch your actions, Vampyre." He spat the word and looked down at the blade he had pointed at her heart. She released him, and he straightened his clothes. Johnathan joined them now.

"What do you want?" he asked.

"I have come to give a message, but the Master said that if I see fit I don't have to, they'll get what they need from the priest you so generously sent to us." He looked at Rosina, hatred filling his gaze. It took everything for her to keep from strangling him.

"Fine, please tell us where he is and what you want us to do," Johnathan spoke in softer tones than she would have been able to.

The man didn't say anything, just stared at Rosina. She was at her limit and had to turn and walk away from him. Finally, he spoke, "She's what you gave everything up for?" His disbelief not hidden.

"Yes." He didn't elaborate.

He stared after her, not saying anything for a long moment then, as if answering his own disbelief, he said, "No matter, we will soon find out why she is so special. Though I will be disappointed to find out that you took her as a lover." He looked towards where she retreated to.

"What if we were lovers?" she said from her corner on the other end of the building, "Is it going to turn him into a goblin?"

"It is forbidden!" He directed it at her, but then turned to talk to Johnathan,

"She isn't even a beauty worth breaking the code for." She growled.

She started coming back towards him, "Not what?"

"We are not lovers, everyone knows that," he had a pain in his voice as he thought of his wife. "You are just trying to pull a fight out of her." Johnathan spoke up, stopping her.

"Well, it seems that it isn't hard to accomplish, just like every other bloodsucker." His disgust was clear.

"She is upset because you took something precious to her; anyone would be, vampyre or not." Johnathan defended her.

At that comment, the other man looked at him, an emotion passing over his face that shadowed shock and disappointment. "You really have changed sides, haven't you. Tell me, Johnathan, what has she done to you that caused you to become this?" he motioned to his ratty clothes and disheveled appearance.

"She cried." He simply said.

"I won't cry for you again," Rosina spat at him.

"Oh-ho, a nerve." The other man said. She reached for him, but Johnathan grabbed her arm and yanked her with him to the corner.

"If you don't keep your tongue in your mouth, he isn't going to tell us about your dear priest!" he whispered harshly at her, "Let me do the talking, and you stay here," he shoved her down into one of the last remaining whole pews. She stared at him as he walked away and felt ashamed. He had scolded her like she was a child, and she put her face into her hands.

"Please, tell us, old friend." He talked softly, and she heard the other man sigh.

"She is to come to headquarters and show us that the priest speaks the truth, though I do not see it yet. She is to come unarmed and prepared for our judgment, which may include death if she fails to provide us with sufficient evidence to this end. And she is to bring the traitor with her." He looked at Johnathan, who didn't look away, "also unarmed and prepared for our punishment for giving away secret details of our headquarters. You will wait until just before dawn. Therefore she is weak and less likely to cause… trouble."

"I am willing to accept any punishment you have in store for me, but you must promise that Samuel will come to no harm." Rosina spoke quietly, she was standing but didn't come closer.

"I cannot make such a promise as he has already been injured." The man said, enjoying the pain in her voice, "But it seems that I have collected some valuable information. If you come to us, we are willing to listen to you beg for his life." He had a laugh in his voice. She could feel her emotions running wild, from worry to anger and her skin started to tingle, but she didn't move, heeding Johnathan's warning.

"We will come," he interjected before it escalated.

The other man stared at Rosina for a long moment. but then finally put his blade away and exited the church. The tension decreased so much she could feel it leaving her body but only to be replaced by worry and irritation of another kind. She waited a few minutes then started walking towards the door, fully intending to fill herself before their morning meeting. Johnathan stood in front of the door, stopping her again.

"Move," she said through clenched teeth.

"I will not allow you to go out and cause 'trouble.' They are going to be watching you, we can only sweet talk to them so much. If you go out and make a mess, you are killing us all."

"Would you rather I go in there hungry and weak from the sun? That is a much worse combination. You should know, hunter." She put all her dislike for the whole group and the situation in that one word. She had no intention of causing a scene, but she also wanted to show the hunters just what she was and to be afraid of her.

"If you need it so much, feed from me." He pulled up his sleeve.

Shock kept her from answering right away, but when she recovered, she laughed. "How long have you been immersed in the world of vampyres? You know it's the hunt that we crave, blood is just the reward, nurishment, if you will, a requirement. But it doesn't taste as sweet if we don't work for it." She got really close to him and licked her lips, "we feed off the fear and the adrenaline, the rapid heartbeat and the sweat just under the collar," she leaned in and smelled his neck. When she pulled back, she said, "you aren't ripe enough for me." She reached under his arm and pulled at the door handle, but he didn't move.

"You'll just have to deal with a sour meal because I'm not allowing you to leave this church." His stubbornness was wearing on her patience.

"Allow me to leave, or the reason for me to be nice and well behaved will vanish, and I'll go in by force to take back what is mine." She allowed her anger to show in her voice. He wrapped his arm around the back of her neck, pulling her close to him. She could feel his heat and found that his resolve was the only thing keeping him from snapping her neck. She smelled the sweat produced from the strain of keeping his cool. His heart was strong, she could feel its beat against her chest.

"You will feed on me or not feed at all, this is not a request." His stern tone in her ear kept her from retorting. He loosened his arm a little allow some room between them and raised his bare wrist to her lips. She glared at him from over his arm.

"You will not enjoy this," she breathed against his warm flesh. He smelled so good she was taken by surprise when her hunger overtook her, her eyes glowing and her teeth aching to bite him. She wrapped a hand around his arm, holding it tightly.

"I'm sure. Gah—" she bit into him and pulled the hot blood from his body. She closed her eyes and thought of nothing but the feast. His blood tasted different than before. Maybe it was just her overthinking, but before when he had been generous, needing her to take from him, he tasted sweet but now when he had forced her to drink it was much more metallic, as if his demeanor was reflected in his blood. She pulled away, but didn't lick his wound, just let it drip blood. She wouldn't let him pull away. Smiling, she watched his blood leave his body one drop at a time, then she pulled it back to her mouth and she slowly licked the lines of blood from his wound, until he pulled away.

"That's enough!" he wrapped his wrist with a cloth in his coat and returned to the tower without another word to her. She remained down in the church and looked at the damage that the mysterious Dracula had left behind. The silence grew, and she paced, trying to make the time pass faster, but it dragged until she heard Johnathan descend the stairs again with his and her bag.

"It's time." Was all he said as he dropped their bags by the altar and walked to the door. He left before she could talk to him about earlier in the night or what the plan was. He walked quickly to the seemingly abandoned building. It was unguarded, but it put up a good front, she would have passed it without a second thought. The door creaked when he opened it, and the inside of the building was no different than the outside. He walked to the center of the abandoned, run-down building and used a metal bar hanging on the wall to pry up a tile. Under it was not a floor but a trap door. He pulled the metal ring up, and the door gave way. He descended into the floor. She looked down into the hole and followed him down the ladder to the floor below. She stepped off onto a dirt floor. He reached up and pulled the trap door down, and she heard not only it but also the tile fall back into place.

"Stay here. Do not move and do not defy me; I *will* let you die." He was still angry about the night before.

She reached out and gently touched him on the shoulder, "I'm sorry," she whispered, "I acted like a child."

"Don't be," he responded before he turned to see the look of fear on her face. He reached up and put his hand on either side of her face, gently holding it. "You are worried, someone else has done something for you and you fear they will die because you allowed them to." He wiped a tear that had appeared on her cheek away and pulled her into a hug. "Even if we can't convince them you are good, I promise you that your priest, Samuel, will leave here alive and unharmed. I will do this even if it kills me. He has helped me, he is risking his life for both you and me, and he did it without a thought to himself. We have to take care of him, because he won't." He squeezed her tight as he felt her start to tremble and then she nodded, consciously pulling herself together. He pulled away and smiled at her, "there, I like this you much better than the one from last night. The raw you is always the best, it gives me energy to be successful!" he turned, leaving her wondering about him, and walked town the tunnel that lay before them.

The stones that made the walls and ceiling were arched and mostly cracked and some missing. She watched him feel his way down the right side of the wall, he was measuring the distance. He pushed a stone in, and she heard a mechanism moving behind the wall and then he disappeared into the wall. She was about to follow when she heard him yell back, "Wait there!"

She waited, hearing different noises ahead of her, scrapping and crumbling stone and gears cranking. Then she heard footsteps, she watched the darkness ahead of her and saw a light, slowly getting brighter. Johnathan reappeared carrying a torch.

"Let's go," she followed him back up the tunnel the way he had just came. They turned right then walked down another hall for a long distance then turn left and went down. She could see where the walls had opened up and where there were booby traps set for those who were not allowed to pass. She noticed that there were no bodies. *They cleaned up their traps,* she suppressed a laugh at the irony, by covering her mouth. The distance from the entrance to the second door was shorter than she thought. He opened it with a key that she noticed he hadn't been carrying when they first arrive. The door was almost like a diamond in a bed of rocks. It was large, taking up the whole wall, ten foot from the floor to the ceiling and was white with intricate golden designs all around its edges. The keyhole was centered in the door, not hidden like she would have expected. It was surrounded with a gold ring similar to that which was on the edge of the door, as if drawing attention to itself. She was weary as he turned the key and she could hear the mechanisms in the door turn and clank as they moved into a different position. There was one final click, and the door popped open. He reached up and grabbed the edge of the door, leaving the key in it. He pulled the door open fully and she was shown an entrance way that matched the door. The ceiling was much higher, and there were stone walls covered in tapestries and candles in holders of crystal. The ceiling was adorned with chandeliers that rained crystal light down on the room. There were cases lining all the walls, holding old texts and weapons behind glass. Two men stood on the opposite wall, guarding yet another grand door. They stood in uniforms that would have caused a maiden of a royal family to swoon. They looked like knights in their light armor draped in red velvet across the chest pieces and waists. It was made to protect, but also to be easy to move in. A decorative sword hung from their waists, and they stood holding spears that were very real. She was awe struck for a mere second until these lovely men were upon her with their spears directed at her chest. She reacted by dropping down into a squat and darting at them, under their long spears. She heard Johnathan call out just before she managed to grasp and pull their legs out from under them.

"Rosina!" She paused, kneeling down before the two knights. He placed a hand across his chest and bowed at them, saying, "We were invited by the Master."

"You are a traitor that dares to bring a vampyre into our place of refuge! You will not be forgiven!" They turned their attack on him, but they didn't get close to them because Rosina grabbed their heads and knocked them together. They both collapsed to the floor. He looked at her as if at a loss for words.

She laughed, "Shall we?" she motioned to the door. They walked towards it, but it opened before they reached it and a dozen more men flooded into the entryway. "I'll take those on the left you get those on the right?"

He smiled but it wasn't one of joy, "We shouldn't resist." She stared at him for a moment, but then she knelt down on the floor and put her head down, showing her submission, hoping they wouldn't abuse that and kill her. She heard him kneel down as well and then a voice saying, "Take them to the cage and search them thoroughly." Someone grabbed her arms and tied them roughly behind her back and yanked her up shoving her towards the open door. Johnathan was treated the same. She was pulled down the hall off the entrance, it looked similar to the first room, but it had a door every few feet, leading off to some other room or hall or stairs. They were taken about halfway down the wall and then she was shoved through a door on the right. The room had nothing in it but a wall of bars in the middle, cutting the room in half. She was alone in the room with the man that had brought her here, the others and Johnathan had not followed. The bar wall had a door that was open, and she was shoved through it. The man proceeded to yank at her clothes, trying to remove them, she reacted out of instinct and kicked him as hard as she could in her position. He stumbled back and ran into the wall. He looked up at her, anger in his face.

"Come back at me again and try to do that again and I won't let you walk away." She said, she was not going to allow this hunter to abuse her, the worse possible scenarios were running through her mind, and she allowed her fear to react for her and cause her skin to blaze. He came at her and tackled her to the ground, startling her and hitting her repeatedly until she drew up her legs and wrapped them around his front and pushed him back down as hard as she could against the floor. She heard his head smack the floor, but because she didn't latch on as she had wanted to it wasn't a hard hit. He recovered quickly and drew a sword and came back at her as she scrambled back away from him, finding the wall and her feet quickly. She moved in time to hear his blade hit the wall just inches from her. She kicked him again, hard in the chest, knocking him down. She straddled his chest as he lay on his back and held him down. He grabbed her thighs, scratching at them as she leaned down as far as she could. Her movement caused her to slide down to his stomach and trapped his hands under her legs.

She leaned into his face, "You are not allowed to do what you want! You are a man of honor, or so I hear. The hunters are respectable, they do not do unnecessary things or things that are born out of temptation." Her fear was showing in her face, and she was overcome by the thought of a man abusing his strength to overcome her and use her for his fun. He had a look of irritation on his face, it seemed he was asking for her to harm him, giving him a reason that would justify his actions. His look that lacked fear caused *her* fear to grow. It was then that she realized that her hands had become loose and she wrapped them around his throat yelling, "You can't have me!" He gasped for breath and struggled under her, but she held him tight.

"Rose!" She looked up, through tears to see Samuel standing with a different guard in the doorway, a look of horror on his face. She looked down at the man on the floor and quickly released him, scrambling back against the corner, completely overwhelmed by her shame and fear; her face was soaked with tears. He ran to her, ignoring the man clasping his throat and coughing on the other side of the room. He held her, felt her trembling and whispered to her, "It's ok, I'm here, it's alright now. I'll protect you." She cried into his chest for a moment longer, but then he was ripped away from her, another man had entered the barred room and was holding Samuel's arm and looking down at her. He was dressed differently than the others: he wasn't wearing armor, but instead an expensive tailored trousers, shirt, and jacket. He also had a sword at his waist, but his wasn't just for decoration. He had short, well-groomed hair, and a smooth face, but his dull brown eyes were empty.

"Pathetic," he said. "We brought him here as a show of good faith to you, but what do we find a weeping girl trying to kill her guard. Tell me, little girl, why should we not kill you now?"

"It's not her fault," Samuel said.

"Father, please remain quiet." He looked at the guard, "What happened here?"

The man that was coughing knelt before him and said, "I was attempting to search her for concealed weapons as I was ordered to when she just attacked me." Samuel looked at Rosina, still on the floor in the corner, she had a look of shock on her face, she had no idea what he was talking about.

"No! That is not what happened. He tried to rip my clothes off! I was defending myself!" Her tears were renewed, and she was ashamed at her fear. She was being belittled and she couldn't even stop her crying, she really was a child. The new man walked over and smacked her in the face with the back of his hand.

"Silence, beast!" He yelled, "you do not speak unless spoken to."

"Ryan, you need to be more gentle with our guest." A soft-spoken man entered the room, he was wearing a robe, similar to Samuels, but he was not that of the church. It was not brown but blue, and even though it was simple it was made of expensive fabric, and he had no visible weapons. He had shoulder length black hair that was tied up at the back of his head, allowing a few strands to fall loose and frame his slender welcoming face and gentle dark brown eyes. He smiled at her as he approached, extending a slender hand towards her. She looked at it, but made no move to take it.

"Come, dear, I mean you no harm. I want to make up for the poor treatment you have thus far received." He glanced over his shoulder, taking in all the other men in the room, the two guards bowed and left. He knelt down before her, she had stopped crying, and her emotions were starting to return to normal. Her skin was burning less, and her marks were fading, they were only a slight red tint on her skin, barely visible.

"I'm terribly sorry, the guards are not used to having a vampyre as a guest. They see you all as an enemy, so your *escort* didn't handle the situation properly. I will not ask you to forgive him, but please understand they were trained to kill your kind on sight not treat them with respect. I will trust that you have no weapons seeing as you decided to use your hands rather than a blade. Now, if you would please accompany myself and Ryan to the council chambers, Johnathan is already waiting for us there." She looked past him to Samuel, and when he nodded she stood up, and the new man clapped his hands in joy as he also regained a standing position, smiling at her.

She refused his hand as she stood and he pulled his hand back without showing any signs of irritation at her refusal. He turned back to the first man, Ryan, and Samuel and walked past them to the door. "Come now, they are waiting." He exited the room, and Ryan shoved Samuel through the door and several guards came in to force her to follow. They went further down the hall and turned left at the end when it made a T. She could hear whispers. She wasn't surprised that there would be people watching and wondering what she was doing here, a vampyre in the headquarters of the vampyre hunter's. She smiled a little, she couldn't help it, she loved chaos.

They came to a double door at the end of the hall, this is where the man in the robe stopped and turned towards them. "I request that you speak only when spoken to and answer all of your questions with honesty, no matter how trivial or probing it may be." She was going to protest at the rules of being treated like she was on trial when she realized that that is exactly what this was. She knew this coming in, but she still tried to resist it.

He nodded to the guards at the doors, and they opened them revealing an even more grand room. It dwarfed even Samuel's beloved cathedral, with its high, brightly lit ceilings with beautiful architetrual arches reminiscent of the Gothic period that was not that long past. Beautiful floor to ceiling windows of stained glass depicting scenes to honor those that have fallen to the vampyre enemy. Some were unbelievable, with men standing in armor holding the decapitated heads of their opponent and others with men helping poor children covered in blood. She couldn't believe the sight, it was beautiful in all its color and gore. She smiled again, and one of the guards took a step away from her. She could smell his fear, which made her smile widen as she winked at him. He made an audible gasp.

"I would ask you to stop teasing our new members." The man in robe said without looking back at her. She looked down, hiding her smile that she couldn't take off her face. They proceeded further into the room. She noticed that it lacked furniture, considering its massive size, she found this strange. She could hear chairs sliding on the floor and the sound of fabric rustling. The sound drew her attention to the far end of the room which came into light as they approached. There was one long arched table that formed a crescent at the end of the room. There were several chairs on one side of it, facing into the room. The table itself was made of thick, dark, sturdy wood as were the chairs; they were high backed and made of designs that would have made any art lover speechless in awe. There were candles spread from many gathered in the middle of the table out to a few at the edges. There were men standing behind their chairs, four in total, two on each side and one man seated in the middle. He was an old man, with a long white beard and glasses resting on the edge of his nose. His beard was tied neatly to keep it in order as was his long hair which was braided down his back with ribbons of gold. He also wore a robe, a dark one, its color undiscernable in the candlelight. He wore very little adornments except for one ring with a crest, she assumed was that of the Order's. It was a shield with a cross on the upper right corner and a spear and sword crossed in the middle. He also wore a necklace that resembled a dagger, it was decorated with one gem, a ruby on its hilt. He raised his hands from the armrests of his chair, welcoming them into the chamber and the two men that had brought them to the room joined him. The well-groomed man, Ryan, on his left dend the other on his right. All six men bowed and took their seats. She looked around, trying to find Johnathan but couldn't. Samuel caught her looking and made a tisking noise to get her attention before she could ask about him. He shook his head at her when she looked, and she had a look of irritation on her face. *I have to be careful what I do and say from here on out, or they will kill Samuel.* She put her attention on the men at the table. Some were wearing robes, and some were wearing similar armor to the guards that were now standing a distance from them, but within reach, if anything were to happen.

"Welcome Father," the old man spoke, "I am the Master of these men here, and I am also a guardian of their well-being." *Well-being my —* "When one of our own veers off the path of those that came before I must take action to correct this so that he does not lead others off the path. Even if that means I must remove him from our order and throw him out on the street with nothing." He spoke without a hint of remorse, as if he was just taking out the trash. "I must protect those under my care. That being said, this is the first time that anyone has tried to appeal the act of the council and it is the first time a vampyre has walked through our front doors alive let alone given an invitation. Do not feel too pleased that you have come this far and do not forget that you are only here because I am allowing it. Be it the delusions of an old man, but my curiosity has gotten the better of me. But when that curiosity runs out, I will not hesitate to remove that which burdens me."

"That being said, please tell us how you were able to sway one of our most convicted men that vampyres , the beasts that took away his wife and child, might not be all that terrible? What separates you from those other beasts that have terrorized innocent men, women, and children for centuries?"

"Someone's holding a grudge ha ha ha ha." She shook her head to clear out her demon's thoughts.

"Perhaps you should ask him." She said gently, no hint of a snide remark.

"He is asking you, vampyre!" the well-groomed Ryan interjected. His face flush with impatient anger.

"There is no need to be rude, Ryan." The soft-spoken man they met earlier said.

"You—" Ryan stood, his temper getting the better of him.

"Sit!" bellowed the master. Ryan quickly followed his instruction.

"Good dog." Her demon cackled. "Mmhmm" she replied quietly.

"Answer vampyre!" the master continued.

"My name is Rosina. I kindly ask that you call me by that name and do not degrade me like a rat." She bowed as she spoke, but her words had the panel of men murmuring. She grinned at causing a ripple of turmoil but hid it when she stood straight again. "I cannot answer your question," more murmuring, "for I have not met any other vampyre save my sire. He was a kind man that took me in as a daughter. He never killed and never turned anyone. He was gentle and brilliant. All he wanted to do was show the world how beautiful his city was, share his knowledge of art and architecture. But he was also a coward. He turned me then left me to be buried by my family. He allowed me to be consumed by hunger and despair and forced me to watch my family suffer. I had to claw my way out of my own coffin, through rotting dirt and worms. My first feed was an innocent child, a child whose face is still burned into the back of my eyelids. I was alone as I stumbled through the darkness that I was left in. I fought my demon, I fought my hunger, I learned a little about what I could do, but even after all that I still feel human. I will not feed or kill for pleasure. I do it only to live and I choose carefully who I feed on. I work hard every day to help others. I would die protecting those I love or leave them if I put them in danger." She glanced at Samuel who was listening with sadness on his face. "And I will fight against those that would harm me merely because I was bitten! And as used as it is, I will bleed red if you cut me and I will feel the pain."

"Your story is saddening," the master spoke without giving a pause, "but you forget we have been watching you for some time."

Thank goodness they didn't see me before the village with Samuel, she thought among the Master's speech.

"And as amazing as it is that you have been able to remain yourself through all that, the fact remains that you *are* a vampyre. And try as you might that fact *will* consume you. The hunger and desire for power will overcome your conscience and your strength of mind and you *will* go mad. You've already removed a building full of people in one evening."

"They—" she tried to protest.

"There were women and children there." The master talked over her. "Women and children forced into slavery, wishing every day for freedom." Rosina stared, wide-eyed in shock at him, *how could he know?! Did Johnathan tell him? Does he know about the demon?*

The master stood, "You think you are so good? You think you are different than the rest of them?" He bellowed at her. "No! You are worse! You pretend to have a soul, but you do not. You hide behind a mask of innocence and pain. You do not even know what you are capable of." She could feel her fear growing. He was right, and her anger started to take over. She tried masking it, but her skin started to warm. "The others do not hide, they show their intent; they show their fangs! They do not skulk in the shadows!"

"Enough!" Samuel shouted, and Rosina looked over to see his hands were clenched into fists held tightly at his side. "That's enough!" The room fell silent, all she could hear was her heartbeat or was that Samuel's? He slowly relaxed his hands and stepped closer to Rosina. She had taken steps towards the table when she was projecting her feelings to the men at the table, pleading with her body and her words. He stood next to her, standing tall, not showing any weakness, "You allowed her to come here to show you that she was not the same as all the other vampyres and yet you sit up at your high table doing nothing but trying to make her fit into the mold! She has shown you nothing but courtesy and respect. She refused to kill both the hunters you sent after her because they were innocent, she refused even if it cost her her life and it almost did. You judge her for massacring," she twinged a little at the word, "that house full of women and children, but you do not know that it was your man and your target, me, that drove her to it. I tried to force her to confide in me though she was trying her best to keep her secret from me and keep me safe. Your hunter being in town was causing her secret to become that much heavier. She had to worry about how to get rid of him without killing and keep me from finding out and coming to harm at the hands of a killer." He did not say if he was referring to her or to the hunter. "She almost died because she was forced into the sun without feeding and cornered by your hunter and she still refused to give in and allow her demon to kill him. It would have been easy for it, but she chose to die rather than harm him."

There was murmuring at the table, she could hear the word demon being passed around followed by a question as if no one had heard of the vampyre demon that lives within all of them.

"This is fun, shall we show them what I look like?" her demon asked, loving the attention.

I would love to, these old men are getting on my nerves, but for the sake of the man we came here to save and now Samuel, we shall wait. We can kill them later…

"Ho Ho! I love what these hunters have done to you! I shall be patient for a little while longer."

223

"Rose?" Samuel whispered in her ear, drawing her attention back to the room. "Are you alright?"

She shook her head slightly, "If you don't stop they are going to kill you too," she was concerned for him but she had a look of appreciation on her face. "You've done your part, now let me speak for myself, I have two legs, let me stand on them." She smiled at him and put a hand on his chest and leaned in to kiss his cheek, "Thank you," she whispered and pushed him slightly back.

She turned back to the men at the table. They fell silent again, "I did not come here to fool you. In fact, I want to show you what I really am. I *am* a vampyre! I *am* a killer, a monster, a beast, whatever word you use to describe me, but I am still human!"

The murmurs turned in to yelling, "Human?! You dare insult us?"

"You are no more human than a snake!"

"Humans do not feed on human flesh!"

"You lie! You came here to trick us. You brainwashed these men and you try to use them against us? Human?! You are nothing more than a filthy rat!"

"You don't deserve to even be in the same room as a human!" With each word her anger grew. She had been treated like dirt from outsiders her whole life, but she was sick of it and would no longer stand for it. With each loud word her skin grew hotter and hotter, she felt that at any moment her clothes would catch fire.

"Silence!" The soft-spoken man stood and caught everyone's attention. "Let us hear what she has to say."

"I agree, Michele, let us listen as she dooms herself," Ryan had spoken up as well.

"Vampyre, you came here to defend yourself and that of Johnathan," he lightly tapped his fingers on the table, and she heard a door open and a scraping noise. She looked to the right of the table to see two guards dragging Johnathan out. He was bloody, his clothes torn and his eyes were half closed. "Then, show us your true colors!" The threw him down in front of her. The smell of his blood was filling up her senses. She closed her eyes to gather herself, grateful that she had fed before they came here, but that much blood still stirred her hunger. She opened her eyes again to a waiting audience. They were still green, she had her hunger in check, but her anger was flaring inside her.

She smiled at them, "What did you expect? Did you think I would go crazy and drink him dry?" She stepped forward and knelt down next to him. She wiped the blood from his face with her sleeve. They had whipped him from head to foot; she grit her teeth. "Are you alright?" she whispered.

He looked up at her, pain on his face. "Please don't do anything rash, they were just testing you, I will heal."

"Testing? They would use one of their own to test me?!" She pulled him to her, holding him close, conveying her sorrow with her arms. She felt tears start to fill her eyes which made her angrier. She looked up at the men at the table, a tear running down her cheek. Her skin ablaze, she felt her marks creep up her neck, she welcomed the burn.

"*Kill them!*" her demon demanded.

"You…. You call me monster?!" She slowly laid him on the floor and stood, his blood covering her front.

"Oh… You resisted, perhaps he is not to your liking. Maybe one you cared for more, would taste much sweeter to you." Before she knew it, one of the guards had grabbed Samuel and the other had drawn his blade. He ripped off his robe and sliced him across the chest where she had gently pushed him. She heard him gasp in pain and smelled his blood. She turned and ran towards him, but a third guard had grabbed her, injecting her with the same thing the old hunter had used to paralyze her before. She felt the numbness seeping into her. She went slack, and the guard held her, yanking her head up by her hair, so she had to watch as the other guards sliced up and down his chest and stomach, his blood was dripping on the floor, but he no longer made any noises.

"Watch your beloved priest die because you are a monster!" the guard holding her whispered into her ear.

"This is what falls on those who have relations with a vampyre." The man with the blade yelled at him as he continued to slice his skin.

She felt tears start to flow from her eyes, she was so helpless.

"*Let me help you, this is too pathetic to watch.*" She felt a warmth overtake the poison and she could feel her strength coming back. She pulled her head out of the grasp of the guard and turned in his arms and stared into his fearful face.

"You better prepare yourself. I am not the worse vampyre there is out there. If you fear me, you will die before your first kill." She whispered into his ear, they howled in laughter as she punched him in the chest and he fell over in pain. She turned to the guards torturing her priest and ran at him. The guard holding him saw her coming, but wasn't quick enough to release him and grab his sword. She was already upon them. She grabbed the blade out of the second guard's hand and turned it on him, ripping off his chest armor and slicing him clean up the middle.

"You are lucky, I'm trying to impress your boss, or that blade would have gone more than skin deep," she said to him as he fell wreathing in pain. She stood up before Samuel and the last guard, he was locked in fear, "I suggest you release him, or I won't be able to keep my hunger at bay," she blinked, and her eyes turned black. He let go and ran full force from the room. Samuel fell to his knees, clasping his chest. She knelt down to catch him.

"I'm so sorry…" She helped him to the wall where he could lean in a sitting position. "Let me heal you." She bent to lick his wounds, but a hand on her shoulder stopped her.

"No, they will misconstrue. They will think you failed their test." When she looked up at him, there were tears in her eyes and fear on her face, "I'll be fine until you deal with these fools then you can lick to your delight," he smiled at her but, when she didn't leave, he whispered, "Please teach them a lesson about kindness." She stared at him, then nodded.

She stood, not turning to the men at the table, "You wish to push me to my limit by hurting those I love. You want to see me fail. You want to see me kill them, so you have a reason to kill me? Well, then, let me show you my true colors!" She yanked off her coat and softly laid it on Samuel, then removed her boots and ripped her trousers halfway up her thighs and her shirt, ripping it up to her chest revealing her skin and her burning markings. She turned to look at them over her shoulder, they were silent, staring at her. She bent her knees and jumped across the room, landing in front of the table.

"This is what happens when I deny my demon the blood it desires, I burn for it!" She motioned to her markings then she bent over the table, both hands on the smooth wood and smiled at them then her smile turned to disgust. She jumped on the table, standing right in front of the Master, the other men gasped and moved back from the table and drawing weapons, all except the Master, Ryan, and Michele, who was smiling with excitement.

She knelt down, so she was at eye level with the master. She leaned in until she was next to his ear, he didn't flinch. She ran her hand over his beard, pulling it away from his skin, his neck was exposed. She leaned even closer until he could feel her breath on his flesh, then he did flinch, only a little, but she couldn't help but smile. "So, even you fear me. That's good because I like a little fear in my prey," she let out a little giggle, her demon was howling with laughter, getting exciting at the thought of the Master's death at her hands.

"If you kill me—" he flinched again when she licked his skin.

"Mmm."

"You will die, and those two will die." His voice trembled.

"You are not quick enough to kill them. All your men will be dead before they can even draw their blades. My demon will make sure of that. It's at the surface, it's so close to you, it begs for your blood, it is impatient with your games." She giggled again, and he flinched. "But!" she said and released his beard and leaned back on her feet, so she was looking at him again, "you misunderstand, I do not intend to kill you, as much as I would enjoy it. I will not exile my family! I protect what is mine, and by killing you, they will be hunted and your son, Johnathan, will not be allowed back into the dysfunctional family that is so precious to him. Do not misunderstand, Master," she reached to him and stroked his neck with her hot fingers, "I resist my demon, my hunger, and my desire to see you and the rest of these fools dead only for them, not for me, but those I love." She pulled back again, "Do you understand?" she asked as she yanked his beard and he was almost touching noses with her, "Master?" she asked sweetly.

She released him and jumped off the table, "You may hunt me to your delight, but harm them or banish him," she pointed at the bleeding Johnathan, "and I will hunt you and all your children in this Order until they are all dead." She walked back to Johnathan and knelt before him. She slowly removed the rest of his clothes.

"I'm going to heal you," she said, loud enough for the other men to hear, then she knelt down and started licking his wounds, he groaned with relief as she worked her way down his body, healing all his wounds until there were none left. She picked him up and carried him to the cushioned settle, she saw on the wall perpendicular to the door he had been brought in. She covered him by ripping down a curtain made of silk, she scoffed at the thought of it, *silk? Fools.*

She then returned to Samuel and was surprised when she saw him smiling up at her, "What?" She knelt before him and felt his forehead, "No fever, you must be delirious from blood loss." She bent down to start healing him but he caught her face in his bloody hands and brought it up to his, he gently kissed her.

"I'm glad," he whispered on her lips, "you're safe."

"Wha—Of course I am," but she couldn't help her tears. She was glad, as well, and she leaned in and kissed him back. She could hear the murmurs again, but ignored them as she started to heal him with her kisses.

When she had finished, she wrapped her coat around him and helped him to the settle next to Johnathan. She then returned to the floor facing the Master and his men. "What would you have me do to allow Johnathan to live his life where he loves and belongs?"

They were taken aback so much so that they did not speak, save the Master and his two men, Ryan and Michele. Michele stood and bowed to the Master and then to her, "May I?" he asked, and the Master nodded.

"You will allow us to keep surveillance on you and at any time you do not withhold our standards, which I will outline for you in a moment, you will be killed on site. You will report to us on an annual basis and even be willing to help us, if needed, with a difficult case." She looked shocked and he smiled a little at the corner of his mouth, "You are the perfect candidate to bring one of us into the house of a master vampyre. Who would suspect a vampyre bringing in a hunter?" His smile widened as the look of shock deepened. "You will not be reckless and create "servants" of any undead nature," she was looking confused, "and by the look on your face, I can see that we won't have to worry about that." He paused to clear his throat that she suspected was hiding a laugh at her expense. "You will not kill innocents or play the game of 'cat and mouse' with your victims. And lastly, you will avoid contact with any other vampyre—"

"No. That last I will not agree to," she interrupted him. "I will not avoid my kind that is like asking you to live in the woods with no contact with other humans. They are my kin, no matter how much you hate them, and I will be allowed to be with them if I so choose."

He opened his mouth to speak when the Master spoke, "Fine. However, you will avoid them if they pose a threat to humans, a threat that we will have to remove. If you are caught dealing with them, we will eliminate you as well."

There was silence then she nodded. *I have no intention of doing any of those things anyway. This is turning out to be easier than I had expected.*

"Fool! They played you! This was their intention from the beginning. They just wanted to torment us first! They wanted you to think it was your idea, you are the better person."

Even so, I will outlive them all, let them think they outwitted me. She smiled to herself.

"The only thing left is to sign the contract." Michele sat and dipped a feather pen into an inkwell and started scratching out words on a roll of parchment.

"You are just going to let her walk out of here?!" Ryan finally spoke up, "She's a vampyre, a killer! She will —"

"Yes," the Master said cooly, steeping his fingers in front of him, "and when she messes up, you can kill her." He stared at her, an ice cold stare that she would never forget. Ryan smiled and sat down, staring at her as well, a look of hunger on his face.

"He would make a good vampyre." Her demon spoke up. She wasn't surprised when it noticed the same as she did. *Yes, he would, but I wouldn't want to go toe to toe with him, even as a human. Perhaps we should speak with him alone and ask him what he thinks?*

"You and I have become more alike." It laughed at her.

She couldn't answer it, it scared her that it realized this as well.

"Come, vampyre, sign the contract." She was pulled out of her thoughts as Michele motioned towards her. She stepped up to the table and looked down at the contract. It said the same as he had earlier so she reached for the pen but it was pulled away from her. "No, you must sign it in your blood." She looked up at him.

"Is this some sort of witchcraft? Why must I sign in my blood?"

"It seals the contract much better than ink." He held out a jeweled blade, and there was murmuring again. She was a little leery of it, but wanted to get out of this place as soon as possible.

"Fine," she reached out and took it. She sliced her hand and allowed the blood to drip onto the paper then took a fresh pen and used the droplets to sign her name on the paper. Michele collected the paper and pen quickly and removed it from the room.

"Now, remove yourself from this place. I do not wish to look upon you anymore. We will send word to you when we wish to see you again." The Master stood and left the table, following Michele through the door behind it. He was followed by Ryan and the others.

She stared after then, not believing it was over just like that. She felt insulted. They had used her, toyed with her and got exactly what they wanted. Then, they threw her out like trash. She slammed her fists against the table and cracked it, "Augh!! What the hell?!"

"Rose," she felt a cool hand on her shoulder, and when she turned, she saw Samuel there and behind him was Johnathan, weak, but smiling. "Let's go." She nodded, and Johnathan showed them the way out. They didn't have to go through the tunnel again. Instead he opened a hidden door in the hallway not far from the door they had been dragged through. It opened out onto a courtyard that was barren, no trees, no flowers, no decoration of any kind, just grass. After all the elaborate decorations from inside the mansion, it was all the more empty. She felt a twinge of loneliness while looking at it. She remembered the rose gardens she had left behind. Much like her heart, it was now without color and beauty, she felt the darkness starting to creep in. She had failed Samuel, allowing him to be hurt and Johnathan had to suffer deep emotional wounds that had long ago been carved into him. And Gabriel, the image of him being dragged off in despair, alone, abandoned and betrayed.

She stopped and felt her tears run anew, "I'm sorry." Both men stopped and looked at her.

"Why?" Johnathan spoke first, "you won. Today is a day to celebrate! I have never seen a vampyre walk into the council room and convince them to allow her to leave alive. That's quite a feat." He had a wide smile on his face, and a new light was taking place of the dark in his eyes.

"He is right, Rosina," Samuel's gentle voice fill her, "You should be celebrating. We should all be celebrating, we all made it out alive and free." He, too, was smiling at her, a new vigor was overcoming him, and she couldn't help herself but smile, even through her tears. She wiped them away, *for now it's alright, right?*

•   •   •   •   •

"Oh, that *is* interesting," Michele looked down upon them from a window of the second floor.

"Michele," he turned from the window at the Master's voice, "explain your reasoning for having collected that monster's blood."

"You go too far, Michele. What experiment do you have in store this time?" Ryan had accompanied the Master.

"Master, Ryan, I have learned something interesting about our guest." He walked over to the wall of books that he had collected in his long years of research, "I have to do some more digging, however, she kept mentioning a demon within her. I believe that it is possible that she is one of the rare humans that was born alongside another being, consuming it in the womb but never fully rid of it. If I am correct in my thinking, then our dear vampyre is much more than she appears."

"Speak clearly," Ryan had grown tired of his beating around the bush.

"I'm saying that that girl is not only a vampyre, but she is also a demon." Michele insisted.

"Don't make us to be fools!" Ryan grabbed the front of Michele's robe.

"I would never do that my dear Ryan." He pulled Ryan's hand away from him and pulled a book from the shelf, opening it to a page that had been folded down. "It says here that once there was a man born to a farmer's wife and grew as a normal human would, but when he reached puberty, he claimed there was another voice in his head telling him to do awful things. They tried to exercise him and failed. He went on to kill the villagers and continued on a rampage. He was uncontrollable until a priest collected some of the young man's blood. He bound the man with it using an old spell. The man never acted out of his own free will from that day on. And, if you recall from our training, the only creature that can be controlled by its blood is a demon, yet this man and that girl seemed to be human. They showed no signs of any demonic power or physical characteristics. That is until the man went mad."

"Are you saying that we might be able to control her?" Ryan asked.

"I'm saying that if we don't, she may be the Revelations that is spoken of in the bible, except she will not spare those faithful to God. She will send all souls to hell, or worse, she will consume them." Michele answered.

"Do you think she knows?" The master's voice was full of concern, but not for her.

"I don't believe she does, but I have ordered men to keep a discreet eye on her. If she seems to act out of normal, they are to sedate her at all costs." Michele answered.

"Very good. Let's keep this between us three." He said turning to leave but paused, turning his head slightly to speak again, "and Michele, get to work finding out any information you can on this subject and how we could control her if it is necessary."

"Yes, sir!" Ryan and Master left and Michele continued pulling books from his shelves, whispering under his breath, "When I control her I will rid this world of all those blood-suckers and take the seat of Master."

*   *   *   *   *

They crossed the street and went back to the hotel to redress. They decided a night out in the beautiful city of Rome was the least they deserved. When they arrived at their room, they found several items had arrived for them. A leather bag filled with Johnathan's weapons and a new, jeweled blade. There was also two boxes, one addressed to Samuel and one to Rosina. Samuel opened his to find a new robe, similar to the one that the Order had destroyed, but made with much finer cloth and a letter of apology for the way he was treated as well as a request that he was to consider joining their order.

Rosina's also contained clothing and a letter, she read the letter:

Vampyre,

I would like to extend our appreciation to you for coming to our humble mansion to share with us your time as well as opening our eyes to a new kind of demon. And also a congratulations for being so cunning. Please take this dress as a sign of our appreciation and apology for your treatment. I do not believe it will suit you, but I refused to purchase rags to replace your old rags. Please...

She ripped up the letter before she finished, "Rose?" Samuel looked at her in concern.

"I hate that man." She replied.

Johnathan stopped replacing all his weapons and looked down at the shredded paper scattered on the floor, "Michele, he's a snake, but he is always right."

"Tsh! He wasn't right about me." She said, irritation filling her voice.

"I beg to differ, we only left the mansion a few minutes ago yet here is our things and that letter." He had a you-can't-deny-it look on his face.

She didn't respond just reached into the box and pulled out the dress. It was a beautiful gown made with flowing white fabric. It was strapless, but the fabric was not stiff. Under the dress was a corset as well as stockings and silver heels that had ties that would go up to her lower leg. There was also a small box that she found contained a diamond necklace, bracelet and earrings.

"Who does he think he is?!" She prepared to chuck them out the window along with the rest of the items, but Samuel stopped her, a starry look in his eye.

"Maybe you should wear them. You know, show him that you aren't phased by his games." He said, covering his desire.

"What?" she said, in disbelief.

"I agree with him, Rosina, wear it." Johnathan also had a look in her eye that she didn't recognize.

"I don't know what you two are thinking, but I'm not wearing it to amuse that man!"

"Fine, but I was thinking of taking you two to a nice restaurant to celebrate, and you would stand out more if you wore your normal clothes." Johnathan turned back to his bag. Samuel removed the robe from the box and put it on, feeling the fabric and making sounds of approval.

"Gah." She took the box and went into the next room and removed her dirty, bloody, torn clothes. She slid the corset on and struggled to lace it by herself, finding she was more successful that she had expected. She pulled the stockings on, they went up to her thighs. The fabric was smooth and fit her well. She pulled the dress up in front of her and looked at it. *It really is beautiful.* She stepped into it and pulled it up to her chest, pulling the ties in the back to find they were made of silk which matched the chiffon fabric that the dress was made of. The front was adorned with crystal jewels, blue and lilac. The skirt was long and had several layers, the top starting at her left hip and gradually going down and around until it reached the bottom. It was not full, it lay down against her to the floor leading to a train that lay two feet behind her.

"Looks like a wedding dress," she mumbled to herself. She ran a comb through her hair and pulled it off the side, using what pins she could find and placed the jewelry on. She couldn't believe that she was wearing something like this from a man that she despised, what was he trying to do with this? She slid on the shoes, they also fit her well, and pulled the soft silver, silk laces up around her calves, twisting them around and tying them at the back of the leg, just below her knee.

She came out of the room to find the two men on the balcony. They turned when they heard her, and neither said anything, just stared.

"There is no need to stare, I'll go take it off," she turned, agitated, intending to go back and change.

"No." She heard Samuel whisper, "wait."

She turned around with irritation, "what?" She found that he had walked up to her and he was close enough to touch her.

"You look beautiful." She looked at him, shocked. He reached up and touched her gently on the cheek, "you have something here," he ran a finger over her lip.

She quickly reached up and put a finger over her mouth finding dried blood there. He leaned closer to her and whispered, "I have the urge to lick it off." She backed away quickly, blushing and went to the washroom, scrubbing her face free of any remaining blemishes.

She came out, her face red from embarrassment. "I've created a monster." She said as she opened the door out of their room. Johnathan laughed and followed. They made their way to a restaurant nearby. Johnathan and Samuel ate, and Johnathan and Rosina drank until they were full and Johnathan couldn't stand.

Rosina helped him up out of his chair, "I think we need to get some fresh air. What do you-?" The lights went out as if a breeze had come through the entire building, leaving very little light coming from the street. Johnathan fell with a thump as she released him because something had hit her on the back. She turned around in time to see a shiny object coming at her, aimed for her chest. She reached up to stop the hand that was holding it, finding that it was a short sword. Her eyes could see in the dark where a human's wouldn't have been able, so they must have been using something else to find her, her smell? Her breathing? The sound of her movement? She saw that attached to the arm was a man that was dressed in armor.

"You're from the Order." He grunted and yanked away from her, she looked around to see that the customers that had filled the room were gone and replaced with men and women all dressed in a similar fashion.

"Tsh, I should have known," she dodged his attack and dove at him, tackling him to the floor, knocking the breath out of him and sending his sword across the room. She hit him again, knocking him unconscious, and was up on her feet just in time to duck away from another attack. She recovered from it, just to have another man attack her. There were several coming at her, she was barely moving in time for any fatal strikes to hit, but she was making a collection of nicks and cuts on her arms from blocking.

"What the hell is going on?!" she demanded.

"The council was foolish when they let you go. We do not allow vampyres to live." A man further back shouted. When she looked at him, she saw him holding Samuel. Johnathan was under the table, unconscious. At the man's head nod, they all came at once. She dodged as best she could, she was much faster than them, but they were coming from every direction she tried to run away, but the dress tripped her up. She found a discarded knife on the floor where she was currently at and slit the dress from her ankle to the top of her thigh and cut off the shoes. She quickly got back up and ran. She reached the furthest wall and turned to see them still coming after her.

"Just give up." The man with Samuel said, "We are trained for years to kill your kind, so a baby like you does not stand a chance of surviving. But we are curious, we heard that something interesting happened at the meeting today and it has our Master and the right hands in quite a tight knot." He stopped walking towards her and stared her right in the eye. "We want to see your demon." He said the last with an evil grin and a redness in his eyes. He smacked Samuel with the hilt of his short sword, and he slumped over.

"Quit toying with me!" she shouted over all the hunters, and they paused in their pursuit of her. She reached up and tore off the jewelry she was given and slammed them on the floor. She felt her skin start to burn. She looked down at the floor, *I don't want this. Why must they treat me like a dog? I am not to be used and thrown away,* "I'm not for your entertainment!" She looked up tears in her eyes her skin on fire and her eyes black with hunger.

"Let's kill them! Make them feel your pain!"

"I'm going to eat well tonight!" Her voice held a note of something different and she realized it was her demon, it was helping fuel her anger. The hunters started coming at her, but they were more cautious. Her glowing skin lit their faces and glinted off their many drawn weapons. She smiled, showing her fangs and laughed from deep within her. "Let's go." She whispered to her demon, "I want to taste their sweet blood!" She ran towards them, her demon's power heightening her senses: her speed was increased almost double, her sight, her hearing, even her taste. She reached for the first's blade and removed it from his hand and quickly slit his neck. Then, moved on to the next and the next, jumping over and under them, dragging them down and slamming them against the floor and wrapping her legs around their necks and twisting. Most she just incapacitated. She made it through the many hunters and finally reached the man still holding Samuel. She could hear some of the fallen hunters rousing and getting up.

"They don't give up do they," she glanced over her shoulder, "I didn't really want to kill them, that's not how I like to do things. My demon doesn't like it, but as long as I feed it enough, it doesn't argue much." The hunters that could still fight started to surround her again. She ignored them and stepped closer to him. He dropped Samuel and pulled out a second sword and took up a fighting position.

She dropped the blade she was holding and shook her head, "No, that's not how this is going to end." She got close enough to him so he could use those swords, but he didn't move. Instead, he watched her, as if he was studying her. She reached up with both hands and grabbed the blades of his swords, grasping them tightly so he couldn't use them. A bead of blood ran down each of them and coated his palm. She pulled them from his wet hands and threw them behind her onto the floor.

He had fear in his face as she drew closer to him. She ignored the blades flying at her, some hitting directly and others grazing her, the once white dress was stained with her blood and that of his hunters'.

"Are you happy with what you see? Do you fear for your life at seeing what hides within, Hunter?" He twitched when she spoke, but stubbornly refused to give in. He reached in his coat for another weapon, but she grabbed his wrist before he could get to it.

She clicked her tongue at him, "Ah ah. Let's not—" She paused when she noticed that he was trembling uncontrollably. Her hunger dissipated and her eyes became their normal gentle green. She felt ashamed for allowing herself to act like them, to toy with him. She pulled his hand out of his coat and held it between her own.

"You've seen my demon," she said softly, "now see my human." She brought his hand up to her cheek, he resisted until he felt her hot tears fall onto his trembling hand. He looked up into her face, surprised. "This is the side of me that I don't want to lose. I fight every day against the demon that hides within," she closed her eyes and continued as if she was talking to herself, "Will I always be in pain, will the demon be the only thing that will ever be seen? I cannot kill them, they are innocent, I will not kill them for the mistakes of their fathers'."

He let out a breath, and his hand stopped trembling. She felt his other hand touch her other cheek gently, wiping away her tears. She opened her eyes to see him staring at her. "Is this what he saw?" He withdrew quickly, as if he was burned. "I will not be manipulated!" He reached behind his back and pulled out yet another short sword, and held it to her chest.

She let her hands fall to her side, "Then kill me if that is what you desire, I will not resist." She grabbed the sword and pulled it into her, cutting into her skin, "I will help you, you will be doing me a favor."

"Tsh!" he grit his teeth and put a foot behind him for more strength., "The Master was right, you are worse than any other," he pushed the sword deeper, closer to her heart, "You will die here vampyre!"

"I'm sorry Gabriel, I cannot come back for you as I had hoped. I had wished to see your face, hear your laugh, and feel your warmth at least once more before the inevitable end."

She felt a warm wind blow across her face, "Come to me, my beautiful, black Rose. We will go to eternity together." She felt her skin burn anew, but she ignored it.

"I am ready, Gabriel."

She felt a sharp pain in her chest that caused her whole body to quiver in pain. She felt as if her very organs were exploding and then they burned. They burned so hot she yelled out and reached up and tried to grasp her chest only to find a cold blade protruding out of it. She knew it went completely through her. She followed the arms that held the sword and found the hunter, a look of evil happiness on his face, a grin that extended from ear to ear plastered on it. For a moment she was scared of him. She tried to step back, but he had a firm grip on the sword, and it was not coming out easily.

"What are you?" she gasped, as the pain became overwhelming, the demon howled with it, causing her ears to ring, it didn't want to die.

"I am a vampyre hunter!" He pulled the sword, and it slid slowly back out of her. She moaned in pain and fell to her knees as soon as the blade was free from her flesh, her blood pouring out of her, "I never miss," he said as he lifted up the sword, it had just missed her heart, a slight miscalculation. "It must be the missing heart that caused that." He held the sword up and examined it, "This blade is made of a metal that I understand is toxic to vampyres. It has been passed down through the Order from generation to generation. It has never failed to kill a vampyre." He looked down at her. She was holding the hole in her chest and gasping, her vision darkening and her markings fading. "I guess it was a good thing I missed, I get to watch you in so much pain," he laughed "That is what you get for trying got manipulate the Order," he took a different stance and raised the bloody sword above his head and prepared to bring it down on her. She tried to move out of the way, but she was frozen in place, her arms and legs would not move, the blood loss was causing her body to die. She couldn't look away, all she could do was stare at the shine from the sword and the evil glint in his eye.

"Stop"

"NO!"

"Wait!"

Three voices in unison found their way to her ears, and the hunter stopped in his swing and looked towards the door. She looked to see Michele along with several guards from the Order standing in the door and a warmth that was not her own holding her up. She didn't realize she was sinking the rest of the way to the floor. Samuel had regained consciousness and was there, as well as Johnathan, leaning heavily on the table where he had been left.

"That is enough Gustave! Remove yourself from this building at once." Michele ordered and entered the room, walking swiftly over towards Rosina and Samuel, Johnathan stumbled over behind him. The man called Gustave left in a huff, slamming the door behind him. The remaining hunters that had attacked filtered out one by one, after collecting themselves and their weapons. One of the last collected Gustave's as well before leaving. She couldn't see well, her vision was going dark, but she could see the damage she had done. She knew she had killed in her fit of rage, but she didn't know how many.

"She needs blood," she heard Michele saying.

"No." she whispered in a frail voice, "don't save me." She leaned her head back and let the black take over, her body numb and welcoming the end.

"No way in hell am I letting that happen!" Samuel saw her lose consciousness and looked for a blade, but couldn't find one. "Johnathan, give me a knife!" He didn't hesitate, just reached into his belt and pulled out one and handed it to him. He quickly sliced his arm and held it to her mouth, but she didn't move to take it. He let it flow in, but she didn't swallow. He shook her begging, "Please, please, take it," he shook her more violently, but still nothing. "Rose! Please! Don't give up!" She remained motionless, and Johnathan put his hand on Samuel's shoulder, but he shrugged it off, "I'm not ready to give up, even if she is." He pulled her close to himself, hugging her as tight as he could. "You can't go yet, you just started to carve out your path. You just started to change the world, you just started to change me! You haven't saved Gabriel yet. He is waiting for you, don't make him wait in vain." He laid his head on her shoulder and whispered, "I love you. If you leave, do it in a way that I know I can see you again." He nuzzled into her hair and waited, they all waited.

He felt her move, swallow, and groan in pain, "Your blood is so tasty. I can't get enough." She turned and nuzzled into his neck, "Can I have some more?"

He laughed and nodded because his voice was caught. But then noticed she didn't move to take it and said, "Yes, for God's sake, take it, take as much as you need."

"I'll take a little," She bit into him, and he felt no pain. So pleasurable was the relief he felt, it flooded into her, and she sighed as she drew his blood into her. She did as she said and only look a little. She withdrew and licked her bite, closing the wound and cleaning the blood from him. Then she sat up, feeling light-headed and almost fell again, but Samuel caught her, again. She wrapped her arms around him and clung to him, "Thank you," she said into his chest, her tears flowing without her control. If she didn't let go, she would be able to stay here. She was allowed to live in this world. He held her tightly while she cried, hiding her from the other men in the room that seemed to be watching her as if expecting something to happen. They were surprised, when they saw her like this, like the scared child she was.

"I'm so tired," she mumbled into his chest then he felt her body slump. He looked down to see her breathing, steady breaths and he let out a sigh of relief. Then he felt her body temperatures increase so rapidly that he felt that she was going to burst into flame. He pulled her away from him to see her markings had returned and her wounds were healing, even the one in her chest.

One of the guards gasped, and he looked up to see all the men watching in awe. Michele had a look on his face, one akin to a scientist making a wonderful discovery.

"That's not right." Johnathan was the one who spoke first. "That wound was dangerously close to her heart and there should be no way it is healing so fast. Even the master vampyres have to go into a healing sleep for several days to heal a wound like this. It is a long process."

"What are you saying?" Samuel asked frantically. He didn't like being on uneven ground. He had very little knowledge of vampyres, and they were talking as if he should know more.

"He's saying that her 'demon' is not an effect caused by her being a vampyre."

Michele finally spoke.

"Speak clearly!" Samuel was becoming frustrated.

"I mean that she is a demon." He said it with joy.

"That's impossible!" Johnathan said. "She was clearly human before she was bitten or her sire would not have touched her. A demon's blood is poisonous to a vampyre."

"I thought so myself, but we can no longer ignore her marks or her rapid healing." Michele said, but when that didn't appease them he continued, "I was curious about this 'demon' she spoke of. At first, I thought she meant the burden of being a vampyre. A guilt. But, when she showed us her marks, I became even more intrigued. I did more research and found a very rare case in which a human is mingled with a demon in the womb." He received confused looks, "There is very little known about this, so we don't know how that happens. The baby is born seeming human, growing human, showing no special abilities or strengths not even accelerated healing. When the child descends into puberty, the demon awakens, and the human is shoved aside while it uses the body to fulfill its desires. The human can try to fight it, but in no case did the demon lose." He paused and looked at Rosina, "There has also never been a case where the creature was made into anything else, vampyre, were, anything."

"But she was sixteen when she was turned," Samuel objected, "She was well past the point of puberty."

"She is truly a special case. Perhaps if she had not been turned, she would have been the first to reject the demon." Michele paused, "Poor thing," He ran his hand through her hair, but he did, as if he was looking at a specimen, not a person, "I would love to observe you more closely."

Samuel pulled her away from him, "or maybe you're wrong." He stood and lifted her into his arms.

"Perhaps." Was all he said, not taking his eyes off her.

"I'm taking her back to my room," Samuel said. "And you will not interfere with her again until you call upon her, and she will come to you. If I so much as see a hair from a hunter's head I will personally remove it along with its owner's head. I will not allow her to be used as an experiment." He stared at Michele for only a moment then turned and left. Michele had a smile on his face but said nothing.

There was a silence that weighed down on them until Michele spoke, "Aren't you going to follow?" he asked Johnathan.

"Technically I am a hunter again," he started for the door, "I will go if he calls for me, but no sooner." He left and, after a short pause, the guards and Michele followed. A short time later several men in robes entered and proceeded to remove the bodies, corrected the tables, cleaned the blood and retrieved any weapons left behind, leaving the place as it had been before any of them had arrived.

• • • • •

Samuel hadn't meant to leave so abruptly, but he couldn't swallow the way that man, Michele, had been looking at her. He made a nose of irritation as he reached the door to the bath house. He was getting looks from all around, but he ignored them. He did not want to have to explain why she was covered in blood. He sat her gently on the floor in a sitting position and removed his clothing before holding her up and starting on hers.

He unlaced the fragments of her dress and corset. He slid them gently over her head and unlaced the tops of her stockings and slid them off as well. He carried her to the large, heated bath and stepped in. He sat along the edge, but was covered up to his belly with warm, aromatic water. He sat her down in the water and used a cup to rinse her. He used his hand to wash off the blood, being careful of her stab wound, even though it was healing rapidly, it was still severe. When he was finished, he wrapped her in his robe and left her bloody clothes on the floor of the bath.

He took her back to their room and laid her down on the bed. As he covered her, he wondered how long she would sleep, and that thought drifted to what Michele had sad.

"What he said couldn't possibly be true, right?" he looked at her, knowing she wouldn't answer. "I'll keep this to myself, for now, at least until I can gather more information. You don't need another burden."

He dimmed the lantern and replaced his missing robe. He went out onto the balcony and looked out on the city, "As beautiful as you are, my lady, I cannot wait to be parted from you. You, who only brings despair."

Chapter Twelve: An Unwelcome Protector

The heat from the ground she was standing on made her sweat, but she welcomed it because she couldn't remember the last time she had. She could feel her heart pounding and smelled a familiar fragrance, she heard a sound that she didn't quite recognize but knew. She opened her eyes to find she was standing on a beach of white sand stretching for miles on either side of her and in front of her clear blue waters crashing gently onto the shore. It looked as if it were the beach that lay below the cliff near her town, but it was several times larger. The sun was high in the sky, and she automatically lifted up her hands to shield herself from it, but when she noticed that it was not burning her, she knew she must be dreaming. She stretched her arms out to each side and allowed herself to slowly fall to the ground. The heat from the sun and the sand melted away her sadness and fear, leaving only happiness. She let out a breath and allowed herself to, just for a moment, remain still, not worry about anything but the sun and the ocean. She could feel the knots in her muscles, and her stomach unfold themselves, and she smiled, she couldn't help herself.

She heard sand shifting then felt a coolness settle over her head and shoulders. She opened her eyes and looked up and was shocked at what she saw.

"You look very good for a dead person," Gabriel was standing over her smiling, "Not that you'll hear me complain." He reached out a hand to her and she took it gratefully. He pulled her up off the sand and right into his arms. He still had his old but beautifully long hair and he smelled the same, as if no time had passed and his thoughts of her had not soured. She felt an overwhelming sadness but she felt no tears and, after a moment of his heartbeat in her ear, the sadness too faded into nothing but happiness.

"If this is death, then I will gladly welcome it with open arms." She said into his chest.

"Always so morbid." She heard another familiar voice from behind Gabriel, who was chuckling.

She pulled away from him to see Marcus standing a short distance from them. Behind him, she saw her mother and father sitting at a small table, shaded by an umbrella, just a short distance off the beach, in the grass that grew right up to the sand, they were enjoying afternoon tea. Gabriel let go of her, and she ran to them and hugged them as she had never done before. There was so much she wanted to tell them, apologize to them, explain to them, beg them, but she couldn't get the words to form, so she just found comfort in their arms.

"My dear," Her mother's honey soft voice drew her attention and her gentle hands lifting up her face, "You look so beautiful, the sun agrees with you." She smiled as if Rosina had never left, had never caused them a day's worth of grief, a smile she hadn't seen in so very long.

"It really does. You should go out in it more, my Rose." Her father's deep voice came from above her; she looked up into his dark eyes that shone like they held the universe of stars and knowledge. She longed to sit and listen to his stories once more in their library or in their garden of roses. "We should come here more often, don't you think, darling?" he asked her mother.

"Father," Marcus said as he and Gabriel had joined them, "Once you retire we can come as much as you like,"
He laughed, a carefree laugh, "Yes, Marcus. But I will not retire until you ask that lovely Victoria to be your bride."

She looked up at Marcus to see him put a hand over the lower part of his face, but she could see that he was blushing, his hand could not hide that. He recovered quickly, "I will do so as soon as these two finally decide to set a date," he glanced down at Rosina, and something caught her eye. She looked down to see a ruby ring on her wedding finger, she couldn't believe it. She looked up at Gabriel who was now looking over at the ocean, his embarrassment clear.

"Now dear, don't rush them. We all remember how long it took him to ask her in the first place, we don't want to scare him off." Her mother was laughing, "Oh! Rosina, dear, your roses look beautiful this year," she reached behind her chair and brought out a bouquet of roses she recognized as her own. Their dark red color and vibrant green leaves and stems stood out against the pale white sand.

"Mother, they are beautiful!" She reached and took them but when she did her arms became covered in blood. The thorns had pierced up and down her arms. She quickly dropped them full of shock, "when did all these thorns grow?" she asked and looked up to see them staring at her, but their life was gone. All that remained were their skeletons in old, worn clothing. She gasped and quickly backed up, stumbling in her long dress and the now wet sand.

"Why did you leave us?" her mother's voice had soured, but it swirled around her.

"We worked so hard for you to be happy, to be given life without hardship; why did you betray us, and cause us to be cast out?" her father was angry.

"You're supposed to take care of me, you are the older sibling." Her brother sounded sad and betrayed.

"I loved you, why did you leave me when I needed you?" Gabriel's voice was faint, but also *the most hurtful.*

"I'm sorry! I never meant any of this to happen! I wanted everyone to be happy!" She felt her throat dry up and the sun become scolding. Her skin was burning in its light and heat. She tried to shield herself, but it was so hot. She fell to the ground and tried to crawl to the ocean, but it was no longer made of water ; now it was fire and the sand was coals, burning her hands and knees. She wept for escape and tried to beg for forgiveness, but no one could hear her. Everywhere she looked was endless fire, everything was burning red, she tried to scream but nothing came out. She felt her skin start to flake, she was turning to ash and bleeding from her chest, so much was flowing out that she should already be dead but she was not; she was burning for eternity!

• • • • •

There was a hurried knock on the door, "Sir?!"

Johnathan sighed before he called out, "What?"

"Urgent letter, sir!" the other man said and Johnathan quickly walked to the door. He opened it to find a young guard holding a folded letter without an envelope or seal. He opened it and it only read:

Johnathan,
Bring your creepy friend and come to our room!
-Father Samuel Coalson

P.S. Have him bring as many books as he can carry.

Johnathan rushed out of the room, leaving the young guard wondering what was going on. He ran to the back of the mansion where Michele, his creepy friend, could be found. He swung open the door and was met by a protest that quickly evaporated when Johnathan said, "Rosina needs help!"

"What's wrong?" he asked closing the book he was reading and taking notes from.

"I don't know, but the priest said to bring as many books as you can carry." He grabbed a bag that was hanging on the back of a chair and started collecting the books on the large table that Michele was sitting at.

"How do you know those are what is needed?"

"If I know you as well as I think I do, you will not have stopped researching this demon thing until you have all the answers and if that were the case, you would have told many, including myself." Michele stared at him for only a moment before helping him gather the rest. They left the mansion by the side as the three had done before and quickly made their way to the inn that Rosina and Samuel were staying. They rushed up to the room and pounded on the door. When Samuel opened it, they saw him covered in blood and Rosina screaming and thrashing behind him on the bed.

"I don't know what to do, she won't stop bleeding, and I can't wake her." He said frantically.

Michele pushed his way through towards her. He watched her for a moment a look of fear on his face that quickly disappear when Johnathan joined him.

"What's wrong with her?" he asked.

"She needs blood," Michele answered, "But I do not know why she is thrashing and why she hasn't healed yet."

"Here," Samuel held out his arm that already had several cuts that were slowly clotting, "I've already tried to give her blood, but she won't take it."

"You can't, you are far too weak," Johnathan said.

"I am the only one that can. It is against your rules for a hunter to give a vampyre blood, and after getting you reinstated…" he drifted off, but Johnathan nodded.

"Are you sure?" Johnathan looked at Samuel's arm, it was shaking, "We can get someone else."

"No, there is no time, and there is no way we will be able to bring someone here and have her drink without that person causing a rucus," Michele said, as if he had done this before.

Johnathan nodded again and looked at Michele who climbed on the bed and placed his knees on her shoulders and his hands on her arms to try to hold her down. Johnathan quickly cut Samuel, and he gasped, but hid his pain behind his worry. He held his arm close to her mouth, but she continued to thrash, and the blood was being spilled everywhere.

"Try over her wound," he pulled up her robe to expose the bloody hole in her chest. Johnathan moved Samuel's arm over it, and his blood dripped into it. When the first drop hit it, she stopped moving and a sigh escaped her lips.

"She's burning up," Michele said, "I've never seen such a thing." Johnathan nodded in agreement.

"Is it her demon?" Samuel asked in a weak voice. Johnathan pulled his arm back and wrapped it with a piece of the sheet form the bed.

"Perhaps." Michele answered, "I've been studying as much as I can, but there is very little written about demons and even less about demon/human mixtures and as you can guess nothing on demon/vampyre mixtures." He moved off the bed and went to the bags that they had brought, pulling out all the books he brought and placed them on the table. He leafed through them as Johnathan attended to Samuel.

"When was the last time you ate?" Johnathan asked.

"At that dinner two nights ago," Samuel answered

"You need to eat," Michele chimed in over his book and notes, "Your blood lacks nutrients and that will do her little good, especially if she wakes up to find you dead of malnourishment."

"I agree," Johnathan said, "I'll go downstairs and see what I can get at the kitchen." He left quietly.

"Rest until he comes back. Your worrying will not make her well, and your restlessness will only irritate me." Michele said without looking up. Samuel was reluctant, but after a moment he slouched down in the chair asleep.

He was woken up to Johnathan and the smell of food he looked around and saw that Michele had changed Rosina out of the robe and into a lightweight white gown and removed the blanket from the bed. "How long was I asleep?"

"Not long." Johnathan handed him the plate of potatoes and chicken. He ate quickly, he hadn't noticed he was that hungry.

"What do we do now?" he asked after taking a few bites.

"We wait," Michele answered, "Hopefully when you are full you can provide better blood, and that will help her." Samuel looked over at Rosina again and saw that she was starting to twitch again, so he finished his meal in only a few bites.

"Uhhnnn… Mother…" He looked up when he heard her voice.

"She's been doing that for a while now." Michele answered his unasked question, "I would assume that she is dreaming, which I would take as a good sign." They sat silent after that, listening to her murmur in her sleep.

After about an hour Michele spoke again, "She's getting worse, perhaps we should try again." Samuel nodded and walked over to her, cutting his arm again. He let the blood drip down into her mouth, and she closed her lips. She seemed to be swallowing, so he put it closer to her, and she lifted her arms and wrapped her hands around his wrist and arm. She pressed her lips to his open wound and began pulling from it, but when she opened her eyes they were not her usual black; They were bright red, almost glowing and her skin ignited with her markings and heat. Samuel tried to pull back, but she was too strong and she just held tight.

He could feel that she was pulling too much blood, "Rose," he said gently, "Rose!" he said a little louder, "Rosina! Release me!" The two other men rushed over to see what was happening and when they saw her eyes they gasped, but Johnathan reached down and tried to pry her off. Even he was not strong enough. Michele pulled a knife from the strap on his calf and, grasping her hair and exposing the side of her neck, held it to her skin. Her red eyes moved to him and finally released. She licked her lips that held a smile that chilled him.

"Demon." He whispered.

She laughed a hollow laugh, "You are correct, Hunter." She slid off the bed and came close to him he stepped back once before steadying himself. "You think to play with me," she did not ask. "You know of me, but you can only learn so much from your books." She walked around him, and he saw the shadow of a long tail coming from under her sleeping gown. She picked up one of the books he was reading and laughed to herself as she dropped it on the floor. She ran her hand across the back of his neck and he tried to stifle a shiver. "You fear me?" she asked even though she knew the answer. "Don't worry, I do not wish to devour your soul," she leaned against him, her chest to his back, wrapping her arm around his chest and talked into his ear, "yet." she laughed again. "You are filthy, but you have so much potential to be very tasty, so I will leave you alone for now." She slid her arm down and across his heart and then removed it all together and came back around him. She wandered around the room, the fabric of the gown rustling with her movement, almost as if she had a wind around her that no one else could feel or was affected by.

"This room is filled with the smell of fear." She closed her eyes and pulled in a breath. When she opened them again, she had a wide smile on her face, and her fangs were replaced by a set of teeth that should belong in the mouth of a leopard. "I love that smell. Too bad I'm not hungry right now, you see, my dear Rosina keeps me well fed." She looked down at herself as if seeing her body for the first time. "She doesn't allow me out very often, but she makes sure that I feed upon the best…" she paused and looked at them, "food."

She walked over to Samuel, "You are a pleasant surprise, she does not allow us to feed on the innocent. You are very tasty, but I require more than blood to live, and your soul is bitter. You see, too much good and innocence is poisonous to a demon. It tasted a little better today than yesterday, you have lost some of your innocence." She put her hand on his cheek and leaned in and kissed him, a hungry kiss, unlike Rosina's. "She has dirtied you, priest," she whispered against his lips, "you will not be able to resist your lust for her." She pulled away and looked him straight in the eye, "You desire her, even now, I smell your need mingled with your fear and that," she paused and closed her eyes as if devouring the smell of him, she opened her eyes again, "is most intoxicating. If I had the strength to overcome her will I would not hesitate to relieve you of your desire. I have never been able to devour one with such a beauty about him." She turned away from him, "But, she will not allow it. She has a stronger hold over me than I would like to admit and she will not stand for me hurting someone she loves or someone that is innocent. Even the evil men she kills she will not allow me to torment, she believes in a quick and… mostly painless death."

She walked to Johnathan that had retreated towards the door, to his bag of weapons. "And you," she stopped him with her voice, "she will not allow me to harm you either." She got close to him and grabbed both his wrists, causing him to drop his knife and gun that he had managed to grab and pulled him back into the room, "That is no matter, your body," she released his wrists and reached down between his legs, grasping him fully as he tried not to pull away, "craves another so much that even your blood is sour." She released him and walked out to the balcony.

"But she needs me, you see, because she cannot live without me and I cannot live without her." She leaned on the railing. "We are one, and we cannot be separated, nor do we play by the same rules as most demons or vampyres. We are writing our own rules." she looked over her shoulder, "be grateful that she has such a pure soul. The light that comes from it," she closed her eyes imagining it, "it lights up my world, with her white light, even the electric red currents from mine only add to its intensity and electrifies it, it cannot be dimmed." She opened her eyes and looked out onto the city. There was a long pause before she started again, "I will not allow you to taint it, this soul is mine! And I will stop anyone that chooses to abuse it or use it for a game or some sick and twisted experiment."

She clenched her fists on the stone railing, "I am stronger than her, and I will eliminate anyone that would try!" she slumped her head and was silent for a moment, "She needs blood, her body, our body, is weak. She needs someone that she can completely devour, she needs someone she can kill." She looked down at the street, watching the people walking along, not knowing what stood above them, not knowing the storm that could wipe them out in an instant. "You must protect her." She let out a sigh and slumped, unconscious on the railing before falling to the floor. They approached her slowly, but when her marks faded, Samuel ran over and leaned her up against the railing. She moaned and slowly opened her eyes, they were cold green, and he smiled, relieved.

He helped her to her feet as the other two watched, cautious of her. "My head," she whispered, "what happened? Why am I out here?"

Samuel actually laughed, "Your other half paid us a visit."

She looked up at him in shock, "What?"

"Your 'demon' decided to take over for a short while and explained to us a few things." He said.

"Did it hurt anyone?" she asked, panic rising.

"Not physically, but I believe we will all think twice before getting on your bad side." He helped her to the bed. Johnathan flinched when she passed, and her hand swung down by her side and close to his nether region. Samuel stifled a laugh which earned him a glare from Johnathan.

"What did it do?" Rosina asked as she sat down on the bed.

"Nothing, really. She likes to talk, but she also has a severe case of self-preservation." Samuel answered.

"Yes, we learned a good bit from her visit." Michele finally spoke. "I have to get back to the mansion," he started collecting his things, "I trust that you two can handle it from here?" he shoved everything in his bags and quickly left the room.

"What did it do to him?" Neither spoke.

"*I told him he has a tasty soul and I can't wait to devour it,*" her demon answered with a pleased tone.

"Soul?" she tilted her head as if trying to listen to something they couldn't hear, but it didn't answer. Johnathan cleared his throat, then went to the closet and pulled out a long coat, tossing it onto the bed next to her.

"You heard her. She needs to eat, and I think it would be best if we took her to the meal rather than trying to bring it to her." Samuel nodded and helped her put on the coat.

"Her? She? Why do you call it so?" She slipped on a pair of slippers

Neither answered right away but just looked at each other. "Well?" she prompted.

"Let's just say that your demon has a strong attraction to the male gender and *it* speaks like a woman," Johnathan answered and walked to the door, holding it open for her and she left the room.

"Where do we even start?" Samuel asked as they reached the street, before Johnathan could answer, she turned left and started walking up the street. She turned right after walking a good distance from the inn and into the alley. They followed her, giving her a little distance.

She walked calmly down the alley, but inside she was shaking. The demon had never taken over without permission or the need to feed. Why this time? And why so completely? She shook her head trying to rid herself of her fears. *Why did you come out?* She asked and waited but no response came.

"Tsh!" she kicked a bottle laying on the ground, and it shattered when her foot hit it. The noise caught the attention of a man that was struggling to stand upright as he walked down the alley towards her.

" 'ey there, 'retty 'ady." He slurred, and he stumbled towards her.

"That was easy," she mumbled quietly to herself. In her weakened state she didn't have time to be picky, this drunk pervert would have to replace her usual more-than-evil-man meal. He reached her and, wrapping his arm around her neck, pulled her close as he tried to sweet talk her. She wanted to pull away from him; she was in no mood for this man, and the smell of wine on his breath was so strong she wanted to gag. However much she was repulsed by her was how strong her hunger was craving him. She felt her throat clench, and her skin get warm, but it was a different heat from the heat that was produced by her markings. It was just pure anticipation and hunger.

She turned so she was face to face with him and put her hands on his chest. She could feel his heartbeat, strong and steady, it called to her. She couldn't contain her hunger anymore and she pushed him against the wall, he slouched against it, knees bent.

"Whoa! You are a 'ady that knowsh wha she wans." He laughed, misunderstanding her.

"Yes, I am." She grabbed his shoulders and pulled herself up and put her knees on either side of his hips and clenched, holding herself up. She pulled his collar aside and bit him, she didn't waste time trying to make him believe that it was anything other than a feeding. She moaned as the first spirt of blood filled her mouth. She pulled the hot nourishment from him. He struggled against her, trying to pull her off but she just clenched her legs and hands tighter. He tried to stand up away from the wall but she had pulled so much blood from him that all he could do was sink to his knees. She extended her legs as he fell and was now leaning over him as she drew out the last of his blood, she could feel his death coming. She pulled away just in time to look in his eyes, and his life left him.

"I am not a plaything!" she pushed him and he fell to the ground, dead.

●　　　　●　　　　●　　　　●　　　　●

By the time they reached the alley she already had a target. They watched as she shoved him against the wall, and climbed him like he was a ladder and just sunk her teeth into his flesh without any ceremony. "Does she always feed this… brutally?" Johnathan asked.

"I never watched her, so I don't know, but I'm sure not. She's been through quite an ordeal and now she just found out that her demon can take over whenever it chooses. You probably would drown yourself in a bottle if it were you, but she doesn't have that option. She has this," he motioned to her. "Blood, violence. That leads her to ecstasy and oblivion. Right now she probably doesn't care to be kind. She just wants blood. She wants to feed, something so basic that it is instinct. She doesn't have to think, something that will drown out everything else. She wants it to consume her."

"She is," Johnathan paused, "so much stronger than I would have expected after learning of her from the master. I am glad that I got to witness this. She has changed my whole outlook, down to my very beliefs. I am grateful that I was saved by her. I just hope that I can help save her in return."

"Yes, she really is—" Samuel was cut off by a gut-wrenching sound that came from Rosina. She was standing over the man, her head down and her hair over her face. She had ripped off the coat and was looking down at her chest. The wound was still there, but was closing in front of her eyes. She looked up at them as she heard them running towards her, a look of panic on her face. Then, she bent over again and let out a scream of pain. She ripped open the front of her gown to see red markings swirling around her wound, but nowhere else. She watched as it continued to close. It seemed as if her flesh was burning, as if she was standing on the beach again, with the fiery sun and molten ocean. She wrapped her arms around her middle, trying to cool it but it didn't subside.

"Mother! Mother! Make it stop!" she screamed. When Samuel reached to touch her, she flinched away. "I'm sorry, Father…" she was trembling, and tears were falling down her face, her fear was washing off her so strongly that even the men could feel it. "I didn't mean to betray you." Her screams drew another man down the alley.

"Is she alright? What are you doing to her?" he asked, concern on his face.

Her head snapped up, her voice quiet and her stare focused.

"No!" Samuel yelled out as she ran past him and jumped the new man, knocking him to the ground. She sank her teeth into the arm he threw up to defend himself. She drew blood from him as quickly as she could, not thinking of anything but the blood. She needed it, she was dying.

"He is innocent." She heard her demon whisper, in shock, but ignored it. *"I could not have guessed that this would have happened so close to your birth."* She could feel it smiling, happy she had given in to its power.

She lifted her head away from the man, "What are you doing to me?!" She yelled into the night.

"Haha!! I am protecting us! I am keeping us alive." Her demon answered.

"Not like this! I will not harm innocents!" The man that she had been feeding on was motionless in fear, "I'm sorry." She said to him and gently pulled a little blood from his wounded arm. She sent in thought about a beautiful beach, and he gently went to sleep. She licked up the blood, and the wound closed. She stepped back and the burning returned. By this time, many more people had started to gather at the end of the alley, but they weren't close enough to see what was happening. She withdrew further into the alley. She felt weak, fighting the hunger and the pain in her chest. She stumbled and fell to the ground and felt her vision swirling, going black.

"I'm sorry, Gabriel. I want to be with you, but I don't think I can. I'm dirty now, your light is too bright for me…" she felt her consciousness fading.

"Gabriel?" she heard Johnathan ask before she found the peaceful darkness.

"Yes, sleep, heal, for our sake."

Chapter Thirteen: A Sour Good Bye

I saw an angel a few nights ago,
She was clad in fluid white cloth,
Her wings glistened, reaching towards the sky,
Their red feathers capturing my eyes,
Their fire burning brightly.
Her dark hair flowing in the soft breeze
That I could not find.
Her green eyes, more gentle than a flower,
Searched me, sought me, found me,
Lost.
Her hands caressed my soul,
Igniting my hidden light
And calming my turbulent indecision.
She left me breathless,
She ne'er touched me,
Only whispered to my trembling body,
"Come to me," her arms opened wide.
I fell to her grace and her dark beauty,
Never again will I love one so full of light and shadow.

She awoke to the comforting warmth of bedding, a different heat from the burning that had now subsided.

"This bed," she said, exasperated, she was growing tired of waking up in it. It made her feel weak. She sat up and felt a twinge in her chest, but it quickly subsided. She pulled her gown away from her chest and looked down to see that the only remains of her wound was a raw patch of skin. She couldn't believe it. She slid her feet off the bed and down to the floor, standing in the dark room. She could see light streaming from under the door to the sitting room and hear muffled voices.

She walked to the door and reached for the handle, but stopped when she heard Samuel's voice. "We cannot tell her! It will destroy her!"

"Do you remember how it made you feel when she neglected to tell you she was vampyre? Imagine that ten times over." She heard another voice, but it wasn't loud enough for her to decern who it belonged to.

"This is different! We are not even sure if it meant what we think it meant. It did not come out directly and say so." Samuel protested again.

"You're right, Father, this *is* different. This is much worse. Be reasonable, she remains ignorant that her demon half is actually a separate being fused with her human half. She believes it is the vampyre within her speaking" the other man spoke.

"I am being reasonable. We do not know that Michele is correct in his assumptions, he could be wrong." she could hear his fear and for the first time, he sounded young and lost, like he was grasping as strings that were falling around him. She stood in shock. "I will not lay upon her any more burden, not until I know for sure the truth." She heard the other man sigh.

Finally, she turned the knob and light swallowed her. She allowed it to wash away her fear of the demon that may be more than it appears. She may not be able to separate herself from it even if she did know the truth. She decided to worry about it later, she wanted to leave this city as soon as she could. She saw Samuel pacing and Johnathan sitting, his right ankle resting on his left knee, seeming calm, but she noticed a slight twitch in his raised foot.

"Rosina!" Samuel stopped pacing and faced her.

"It is not polite to speak of someone while they are not present." They reacted as she had expected: tense, cautious. "I am not going to break, though I may be a little sore for several days." She looked at them both and forced herself to smile, "I am fine, please do not worry." She felt the tension in the room decline.

She looked at Samuel, still not looking convinced, "Angel, do you think we can leave this city soon?" she looked over at Johnathan, "If everything with the Order has been smoothed out."

"Everything is as it was before I was banished," Johnathan spoke. "They insult me with the menial tasks that they have given me, but I believe it is their way of punishing me for sullying their precious mansion." He stood and walked towards her. "I hope that you are alright, I fear for you and your soul," he leaned down and kissed the top of her head, "If the demon threatens to devour you, please do not let it."

"If it tries, I will kill it." She said, and he knew she knew that meant killing herself.

He laid his hand gently on her shoulder, "I hope to see you again soon, you make a good partner, and I would be glad to have you by my side again." He paused for only a moment and then he was gone, gathering his stuff and was out the door.

"Can we leave?" she asked again.

"Yes, of course, we can't leave fast enough." He stared at her as if waiting for something to happen, but when nothing did, he said, "We can leave in the morning if you wish."

She nodded, "Thank you. I'm sorry I put you through so much," *This will be the last time,* she thought but didn't say.

"Don't be, I made the decision to come even though I knew that my life might be in danger, but I cannot turn from a child in need," with that sentence he grew into the man she had come to know and she was saddened but glad to see him again. He drew a line between them again, now that he didn't cling to the fear of death, he no longer needed to lean on her.

She suppressed the sadness clawing at her. She smiled and said, "I'm glad to see you back to your normal self. You were rather whiney." She laughed, "but it was refreshing to see that side of you, to know you are human."

He walked over to her and put his hands gently on her upper arms, "I am more human than I want to be, I'm supposed to be more spiritual than this." He looked away from her, "But I guess I still have a long way to go." He looked down at her again, "I'm glad that I could be of some use," she could hear the disappointment in his voice even though he tried to vail it. He let her go and walked past her to the bedroom.

"I wouldn't be here if not for you." She said, without moving, "Johnathan would have died in a drunken stupor if not for you. You have done more than enough. You have done more than either one of us. You partook in something dangerous, you risked your life for a lost vampyre and a drunken hunter. If not for me you would still be in your church living a peaceful life. You would not be tied in knots and sullied by me." She heard him coming back into the room, taking quick heavy steps.

He grabbed her and shook her, "Do not speak such lies! I have done nothing! And you have not dirtied me any more than I have dirtied you! I made my own choices, and I do not regret them." He let out a breath of frustration, "I have never been touched by one so beautiful. Your demon said that your soul shone so brightly that even it couldn't touch it and I have seen that light! You have made my life better, fuller, more colorful. I did not know the meaning of the gifts of God, until you walked through my front door. It matters not what you are."

"How can you say that? The very definition of me is a creature send forth from Hell, I am a minion of the devil himself."

"You believe this?"

"Yes,"

"Then you are blind!" he let go of her and started pacing, "I wish I could show you that you are a creature of God. The very fact that you still stand and have not been cut down is because of Him, He loves you! He put you here for a reason, can you not see that?"

"I cannot. All I see is the demon, and all I feel is its hunger, be it the vampyre or a true demon, matters not!"

He stopped pacing and walked over to her, wrapping his arms around her and pulling her into him, "If you will not believe, then I will for you."

"Everyday I believe less and less that God is there and that he watches over us." She said quietly into his shoulder.

"I know."

•　　•　　•　　•　　•

Morning came quickly, and they left the inn, "Wait! Sir! Miss!" The receptionist called out to them. He ran out to them and handed them a letter, and an item wrapped in cloth.

"Thank you," Samual said as he walked back in the building. Rosina opened the letter:

Rosina and Father Samuel,

I wish you well on your travels, but I want to give you a few words to help lead your way. Father, do not stray too far off your path, it is one of holy abundance. You can help so many and lead them to a life that is full of happiness and peace. Be patient, not only with the flock but also with yourself. You have been tested these past few months, and you will be tested again, but you will not fail if you hold your faith. God will see you through as He always has. Watch the dark rose at a distance and allow it to grow as it will. It will be beautiful in its own right, all you need do is water is when its tears dry up.

Rosina, I do not know what your plans for the future are, but I suggest that you focus on something that way you do not grow bored, and you do not feel out of control of your faculties. I have heard that the bounty hunting business is very lucrative. It will give you the hunt you so require and allow you to put some roots down. Perhaps? Try not to dwell on the past, your sight should be toward the future. You will make many mistakes, but you have much time to fix them or to forget about them. Visit your family, if not in person at least visit your grave. Allow yourself to mourn for the loss of that life but do not allow it to be forgotten, allow it to lead your new life, savor the fond memories of it. It is your beginnings, and you will always have strong roots there, they will lead to your beautiful flowers. And please do not keep away from us, we love you in the way brothers love their little sister.

Farewell for now,

Johnathan Lockard

Behind the letter was another sheet of parchment. It had on it a drawing of a man's face, he looked angry and unkept. Under the image were the words: Wanted for Theft and Destruction of Local Bank. Reward: 10 Silver.

"He looks familiar," Samuel said over her shoulder.

"Mmm." She agreed, "From one of the taverns on the way here, close to the village."

"Perhaps we should look into this?" he said, a little excited.

"Or perhaps we should get you back to the cathedral, where you belong. I fear you are getting a taste of this life and you are enjoying it far too much." She had a small smile in her voice.

He looked at her sideways, as if to refute her statement then paused and said, "you may be right." She couldn't help but laugh.

"Plus, I thought you hated bounty hunters?" she asked, but he ignored the question, and she just smiled.

"What's that?" he pointed at the other item. She untied the twine holding the cloth and slowly unfolded the cloth. It revealed a blade that was between a dagger and short sword in size. She pulled it from its leather sheath, the blade was curved and engraved with words of Latin, "Vos may interficietis daemonium," meaning "May you slay your demon." The handle was simple, but was adorned at the end with a single square ruby, and the hilt was newly wrapped in leather. There was another slip of parchment in with it, "*A parting gift. I thought you might need this and it seems to suit you.*" She held the blade in her hand, and it fit perfectly as if it had been made for her.

"That was a nice gift." She nodded, resheathed it, and placed it in her bag.

•　　•　　•　　•　　•

They left the beautiful city behind as the sun made its last stand and fell beneath the horizon. Along the way they talked and acted as if nothing had changed, but as their home grew near they could both feel the tension building with each mile.

"Are you going to be alright?" Samuel asked with concern.

"I'm fine. Why such a question at a strange time like this?" She tried to laugh it off, but Johnathan and Samuel's conversation still rang in her mind. He just stared at her as if to say, 'come now, I know you better than that.' After a moment she said, "I'm… Alright. I am not really sure what is happening or what is going to happen in the future. I am on very quickly sinking ground, but I think I will survive. I am not sure if I will like the outcome, but I will live." She paused again then continued, "To be honest, I am not sure that I am ready to know, yet. I am scared of what I am, all this time I thought the demon was part of my vampyre. But now I find that we have been one since sometime before then, but when? Am I possessed like all the priests and bishops said… but that doesn't sound right. I'm making all my own decisions, I believe. If not that, then does that mean I am a demon? Or are we just sharing one body? Will it take over at some point, will I be lost?" He watched her talk herself into a panic, but said nothing. He just pulled a thick envelope with a bright red wax seal, endorsed with a crest that she didn't recognize, from his bag. He placed it on her shaking hands that sat in her lap. She looked at him, puzzled.

"I didn't want you to find out the way you did. I wanted to search for answers for every question you would have, to go through it with you, to support you, hold you and if necessary give you a good slap if you get out of control." She just continued to stare at him. "It's a letter," he looked at her with sympathy in his eyes. "It contains everything I know about your other side. Michele, Johnathan, and I talked at length about it, and everything Michele could find out is in there." He pointed at the paper that was laying in her lap.

She stared at it, as if afraid to touch it with her own hands. "You don't have to open now or ever, but I want you to have the knowledge, should you ever need it or want it. It's there for when you are ready." He took her hand and squeezed it, drawing her attention to him rather than her fear of what the letter contained. "I will be here when you are," he smiled gently at her before turning back to the road.

After a long silence she spoke in a small, scared voice, "What then? Will I be able to live with it? Will others accept me? What about the other vampyres, will they kill me or use me as a tool?" her voice started to grow tense and her breathing harsh.

"Hey," he tried to get her attention, "Hey!" she looked at him, fear in her eyes. "I know my knowledge of vampyres and demons is limited, but you are you as you've always been. You've had this other side since before birth and it never stopped people from loving you and caring about you. This new realization will not change you, it will just be a small bump on your road. Perhaps you have gained a new ally in this so-called demon. She seems to care… well, she is, excuse me, hell-bent on protecting you at all costs. I would say she cannot be all that terrible if she passed up three, well two, easy meals to tell us she wouldn't put up with anyone harming you, emotionally, physically, or otherwise." He gently squeezed her hand again.

"I remember seeing an angel the other night. She was clad in fluid white cloth, her wings glistened and reached towards the sky…" She listened to him speak, tears filling her eyes. He saw beauty in her darkness, and he loved her all the more for it, but he was also fearful of it. She knew he would not be able to handle the demon that resided within her and her decision to leave was made all the more right by this.

She began eating less, woke when she should be sleeping, and her quick, clever come-backs were slower and lacked spark. The tension was distracting her, and no matter how he tried, he just could not ease her. She was fighting something he did not know, but he understood her fear, her suffocating, overwhelming, dark fear. He knew he couldn't hide his concern for her, but he also knew it wasn't helping. He could tell by the look in her eyes she planned to do something stupid and he knew she needed to bring herself back from the grasp of the demon and he had to let her. But that didn't mean he had to like it.

"What is going on with your face?" she asked.

"Huh?" he had been lost in thought and didn't realize she was watching him. He sat with his arms crossed and slightly crouched over himself, irritation over the whole situation clear.

"You're scowling." She poked him in the cheek, and he was so shocked that he jerked back and almost fell off the wagon. She grabbed his hand and pulled him back to his seat. Her laughter filling his ears. "I'm sorry, did I startle you?"

He joined in her laughter, until she suddenly stopped, her gaze on the road in front of her. "I didn't realize we were this close to the village," she said, and his concern returned.

"Yes, we will reach the cathedral before the sun sets again." He said.

"I have to get off now." She said abruptly.

"What?" he didn't understand.

"I can't go back there." She said.

"Of course you can. What are you talking about?" he could feel her slipping away.

"No, I can't. Not after how I left. They will hunt me and they will kill you for hiding me," she spoke the truth.

"They have no idea what they saw. You defended yourself, and they have long forgotten it by now." He tried to convince not only her, but himself.

"I chased those three men down like animals and fed upon them like a beast."

"I will set them straight. Now is not the time for you to wander around the countryside. You need—"

"You are a most precious angel, but I cannot stay." She interrupted him, "I need to find what resides in me and test its resolve. I cannot do that in a place like this, I may end up killing everyone," she looked at him, "including you." She gently ran her hand over his cheek, his warmth almost burning her. She looked into his eyes, their dark brown searching her for the answer, desperate to help her, to keep her safe. "I love you, and I cannot put you in danger any longer. I never thought I would feel like this again, care about another person enough to worry day and night. You showed me so much, your light guided me when I stumbled around in the dark. Thank you, I cannot tell you how I appreciate you, no words would be enough." She removed her hand and reached behind her and grabbed what little belonged to her and jumped off the wagon.

She heard the wood squeak as he got off as well and came after her. His hand grabbed her wrist harder than she had ever felt his grip. "You cannot leave." He pulled her back, and she turned into his arms. His heart was beating hard in his chest. She thought she could hear it breaking; she fought the pain in her chest. His breath was ragged, and she felt the warmth of tears fall onto her cheek. She looked up to see his face was twisted in pain. He lifted his hands to her face, and he held her there.

"You can stay. I will take care of everything, no one will harm you. I will cross all the lands to find out what this demon is and what will happen to you. I will do whatever it takes to make sure you are safe. Everything to keep you who you are, to make you smile and dry your tears and allow you to see the beauty in everything. You will never be lonely. Every day will be filled with joy, and you will never be left wanting. I know you do not seek material things only to be loved and accepted. You will find that here, every day and night I will look after you." His tears burned her face and mingled with her own that now fell from her eyes.

She placed her hands on his forearms, "My beautiful angel. I cannot condemn you to a life of slavery to a vampyre. I will find happiness, it may not be tomorrow or for years to come, but I need to find it myself. I cannot force you to provide me with it, that is not true happiness,"

"Bu—" she put her fingers over his mouth.

"What you say means so much to me and will provide me with a light to move forward, to sustain me until I can find my own way. Your essence will forever be within me. You have brought my heart back to life, it beats for you, my love." Her tears fell harder than they have ever before. She reached up and pulled his head down to hers, resting his forehead against hers. "You are the most amazing thing in this world. I will never be left wanting for that, the only thing I want is for your happiness, your joy, I will not allow you to follow down this black path that is ahead of me."

"You cannot go alone, even with your unending strength, you cannot do this alone. No one should ever be alone." He whispered.

"I will never be alone." She smiled, "you will always be with me. Your presence is like the air, it will sustain me even when I cannot see you." He pulled her in with strong arms that have gone weak. He held her even though he trembled and she wrapped her arms around him and held on tightly. She didn't shake, but the pain in her body was almost more than she could bear. She needed to get away from him for she was too weak.

"Please reconsider," his deep voice vibrated through her.

"I cannot condemn you more than I already have. You promised your life to God, not to his enemy's spawn."

"God would wish me to help you not allow one of his lambs stumble around in the dark."

She laughed, "Lamb, huh? Thank you for that." She pulled away from him and looked him in the eyes, "You really are amazing, even knowing all you know you refuse to turn from me."

He reached under his robe and pulled out his rosary. It was made of white stone with a gothic style cross hanging off its end. He took it off and placed it around her neck. "This is to keep you safe."

She had a gentle smile on her face, and that made his pain even worse. She pulled him down to her and kissed him, a soft, farewell kiss that said more than she could with words. She pulled away quickly and turned and walked swiftly in the direction away from the village, towards the forest where she disappeared from his sight. He slowly knelt to the ground and cried silently as he prayed for God to keep her safe and help her find her way back to his light and to help him understand why she left.

She found the first tree that would hide her from him, and she fell to the ground. Her tears overwhelming her and her sobs so loud she thought he may hear her. Her pain cut through her body like a thousand blades. She couldn't move, couldn't breathe, she could only tell herself that this was the right thing to do. It was what was best for him and for once in her life she was doing something that would help someone other than her. He had taught her what it was like to not be selfish, he taught her so much, she already felt lost without him...

"You could go back, you know he waits for you." For the first time since she left Rome her demon spoke. Her shock caused her to physically jump.

When she realized who had spoken, she said, "You have no right to speak of him. This is your fault. You are the reason I had to leave."

"We both know that is not the truth."

She wanted to play stupid, act like she didn't know what it meant, but she couldn't, she knew, and her demon knew.

"You run away, not because of me but because of your own uncontrollable selfishness and insecurities."

"No…" she whispered.

"Yes. You left him because you knew that if you stayed you would hurt him, kill him or worse, make him your slave. But leaving was not for him, it was for you. You want to explore this new strength that you never knew you had. You want to push it to its limit, and you know he will not recognize you when you have reached your goal."

"No! I left to save him. If I was being selfish, I would have stayed and made him fulfill the promises that he made, even knowing he couldn't possibly make someone like me happy. I left to save him." She paused, waiting for it to chime in, it was clever, seeing what she truly wanted, even her darkest desires.

"Maybe you are right," she said without when it didn't speak. "But we are one. For you and I to have different wants and needs would cause turmoil and neither of us would survive. I have to give up the façade of being good and give in to you or I will die."

"You finally understand. We have no limit to our strength. We will rise above all the fools that have turned us away, and you will never doubt yourself again. You will never be afraid or in danger of the humans taking anything you hold dear. They will curse the day they let us walk out of their manor alive." She listened to the demon ramble. It sounded like a power crazy man about to do something incredibly stupid, and she was not going to allow it.

"One thing at a time, I'm still not sure if this is real or if I'm going crazy. You'll have to give me time to adjust, and we'll take it one step at a time." She pulled out the parchment with the wanted man's face on it. "Let's test out this new bond on catching this bastard. We will need money to purchase a place of our own, somewhere secluded, where we can gather ourselves." She felt the demon agree.

"Is there any chance you could give me some time alone?" she asked quietly. Instead of answering the demon's presence just faded.

She never felt more alone than she did in that moment. All the warmth she held dear to her was now gone as her hope for being loved vanished. Her heart hardened as her tears fell. She was allowed to have two angels in her life, and both times she disappointed them and hurt them. Why did she keep getting opportunities to be horrible?

She looked up to the sky and cried out to God, "Stop testing me! You know

I'm not worthy of these blessings. You know I don't deserve them! Stop reminding me of what I am, of what I do every time someone loves me!" she ripped off the rope Samuel gave her and threw it from her, she stood in the night with her tears falling onto her bare skin. "Take me if that's what you want! But know that there is no place that will not be more like hell than this place!" she screamed at God, whom she knew was not listening. "That's right! If you were there, you would have already listened to your child's please and taken me from this earth. I know you have abandoned me but can you please, just this once, listen and help me. Please take me my Holy Father, don't abandon the man that has sacrificed his whole life to you. Prove me wrong and prove him right, do what is right by your holy sun," she begged Him for the last time, her faith finally completely shattered.

He sat in the cold stone building. It was so empty without her presence. He could still hear her voice resonating off the walls, and her smile was burned into his mind. He sat on the floor where he fell, not even making it halfway to the altar. His tears burned with their betrayal. He knew she didn't feel as he did and he shouldn't even feel how he felt, but he couldn't help himself. He had fallen in love with her even when he knew from the beginning he could never have her.

He chucked through his pain, "This must be how mistresses feel, always second best to another man." He leaned against a pew and his head hung down over his chest. "I was hoping for more than this. Father, I'm sorry for straying. I wanted to save her from herself, and in the end, she was saving me. I lost sight of what I was doing, trying to use her methods against her. I was left alone after all. I tried so hard to find a place in this world, but it appears I cannot." He pulled his robe off and let it fall onto the dusty floor.

•   •   •   •   •

She slowly climbed up the roof and sat next to the stone chimney, looking down on the town that was all too familiar to her. She watched the people walk by, oblivious of her presence, but the man she was seeking was nowhere in sight. She recognized many faces, though, most were attached to memories that she would rather forget. The irony was not lost on her that many of them had called her a demon, possessed by the evil of the fallen angel.

"If they only knew," she whispered to herself, and her demon cackled in her head.

"Shall we show them what we really are?" she shook her head. As much as she wanted to show them that she wasn't a lost lamb, she decided that just ignoring them was best for them *and* her. She was thinking about how she could teach them about her in a way that would leave them afraid of every shadow, when she caught a familiar voice.

She sat up on her heels and looked down close to the building she was on. She saw the top of his head, his hair was short now, she felt a pang of sadness at that. He said goodbye to the shopkeep and started walking down the street. He was tall, as she remembered, but he was no longer skinny. He had built up his body and was now a full man, from his thick beard to his well kept, tailored suit, and shoes. He placed a low-key top hat on his head and hid his face from her. She followed him, jumping silently from roof to roof. He had changed a lot, but his walk was still the same. He had that confident, cocky strut that projected his lack of need for anyone to make him feel good. "I've got this," she remembered him saying. Watching him now, she believed him, even after all these years, he still had it.

She jumped down to the street and hid around the corner when he stopped at a shop for another business meeting. "I have no right to be here," said to herself.

"But you cannot help yourself, right?"

She watched him talk to the man in the shop and then shake hands and came back outside. He looked up into the sky and sighed. She was close enough to him that if he had the nose or ears she did he would know she was there. He turned slightly, and she caught sight of his eyes, still as beautiful as always, clear and shining, so full of life. *I cannot interfere, just watch.* She closed her eyes and took in a deep breath, preparing to leave him, again, but the scent she expected was somehow unfamiliar, tainted, almost soured. She opened her eyes and studied him more closely, trying to figure out what had changed about him. He had aged several years, but that wasn't it. His clothes were clean, she could still smell the soap on them, and he was well kept, his hair clean and in place, as it should be. Everything about him looked different but, other than a few things, he didn't act differently. That was to be expected, he was just a teen when she left and now he was a man. Perhaps it was that, he had become a man it was only natural that he would seek comfort in a woman. She felt her jealousy spike, and her skin started to burn.

"*If that is what a woman smells like then I am very glad that you died at sixteen.*" She thought about the demon's disgust and realized that it wasn't a woman. It smelled dirty, almost like an animal. She had to cover her nose because it was making her nauseous. She retreated away from him. He was the same, but now he was different, and her curiosity was about to get the best of her.

•   •   •   •

He turned towards the alley that was cloaked in the shadows of the night. He caught a glimpse of red light, but it was gone as quickly as it had come. He heard a familiar voice and smelled a familiar scent that had long ago died. He cocked his head to the side and listened, he heard footsteps growing quieter. He followed them but found nothing, not even the warmth that would have been left behind if a person had been standing there. He sighed, a ghost from his past. The ghost that haunted him and kept him awake at night. He wished this ghost would leave him be. She was gone, and she was never coming back. He turned back to the street to complete his even business before returning to his empty mansion and cold hearth.

About the Author

H.N. Benson grew up all over the United States from Idaho to Pennsylvania. She currently lives in Pittsburgh where she loves spending time with her dog, Ivy, and her three cats. As well as enjoying art, writing, and being outdoors, she loves spending time her family, especially her two nieces and nephew.

Thank you so much for reading one of our **Paranormal Fantasy** novels.
If you enjoyed our book, please check out our recommended title for your
next great read!

The Graveyard Girl and the Boneyard Boy by Martin Matthews

"... a compelling and eminently likable cast of characters." —*Authors Reading*

View other Black Rose Writing titles at www.blackrosewriting.com/books

and use promo code **PRINT** to receive a **20% discount** when purchasing.

www.ingramcontent.com/pod-product-compliance
Lightning Source LLC
Chambersburg PA
CBHW011130100726
47898CB00009B/2929